TWISTING, SHANNON FINALLY FREED HERSELF FROM ALEXANDR. "THAT'S FIGHTING DIRTY."

"What do you expect, given our profession?"

"Next time, I shall be on guard against any trick."

"Or any thrust?" He smiled, a sinful, sensual curling of his mouth.

Shannon's cheeks, already flushed from the physical exertion, took on a deeper burn. *Damn the man.* And her own wicked body for yielding a sign of weakness.

She knew she ought to slap him . . .

As if anticipating her thoughts, Alexandr tightened his fingers around her wrist. "In chess, I would call this a checkmate."

"But we are playing a different game." Shannon twisted out of his grasp and in a whirl of spins and steps threw him over her shoulder.

~

"Ms. Pickens is a talented writer. Her characters are real and the setting is beautifully drawn, while the dialogue is snappy and period-appropriate. For readers of romance, who enjoy tales of fighting women and the men who love them, this book is worth adding to your reading list."
—*Historical Novels Review* on *The Spy Wore Silk*

"Saucy . . . aud[...]cy espionage romantic [...]roine and a strong suppor[...]

—[...] *Wore Silk*

D1011802

Also by Andrea Pickens

The Spy Wore Silk

Midwest Book Review on *The Spy*

Seduced by a Spy

ANDREA PICKENS

FOREVER

NEW YORK   BOSTON

Cover illustration by Alan Ayers
Handlettering by David Gatti
Book design by Giorgetta Bell McRee

Forever
Hachette Book Group USA
237 Park Avenue
New York, NY 10017
Visit our Web site at www.HachetteBookGroupUSA.com

Forever is an imprint of Grand Central Publishing. The Forever name and logo is a trademark of Hachette Book Group USA, Inc.

Printed in the United States of America

First Printing: March 2008

10 9 8 7 6 5 4 3 2 1

*For Ellen M. Iseman: Your wit and wisdom in presiding
over our monthly Library Committee
meetings are a constant source of inspiration
and affirm the magic of
words, ideas, and the printed page.*

Seduced
by a Spy

Chapter One

*T*he wind whipped against her cheeks, a hard, biting cold that cut down to the bone. Ignoring the pain, Shannon ducked low in the saddle and spurred her lathered stallion toward the high stone fence.

"Fly, Ajax, fly," she whispered, feeling her own muscles tense at the sight of the rocks standing in sharp silhouette against the scudding mists. "NOW!"

Soaring high into the air, the big animal hung for a heartbeat above the jagged teeth before thundering back down to earth in a blur of heaving flanks and flailing legs. The ground was slick with rain and the stallion stumbled, but Shannon gathered the reins, steadied its head, and angled for the narrow path between the grove of oak trees.

Faster. Faster. A mere fraction of a second could make the difference between life and death.

Despite the chill, her face was sheened in sweat. *The pistol.* Surely it was just up ahead, where the trees thinned to a small clearing. Straining, she caught sight of the telltale glimmer of steel among the fallen leaves.

Shannon leaned forward. Gripping the leather pommel with one hand, she kicked a leg free of its stirrup and swung low. Thorns scraped her fingers, but she managed to snag the weapon. A hard twist, a turn of her hips, and she was back upright.

Steady. Steady. No mistakes—not now. Not with all that was riding on her ability. Her pulse was racing nearly as fast as her stallion's gallop. Her heart thudded against her ribs, its rapidfire beat echoing the cacophony of pounding hooves and snapping twigs. Drawing a deep breath, she willed herself to see only the leering face up ahead—the coal-dark eyes, the menacing snarl, the broad bulk of shoulders cloaked in black . . .

Without hesitation, Shannon took aim and squeezed off a shot.

A hoarse cry rang out as the bullet exploded, tearing a gaping hole in the figure's chest. She slowed to a trot and circled back, the acrid smoke of the gunpowder still heavy in the air. From the corner of her eye, she caught a ripple of movement in the trees. A young man stepped out from the sheltering branches.

"Is he dead?" she demanded as he crouched down over the jumble of cloth.

"Dead as a doornail." Giovanni Marco Musto—Marco to all his friends—grinned as he poked at the singed straw. A tall, well-muscled Milanese mercenary, he served as the assistant riding and fencing instructor at Mrs. Merlin's Academy for Select Young Ladies. "*Bravissimo.* You hit him square in the heart."

"No real harm done." She repressed a twitch of her lips. "Jem will fashion him a new one by morning."

"*Sí,* but God help any flesh-and-blood enemy who stands in your path." He consulted his pocket chronometer and the pearly flash of teeth stretched wider. "A *magnifico* time, *Signorina* Shannon." He gave a jaunty salute as he snapped the gold case shut. "You've shaved another second off the Academy record. None of the other students come close to matching your equestrian skills." Standing in profile accentuated the artful tumble of his dark hair. It curled in Renaissance ringlets around his open collar, looking soft as silk in contrast to the sculpted muscles of his broad shoulders. The very picture of masculine beauty.

And well he knew it, she thought wryly. The Academy—a small school hidden in the pastoral countryside outside of London—required both its teachers and students to possess a unique range of talents. Marco was apparently picked not only for his finely honed skills with spurs and sabers, but also for his perfectly chiseled body. The young Italian was often called upon to model for the advanced drawing classes. A position he flaunted with shameless bravado.

Marco held his pose for a touch longer before turning with a suggestive cock of his hips. "Now, if you wish to have expert instruction in the art of swordplay, come by my quarters after supper. A private tutorial is yours for the asking."

"Steel yourself for disappointment. If we crossed blades, you would not come out on top."

"All the better, *bella*."

"I doubt you would be singing the same tune as a *castrato*."

Marco accepted the set-down with a good-natured laugh. "I can't help myself, *cara*. We Italians are born with a lively appreciation for beauty."

"Keep your lively appreciation buttoned in your breeches. Mr. Gravely would not be at all amused if he were to get wind of you trying to cut a swath through his students."

His face lost a touch of its waggish cant. "*Porca miseria!* You won't . . . hay on me, will you, *Signorina?*"

She bit back a laugh. "No, I won't *grass* on you, Marco. I stand by a friend. Even when his boudoir braggadocio threatens to get out of hand."

"*Sí.* We all know of your steadfast loyalty." Suddenly serious, he kicked at a wisp of straw. "It is a pity that *Signorina* Siena has taken her leave from our ranks."

Shannon swallowed hard, trying not to dwell on the fact that her own departure from the Academy might also be imminent. The difference was, her friend and former roommate Siena had taken up an even more challenging position, while she . . .

She looked away to the shadows, loath to let anyone see a flicker of pain in her eyes. She was, after all, one of the select few who had made it through to the Master Class. Its badge—a black winged merlin tattooed just above her left breast—marked her as a hardened warrior, a trained killer.

Softer sentiments had no place in such an arsenal of talents.

"I miss her," mused Marco.

"As do I."

He slanted a searching look at her. "It will only take me a bit longer to finish up here. Wait and I will ride back with you."

"If you don't mind, I'd rather go on alone."

Before he could argue, Shannon gave a flick of the reins and spurred her stallion for the stables. Her body relaxed, instinctively matching the rhythm of the canter. Would that she could exercise such easy mastery over her mind, she thought. Daredevil acrobatics came naturally to her. The steel of a sword or pistol fit her hand like a second skin. But when it came to controlling her tongue or her temper, she was awkward, unsure. Damnable inner demons, they seemed to have a will of their own.

"Bloody hell." The oath slipped from her lips as the whitewashed walls and peaked slate roofs of the stables took shape from out of the fog. Her fears, sharp and pointed as the weathervane crowning the center cupola, formed into a palpable presence in her chest. Like the talons of the weathered copper hawk, they clenched and would not let go.

Would Lord Lynsley expel her from the school? She had broken a frightening number of rules by interfering in another Merlin's mission. But as of yet, the marquess had been ominously silent as to her future.

Looking around her, Shannon felt regret, recriminations dig even deeper. The shooting ranges, the fencing fields, the spartan classrooms and dormitories—all were so achingly familiar. It was hard to imagine an existence outside the ivy-covered walls. After all, it had been home since . . . a life she did not care to remember.

The fears, the filth, the violence had been left behind in the slums of London. Even her real name, if ever she had possessed one, lay buried in the shadows. Like all new students, she had been ushered into the headmistress's office, a skinny, frightened little girl uncertain what to expect. One of the first things Mrs. Merlin had done was show her an ornate globe, and as the orb was set to spinning, she had been told to pick out a name from the myriad cities dotting its surface.

A new name for the new world she was about to enter . . .

Seen from afar, Mrs. Merlin's Academy for Select Young Ladies was undistinguishable from the other boarding schools that polished highborn daughters of the English aristocracy into Diamonds of the *ton*. The pastoral grounds, the tidy brick buildings sheltered by the high, ivy-covered walls. However, outward appearances could be deceiving. The difference was . . . day and night.

Shannon's grip tightened on the reins. Here, the students were not pampered young misses admitted on account of their family's pedigree and purse. They were streetwise orphans, handpicked by the Marquess of Lynsley from the rookeries of Southwark and St. Giles.

Shannon wondered what he had seen in her. A surly toughness that refused to knuckle under to the grim realities of the stews? Even as a small child, she had been awfully good with a blade.

With her fists and her fury, she had fought her way to the top of the class. Unlike the other finishing schools, the Academy's curriculum was not designed to cast its students in a rosy light, but rather to thrust them into the heart of darkness. To be sure, there were instructors to teach dancing, deportment, and all the other social graces. But while other girls studied the art of watercolors, Merlin's Maidens studied the art of war. They were England's ultimate secret weapon, dispatched by Lord Lynsley to take on the most difficult, dangerous assignments. Their master classes included rigorous training in the traditional martial arts of fencing, shooting, and riding, along with the more exotic Eastern disciplines of self defense and yoga.

Would that she had paid a touch more attention to the

lessons on self-control. Action came so much easier than introspection.

Blinking the beads of moisture from her lashes, Shannon forced her chin up. She would not surrender to self-pity. Discipline, duty, and a dispassionate detachment from emotional excess—those were the rules that Merlin's Maidens swore by. If her superiors deemed her unworthy of the name, she would go out with her head held high.

Disobeying orders was a serious transgression. It was understood by all that a Merlin was on her own when dispatched on a mission. But on learning that her roommate was in dire danger while trying to trap a deadly traitor, Shannon had slipped away from the Academy without permission in order to ride to the rescue.

She had violated the spirit, if not the letter, of the law, and yet she could not truly say she was sorry. Part of the basic training taught that in their profession, there were no rules. So she had obeyed her heart rather than the Hellion Handbook that each student was required to memorize.

Right and wrong. Discipline and duty. That her intervention helped defeat a dangerous traitor did not, according to the headmistress, diminish the gravity of the offense.

No one questioned her courage, merely her character.

"Shall I rub 'im down fer ye, Shannon?"

Roused from her reveries, she shook her head. "Thank you, Jem, but no. I shall see that Ajax has his oats before I go in to my own supper." She patted the stallion's sleek neck before slipping down from the saddle. Her legs wobbled a bit as her boots struck the cobbles. She had pushed herself at a punishing pace all afternoon—

fencing, karate, and the cross-country shooting course. As if pain could make amends. But at least the aches and exhaustion kept her from thinking too much about the future.

Her hands, stiff with cold, fumbled with the buckles of the bridle. "You will find barley vastly more tasty than hair," she murmured, fending off the velvety nuzzling to her neck. Ajax's nickering formed soft puffs of vapor in the twilight chill as she untangled the loosened strands of her chignon from the leather and brass.

After currying the stallion's coat to a gleaming chestnut sheen, she pitched a few forkfuls of hay into the stall and latched the door. Duty done, there was nothing to keep her from joining her comrades in the dining hall. And yet she lingered, loath to see the glimmer of sympathy in their eyes. Pity only piqued her wounded pride.

Dipping into the stone cistern, Shannon splashed a handful of cold water over her face, determined to shake off the maudlin mood, along with the gray grains of gunpowder still clinging to her cheeks.

"Need a hand?"

She watched her roommate slip out from the shadows. Sofia always appeared so assured, so elegant, moving with a natural grace that would have been right at home in the ballrooms of Mayfair—save for the foil and saber tucked under her arm.

"It looks like you had a rough afternoon," added Sofia.

"Not bad."

"Don't beat yourself up. You made the decision you thought was right, and would do it again in a heartbeat."

"Thanks for not saying I told you so." Shannon essayed a smile.

Sofia uttered an unladylike oath. "I'm not such a fair-weather friend as that." She quirked a wry grin. "Besides, it isn't as if I'm entirely innocent of wrongdoing. Marco still hasn't forgiven me for sneaking your stallion out of the stables."

"You are the best of comrades, Fifi. And you shouldered more than your share of the blame. I'm sorry you were stuck with so many demerits."

Her friend cut a jaunty flourish through the air. "I am learning a great deal about the fine points of weaponry, seeing I have been set to polish the whole damn armory."

She winced. "Lud, Da Rimini is a bastard—"

"SHANNON!"

She snapped to attention at the sound of the stable-master's stentorian shout. Hopkins did not often raise his voice above a growl. "Here, sir!" she answered.

"You are wanted in the headmistress's office."

Mrs. Merlin wished an audience? Her heart gave a lurch, hope warring with trepidation.

"NOW!"

Muddy boots and cockleburred buckskins did not help to inspire much confidence. She would have preferred to appear more polished and poised, rather than as a be-draggled gun rat.

"Good luck," murmured Sofia. "And godspeed. You heard him—march!"

Turning smartly, Shannon maintained a military stride until rounding the barn door, then broke into a hell for leather run.

"Za Zdorovie."

Alexandr Orlov accepted the glass of clear spirits.

"Cheers," he murmured, tossing back the potent vodka in one gulp.

Prince Yuri Feodor Yussapov, head of Special Intelligence Services for the Imperial Russian Ministry of War, chuckled as he switched to a bottle of ruby port and poured them both another round. "I trust you enjoyed your sojourn in England?"

"It had its high points, Yuri."

And its low ones as well. Orlov pursed his lips, aware of a slightly sour taste in the back of his mouth despite the sweetness of the wine. The covert mission had not gone quite as planned. In truth, he considered it somewhat of a personal failure, though the end result had proved satisfying to his superiors.

He had been dispatched to London to retrieve a stolen document. The fragile alliance between England and Russia depended upon keeping it out of French hands, and the Tsar had been unwilling to trust Whitehall's agents to get the job done.

Perhaps because not in the wildest flight of fancy would anyone in Russian Intelligence have imagined what shape and form the English counterattack would take.

Orlov stared moodily at his port. The paper had indeed been found—but not by him. Though to be fair, he had made a certain contribution to the success of the venture. The two traitors would not be sending any more state secrets across the Channel. Still, the thought of being outmaneuvered by a rival operative stuck in his throat.

Swearing a silent oath, he drained the rest of his drink in one gulp.

Never one to hold his punches, Yussapov threw in another sly jab. "Don't look so glum about being bested by a female, *tvaritsch*. Lord Lynsley's winged ladies are said to be birds of a unique feather."

"They are that." Both he and the prince had been astounded to discover that Whitehall's most trusted agents were a secret force of highly trained women warriors.

And they were good. *Damn good.*

So was he. Yet it was only by the skin of his teeth that he had eluded the embarrassment of being captured. Sitting here, in the comfort of the Stockholm embassy, it was easy enough to crack jokes. But at the time, it had been no laughing matter.

Taking up the prince's Cossack dagger, Orlov spun its point upon the leather blotter. "However, you might have given me—and Lord Lynsley—fair warning that the mission was a joint venture. As it was, the wrong man nearly ended up with his throat cut."

"Bah." Yussapov brushed off the retort with a cavalier wave. "All's well that ends well. Is that not how your famous Bard put it?"

"As I am half Russian, I am wont to look at things from a more melancholy perspective," he replied dryly. "It is easy for you to laugh from the comfort of your armchair and lap robes, but the whole affair came dangerously close to disaster on account of not knowing who was friend and who was foe. If we are allies with the British, should we not try to work together a bit more closely?"

"We are uneasy allies, Alexandr. The Tsar is not quite certain he can trust the Mad King and his ministers."

"Still, it is cork-brained not to share intelligence with Whitehall." Light winked off the razored steel. "While we circle each other with daggers drawn, Napoleon's agents steal a march on us."

"You have a point." The prince stroked at his beard. "I shall raise the issue with His Imperial Highness."

Orlov felt marginally better for having voiced his opinion. Yet his mood remained surprisingly discontented given the superb quality of the aged port and Turkish cheroots. Leaning back, he propped a booted foot on the desk and blew out a ring of smoke, hoping to rid himself of his black humor as well. It hung for an instant in the air, a perfect oval in harmony with itself, before disappearing in a sinuous swirl of ghostly vapor.

Ashes to ashes . . . What strange musings had come over him? His Slavic penchant for brooding introspection was usually balanced by the more devil-may-care spirit of his English heritage. His mother, a lively Yorkshire beauty, had proved a perfect foil for his Muscovite father's proclivity for solitary sulks.

Orlov drew in another mouthful of the pungent tobacco smoke. He was aware that many would say he had inherited the worst traits of both parents. His cynical outlook on life and acerbic wit offended most people. Deliberately, he conceded. He was the first to admit that he was an unprincipled scamp, a rapscallion rogue. A man possessing a finely honed sense of honor would have difficulty doing the things he was called on to do. Lies, thievery, seduction—and yes, even murder. His conscience, if ever he had had one, was certainly long dead to remorse and recrimination.

"Another drink?" Yussapov was eyeing him strangely from beneath his shaggy silver brows. "You appear—how do the English say it?—red-deviled tonight."

"*Blue*-deviled, Yuri." Forcing a sardonic smile, Orlov held out his glass. "Stick to Russian if you wish to employ subtle sarcasm. It loses something in the translation."

"*Moi?* Sarcastic?" Assuming an air of injured innocence, the prince toyed with the fobs on his watch chain.
"I am merely concerned for you, *tvaritsch*. As a friend, I
fear that of late we are asking too much of you."

Orlov nearly choked on a laugh. "I am greatly touched
by your tender sentiment," he replied after swallowing
the port. "Not that I am fooled in the least by what moti-
vates it. I take it you have another job?"

A flicker of hesitation, and what seemed to be a flash
of warmth. But Orlov quickly dismissed it as a quirk
of the candlelight. Or a figment of his own overheated
imagination. For when Yussapov spoke, it was with his
usual ruthless candor. "As a matter of fact, yes. This one
will not require your celebrated charm with women."

"You are skating on dangerous ice, Yuri," he growled.
"That particular joke is wearing thin."

"You *are* in an odd mood." The prince folded his
hands on the desk. "But I shall take heed of the warning
and skirt the issue—"

Orlov's glass thumped down beside the fallen dagger.

"My, my, such a sensitive skin tonight, *tvaritsch*. But
very well, I shall refrain from any further mischief." His
expression sobered. "There is, after all, nothing remotely
amusing about this next mission."

"Which is?"

"Our head of Intelligence in Brussels was murdered
last week. We have good reason to think it was done by
D'Etienne, the same fellow who dispatched the Prussian
envoy in Warsaw."

"I have heard of him," murmured Orlov. "He is said to
be the most dangerous agent the French have. And very
good at what he does." A wry grimace thinned his lips.
"Apparently the rumors are not much exaggerated."

"Good, yes." Yussapov swirled his ruby port. "But not, I trust, as good as you."

Muscles tensing, he straightened in his chair. "What is it you want me to do?"

"Kill him, of course."

"Of course," repeated Orlov softly.

"As you know, we have resumed negotiations with England about forging an alliance between us and our Western compatriots. Through murder and mayhem, the French hope to disrupt any agreement between our countries."

"Where is D'Etienne now?"

"In Ireland. He's staying for several weeks to foment trouble with the Irish nationals. From there, we believe he is scheduled to move on to Britain, in order to assassinate Angus McAllister."

"The Scottish ballistics expert?" Orlov frowned. "That would indeed be a blow to the British efforts to improve their artillery units."

"So you understand the gravity of the situation."

He stared at the blood-red refractions of light from the crystal. "You have no need to offer moral explanations. I am far from faint-hearted."

"You are human, Alexandr. As am I. I do not ask you to take a life lightly," said Yussapov quietly. "But however repugnant, the action may save a great many good men."

Orlov merely shrugged.

"You look tired, *tvaritsch*."

"I'm not getting any younger," he snapped.

A wink of gold flashed in the candlelight as Yussapov toyed with his signet ring. "Perhaps the time has come to think of settling down. Of getting a wife."

"God forbid." He grimaced. "Can you really imagine me legshackled to a proper little London belle or Muscovite miss?"

The prince contemplated the question for all of five seconds before giving a bark of laughter. "I confess, I cannot picture you leading such an ordinary life."

"Work may be a hard mistress, but it's far preferable to the boredom of matrimony." A sardonic curl lingered at the corners of his mouth. "I trust you have the logistics for this assignment arranged."

"A schooner is ready to sail on the next tide."

"Ah, and here I thought I would have a chance to explore the Nordic delights of Stockholm. A pity—a blond Valkyrie would be just the thing to appeal to a man of my tastes." He rose. "Perhaps next time."

The prince pushed a packet of papers across the desk. "All the background details are there, as well as maps and a list of contacts."

Orlov slipped it into his coat pocket. "When do you return to St. Petersburg?"

"I still have several more meetings with the Minister of War and his deputies regarding the Polish question. After that . . ." He shrugged. "God knows where I shall be. Like you, I am dispatched to wherever it is necessary to fight fire with fire."

"Do have a care not to get singed, Yuri."

"And you, Alexandr. Contrary to what you think, I *am* a sentimental old fool. I would be greatly upset to hear of your demise. So do try to return in one piece rather than go out in a blaze of glory."

Chapter Two

I am not quite sure what I should do, Charlotte." The Marquess of Lynsley settled down on the sofa, his coal black coat and pantaloons a somber smudge on the pastel floral chintz. "I do not make a habit of second-guessing my decisions, but in this case . . ."

"It is, I know, an onerous one, Thomas. But that is why the Academy exists—because there are no easy or pretty answers to the threats our country faces in times of war." A frail, feather-thin widow with a cap of dove gray curls framing her narrow face, Mrs. Merlin had presided over the school since its inception. Age had softened her features and blunted the poke of her prominent nose, but behind the oversized spectacles, her silvery eyes gleamed with a hawkish intensity. "The girls understand that."

"I know." Lynsley pinched the bridge of his nose. "Yet it does not make it any easier to sleep at night."

"Rest easy," she counseled. "Protecting England from enemies who would seek to destroy its sovereignty, its freedoms, is a cause worth fighting for. Victory does not come without sacrifices."

"Thank you for serving up a generous helping of sympathy along with your superb Oolong tea and strawberry tarts." He leaned back from the light and sipped at the fragrant brew.

Despite his wealth and rank, the marquess chose to spend much of his time in the shadows. And by design, he would not stand out in a crowd. Over the years he had learned a number of subtle mannerisms to appear slighter and shorter than he really was. As for his features, they were austerely patrician, but by cultivating a self-deprecating smile, he softened the edge of authority. His hair was neither long nor short, and its mouse brown hue, now turning silver at the temples, was echoed in the somber tones of his clothing. Many people thought him a bland, rather boring bureaucrat. A fact that suited him perfectly.

His official title—Minister to the Secretary of State for War—was a deliberately vague cover for his true responsibilities. Charged with countering espionage and intrigue, he dealt with the most dangerous and diabolical threats to England's sovereignty. The Academy had been one of his most unorthodox ideas. The Prime Minister had thought him mad at first, but he had convinced the government to give him an old estate, which had been used as cavalry pastures. He paid the operating expenses out of his own pocket, and Mrs. Merlin oversaw all the day-to-day operations.

"I know you take these decisions very personally, Thomas. After all, it was you who picked each of our students from the rabble of orphans roaming the slums."

Lynsley drew a deep breath. "Regrettably, I have a

great many from which to choose." Each year, a select few were added to the ranks of the school. He looked for signs of courage and cleverness in a girl. And looks. Beauty was a weapon in itself.

"Life can be unfair, as we both know," replied the headmistress. "However, the girls take pride in the fact that they have been given the weapons to fight for a higher good."

"So, would you care to offer any last-minute advice on my choice?" he asked.

"To be frank, I am not sure you *have* any choice." Peering over the rims of her spectacles, Mrs. Merlin slowly squared the sheaf of papers on her desk. "The latest evaluations from Shannon's instructors only confirm what I've observed for myself. No one else here can come close to matching her skills with weaponry."

"I have no doubts about her physical prowess," said Lynsley softly. "It's her mental state that is cause for concern. If ever an assignment called for a cool head and steady nerve, it is this one. An impulsive move, an unnecessary risk, and she will die. As will others, as a result of her failure." The marquess stared into his cup, as if trying to read the tea leaves. Throughout the first few months of 1812, Napoleon had won one military triumph after another on the Continent. England desperately needed a victory—even a small one—to show that the Emperor was not almighty. "I have read the disciplinary reports on the top of your pile. Knowing of a weakness beforehand makes me wonder whether I am morally justified in overlooking it."

"Sometimes a weakness can be a strength. It's all a matter of timing and degree," replied Mrs. Merlin. "Being decisive, even dangerously daring, can often snatch victory from the jaws of defeat."

He made a wry face. "You are very persuasive."

"That is why you pay me so well to teach a master class in rhetoric and logic." A twinkle reflected off the lenses of her spectacles. "However, I take it you have not made up your mind?"

"No."

"Let us go ahead and call her in. If you decide at the last minute on a change of strategy, then we will regroup and come up with another plan of attack."

At Lynsley's nod, the headmistress rose and went to the door.

Wiping her hands on the backside of her breeches, Shannon tried to remove the worst of the black powder and gun oil. A sidelong glance in the windowpane showed a face streaked with sweat and a spattering of mud, its sharp angles framed by untamed tendrils that had pulled free of her hairpins. A picture of recklessness rather than restraint.

She sucked in her breath, trying to keep her emotions under tight rein. If they expected parade ground precision, they would be disappointed. And not for the first time.

Squaring her shoulders, she shook off such negative thoughts. If defeat were inevitable, she would show grace and grit and . . .

Goddamn it, she would fight like the very devil to change their minds.

"Ah, I see Hopkins passed on the message," said Mrs. Merlin as Shannon snapped off a quick salute.

"Yes, ma'am. I came as quickly as I could."

The headmistress eyed the trail of mud and straw now befouling her hallway runner. "So I see."

"Sorry. I should have—"

"Come in, come in." The headmistress waved off the apology. "Lord Lynsley is here, and we have several things we would like to discuss with you, my dear."

If one lived by the sword, one should not be afraid to die by the sword.

"Before you begin, sir, might I first say a few words in my own defense?"

"This is not a court-martial, Shannon," said the marquess softly. He smiled, though the crinkling of humor could not quite hide the lines of tension etched around his mouth and eyes.

"It is what I deserve, sir," she replied. "And yet . . ." Lynsley was always so kindly. Like the father she had never known. As she met his gaze, she found herself wondering about his age. It was hard to tell. His hair, though threaded with silver, was still thick and his body still looked lean and strong beneath the elegant tailoring. She had heard rumors of his youthful exploits for Whitehall, tales that seemed at odds with his refined features and courtly manners—

His brow quirked ever so slightly. "And yet?"

Roused from her momentary study, she quickly finished her request. "And yet, I should like to offer a rationale for what I did."

"Would you care for some tea first?" murmured Mrs. Merlin.

Shannon shook her head, afraid the rattle of china might betray the true state of her nerves.

Lynsley set down his cup and folded his well-tended hands in his lap. "Go on, then."

"According to Sun Tzu, the great Chinese military strategist, *yin* and *yang*—hot and cold—are essential elements of the art of war. They must be balanced, of course." She swallowed hard. Did she dare go on and risk sounding insubordinate? There was still time to pull back and take cover in convention. The clotted cream and cakes looked inviting. "Which is to say, sir, that victory cannot come from wisdom, organization, and discipline alone. Such sterling qualities must be complemented by flexibility, imagination, and surprise."

"In other words," said Lynsley slowly, "a general must trust the *ch'i*—the spirit—of his officers in the field?"

Shannon wished she could read his reaction. The marquess was always in command of his emotions. Neither his inflection nor his expression gave anything away. She slanted a look to Mrs. Merlin, but the elderly lady was busy jotting a few lines in her notebook.

"Yes, sir."

"A very incisive and intelligent summation of the legendary manual of war. Based on such principles, how would you assess your own recent performance?"

What did she have to lose?

"In retrospect, sir, I would not have done anything differently." She forced a ghost of a grin. "Save perhaps for not cutting the Russian rascal's throat when I had the chance."

Was it merely a flicker of the candles, or did Lynsley's lips twitch? In her defense, the mysterious Mr. Orlov had proved just as slippery in eluding the marquess's efforts to nab him. Despite a tight surveillance of all the Channel ports, the man had disappeared as if into thin air.

But it was not Orlov's fate that was under discussion—it was her own.

"Let me explain myself more fully," she went on quickly. "When you asked me those questions concerning Siena's loyalty and commitment to the Academy, I judged that her mission must be of the utmost importance." Forcing a calmness that belied the churning of her inside, Shannon paused for a fraction. "I also judged that it was in danger of failing for two reasons—Siena was a traitor, or she was in trouble. Either way, I decided I could be the difference between success and failure."

Mrs. Merlin looked up from her notes, her gaze intense, unblinking. The resemblance to her namesake hawk was uncanny. "And what if Siena had betrayed the principles of our Academy?"

"I did not truly believe it would come to that. But if it had, I trust I would have had the strength to do the right thing."

Coals crackled in the hearth. Papers shuffled with a feathery whisper. Shannon watched steam curl up from the teapot, wondering whether her hopes of remaining at the Academy were dissolving just as quickly.

"Sit down, Shannon, and take some sustenance."

As Mrs. Merlin's gentle urging had an undertone of command, she perched herself on the edge of the nearest chair and accepted a plate of shortbread.

"Well, Thomas?" murmured the headmistress after she had finished refilling his cup. "Satisfied?"

Shannon sensed Mrs. Merlin was not referring to food or drink.

Lynsley touched a hand to his temple.

To Shannon, the silence spoke volumes as to his lingering misgivings. "Sir, before you answer, I have one last thing to add," she said. "If I may."

He nodded.

"Rather than make a final decision, why not give me a trial? A chance to prove myself in an assignment of my own."

A frown furrowed Lynsley's brow. "A trial by combat, so to speak?" He considered the idea a moment longer. "The idea strikes me as somewhat barbaric. If I am to ask you to risk your life, it ought to be as—"

"Think of it more as an apprenticeship," she interrupted. "In truth, you can't be expected to admit me to the ranks of the full-fledged Merlins, seeing as my first flight was erratic. However, it would be a shame to waste all the years of training without giving me one more chance to prove my wings."

His grave expression betrayed a flicker of bemusement. "A skillful negotiation."

Shannon had once been told by Mrs. Merlin that the marquess had been inspired to create the Academy after reading a book on Hasan-I-Sabah, a Muslim caliph who raised a secret society of warriors at his mountain citadels. His men were known for their deadly skills and fanatic loyalty. And legend had it that they never failed on a mission. The very name *Hashishim*—or Assassins—was enough to strike terror in the heart of the Master's enemy.

Like them, she would do anything to prove her unswerving dedication to Lord Lynsley and his ideals.

"Though it may not seem so, sir, I do understand that victory is not always achieved with a sword," replied Shannon. "A good general knows that compromise can be a powerful weapon." She hardly dared to breathe. "What do you say?"

In answer, the marquess slowly pulled an oilskin packet from inside his coat and put it on the side table.

Her throat went suddenly dry. Marching orders, no doubt. But to where?

"I admit that I have had mixed feelings about you, Shannon. On one hand I admire your courage, your conviction. On the other hand, I worry that your bravado is dangerous. Not only to you, but to all those who depend on you to get the job done."

She nodded.

"But Mrs. Merlin is of the opinion that you should be given a second chance."

Hope soared in her breast. "I promise I won't let you down, sir."

His lips compressed. "Don't thank me quite yet. The assignment is a very dangerous one, Shannon. If I had a choice, I would not rush you into action so soon." His fingers drummed upon the packet. "However, Mrs. Merlin tells me I do not. The job calls for a full arsenal of deadly skills. You are, without question, the best we have."

"Thank you, sir!" Ignoring his admonition, she broke into a wide grin. But much as her fingers itched to snatch up her orders, she held herself back.

"As I said, you may soon be wishing me to Hades, rather than heaven, once you learn the particulars," he replied dryly. "The details are all spelled out in your orders. I do hope you are not prone to seasickness."

An ocean voyage? A wave of excitement washed over her. "No, sir. My stomach stays on an even keel." After a moment she added, "As will my resolve. I won't go off half-cocked."

"I am counting on that, for the man you are matching up against is a consummate professional. The smallest slip on your part could prove fatal." He glanced at the clock. "We have time for only a brief overview before you must leave. A coach is waiting outside to convey you to the coast."

"I promise that I shall watch my step, sir." Shannon schooled her voice to a flat calm. "What is it you want me to do when I come in contact with him?"

"Kill him, before he assassinates another one of our key allies." Lynsley stood and went to warm his hands by the fire. No spark, no flame reached his face. Wreathed in shadow, his eyes appeared gray as gunmetal and the weight of his responsibilities seemed to hang like cannonballs from his shoulders. She did not envy him his job.

"Tell me when, and where." Was she headed to France? To the Low Countries, to . . .

"Ireland," he said. "We have received word that for the next fortnight he is residing at a remote castle of the O'Malley clan near Killarney. The French have sent him to instruct several of their members in the tricks of his trade before moving on to Scotland for his next attack."

"An isolated location, a fortress bristling with armed guards," she mused. "Let us hope he has a weakness for women."

"D'Etienne is French," replied Lynsley dryly. "And is said to have an insatiable appetite for feminine flesh. Which is another reason why you have been chosen over one of my military operatives."

"He is about to get a taste of a *femme fatale*." She thought for a moment. "Any preference for how it is to be done?"

"I leave the choice to your discretion, Shannon."

"Is D'Etienne the only target, sir? I have heard that O'Malley and his bunch are a brutal lot."

Lynsley appeared to measure his words carefully.

"D'Etienne is our main concern. Don't risk the mission by going after the others. But an Irish rebellion would be a serious threat to our government at this time. If there are other casualties . . ." He did not need to finish the thought.

"I had best go collect my weapons." She stood up.

"Sofia had already been instructed to load them in the coach." Mrs. Merlin consulted the small gold watch pinned to her bodice. "You have a quarter of an hour to change your clothes and pack the rest of your gear."

The marquess pressed the document packet into her hands. "I would not have you think this is a punishment or a penance," he said softly. "Don't go up against insurmountable odds. I would rather have you return, ready for another try, than die a hero's death on the ramparts."

"I understand, sir. Discretion is the better part of valor." Shannon flashed a rueful smile. "Contrary to what some of my classroom teachers think, I *do* listen to their lectures."

"So I am learning." His expression of grim foreboding had lightened somewhat. "I have sent my carriage on ahead and shall ride with you for the first few miles to go over the logistics of the mission. Certain details I cannot put down in writing. The rest of the information you will have ample time to study while you are at sea."

"Godspeed, Shannon. Now go." Mrs. Merlin fluttered her hands.

She snapped a salute and moved off swiftly through the arched hallway. It was an unspoken rule that sentiment played no part in Academy farewells. Still, on crossing the courtyard, she felt a small lump form in her throat. *A rite of passage.* From the familiar—the nicked gargoyle, the cracked tower bell, the loosened gate latch—to the unknown. For the first time, she was no longer a student but a full-fledged agent.

One of Merlin's Maidens.

She must now prove herself worthy of her wings.

Hurrying her steps, Shannon took the stairs two at a time up to her room. Not that packing would occupy a great deal of time. A proper young lady of the *ton* might require an army of trunks to transport her wardrobe, but for her, a single canvas seaman's bag would do. A rain cloak, a throwing knife, a set of picklocks from—

"Take this as well." Sofia jammed a small leather-bound book in between the slivers of steel. "You may have a few moments of peace in which to read."

"But you haven't finished it." Shannon didn't look up from rolling her riding gloves into a tight ball.

"Which is why I expect you to bring it back in one piece. It cost me an arm and a leg."

"Thanks, Fifi. I will do my best to keep it unscathed."

"See that you do." Her roommate perched a hip on her desk. "Or I'll take a birch to your backside."

"You could try." Shannon tested the flex of a braided rope and added it to the bag. "But you might find yourself too sore to sit down for a fortnight."

Sofia grinned and mimed an intricate ballroom twirl. "Not if I dance out of reach."

Both understood the feelings that lay beneath the banter. Thrown together, skinny little orphans plucked from the sordid stews of London, they had become close as sisters during their years at the Academy. The only family each had ever known.

"Your prowess on the parquet far exceeds mine," admitted Shannon. "Of the three of us, you have always been the most ladylike." Seeing her friend scowl, she hastened to add, "Not that I am disparaging your fighting skills, it's just that grace and charm are your weapons, while I must rely on a steel wrist and a sharp aim to vanquish a foe."

Her friend leveled a long look her way before answering. "Don't underestimate your strengths, Nonnie."

As she tugged her shirt over her head, Shannon caught a glimpse of her own reflection in the looking glass. Though slender as a rapier, she could hardly be described as delicate. Not with her height, and the hint of lithe muscle accentuating the more feminine curves. Marco had once compared her to a lioness, pointing out her blonde mane and explosive athleticism. He had also remarked on her gaze, calling it piercing, predatory. *The eyes of a hunter.*

Shannon stared at the glitter of green for an instant, then ducked away. How strange. She saw doubt where others saw determination. As for her face, while others described her features as striking, she considered herself quite ordinary.

Smoothing the folds of the fresh linen, she stripped off her old breeches and donned a clean pair.

"Know thyself as well as the enemy," she said softly, quoting another precept from Sun-Tzu's classic treatise on the art of war. "I shall take great care to avoid any mistakes in judgment."

"You have nothing to prove, you know." Sofia fingered the thin filigree chain at her neck. "To yourself or to others."

Not trusting her voice, Shannon jammed a last bit of clothing into her bag and pulled the strings taut.

"One last thing . . ." Unfastening the clasp, Sofia took

the length of silver and the hawk-shaped pendant and pressed it into Shannon's palm.

"T-this is your lucky charm!"

"I am counting on you to bring it back, along with my book, so that I may depend on its powers when it's my turn to fly."

Fisting the tiny talisman, Shannon gave her friend a fierce hug. "Time to go."

Fog. Rain. The bone-chilling dampness pervaded every cursed corner of the creaking timbers. Orlov wrapped his cloak a bit tighter around his shoulders. Not even a layer of thick sable could keep it at bay. Glowering at the gray waves, he took yet another turn on the narrow deck.

"You are not at home on a ship?" The Dutch captain fell in step beside him.

"I prefer space to stretch my legs." The schooner gave a yawing lurch. "And *terra firma* beneath them."

"With this wind, we shall soon be reaching our destination."

"It can't be soon enough." Orlov added a rather salty oath.

The officer immediately knocked his knuckles on the wooden railing. "We sailors are a superstitious lot. It is bad luck to insult the sea gods."

"Then it is fortunate I have no ambitions for a nautical career. I hold very little sacred, save my own skin." Wiping the drops from his brow, he grimaced. "Which may soon turn into fish scales."

"This is no more than a passing drizzle."

Cold comfort indeed. "I think I shall go below," he said, though his dank cabin was designed for someone only marginally larger than a bilge rat.

Once he had wedged his lanky frame into the narrow berth—a feat that forced him to draw his knees to his chin—Orlov lit the lamp and thumbed through the sheaf of documents. He had, of course, read over them before.

Ad nauseam, he added wryly as his stomach gave an unpleasant heave. A touch of seasickness brought on by the foul weather did not improve his mood. By the bones of St. Sergius, he hated traveling by ship.

He turned his attention back to the papers. Yussapov's spies had been quite thorough. D'Etienne's background and accomplishments were spelled out in grisly detail. The man was, by all accounts, a ruthless bastard whose list of victims included several women and a young child. Orlov's expression clouded. He freely admitted to having precious little claim on morality, but he did not make war on the families of his foes. His profession was a dirty business, and killing a sordid necessity, but in this particular case he would not suffer any twinge of conscience.

The maps appeared excellent as well. Routes were drawn, landmarks described, and several bolt holes marked along the way. He spent some time committing the information to memory, before nausea and a piercing headache forced him to extinguish the flame. However, the pounding of the waves against the hull was still foreign to him and he had trouble settling into the rhythm of the ocean.

Were the sea gods seeking vengeance for his verbal slight? Or was it some more earthly demon prodding a trident into his skull?

He could not shake the feeling that something was not quite right. As of yet, he could not put a finger on it. The feeling was nebulous, like the crosscurrents of fog rising up from the sea. Impossible to grab hold of, but its swirl stirred a prickling at the nape of his neck. It might be only the ill effects of the *mal de mer*.

But he didn't think so.

Instinct, a sixth sense for survival, had warned him in the past of impending danger. He had learned to trust these strange twinges—a leap of faith for someone who tended to view the world with sardonic detachment. Trust was, after all, not a very practical attribute in his profession. Deception and duplicity were far more useful. Lying had become second nature . . .

Pressing his fingertips to his throbbing temples, Orlov sought to hold such disquieting musings at bay. It wasn't often that he gave a second thought to the morality of what he did. *Right and wrong? Good and evil?* Perhaps a true gentleman would believe in absolutes. But it seemed to him that the world was not black and white, but rather shaded in an infinite range of grays.

And yet, he did have *some* principles. Though he would be loath to admit it aloud, he did care—if his actions helped stop the spread of tyranny and injustice, then perhaps his benighted soul would not roast in damnation for eternity.

He made a face. The Almighty might be forgiving, but there was a young lady who would like to see his soul—or more likely his liver—fried over the hottest coals of Hell. Not that he could blame her. He had made several uncharacteristic mistakes during his last mission, a fact that might very well be exacerbating his present malaise.

Was he losing his touch?

Damn Yussapov. And damn the sudden stirrings of his English sense of honor. Somehow the tumultuous seas had churned up the oddest mix of sensations. In his mind's eye, he suddenly saw the prince's beaded face, melting into visions of a blond Valkyrie, and then a soaring hawk. From high in the heavens came a cry, cursing him roundly for his misdeeds.

That it echoed some of his own recent musings amplified its accusations. However, the Russian part of him knew how to drown such melancholy brooding.

Growling an oath, Orlov reached for the flask of spirits.

Chapter Three

This godforsaken part of Ireland was not for the faint of heart.

Shannon surveyed the forbidding stones. Lynsley had not exaggerated the isolation of the McGuillicuddy Reeks. *Desolation*, she corrected. Famine had left the hardscrabble moors deserted, and although there was a bleak beauty to the landscape, she knew it was a harsh, hostile environment for anyone trying to eke out a living.

Returning her attention to the wind-chiseled walls of the O'Malley stronghold, she trained her spyglass on one of the outer towers. A primitive garden cut between its base and a copse of stunted live oaks. The tangle of branches would cover her approach, and the turreted roof would afford an excellent anchor for her climbing rope. Lynsley's spy had informed her that the second-floor library was rarely used. From there, she would find a short corridor and connecting stairs to the chambers where the French assassin was quartered.

Her own surveillance had confirmed that the library was deserted at night. And while she would have liked to double-check every detail on the informant's sketch of the castle layout, she had seen enough of the actual interior to feel she could trust the basics.

She shifted her position behind the outcropping of granite and gorse. Lynsley had also been correct in figuring that a female would have a distinct advantage in completing this mission successfully. A male stranger in the area would have raised suspicions, but a mere woman . . .

Disguised in rags and greasepaint, she had approached the castle on foot, timidly asking if there might be an opening for a scullery maid. None of the armed guards had viewed a haggard crone as any threat. Allowed to pass through the gates, she had been shown to the kitchens and offered a bowl of gruel before being told there was no position open and sent on her way.

Irish hospitality was legendary—as was their low opinion of a woman's ability to do aught but bear children.

A grave miscalculation on their part.

The inside glimpse of the fortress had been quite helpful. But even before her inquiries, Shannon had decided that using seduction as a strategy against D'Etienne was too risky. Given the isolated location, a flirtatious young stranger would draw too much attention from the other men. As for the other serving women, they were likely all members of the O'Malley clan, and would watch her every move.

Her attack would instead depend on stealth.

Satisfied that she had seen enough, Shannon crept down from her perch and returned to the hollow where she had hidden her horses. Her arsenal, supplemented from the supplies of the navy sloop that had brought her to Ireland, offered a choice of ways to attack the target. Flexibility was key, and she had spent the interminable hours aboard ship planning for every contingency.

Lynsley would have no reason to fault her for making an impetuous move, she vowed.

After watching the routine of the stronghold for several days, she had decided on the simplest strategy. O'Malley's men had grown lax in their nightly patrols of the grounds, perhaps overconfident that the deep gorge and narrow stone bridge would deter any unwanted visitors. They spent most of the midnight hours drinking and playing cards in the kitchens. Shannon was certain she would have no trouble entering the castle unseen and completing her assignment in brutal silence.

She ran a thumb over the edge of her knife. *In and out.* That was the plan. But in case anything went awry, she would have a few tricks up her sleeve.

Nothing would be left to chance.

Fog hung low over the battlements, softening the jagged silhouette of the ancient crenellations. Orlov took one more look around the castle grounds before inching through the bushes. The trap door, its hinges thick with rust, was just where his map had indicated. Hoping that the rest of his information was accurate, he brushed aside the moss and went to work on the lock.

As the hasp yielded with a dull snick, Orlov shouldered a small canvas sack and slipped inside. By his sketch, the old root cellar led up to the pantries, and from there, a circular stairway gave access to the rooms where O'Malley was quartering his visitors. He felt his way through the pitch-black gloom, finding the passageway behind a stack of rotting crates.

So far, so good.

The smells of roasted beef and spilled ale wafted out from the kitchens. Orlov paused to cock an ear as several men finished off their meal and prepared to relieve the guards on patrol. A nugget of useful information could often be picked up from the muddle of rough laughter and crude curses.

After listening for some moments, he edged back into the shelter of the stairway, swearing a silent oath of his own. *Time to improvise.* A mission of this nature rarely went like clockwork, he reminded himself. Which was why he had come prepared.

The rope slithered over the roof slates, its loop tightening over one of the iron stanchions. Shannon tested her weight against its hold, then wrapped a turn around her hand. As if on wings, she rose noiselessly up the face of the wall and landed lightly on the library ledge. Her blade released the window latch, allowing her to crack open the casement.

Once inside, she took a moment for her eyes to adjust to the darkened room. Between the scudding clouds and the waning moon, there was barely a glimmer of light filtering in through the mullioned glass. Just enough to show a massive oak desk, which looked to date back to Elizabethan times, bookcases crammed with mismatched tomes and . . .

A slight scratching sounded from the far corner of the room.

Crouching low behind a curio cabinet, she thumbed

back the hammer of her pistol. A mouse, perhaps? Taking no chances, she loosened her knife in its sheath.

The sound came again, louder this time, followed by a flicker of movement.

No, it could not be.

A stab of moonlight cut across the room, catching another glimmer of gold.

"You!" she growled. There was no mistaking the lean, lithe form that materialized from the shadows. *The Russian scoundrel.* She would have recognized that distinctive blond hair and glittering wolf's-head earring through the brimstone smoke and fire of hell.

"You," he echoed softly, sounding no more pleased than she was at the encounter.

As they slowly lowered their weapons, Shannon saw he had a gold snuffbox in his other hand. "You have chosen an extremely dangerous place for petty thievery, Mr. Orlov. Get out, before you pay for your hubris with your life this time."

The Russian flashed an infuriating smile. "Hardly petty, *golub*. This is a Renaissance work of art crafted by Cellini. And worth a fortune." He pocketed the tiny treasure. "As for taking a leave of this place, I was just going to advise you to do the same." He cocked a glance at the case clock. "Now."

"Thank you, but I've come for more than a golden bauble."

"D'Etienne is not here. He moved on to Tralee two days ago."

"How—" she began.

"Trust me."

"*You?* I'd rather trust a snake."

"There are no snakes in Ireland, thanks to St. Patrick." Orlov looked again at the clock.

"Afraid you are going to be late for an assignation?" she hissed. "I'm sure the lady won't quibble if you are a moment or two late."

"What I am afraid of, *golub,* is that if we linger here much longer, there won't be any body parts big enough to identify, much less pleasure." He took her arm and pulled her none too gently up onto the window ledge. "Let's go."

"What the devil do you mean?" Shannon wrenched free, her pistol coming up to take dead aim again.

"I've set a charge of explosives in the room where O'Malley has stored his shipment of French gold. Its loss will have serious repercussions on his ability to foment trouble in these parts, at least for a while." He shrugged and stepped up to the lintel. "But suit yourself. If you would rather blow yourself to Kingdom Come for no reason, that's your choice. I shall send my condolences to Lord Lynsley and tell him you died bravely. Foolishly, but bravely."

Shannon hesitated, wondering whether to believe him.

"Need a hand?" he asked. "Perhaps yours is still a trifle weak."

Her cheeks reddened at the reminder of their last encounter, when he had nearly broken her wrist. "Keep your paws to yourself," she warned as she joined him out on the stone ledge. "I don't need—"

Further retort was cut off by the sound of a key turning in the lock.

"Damn," muttered Orlov.

They quickly separated, and took cover on either side

of the window. Shannon flattened against the outer wall just as the door opened and a half dozen men trooped into the library.

"You see, there's nothing amiss, Frenchie," said one of them, holding a lantern aloft. "You saw naught but a shadow."

"Or a castle ghost," said another. "O'Malley's ancestors have more than enough evil deeds to lament."

Laughter greeted the quip.

From her vantage point, Shannon could see they were all armed, their weapons primed and cocked. She swore a silent oath. Whether the Russian was lying or not, any hope of completing her mission had just gone up in smoke. The only option was retreat. Still, she didn't dare move quite yet. The slightest sound and all hell would break loose.

With luck, they would move off in a moment.

"It was no shadow, or stirring of the dead," insisted a weasel-faced man with a heavy Gallic accent. "I tell you, *mon vieux*, someone has slipped through your guard."

"Impossible," scoffed the man with the lantern. Angling its beam into every nook and cranny, he swept the light in a slow circle over the bookshelves. "What say you, O'Malley? See anything amiss?"

The Irish leader, a red-headed giant with a massive face half covered by a bristling beard, slanted one last glance around the room. "Nay. All looks to be—" His words gave way to a roar of rage. "The Cellini!"

Whipping around, he broke for the window, but got no more than a stride before a bullet slammed into his chest.

"Jump!" cried Orlov. "I'll hold them off."

"With what—your bare hands?" Shannon's shot cut

down the man with the lantern, as a bullet whizzed by her head.

That left four men, and three shots . . .

Two, she corrected, throwing herself back against the castle wall in the nick of time. Lead ricocheted off the stone, the chips cutting a gash on her cheek.

Orlov pulled a second pistol and dropped the man by the desk before he could reload. But the Frenchman dodged through the smoke and took cover behind the curio case, gaining a perfect angle on the window opening.

Shannon saw his weapon rise. Off balance and pinned against the stone, she had nowhere to turn, nowhere to hide . . .

"Jump, damn it!"

Orlov flung himself forward and pulled her down just as a shot exploded. His second shove pushed her over the ledge. The drop was short and the damp turf cushioned the impact. Rolling over, Shannon was on her feet in an instant. The Russian fell awkwardly by her side. He was not so quick to rise.

"Run," he gasped.

She saw blood seeping through the rent in his jacket. Already his shoulder was dark with the spreading stain. Reaching down, she caught hold of his uninjured arm.

"Every man for himself," he snarled, trying to shake her off.

"I work by different rules." She hauled him to his feet.

"Go, damn you. They will be quick to reload."

Shannon had already turned and lobbed a small silk sack through the open casement.

Whoomph!

Flames shot up in a shattering of glass and black smoke belched through the broken mullions. From inside came a bloodcurdling scream.

"How the devil . . ." Orlov's eyes narrowed. "You had no lucifer, no flint—"

"Mercury fulminate. A sharp concussion sets it off." She spun around. "That will cover our retreat for the moment." She pushed him toward the footpath cutting between the boxwood hedges. "This way."

Setting a bruising pace, Shannon led the way over the loose gravel. The Russian kept slipping, and his breathing grew more ragged, but somehow he managed to keep up. A last twist brought them down to a narrow stone bridge, where finally his step faltered.

"They will soon be in hot pursuit. I'll only slow you down." Leaning back against the railing, he waved her on. "Go. I'll take my chances."

"Which are nil." Without waiting for further argument, she took hold of his coat and hustled him across the divide.

"*Now* what are you waiting for?" he said through gritted teeth as she knelt down. "A band of angels to strike up a funeral dirge?"

Ignoring his sarcasm, she scraped a flint to steel, setting a spark to a length of fuse snaking down to the base of the bridge. "You are not the only one who came prepared for pyrotechnics."

"It's wet out here—" he began.

"I've accounted for that. The gunpowder is corned to a special grain, with an extra measure of saltpeter." She edged back. "The charge will fire."

A loud explosion punctuated her words. Flames flared up from one of the castle towers, lighting the shower of roof slates and flying stone with an unearthly glow. "It appears your handiwork will slow them somewhat. As will the destruction of the bridge." Shannon peered down into the deep ravine. "Amid the confusion, rigging a makeshift one will take some time."

The Russian started to speak, but his words were sucked up in a harsh intake of air.

"This way." Steadying his stumble, she led him down to her horses. "Here, I had better have a look at that wound."

He made no protest. No doubt, she thought, because he was having trouble enough trying to catch his breath.

Opening his shirt, Shannon saw the bullet was still lodged deep in his flesh. Her expression turned grim as she gingerly probed around the jagged hole. He would need a surgeon, and soon. For now, all she could do was try to stanch the bleeding.

Reaching into her saddlebags, she located a roll of linen. Once she had wiped away the worst of the cloth fragments and burnt powder, she tied a makeshift bandage in place.

"Drink this." Whiskey from her flask splashed over his lips. "Be prepared for a long ride," she warned. "Over rough ground."

"Where to?" grunted the Russian.

"Kenmare."

He nodded, his face pinched in pain.

Wasting no more time in words, she helped him into the saddle.

The rocky trail dipped into a narrow valley and threaded through a tangle of live oak and thick ferns. The hide-and-seek moonlight gave the gnarled branches an even more forbidding twist. They rode in grim silence, the splash of water over the granite outcroppings and the soft thud of hooves the only sounds stirring the damp air.

Shannon strained to hear any signs of pursuit. Nothing so far. The castle was likely still reeling from the first impact of the assault, but she couldn't count on confusion reigning for too much longer. The clansmen would be out for blood. She had to keep moving.

Once again, she gave thanks that Lynsley's network of agents was trained to provide the very best. Her horses were two blooded hunters, thick-chested beasts bred for strength and stamina. She had brought along an extra mount for her supplies, and for any unforeseen emergency . . .

Slowing to a walk, Shannon looked over her shoulder. Orlov was slumped in the saddle, but managing to keep his seat. For how much longer she didn't dare hazard a guess.

She turned and stood in stirrups, praying she hadn't passed the telltale landmarks. Gorse scraped against her boots, a prickling reminder that she could not afford a misstep. As she rounded the tangle of thorns and thistle, she spotted the pale cairn and heaved a sigh of relief.

But now, a decision had to be made. The stones marked a shortcut, but the way was steep, with even less of a trail to follow. She had no doubt of her own ability, but the Russian looked shaky.

Reining to a halt, she dismounted and uncorked her flask. "Here, let me help you to another swallow." Her hand grazed Orlov's cheek. It was already warm, and up close she could see his lips were parched and his flesh was taking on a feverish flush.

Damn.

That decided her. She shook out a length of rope and

knotted it around his waist. "Going up and over the moors will cut several hours off the trip. I know the way, and the horses are game. But it will hurt."

He managed a gurgle of laughter. "Then you will, no doubt, enjoy every step of the way."

Her lips quirked. "I'm not a sadist, Mr. Orlov. Though I am going to have to lash you to the saddle."

"A pity I am not in any condition to appreciate such interesting ministrations."

"Save your strength for . . ." Shannon left off her retort as he fell unconscious in her arms. "A maidenly swoon, sir?" she murmured. "Be assured I shall never let you hear the end of it."

A glance across the valley showed no signs of O'Malley's men. Swinging up onto her own mount, she took a small sip of the whiskey and started up the long climb.

Chapter Four

My information said there was to be only one person," said the man who opened the barn door.

"Change of plans," replied Shannon curtly as she slid the wooden bar back in place.

"The risk is twice as great."

"So charge me double." A shake of her purse silenced the complaint. "I need a doctor as well."

At that, her contact—a wiry little crofter with a shock of silver hair—snorted and shook his head. "Too dangerous."

Shannon flashed a glimpse of gold. "I shall make it worth the risk."

The man rubbed at his jaw. "There's one who may be willing to help. But it will cost you dear."

"Get him," she ordered. "Quickly. I will unsaddle the horses and rub them down."

Orlov did no more than groan as she lowered him into the straw. The bandage was soaked with blood. *Hell and damnation*. The man might be a thief and a rogue but she did not wish him to the devil just yet.

She checked her pocketwatch. Not much time before the tide changed. Kenmare was only a mile away, but she couldn't afford to cut it too close.

Her contact was back within a quarter hour. "No luck," he muttered. "One of the peat cutters suffered a severed toe. Enniscrone won't be returning before midnight."

She looked at Orlov's feverish face. "And if I leave him here to be cared for?"

The man drew a finger across his throat. "I don't know what your business was in the area. Nor do I want to know. But strangers are not much welcome in these moors. Especially if there's a chance they have stirred any trouble with the O'Malleys."

Her jaw set. Lynsley's lecture on misplaced loyalty echoed in her ears. As did her training. Duty often called for dispassionate decisions.

Still, the damn fellow had saved her life by risking his own.

"Help me get him to the docks."

Her contact gave her a hard look. "Nay. No amount o' gold is worth tha' sort of risk. O'Malley would have me head on a pike if I'm seen."

"At the moment, O'Malley is the lesser of two evils." She drew her pistol. "He is dead, while I am quite alive."

He cursed under his breath, a foul-mouthed imprecation on plaguey females.

Shannon responded with a tirade that would have blistered the ears of a dockyard stevedore.

The man blinked, then gave a rueful smile. "Ye must be Irish yerself, missy." Threading a hand through his hair, he pursed his lips in thought. "Look, if I don't get these horses back to Mulligan's stables by the appointed hour, I'll be no further use te yer people. But I have an idea. Take the gig and pony yerself. There's a cart track that skirts the village, and at this hour ye won't have any trouble making it down to the harbor unseen." He described the outer dock where the unmarked naval cutter was moored. "O'Malley's men will assume ye stole it, and I'll be free o' suspicion."

She nodded. It was a fair enough suggestion. And Orlov's unconscious form would be a fact in their favor should anyone observe their progress from afar—slumped against her shoulder, he would look to be just another drunk, in need of assistance home.

"Help me harness the pony."

The directions proved accurate enough, and Shannon made it to the docks without mishap. The sailor on watch looked surprised at finding two cloaked figures seeking to board the vessel, but helped her maneuver the Russian up the gangplank without comment.

The captain, a flinty Scot with a burr as rough as the rocks of Islay, was quick to take command of the situation. "I've a cabin cleared for your use," he murmured, shouldering aside his subordinate and assuming most of Orlov's weight as they headed below deck. He was the only one who knew that the special passenger was a female, and sounded none too pleased at a further complication. "But we are cramped as it is. I can't afford to allot any more room."

"Not necessary," she assured him.

Down in spartan space, they laid Orlov on one of the narrow berths.

"We need to get a bullet out of his shoulder," whispered Shannon.

The captain looked grim. "Cast off," he called up to the crew. He struck a flint to the oil lamp. "He will have to hold on a bit longer. The tides are damn tricky here. I can't spare a hand until we have navigated through the channels and are well out to sea."

Left alone, Shannon made her companion as comfortable as she could. The bunk was not built for someone of Orlov's height, but somehow she managed to strip off the layers of wet wool and linen, and pillow his head against the bulwark with her folded cloak. His boots hit the floorboard with a soft squish, reminding her that she, too, was soaked to the bone from the squalling rain showers. However, her own discomforts dimmed as she peeled away the bandage and looked at the jagged flesh.

Her lips pressed tight.

Finding the flask of brandy in her bag, she shredded a tail of his shirt and set to cleaning the wound.

Orlov muttered something in Russian. An oath, no doubt, for it was followed by several English curses.

"Stop complaining," she growled. "You are damn lucky to be alive."

His golden lashes fluttered, and a glimmer of his usual arrogance shone through his pain. "Luck is said to be a lady—and females find my charms hard to resist."

"More likely you are bedfellows with the devil." Shannon frowned on seeing his inflamed flesh, a raw red that sparked a fresh stab of concern. "You had better pray he does not decide to seek closer company with you."

The Russian winced, yet somehow managed to maintain a show of cocky humor. "You wish me to hell, I know. I am usually happy to oblige a lady, however . . ."

His words segued into a sharp sigh as she probed at the jagged hole in his shoulder.

"Sorry," muttered Shannon. The bone did not appear broken, but the risk of infection was a real danger. Despite the chill of the salt air, he felt hot, clammy to the touch.

Smoothing the tangle of hair from his brow, she wiped away the beading sweat. Orlov's manners might be abrasive, and his motives a mystery, but she was not quite so callous as to be able to ignore his suffering. A quick search of the surroundings turned up a basin, blankets, and a flask of water. When at last she had sponged the worst of the grime from the wound and applied a cold compress to his brow, she leaned back against the hull, feeling a wave of exhaustion roll over her.

Bloody hell. This was a complication she did not need. Not when her mission had, quite literally, blown up in her face. Lynsley would be disappointed enough that she was returning with naught to show for her efforts. To appear with an unexpected companion . . .

Her gaze strayed to the Russian's pinched profile. On the other hand, there were still a great many unanswered questions about Orlov's involvement in the earlier mission involving her roommate Siena. Two English peers had been found with their throats cut. Traitors, to be sure, but the confusion had nearly cost the lives of her fellow agent and an innocent earl.

Not to speak of her own.

So perhaps Lynsley would welcome the opportunity to have a leisurely chat with Orlov, seeing as the fellow had slipped through the marquess's capable fingers that night. Her hands fisted. The elusive Russian had certainly gotten the better of her as well. Feeling the fool at how easily he had manhandled her, she had sworn to herself that one day he would pay for the damage done to her wrist. Not to speak of how he had added insult to injury by stealing her prized dagger, a silver-handled Andalusian blade that she had won for being at the top of her class in weaponry.

The encounter had been a blow to her pride as much as to her person, Shannon admitted. Which stirred a slight twinge of conscience as she wet his lips with a touch of water. Perhaps it was petty to seek revenge for personal reasons, rather than affairs of state.

She found herself fighting down a flush. It was *not* pique but professionalism that colored her thinking. If she could not bring D'Etienne's head on a platter . . .

The captain ducked through the doorway, putting an end to her musings. He untied a canvas roll of surgical instruments and laid them out on the empty berth.

"I take it you have some experience with gunshot wounds," said Shannon, eyeing the razor blades and probes with a sinking stomach. She had received some rudimentary training in tending to battle wounds, but hoped he didn't expect her to handle the job. Much as she would have relished the chance to needle Orlov under other circumstances, the Russian was too vulnerable now. An unfair advantage, if ever there was one. She wished to best him on equal terms.

And she couldn't quite dismiss the fact that he had saved her life.

"Commanding a small vessel in wartime, one becomes adept at a great many tasks," replied the captain. "I've ordered hot water from the galley. However, I must ask that you serve as my assistant. Even though the crew is hand-picked, Whitehall feels that the less they know of the particulars of this mission, the better." He rolled up his sleeves and cut her a sidelong glance. "You aren't one of those females who faints at the sight of blood, are you?"

"I think you can count on me not to fall into a swoon," she said dryly.

The captain rose to answer the knock on the cabin door. A pot was quickly passed over and the latch set back in place. "Then we had best begin," he said, handing her the battered iron without further ado. "The weather looks to be taking a turn for the worse, and I would rather not slice off the fellow's arm by mistake."

In the binnacled lamplight, Orlov looked pale as death. Swallowing a strange surge of regret, Shannon braced herself against the roll of the hull and nodded, thankful that he was still unconscious.

Cutting away the bandages, the captain made the first probe.

The Russian's eyes slitted open, their arctic blue color dulled to a gunmetal gray.

Shannon held up the small roll of leather used to bite back pain.

He managed to shake his head slightly. Teeth gritted, he pressed his lids closed again, enduring the probing with stoic silence.

"Bloody hell, can't you go any faster," she blurted out. Orlov's face was sheened in sweat. Without thinking, she reached for his hand, curling her fingers with his.

"I am trying not to do any permanent damage." A wave nearly knocked the instrument from the captain's hand. "A slip of the scalpel could cut through the muscle, leaving the arm useless."

"Take your time." Orlov's white-lipped whisper held

a hint of dry humor, despite his obvious pain. "I'm not going anywhere . . . I hope."

"Brandy?" asked Shannon.

"Thank you." He managed a small swallow before lapsing back into oblivion.

It seemed like an age before the captain gave a low grunt. "I think I have it." Digging in with the tips of the tweezers, he managed to extract a misshapen ball of lead.

"Thank God." Shannon realized her hands were shaking.

"Aye, and it looks to have come out cleanly," observed the captain with some satisfaction. Holding it up to the light, he made a closer examination. "Leaving any fragments behind would be dangerous, but I think we need not worry." The bullet made a dull *thunk* as it dropped into the bloodied basin. "The worst is over."

Shannon was not quite sure she agreed as she watched him pick up a gargantuan needle and thread it with black silk. "You are stitching flesh, not canvas, captain."

He shrugged. "Can't leave it flapping loose, can I?" He finished the job with blessed quickness and leaned back to admire his handiwork. "Not bad, under the circumstances." Flexing his bloodstained fingers, he reached for a towel. "Can I leave it to you to handle it from here?"

She nodded.

"Excellent." He, too, looked relieved. "Again, I apologize for the cramped quarters. But given ship's size and the need for secrecy, I have no choice but to ask that you share this cabin. And keep to it for the duration of the journey. My orders stressed that we don't wish to call attention to the fact that a female is aboard, correct?"

"Correct," replied Shannon.

He gave her a fishy stare, clearly wondering what sort of woman was under his hatches. "I shall clear the quarterdeck each evening and escort you topside for a short stroll. Other than that, you are not to stir from here."

"Understood." She matched his clipped tone. "You need not worry about me. I am used to far worse conditions than these."

Though the idea of being cooped up with Alexandr Orlov for the duration of the journey might test the limits of her endurance, she added to herself. If the rascal didn't die of his gunshot wound, there was always the chance that she might murder him with her bare hands.

Tossing, turning . . . no matter which way he moved, he could not seem to escape the hellish pain. Red-hot pitchforks stabbed at his shoulder, while fire singed his brow . . .

Orlov drifted in and out of disorienting dreams for a moment longer before he slowly opened his eyes. Though it was black as Hades, the creaking timbers and rocking motion told him that he was aboard a ship. He lay still, wrestling with vague recollections, disjointed images of what had brought him here. *Smoke. Blinding pain. A shower of sparks. A golden Valkyrie.*

The events of the ill-fated sortie suddenly exploded in his brain.

Ah, yes, the lady. He remembered her all too well. An oath slipped through his cracked lips. Of all the cursed coincidences. But now that he thought on it, he should have realized that the British government would be even more anxious than his own to put a period to the French assassin's existence. Or, more precisely, Yussapov should have considered the possibility.

The deadly dance of espionage was dangerous enough without worrying about tripping over an ally's foot.

Or other, more shapely limbs. Even in his muzzy state of mind, he had no trouble imagining every last inch, every subtle curve of his fair-haired adversary. She was, in a word, magnificent.

He ran his tongue over his lips, tasting the bitter residue of laudanum. Maybe it was the effect of the narcotic, but he had to admit that he had fantasized about her quite a lot in the past few weeks since their first encounter. *Naked in his bed, her glorious limbs entwined with his, her spitfire passions heating his blood to a fever pitch.* Hot and cold, a shiver spiraled through his veins. He wasn't sure whether the image eased his pain, or simply stirred an entirely new physical discomfort.

Damn. He had yet another bone to pick with the prince. After his last mission, he had been counting on a well-deserved interlude of rest and recreation in Stockholm, rather than another difficult assignment. Frustrated, Orlov gave a baleful sigh. It had been far too long since he had enjoyed the intimate pleasures of the opposite sex.

As for combat . . .

He grudgingly admitted that Lynsley's winged warriors were a match for any man.

Lithe, lovely, lethal.

It was a potent combination. No wonder that the few people who knew of Merlin's Maidens waxed poetic on their unique talents.

He, on the other hand, was far too jaded to indulge in soulful stanzas. His world was crafted of steel and shadows, not sonnets. To yield a fraction to softer sentiment was a grave mistake for someone in his profession. As was now painfully clear.

Bloody hell. What momentary madness had prompted him to risk his own skin for the female Fury? "Every man for himself" was the creed he had lived by for as long as he could remember. It was a little late for a change of heart.

Wincing, Orlov turned his face to the bulwark and sank deeper into a haze of fitful dreams.

Shannon looked down at the sleeping Russian. His fair hair was matted with salt and sweat, his jaw stubbled with whiskers that gleamed gold in the lamplight. Like points of fire. How could a man appear so devilishly handsome in a disheveled state, while she . . .

A reflection in the polished brass showed that she looked like hell.

Her lips curled in mocking irony. He, on the other hand, looked artistically pale, perfect. A gilded icon. Though she knew all too well that he was hardly a saint.

Indeed, he was Lucifer incarnate, she reminded herself sharply. A brimstone beast from the netherworld, breathing smoke and lies. It would be a cardinal sin to see him in any brighter light.

Orlov opened his eyes.

Embarrassed to be caught staring, Shannon forced a frown. "Finally awake, are you?" She fumbled with the flask of water. "Here, you must be thirsty."

He accepted a draught with a murmur of thanks. "How kind. However, I would prefer port. A ten-year-old tawny, if possible, served with a selection of Stilton."

"Hmmph." She tried not to dwell on the supremely sensuous shape of his mouth, or the thick lashes fringing his eyes. "Swallow your sarcasm, sir." She brushed a bedraggled lock from her cheek, reluctant to admit that his dry humor was rather amusing. "I'm not much in the mood for it."

Orlov looked around the cramped confines of the cabin. "Forgive me. It appears my unexpected presence aboard this ship has created an uncomfortable situation for you."

"You keep turning up where you are least wanted, Mr. Orlov. Which begs the question of how you came to pick such an isolated fortress as the target for your thievery."

His gaze shuttered. "I had heard that O'Malley was hiding some special treasures. As you see, I wasn't wrong."

"You nearly paid dearly for them."

"Great reward does not come without great risk."

She was not about to let his glib parry deflect her probing for answers. "True. Nonetheless, it is quite strange that you somehow appear, as if by magic, at places whose treasures are not common knowledge."

He turned to the shadows. "Not really. I make it my business to know about such opportunities."

"What business is that, Mr. Orlov?"

"Like you, *golub,* I have my secrets."

"It's no secret that you are a thief. And word has it you make an obscene profit selling your ill-gotten gains."

Orlov contrived to look injured. "The Earl of Kirtland got a bargain. He would have paid a great deal more had the books you speak of actually come up for auction."

"They were not yours to sell."

"Let us not haggle over the fine points of morality. I could have sold them for far more money to another collector."

"Why didn't you?"

"Am I being subjected to an interrogation?" His eyes

followed her movements as she took up a small knife. "Or perhaps an Inquisition."

"The bandage must be changed regularly to avoid infection." Shannon started to cut away the linen, trying hard not to touch his bare flesh. That his pithy retorts were every bit as appealing as his sculpted muscles was a fact she wished to keep under wraps.

He seemed to sense her discomfort and smiled. "How churlish of me to make light of your patience and kindness. You are truly an angel of mercy, *golub*. I pray that at some point, I may return the favor."

"God, I devoutly hope not." Lapsing into a surly silence, Shannon hurriedly applied a fresh dusting of basilicum powder and snugged a new length of linen around the wound.

Whether or not the Almighty heard her implied prayer, a soft rap on the door signaled that her daily reprieve from the cramped quarters—and the Russian's company—was at hand.

"Now, if you will excuse me, I need a breath of fresh air."

Chapter Five

Stop squirming, sir. You are not strong enough to sit up."

His fever had broken during the night, and Orlov was already chafing to escape his sickbed. "Care to test that assumption, *golub*?"

"It would hardly be a fair fight," she snapped. "Perhaps when you are at full strength."

"Is that a challenge?" He couldn't resist provoking her. With her color up and her eyes ablaze, she looked even more alluring.

"Take it as you will . . ." Shannon looked away. "With any luck, we won't have any more of these chance encounters. It is not healthy." She flexed her wrist. "For either of us."

"I *did* apologize for our past encounter," he murmured.

"Quite handsomely," she conceded. "But be that as it may, you can't deny that sparks fly when we rub together." Turning back to small chart table, she resumed her writing.

The lamplight moved in a rhythmic dance across her profile. Though his head was still muzzy and his shoulder ached abominably, he held off from closing his eyes in order to study her features. It was, he realized, the first time he had had the chance to observe her at any leisure. Up until now, he had only seen her in violent action—a blur of spinning limbs and flashing steel.

In studious repose, her features were sharp cut, strong, yet surprisingly delicate. Like fine porcelain, her face had a luminous glow, highlighted by sultry green eyes that appeared an intriguing shade of smoky jade. Her nose was straight, in contrast to lushly full lips, whose soft curves invited the imagination to think of how they would taste, how they would feel.

Orlov felt his mouth go dry. There was something fascinating about her fierceness. She was quite unlike any female he had ever known. Which, given the swath he had cut through the boudoirs of Europe and England, was a number he did not care to count up. In truth, none had been very memorable. Women seemed to tumble so easily into his bed.

At that thought, his expression hovered between a grin and a grimace. She—when the devil would she tell him her name?—would put up an admirable fight on that score. Was that part of the challenge, the allure? God knows, he didn't desire anything deeper from a woman than a fleeting coupling. Flesh entwined, then parting. Passion flaring hot, then cooling just as quickly to the ashes of memory.

Emotional entanglements? That was only asking for trouble.

Distance, detachment. Adhering to hard-and-fast rules was how one stayed out of danger.

Still, he could not help but remark, "Speaking of unfair advantage, *golub*, You know my name, but have yet to reveal your own."

The faint scratch of her pen was the only answer.

"Perhaps, as Bonaparte did with his Creole bride, I shall simply christen you with a name of my own choosing."

She snorted at the suggestion. "You are implying there is an intimacy between us? Hah!"

Stung by her scorn, Orlov frowned. "More a mutual respect, forged in the heat of combat. There is always a certain camaraderie between soldiers, even if they are on opposing sides."

Shannon refused to look up from her paper. "There is *nothing* between us, Mr. Orlov."

"Methinks the lady protests too much," he murmured under his breath.

"Do not misquote Shakespeare." She kept up her furious scribbling, pausing only long enough to slap a fresh page atop her pile.

"I assure you, the words are quite accurate. I studied English literature at Oxford."

"I assure you, the sentiments are not. Though the fact may be a grievous blow to your vanity, not every female in Creation is longing to toss her skirts up for you."

"Indeed. I have never seen *you* wearing aught but breeches."

She flushed and fell silent. But not before muttering something that included the words "odious" and "ass."

Still scowling, Shannon finished writing her report and read over the pages. Lynsley ought to be satisfied with the account. She had been thorough in recording all the details of the mission. Perhaps too thorough. It was a pity that Orlov's presence had to be mentioned. Some things were best left unsaid.

Such as an inexplicable attraction to a rogue.

Was his allure yet another indication of her unsteady temperament? By all rational measure, it made no sense. She fought for noble principles while he scavenged for personal gain. She should, by all rights, loathe him. And yet . . .

A groan, hardly more than a breath of air, gave her a guilty start. To be fair, the Russian was not all bad. He possessed a stoic courage and an ironic sense of humor. Not once had he complained of the pain, or the quirk of fate that had caused the bullet to rip through his flesh rather than hers.

Luck? As Shannon fingered the silver charm beneath her shirt, she found herself wondering about that moment. What had moved Orlov to leap to her rescue? *A code of honor?* By his own admission, he had none. She made a face. Perhaps he had simply tripped in his haste to save his own skin.

But there was no point dwelling on uncomfortable abstractions when there were more practical matters to deal with. Setting aside her pen, she rose and reached for her knife. "This pains me more than it does you, Mr. Orlov. But it's time to change your bandages."

"I am always ready to rouse myself to your touch."

"While I cannot wait to be done with the onerous task, duty demands I set personal feeling aside. Let us try to get it over with as quickly as possible."

Catching her hand, Orlov turned it and kissed the inside of her wrist. "You wound me anew with your scorn, *golub*. Come, let us agree to be friends, at least for this fleeting interlude."

Shannon was suddenly aware of a heat shooting through her. A strange fire, that threatened to melt her defenses. For a flickering instant, she found herself tempted to surrender to his suggestion. Then, coming to her senses, she yanked her fingers free. "You are wasting your charms, Mr. Orlov."

Her skittishness provoked a smile from him. "Am I?" he murmured with a smoky seductiveness. His accent added an exotic edge that made her itch to touch the golden stubbling on his jaw. "I wager I could make you ask me to conquer you, *golub*," he added, fixing her with a lazy, lidded gaze. The gleam of his pirate earring added a rakish wink.

"You are very sure of yourself," she snapped.

"I know my desires. Do you?"

She didn't answer. *What a ridiculous question*. Of course she knew what she wanted. Not him—that was for sure. The last thing she needed in her life was an arrogant, infuriating male.

Yet beneath the show of acerbic wit, was there a glimmer of some deeper emotion in his eyes? At certain moments, an odd sort of stirring seemed to peek through the cocksure banter.

Longing? For what?

"If we are to be sequestered in each other's company, we could at least try to converse." His sardonic drawl cut short her musing. "Tell me something of yourself. What brought you to join Lord Lynsley's flock?"

Shannon set her teeth. "I am not about to share the intimate details of my life with you, Mr. Orlov."

"If I were seeking intimacies, I would know just where to find them, *golub*."

"What you would find, sirrah, was your head handed to you on a platter." Cutting through the twist of linen, she set it aside and reached for the jar of salve. "And stop calling me by that ridiculous name. It means 'pigeon,' does it not?"

"In Russian, it also means 'dove.'" The low lamplight limned the nuanced curves of his mouth. A pliant, playful humor curled at its corners, at odds with the arctic chill that sometimes hardened his eyes to slivers of ice. *That* was a look that sent shivers down her spine. At the moment, however, there was naught but a faint twinkle. "It was meant as a peace offering of sorts. What would you prefer that I call you? Olive?"

Shannon bit back a snort, hoping she sounded angry, rather than amused. She did not wish him to know she found his irreverent teasings entertaining.

"I don't imagine Olivia would be any more acceptable."

"Indeed not. It reminds me of a spinster aunt, who makes herself useful by darning stockings."

Orlov exaggerated a shudder. "I can imagine you engaged in many activities involving a pointed implement, but darning is not one of them."

"Do you never tire of making sexual innuendoes?" she challenged. "If you are hoping to put me to blush, you are wasting your time. My sensibilities are not those of an innocent maiden."

"And yet . . ." Steepling his fingers, Orlov ran his gaze the length of her body. "You *are* innocent."

To her dismay, she felt her cheeks begin to burn. "You don't know anything about me," she replied. Even to her own ears, the retort sounded shrill. Covering her confusion, she turned away and took a book from her bag of supplies.

"Not your name, perhaps. But there are other elemental things that a woman expresses without words. They are in the way she moves, the way she smiles—"

"Bollocks," she swore. "You see what you *want* to see, Mr. Orlov. And your vision is colored by your own hubris." She snapped open the travelworn cover. "Don't think for an instant that I will ever be impaled on your conceit."

After a stretch of silence, he shifted in the narrow bunk. "If we can't converse, then might I at least ask you to read aloud?"

"I doubt you would like the story. It offers a scathing satire on male pride."

He angled a glance at the title. "And female prejudice, for in truth both sexes are skewered with the same ruthless wit."

Surprised, Shannon looked up. "You are familiar with Miss Austen's works."

"As a matter of fact I find her observations on society immensely entertaining."

She wondered if he was merely making sport of her as he added, "Miss Elizabeth Bennett reminds me a little of you. A bold young lady, unbowed by conventional expectations, unafraid of standing her ground."

Shannon felt an odd fluttering in her fingertips.

"Would you agree that her one fault may be her tendency to rush to judgment?"

Her gaze fell back to the book. "I—I should not wish to venture an opinion until I have finished."

"Ah. A wise strategy." Lacing his hands behind his

head, Orlov closed his eyes. "Then let me not keep you from enjoying the story."

Shannon turned the page. "Oh, very well," she muttered. "'*There are few people whom I really love, and still fewer of whom I think well . . .*'"

Orlov settled back against his pillow, enjoying the play of light over her face as she read. Like the story, her features offered a compelling play of nuanced emotions. He found himself even more intrigued by her expressions than by Miss Austen's words. For all her beguiling character, Elizabeth Bennett was no match for the flesh-and-blood female who was sharing his cramped quarters. He was acutely aware of her, though she edged her stool as far away from his berth as possible. Heat prickled across the narrow sliver of space.

She was still angry. He had come to recognize the subtle signs of her ire—the tilt of her chin, the flare of her gaze, the exact crimson shade of her flush. However ungentlemanly it was to admit it, he had gone out of his way to provoke her. He liked her show of fighting spirit. He imagined she would not back down from a duel with Satan himself, if the devil dared to displease her.

"Am I boring you?" Shannon looked up abruptly.

"You are a great many things, but never boring, my dear."

Her eyes flashed like daggerpoints.

"Before you take offense, allow me to say that I meant it as a compliment."

"I would rather you keep your flirtations to yourself," she replied. "Along with your hands."

He cocked his head. "What are you afraid of?"

"Not you," she shot back. "Nor any man."

"No," he agreed. "I would guess that your own inner demons are a far more dangerous opponent."

Shannon laughed, but its echo sounded a bit hollow against the oak planking. "The opium has addled your wits, sir. You are talking nonsense."

"Then why are your cheeks turning such a delightful shade of pink?"

"Because you would test the patience of a saint. And God knows, I have little heavenly tolerance. I am not known for suffering fools gladly."

"I can well imagine that you have a temper," he murmured. "And a short fuse to setting it off."

His comment sparked a snort. "Bloody hell." She kicked back from the chart table, but could not stalk more than several strides before coming up against the door. Spinning around in frustration, she flung herself onto her own berth. "Imagine what you wish. Since you seem to prefer your own fantasies to Miss Austen's fiction, I won't bother to keep on reading aloud."

Orlov immediately regretted that his teasing had caused her to lapse into an angry silence. He had been enjoying the melody of her voice more than he cared to admit. It had a lushness to it—like her hair, it reminded him of sun-dappled honey, rich with a nuanced texture and hue.

Swallowing a sardonic reply, he said softly, "Forgive me. I should not vent my own foul temper on you. If I promise to refrain from further interruption, might I ask you to continue, *golub*?"

Shannon hesitated, but after a long moment sighed. "Very well. And I suppose I might as well tell you my name, if only to avoid being called *golub* for the entire trip. It is Shannon."

As he let the words wash over him, Orlov could not helping thinking that perhaps she was right. The narcotic was doing strange things to his brain. Not only had it dulled the pain of his wound, but it had also affected his usual sense of detachment. How else to account for the inexplicable allure of a feisty female Fury? One who would rather slice out his liver than read him a novel.

He turned to the bulkhead, but even with his eyes closed, he could not put her out of his mind.

Fire and ice. By all conventional rules of chemistry, the combination should fizzle, rather than ignite an explosive attraction. Damn. As soon as the drug wore off, he would be back to his normal self.

He wasn't aware that he had drifted into a fitful half sleep, but when next he looked up, he found Shannon sitting on the edge of his berth, a glass in hand.

"Drink this." Her tone had softened to a note of concern. "You've been thrashing about for the last half hour."

"I've had enough of laudanum," he growled. "I would rather leave off its use."

"Yet you are still in a great deal of pain."

"I've seen too many men become dependent on it. I would rather suffer through a bit of discomfort than become a slave to its power."

There appeared a brief flash of respect in her gaze as Shannon nodded. "I think I would make the same choice. But I imagine you will be in for a rough night." Setting the medicine aside, she started to rise.

He caught her sleeve. "There are other ways of taking one's mind off of pain."

She was no longer looking quite so sympathetic. "Mr. Orlov—"

"I was not referring to anything physical," he hastened to add.

"Hmmph."

He couldn't resist. "Though I daresay a certain activity might relieve the tension between us, Shannon."

Her eyes narrowed.

"But enough of my ill-advised humor. I see you are not amused." Orlov shifted beneath his blanket. Sweat was beginning to bead on his brow, and his shoulder ached like the devil. "What I meant was, perhaps we might talk for a bit," he continued. "About . . ."

"About what?" she asked slowly. "Are you going to suggest again that we reveal something of ourselves?"

"For a start."

"And what are you going to tell me? That you are a thief and a murderer?"

He nodded. "That goes without saying."

"Indeed it does. You took my dagger, which I won . . ." She bit her lip. "And god knows what other crimes you are guilty of."

"You, of all people, are in a position to know the sordid secrets of the shadowy world in which we both work," he replied. He meant to sound sardonic, but his voice had an odd edge to it that took him by surprise. "It's one thing for a scoundrel like me to indulge in a life of skullduggery. But Lord Lynsley strikes me as a rather honorable chap. I wonder what possessed him to draw innocent females into such a dirty game as espionage."

"You have no right to criticize him," she snapped, quick to come to the marquess's defense. "In truth, he offered us a life far better than the ones we had."

He frowned. "You mean to say your families were unkind?"

"None of us have families—" She bit her lip, looking aghast that she had let such a detail slip out.

"Orphans." It was more a musing than a question.

"Yes, bloody orphans," she said. The shadows rocked, light and dark playing over her fine-boned features.

Orlov watched the flicker of coppery highlights in her hair. "Your parents were Irish?"

"How the hell would I know?"

"The name of Shannon must have some significance—"

A harsh laugh cut him off. "None whatsoever. It was a mere spin of serendipity. A rite of passage. Our Academy has a large globe, a beautiful orb of varnished wood and lacquered paper showing all the wonders of a world outside the slums of St. Giles. On my first day, our headmistress bade me choose a new name for a new life. So I set the sphere in motion and watched the cities turn slowly." She shrugged. "Shannon had a nice ring to childish ears."

"That it does." He leaned closer and murmured in her ear. *"Sionainn."*

"What—"

"It sounds even lovelier in Gaelic."

She swore, but there was little force behind it.

"And far more interesting than Alexandr." He gave the name a distinct Russian inflection. "No doubt it was yet another compromise of conflicting cultures—my father would likely have chosen Rurik or Yaroslav while my mother would have favored John or George."

Shannon could not quite hide a smile. "*You* settling for any sort of compromise? I am surprised you did not pop out pronouncing your own wish in the matter."

"I was a very well-behaved child. Or so I am told."

"Ha! More likely you terrorized your nursemaid and sent your mother into permanent decline."

"No, that deed I left to my father."

She regarded him thoughtfully before speaking. "Did I strike a raw nerve?"

Damn. He should have known she was too sharp to miss his tiny slip. "Not at all. There is precious little that can penetrate my hide, save for the stray piece of lead or steel." Orlov blotted his brow on his sleeve. The tiny cabin seemed to be rocking more wildly than before. "Speaking of which, is there any brandy left in your flask?"

Shannon fetched it without comment and waited while he downed its contents in two quick gulps. Turning away, she extinguished the lamp. He heard the creak of wood as she lay down in her berth.

"Sweet dreams, Alexandr."

His lips twitched. In one way, at least, she *was* a typical female. It was just like a woman to feel she had to have the last word.

Chapter Six

"What is taking so damnably long?" demanded Orlov. "We should have reached Southampton long before now."

Shannon took her cloak down from its peg. "The captain heard rumors of a French corsair cruising off Land's End. He was forced to head north around the Scilly Islands to avoid any chance of an encounter. And now . . ." She paused, listening to the crack of canvas and the thud of footsteps on the deck above. "The weatherglass shows a storm approaching. I imagine it will mean further delay."

He muttered an oath.

"If I were you. I would not be quite so eager to set foot on English soil."

"Newgate would be preferable to this cursed hellhole. At least its floors do not dance around like a damned dervish." Orlov drew in a breath and let it out in disgust. "And surely the stench could be no worse than this god-awful bilge water."

Shannon couldn't blame him for being in a foul temper. She, too, would be swearing if she were confined in such a dark, damp space. A sidelong glance showed that the Russian was looking pale as the underbelly of a dead fish beneath the stubbling of fair whiskers.

Their eyes met and she saw his jaw tighten. "Let me come with you."

"The captain's orders . . ." she began.

"To hell with his orders." Defiance flashed in his eyes, along with an unspoken plea. "Bloody hell, it is like being trapped in a coffin down here. I am not used to such inaction. Surely you can appreciate what I mean."

A knock on the door signaled the appointed time for her exercise on deck. She pulled up the hood of her cloak and slipped out. But in a few minutes she returned with an extra oilskin. "Here—and be quick about it, before he changes his mind."

Though his movements were stiff, Orlov managed to navigate the steep ladder and hatchway without a slip. Crossing the deck, he leaned on the ship's rail, and lifted his face to the salty breeze. "Thank you," he murmured, after drawing in a deep breath. There was no trace of his usual sarcasm.

She took up a position by his side, ready to steady his footing against the pitch of the deck. They stood silent for some time, a strange harmony flowing between them as they listened to the wind sing through the rigging and the waves drum against the hull.

Then, moved by his pensive expression, she ventured a question. "Are the Russian steppes as vast as the ocean?"

"Yes," he replied. "There is the same sense of freedom, of a limitless horizon, despite the trees." He glanced upward. "And the sky—it is the same. A stretch of infinite possibilities."

Shannon looked thoughtfully at the constellations. "I should like to learn the art of navigating by the stars."

His brow winged up, mirroring the sliver of crescent moon. "Do you ever feel lost?"

She wasn't quite sure how to reply. The truth would expose a weakness, make her vulnerable. She could hear her fencing master's exhortations ringing in her ears— *Non, non, non, Falconi! Never drop your guard—a skilled opponent will seize an opening, mental or physical, and drive his blade home.*

Orlov seemed unaware of her hesitation. Before she could speak, he ran a hand through his hair and gave voice to his own answer. "Orion and Ursus Major look so sure of their position in the firmament. While I often fear I have drifted to some dark corner, far beyond the reach of any light."

Such melancholy musings took her completely by surprise. She knew that the man had cavalier courage and a rapier wit. But this abstract brooding was a whole new facet of his character. A man who was capable of self-doubt? He suddenly seemed more . . . human.

The illusion lasted no longer than the scudding glimmer of starlight on the waves. His mouth quirked, and as he turned to light up one of the captain's cheroots, he gave a curt laugh. "But then, I awake in the arms of some sumptuous ladybird and find I am exactly where I belong."

The cynicism sounded a bit forced. Rather than react with a barbed retort, she slanted another look at the heavens. "According to Greek mythology, Orion was a hunter pursued by the goddess Diana. When she accidentally killed him, she begged the gods to immortalize him in the night sky. If you follow the line of his belt, it leads to the North Star."

"Is that supposed to have some special significance for me?" he asked coolly. "An arctic star for an arctic soul?"

Shannon matched his nonchalance. "Only that there are times when we all can use a guiding light."

He seemed lost in thought for several moments. "What of you, Shannon? You seem to march along with steadfast steps, undaunted by any obstacle in your path. It's hard to imagine anything coming between you and your chosen destination."

Did she appear so certain of herself? Feeling that the conversation was drifting into uncharted waters, she didn't answer. There were too many dangers on which to run aground.

To her relief, the Russian seemed content to steer clear of further questions. Leaning back, he exhaled a series of perfect smoke rings.

"Clouds are blowing in fast from the west," she said at last. "No doubt we are in for some rough sailing. We had better go below."

The smoke dissolved in the gusting wind. He drew in one more mouthful of the pungent tobacco smoke, then tossed the butt overboard. "Shelter in a storm? By all means, lead the way."

The deck was already heaving wildly as Orlov stumbled into their cabin. How he hated ocean voyages! On land he could cling to the illusion of having some control over his destiny.

Shannon caught him as his knees buckled. "In your weakened condition, you ought not be on your feet, sir."

Her cheek grazed his, igniting his simmering frustrations. Turning, he captured her mouth in a hard, hungry kiss. "Is that an offer to warm my sheets, *golub*?" The touch of her lips sent heat spiraling through his limbs. He deepened his embrace, holding her tightly, like she was his only lifeline.

It was as if he had broken loose of his moorings and would be lost at sea without her.

"Damn you!" Outrage flooded her voice as she fought to break away.

Beneath his hands he felt the ripple of lithe muscle. Her shoulders were smooth, sleek, and the sudden twist caused his hold to slip . . . but there was nothing unyielding about her breasts. Soft and sweetly rounded, they fit perfectly into the curve of his palm.

"Damn you." But the force was gone from her voice. When he looked into her eyes, he saw something other than anger. In the wildly swinging arc of the binnacled lamp, her eyes were a swirling seafoam green. A hue of unfathomable intensity. A man could drown in their depths.

He kissed her again, mindless of the rising fury of the storm. Everything was spinning. The hull shuddered, the beams groaned. Or was it his own rasping sound as he thrust his tongue deeper, reveling in the velvety softness of her mouth? Orlov closed his eyes for an instant, willing the moment to last for an eternity.

"Valkyrie." She tasted of salt and a sweetness beyond words.

Was it merely the gusting gale or were her hands threading through his hair, drawing his body into hers?

Her legs slid apart on the bucking floorboards and he lurched forward, pinning her up against the bulwark. Desperately aware of her heat against his hardness, he slid his hands down to her hips and found the fastenings of her breeches.

"No."

The sea witch spell was broken by the whisper of her breath. Orlov reluctantly loosened his hold, allowing a sliver of space to come between their faces. "Very well," he rasped. "I shall not force my attentions on you again." Summoning a ghost of a grin, he added, "Not until you ask."

"Ask you to ravish me?" She hesitated, her expression lost for a fleeting moment in the rocking shadows. "Hell will freeze over before that happens."

"Cold comfort, indeed."

Her hands unclenched from his collar, but did not fall away. "You are quite fond of using your biting wit as a weapon," she said slowly.

"Most of the time, humor is infinitely preferable to the alternative." Orlov looked away, afraid she might see the uncertainty in his gaze. He suddenly felt vulnerable, and hated himself for it. His voice hardened. "One day you will learn that it is one of the keys to survival in the grim world we both inhabit. Even more so than bullets and blades."

"And you wield it very well. It's only now that I see how skillfully you use it for defense as well as offense."

He forced a sardonic curl to his mouth. "Do not presume to know the full range of my arsenal, Shannon. Or how I may choose to employ it."

"Warfare is the Tao of deception," she murmured. "I am trained to parry whatever weapon you wield."

"I, too, can quote from Sun-Tzu—first make yourself invincible. Are you invincible, *golub*?"

"Are you?" she countered, refusing to be distracted.

At that moment a monstrous wave slammed into the hull, knocking them up against the shuddering timbers. His jaw tightened as his face fell into shadow. "The devil take it, is there not another stash of brandy somewhere in here?"

This time it was he who tried to break away, but Shannon kept hold of his coat. "It's not drink or drugs that you need."

"Spare me the lecture on morality," he snarled. "I don't need advice, I need oblivion."

"Yet yesterday you claimed to be in harmony with your own inner demons."

"As you see, I lied." He shrugged. "It's an unfortunate habit of mine."

Her fingers threaded lightly through his tangled hair, brushing it back from his brow. "You need not be embarrassed. We all have moments when we feel . . . alone."

"Trust me, *golub*. There is nothing I would like better than to be alone at this moment. I am by nature a lone wolf, and aside from the occasional wench to warm my sheets, I vastly prefer my own company to that of anyone else. So, unless you have changed your mind about offering up your maidenhood, let us seek our own beds." Orlov saw her cheeks flame in anger as he pulled free of her touch. He much preferred the look of ire to one of sympathy.

"Parting is such sweet sorrow," she said caustically. "Obviously, Shakespeare never met the likes of you." With a toss of her curls, she turned away. "To my mind, the final lines in this farce cannot come quickly enough."

"Land ho!" The cry echoed through the cabin as the ship broke through the fog and tacked for the harbor of Southampton. The storm had broken during the early morning hours and the seas had subsided to a gentle swell. Footsteps thumped over the deck and shouts rang out from aloft, punctuated by the snap of wet canvas as the crew trimmed the sails.

"So, what are you going to do with me?" Orlov's brow quirked in question as he watched Shannon begin to stow her belongings in her bag.

A good question.

She looked away. *Damn the man.* Duty demanded a dispassionate assessment of the circumstances. The Russian had escaped once from Lynsley's pursuit. Now that she had him as her prisoner, there was no question that the rogue should be handed over to her superiors.

Or was conscience a higher authority?

Sensing her dilemma, he shrugged. "Don't torture yourself, *golub.* Perhaps the marquess will be in a merciful mood and not hang me out for the crows at Newgate."

"Damn you." This time she muttered the oath aloud. "No doubt I should be strung up from the yardarm for dereliction of duty, but . . ." She sighed. "I shall turn my back for one moment once we are on the docks. *One moment*—is that clear? When I look back, you had better be gone."

"I owe you a rather large debt of gratitude, Shannon." As he bowed, his sweeping salute slipped inside his boot. "Allow me to hand over a parting memento before

I go." He tossed her silver dagger atop her sea bag. "I trust it is none the worse for wear."

"If you truly wish to repay me, you will do your best to make sure we never meet again."

Chapter Seven

*T*ugging the brim of his hat down low, Orlov slipped in among the throng of sweating stevedores and sailors. His nondescript clothing, scrounged from the ship's supplies, blended in well with the crowd. In a moment, he would be lost from sight.

Squinting in the sunlight, he stopped at the end of the wharf and filled his lungs with the briny smell of pine tar, oakum, and salt spray. After days in the dark, what he needed was a breath of fresh air to clear the noxious memories of his recent confinement.

Freedom. He should feel a rush of elation. Yet oddly enough, his mood felt strangely flat as he forced himself forward. His steps scuffed against the cobbles and he had to resist the urge to turn and scan the crowd for a mud-brown cloak.

He had never been alone that long with a woman before, thought Orlov wryly. A night—two at most—then he always moved on. Deep discussion was not exactly part of the experience. Yet he had enjoyed the conversations with Shannon. Indeed, she was even more intriguing now that he had seen a glimpse of what lay beneath the lithe muscle and fierce grace of her splendid body.

An attraction that was not merely sexual but cerebral?

He grunted. His mind must still be fuzzed from the lingering effects of the opium. What he needed was a drink to wash the dregs away.

Edging past the docks, Orlov crossed the street, watching that no one was mirroring his movements. After he had walked a way up the hill, he chose one of the coaching inns at random. Over a pint of lager, he would decide how to proceed. Heading to London seemed the logical choice. It would be easy enough to arrange a quick conference with the Russian chargé d'affaires. Only the Almighty knew where Yussapov might be right now.

He was about to enter the Golden Dolphin when a man jostled his shoulder. Biting back a wince, he was about to make a rude comment when the fellow paused and looked up to the skies. "By the bones of St. Sergius, there looks to be a wind blowing in from the North."

Orlov went still. "You don't say? By my reckoning, I would guess it to be coming from the east."

"I daresay you are correct." The man stuffed his hands in his pockets and, without further comment, continued on his way.

Orlov gave a longing look at the taproom but followed his new acquaintance into a nearby side street.

"A coach is waiting for you at the Pink Mermaid, off Groton Lane. You had best hurry. My orders said the matter is urgent."

"How the devil—" Orlov knew better than to go on.

The other man confirmed his ignorance with an exaggerated shrug. "I'm just the messenger, guv."

He ought to be grateful that Yussapov had tracked him down, rather than its being the other way around. And yet, Orlov could not help finishing his question . . . How the devil had the prince gotten wind of the fiasco in Ireland? He must have his own flock of sharp-eyed hawks circling the globe. That, or a damnable crystal ball.

His own powers of divination were at a low ebb. Nothing was making any sense—not his foul mood, his sudden summons, or his inexplicable sense of regret. Tired, hungry, he was tempted to make his superior cool his heels while he enjoyed a leisurely meal and a much-needed bath. As for sleeping in a real bed . . .

Damn. He couldn't remember the last time he had enjoyed the comforts of clean sheets and plumped pillows.

Though his steps slowed for a stride, he shrugged off the idea of mutiny. His lovely Merlin had not shirked her duty to report to Lord Lynsley right away, no matter that she might very well end up in hot water on account of her actions.

He, too, could marshal a sense of discipline when it served his purpose.

And come to think of it, he was looking forward to the rendezvous with Yussapov. The prince's sartorial splendor would suffer no material harm, but his ears would be royally blistered by the time the meeting was over. Once again the lack of communication between English and Russian Intelligence could have proven disastrous.

Shannon flung herself against the squabs of the waiting carriage, trying to keep her gaze from stealing to the windowpanes. She did *not* ever wish to see that dratted man again. Alexandr Orlov was nothing but trouble. A harbinger of perils.

Her jaw set. He was perilous to her peace of mind, that was for sure.

She looked away from the swearing stevedores, the barrels of beef and rum jumbled in among the cordage and spars. Every man for himself, she repeated to herself. Orlov was on his own. But even in the midst of a foreign naval port, she was sure that the Russian would have no trouble keeping his head above water.

Her concern ought to be with surviving the coming meeting with Lord Lynsley. Though the primary failure was not her fault, she was a good deal less certain of how he would judge her ancillary actions. She could, of course, omit the information pertaining to her erstwhile companion. However, even if by some prayer the ship captain did not see fit to make mention of the extra passenger, she could not in good conscience keep any of the facts from the marquess.

Conscience. Bloody hell. Such sentiment was a cursed inconvenience for a hardbitten warrior. Perhaps Lynsley had been right to question her mental toughness.

Such disquieting musings kept her occupied through the interminable hours of bouncing across the countryside. The driver, a whipcord figure with a face as leathery as the reins, broke the journey only long enough to change the horses and order a hurried mug of hot tea. Still, it was long past dusk before the coach turned up a gated drive and finally ground to a halt.

"We are here," he called, climbing down from his perch.

Between the surging seas and rutted roads, Shannon's legs were a bit wobbly. "Thank you," she murmured, hoping that no one had witnessed his having to steady a maidenly stumble.

"You are to go inside. First room on the right."

A glance around as she passed under the entrance portico showed that the manor house was a stately stone structure surrounded by expansive gardens. No lights shone from the windows and aside from the crickets and the lone hoot of an owl, there wasn't a sound to disturb the country silence.

An odd venue for a battlefield report, mused Shannon. But Lord Lynsley was often unpredictable, a trait that no doubt contributed to his formidable success in the art of war.

Too fatigued to puzzle overlong on the marquess's motives, she shifted her gear bag and knocked softly on the paneled door.

"Come in." The female voice was warm and welcoming.

Her brow furrowed. She took hold of the latch, yet instinctively her other hand slid to the pistol inside her cloak.

"You must be exhausted from your travels!" A small, plump woman with a frizzle of gray hair sticking out from under her mobcap hurried across the entrance hall. "Come, warm yourself by the fire while I order some refreshments. Then I am sure you will welcome a hot bath and a soft mattress." She clucked like a motherly hen as she rang a small silver bell. "Shipboard travel can be so dreadfully uncomfortable. I do hope you are not prone to seasickness—such tossing and turning always left me feeling that I didn't know up from down."

Shannon felt a bit dizzy herself. "I . . ."

"You are no doubt wondering where His Lordship is."

She nodded mutely as she set her bag down on the Turkish carpet and flexed her stiff fingers.

"He asked me to see to your comforts." The woman

paused to give a flurry of orders to the maid who appeared in doorway. "By the by," she continued, turning back to Shannon. "I am Mrs. Hallaway, housekeeper of Greenfield Hill. Tea is on the way, but perhaps you would prefer something stronger after your journey?"

"Tea is fine." Rubbing at the crick in her neck, Shannon took a moment to let the housekeeper's words sink in. *A steaming bath? Starched sheets?* A small moan nearly slipped from her lips. But duty dismissed such decadent thoughts, at least for the present. "Surely Lord Lynsley wishes a full report before I retire?"

"Your meeting has been put off until morning."

"Why?" she wondered aloud. Unlike a greengrocer or milliner, the marquess was not wont to keep regular hours.

"Oh, as to that, I wouldn't know." The housekeeper's cheery voice dropped a notch. "He and the other gentleman have been locked in the library for hours. Cook has already set the supper back twice." Another cluck. "I fear the roast will be burnt to a crisp."

The other gentleman? As Shannon began to wolf down the cold collation that was brought in a few moments later, she tried to imagine who *he* might be. Had word already reached Whitehall of her abject failure?

Swallowing the morsel of custard tart that had lodged in her throat, she dusted her hands and decided there was no point in torturing herself over the possible scenarios. Whether morning would bring redemption or disgrace, she would hold her head high. She had done her best, given the circumstances. That was all she could demand of herself.

If Lynsley wanted more, then so be it.

As she finished off the repast, Shannon was suddenly

so weary that she could barely stand. Mrs. Hallaway returned to take her under her wing. "Come, my dear. I shall have you tucked away in a tick."

Shannon allowed herself to be led down the corridor. Passing one of the closed doors, she caught the murmur of male voices. Hushed tones, redolent of brandy and smoke. She would have liked to linger for a moment, but her escort hurried their steps for the marble foyer.

"Just up these stairs and to the right. The sheets have been warmed, and the fire banked. Sleep well."

Though she was dressed and ready to report for duty at dawn, the summons to appear downstairs did not come until midmorning.

"Ah, there you are." Lynsley stood and motioned to a chair facing the massive pearwood desk. "Please make yourself comfortable."

Shannon laid a sheaf of water-stained papers on the blotter before doing as she was bid. Seated half in shadow was a bearded gentleman, but as Lynsley made no move to introduce him, she acted as though he was not there. "I have written up a full report, sir. I'm sorry it is a bit worse for wear."

"Hmmm." Donning a pair of spectacles, the marquess scanned over the first few pages, then set them aside.

"I take it from your notes that there were . . . complications." Even for the marquess, a man of unflappable demeanor, it was rather an understatement.

"Yes," she replied, matching his laconic style.

The stranger stirred slightly and crossed his legs, revealing boots of buttery soft leather. It was not only their texture, but also their color—a burgundy red—that drew her eye. *A peacock?* An odd bird to be keeping company with a Merlin.

She skimmed her eyes over his bottle-green pantaloons and richly embroidered waistcoat. Patterned with an intricate design of swirling jewel tone colors, it was an even more glaring contrast to Lynsley's austere shades of black and cream. However, as her gaze locked for an instant with that of the stranger, she saw the same penetrating alertness, the same cool calmness that gave the marquess an aura of command.

She quickly revised her assessment. Whoever he was, the stranger was not a man of preening pretensions.

"Hmmm," repeated Lynsley. Confirming her guess, he handed the documents to his companion. "Perhaps you would care to have a look at these, Yuri."

"Da."

Shannon snapped to attention in her chair. The gruff syllable had sounded suspiciously like Russian.

Nyet, she assured herself. It was merely her mind playing tricks on her. Orlov was still plaguing her thoughts. To get her attention off her own inner demons, she cleared her throat and ventured to speak.

"I am sorry that I failed in my objective, sir. I studied the surroundings, did a reconnaissance of the castle, but did not learn until it was too late that the target had left the area."

"D'Etienne escaped your bullet, but it appears that Seamus O'Malley did not," mused the marquess.

She drew a deep breath. "Actually sir, it was not me who shot him. It was . . ."

She saw the stranger pause and look up from his reading.

"It was the Russian, Orlov."

"Ah, so our friend was up to his old tricks," said Lynsley.

"Yes, sir," she said through clenched teeth, none too happy about the reminder that the rogue had once again upset her plans. "If—"

A loud clapping, punctuated by a hearty laugh, interrupted her explanation. "Bravo, I commend you on the unflinching honesty of your agents, Thomas. There are many who would have sought to take all the credit for eliminating an enemy like O'Malley."

"I am not in the habit of exaggerating my exploits," she muttered.

Lynsley covered a cough with his hand.

"I have also heard that Mr. Orlov saved the young lady's life," continued the stranger. "By nobly sacrificing his own person."

Her cheeks flamed. "That is true, sir," she said hotly. "But if the damn rascal hadn't pocketed a very valuable gold snuffbox, all hell would not have broken loose. He had been spotted skulking through the castle hallways, and O'Malley came to search the library."

The marquess arched a brow at his companion. "She does have a point. That was careless of Mr. Orlov."

"And besides," she added, "I repaid the favor."

"Yes, yes," murmured the stranger. "I have heard something along those lines. As for the other accusations . . ." A sly glint came to his gaze. "Perhaps we should let the man defend himself."

Lynsley nodded. "Most certainly. Call him in."

Bloody hell. Shannon had risen but now sat again rather quickly.

To his credit, when Orlov entered and saw her, he looked just as shell-shocked.

"Perhaps we ought to make formal introductions, to clear up any lingering confusion," murmured the marquess. "Shannon, the gentleman on my left is Prince Yuri Yussapov, my counterpart in Russian Intelligence. And this . . ." he gestured at Orlov. "This man, with whom you are already acquainted, is one of his most experienced agents. A fact, I might add, that would have been helpful to know before now."

The prince clicked his heels and bowed. "I have already tendered my humble apologies on that score, my lord."

"For which I am extremely grateful, Yuri," said Lynsley with a gracious nod. "In turn, allow me to present my agent Shannon to you. As for Mr. Orlov, I believe he needs no further introduction to either of us."

Chapter Eight

$\mathcal{F}$olding his arms across his chest, Orlov assumed an air of nonchalance, though he was seething inside. This dirty game they all played had few rules, but he did not appreciate being made to feel like Yussapov's pawn in whatever cat-and-mouse game Russia was playing with England.

"What a pleasure to see you again, Lord Lynsley," he drawled. "I regret not offering a more polite farewell at Marquand Castle, but I was in somewhat of a hurry."

"Leaving a rather untidy mess behind you," replied the marquess dryly.

His lip curled in a cool smile. "On the contrary, milord. I believe I tidied up quite nicely. If there were a few odd spills to mop up, well, I trusted that you had quite enough help on hand to finish the job." Out of the corner of his eye, he saw Shannon's face scrunch into a fearsome scowl. Her lips moved, but he couldn't quite make out her words.

Which was probably all for the better. Lynsley flicked

a warning glance her way, but his eyes betrayed a ripple of amusement.

"Let bygones be bygones, yes?" said Yussapov with an expansive wave. "However, before we continue, allow me to express my great pleasure on meeting one of the famed Merlin's Maidens." His jeweled ring flashed as he stroked his beard. As did his eyes. "Your reputation does not do you justice."

Shannon replied with a stoic stare.

"Returning to the present problem," said the prince. "We were just discussing the Irish mission, and the reasons for its having gone awry."

"You are staring the problem in the face." This time, Shannon's comment was quite audible, earning her another silent rebuke from her superior.

Orlov countered with exaggerated politeness. "Much as I hate to contradict a lady, the mission had gone sour before either of us ventured onto O'Malley's turf. D'Etienne was gone by the time we got there."

"I don't see how he could have been tipped off," mused Yussapov. "I told no one my plans, save for you, Alexandr." He cocked a glance at Lynsley, who slowly shook his head.

"I was equally discreet. The success of this mission was of grave importance to our government."

"Hmmm." The prince's hand fell to fingering the double-headed eagle on his watch fob. "Sometimes chance flies in the face of the best-laid plans. It appears we were unlucky."

"A fact exacerbated by Mr. Orlov's penchant for petty theft," muttered Shannon. "Sir," she added, turning to address Lynsley. "If I may be allowed to say so, the exchange of gunfire with O'Malley—while resulting in the elimination of one enemy—was an unnecessary complication that may have alerted our true target that we were on his trail."

Orlov caught the murderous look she cast his way.

"Indeed, I would venture to say we haven't a snowball's chance in hell of getting near him in Ireland again," she finished.

Lynsley opened a dossier and thumbed through the papers. "My sources inform me that he has already left the country." Pinching at the bridge of his nose, he asked, "Any comments, Yuri?"

"I shall let my man answer for himself."

"Again, though it pains me to contradict a fellow operative, I did not purloin the snuffbox for mere personal gain. I was not as much interested in the bauble as in what lay inside it."

"Hah!" Yussapov gave a bark of laughter. "You see, he had heard of O'Malley's habit of hiding his orders from the French inside the treasure. I will pass over just how he coaxed such sensitive information from a member of the Irishman's household, as it is irrelevant to the mission. But suffice it to say, the tip proved accurate."

Orlov allowed something akin to a supercilious sneer to alter his expression. He did not normally gloat, but Shannon's scorn had stung. For some reason, he wished to disabuse her of the notion that his highest pursuit was that of money. To be sure, he *was* a rogue, who saw no reason why he shouldn't profit from the risks he took, if the opportunity was there for the taking. But he had never compromised a mission for mercenary motives.

"All in all, when you add up the score . . ." One by one, the prince ticked off the list with a jab of his well-tended finger. "The demolition of the French gold, the demise of O'Malley, the capture of the French document . . . I would say that my man came out on top."

Steepling his hands, Lynsley smiled. "In the spirit of friendly competition, let us give Shannon a chance to reply."

This time, Orlov noted that she didn't so much as deign to glance his way.

"Mr. Orlov's accomplishments, marvelous as they may be, would not have been quite so impressive if I had not managed to haul his unconscious hide, along with the hidden document, over the moors—at no small risk to my own person—and get him aboard a British naval cutter. Where the captain and I performed surgery to remove the bullet from his shoulder."

"Better there than in your skull, would you not agree?" he retorted.

She had the grace to flush.

The prince chuckled. "You see how well they work together, Thomas. A formidable team, to be sure."

"Hmmm." Lynsley's look was a trifle more skeptical. "They appear to get along like . . ."

Like fire and ice, thought Orlov to himself.

"Like steel and flint," blurted out Shannon. "The sparks put the pyrotechnics of Vauxhall to blush."

"Like cats and dogs," finished the marquess. "But then, England's arms feature a lion, while Russia is famous for its wolves."

If a merlin had fangs, thought Orlov, *they would likely be sunk in his throat*. Reacting with his own flash of teeth in the lady's direction, he tugged at his earring.

"Well said, my dear Thomas. As usual, you see right to the heart of things," observed the prince. His grin of unholy amusement made Orlov wish to aim a kick at his well-tailored rump. "I give thanks to St. Georgi that we—and our fearless agents—are allied on the same side."

Very little escaped Lynsley's notice, agreed Orlov. Whether it was a blessing or a curse remained to be seen.

"St. George is a patron saint of our country as well, Yuri," added the marquess. "So perhaps we can consider it a match made in heaven."

Or hell. The exchange of civilized banter between the two titled gentlemen stirred the hairs on the nape of Orlov's neck. "Yuri," he growled. "If you have finished having your fun, I should like to finish briefing you about the rest of the mission, and its consequences. In private, if you please."

"Ah, but you were the one who suggested we have no secrets from our ally, *tvaritsch*. This matter of D'Etienne is of vital concern to both the Tsar and the King. So Lord Lynsley and I have agreed to coordinate our efforts to eliminate the threat."

Orlov felt the prickling sensation turn into a stab of dire foreboding.

"Between our informants and the secret orders you so cleverly captured from O'Malley, we are quite certain that the Frenchman is on his way to Scotland," continued the prince. "While he was lucky in escaping our pursuit in Ireland, it seems that Fortune may have finally turned her smile on us."

His mouth stretched a bit wider. "We believe we may have a way of getting to him. But the operatives will need to be masters of cunning and deception. Not to mention deadly force. Seeing as our two best agents have already shown an ability to work together, we see no reason to alter the arrangement."

"No reason?" repeated Orlov softly. For a moment he thought his superior might be indulging in his peculiar sense of humor. But a look at Yussapov's face showed he was deadly serious. "I shall be happy to write you a list of reasons—in both English and Russian so there is no misunderstanding," he replied. "Assuming, of course, that Lord Lynsley has a ream of foolscap at his disposal."

"For once I agree with Mr. Orlov." Shannon was quick to second his objection. "It won't work."

"Why?" asked Lynsley mildly.

"Er . . ." She looked uncertain. "I . . ."

"I work alone," finished Orlov. "And that's flat."

Yussapov tilted back in his chair and looked up at the painted ceiling, appearing for all the world as if the *trompe l'oeil* cherubs cavorting across the celestial blue were his only interest.

Orlov muttered something in Russian that brought the legs back to earth with a thump.

"Now, now, Alexandr, let us not be hasty," soothed the prince.

"Us?" he said with poisonous politeness. "It is *my* hide that is at risk."

Ignoring the interplay between the other men, Lynsley turned to Shannon. "As I have said, D'Etienne is a grave threat to both England and Russia. But I would never ask you to undertake a mission against your will. If, for personal reasons, you feel that you cannot perform what is required of you, I shall of course accede to your feelings. One of the other Merlins—"

"No, sir!"

Orlov saw her chin rise, its angle sharp as a sword thrust. *Damn.* The marquess had skillfully maneuvered her into a position of no retreat.

"I am ready to ride from here to Hades, if that is what is needed, sir. Alone or in whatever company you so order." Her voice, while it carried conviction, was decidedly lacking in enthusiasm.

"Perhaps if I explain the circumstances, it will help," continued the marquess with the same mild manner. He might have been ordering port and cigars at White's rather than the covert assassination of a dangerous enemy. "Angus McAllister is a scientific wizard in the art of munitions. His innovations in artillery design and ballistics could help swing the balance of power to our side in the upcoming Eastern campaign."

Yussapov began to drum a martial tattoo upon the tabletop.

"However, he is not only a scientist, but also a devoted family man," continued the marquess. "And serves as guardian to his orphaned niece and nephew—a responsibility that is dear to his heart. At our government's urgent behest, he has reluctantly left them in the care of the children's grandmother, an elderly widow living in a remote corner of the Highlands, in order to work with our military experts on cannon design."

Orlov saw Shannon flinch at the mention of the orphaned children. "You need not explain the reasons, sir," she interrupted. "I take your word that the mission is a vital one."

"In this case, I believe it imperative that both of you understand the full import of what is at stake. You see, we believe D'Etienne's next target is . . . but I am getting a step ahead of myself."

"Da," said Yussapov. "Let us back up and explain just what it is that we have in mind."

Orlov had a sinking feeling that he knew where this was going.

"Imagine, a frail old babushka and two young children at an isolated estate." Indulging in the Russian flair for storytelling, Yussapov was quick to warm to the subject. "Alone, save for the wolves and hawks that hunt in the surrounding hills."

"There are no wolves in Scotland, Yuri," muttered Orlov.

The prince ignored him. "An easy target for anyone, much less a trained assassin."

Shannon let out a gasp of disbelief. "You don't mean to say that he intends to murder the children?"

"Attack what they love first—it is one of Sun-Tzu's precepts for defeating an adversary," said Lynsley softly. "War is, by its very nature, ugly and immoral, Shannon. Our enemy will strike where he believes it will hurt the most. Angus McAllister would be devastated if his wards came to harm. And who could blame him if he held us as responsible as the French for his loss?"

She paled but Orlov saw her eyes turn the color of windswept granite. A hard, unyielding shade of green-gray.

"We believe that D'Etienne will first seek to take the children as hostages," explained the marquess. "In some ways, they are more valuable to the French alive than dead. But if the opportunity does not present itself, he will not hesitate to kill them."

"What is your plan?" It was clear that she had surrendered any reluctance to the mission.

"To dispatch you and Mr. Orlov to Dornoch. It will

seem natural enough that McAllister would engage a governess and tutor for the children during his absence. Such an arrangement works to our advantage. You will be in a perfect position not only to guard the McKenzie children, but also to ensure that this mission is D'Etienne's last."

"You English have a saying, I believe," offered the prince. "One that refers to killing two birds with one stone."

"Or, in this case, killing one bird with two stones," said Orlov dryly. "A strategy designed to be doubly effective."

Shannon ignored his quip. "When do you wish for us to leave?"

"We have a cutter ready to sail from Margate," replied Lynsley.

Orlov gave an inward wince. *Not another damn ship.*

"A few more briefings on the particulars, an interlude to assemble the necessary equipment, a surgeon to examine Mr. Orlov's wound . . ."

"I am touched by your concern for my well-being, my lord." He exaggerated a bow to the marquess.

"We will aim to have the ship sail on tomorrow morning's tide."

"Yes, sir." Shannon snapped off a salute.

"Alexandr?" asked the prince.

His lovely counterpart was not the only one who had been maneuvered into a corner. Masculine pride—and perhaps some other, even more primitive emotion—prevented him from ducking the challenge and slinking away with his tail between his legs. "Bloody hell, I suppose I might as well finish the job." Orlov sighed as he regarded the prince with a baleful grimace. "The English have another saying—in for a penny, in for a pound."

* * *

"If you have any lingering reservations, I would prefer that you voice them now." Lynsley was nearly indistinguishable from the corridor shadows, his somber tailoring blending in perfectly with the shifting shades of light and dark. "Before it is too late."

Light and dark. Their world was defined in black and white, thought Shannon. Though in reality, the boundaries often blurred to a muddle of grays.

"I—I regret my initial outburst. I have no doubts, sir," she replied quickly. "I won't let you down."

"You have nothing to prove, Shannon."

His voice was, as always, kindly as he stepped into her bedchamber. *Fatherly.* Or so she imagined in the rare moments that she let herself indulge in sentiment. Thoughts about fathers or family had no place in her world. The Academy was home, her comrades were her sisters, her sword was . . .

Shannon tightened her grip on its hilt as she ran an oiled rag over the blade. "No?" The word echoed softly, half question, half statement, before she hurriedly added, "I understand the urgency and the import of what needs to be done. There will be no mistakes, no miscalculations. You may count on me to see it through to the end, sir."

"Yet you hesitated at first. Why?" The marquess, for all his affable air, was relentless when it came to business.

She let out her breath as she carefully sheathed her sword and set it inside the traveling case. Questioning Orlov's temperament might only cast doubt on her own unsteady character. And yet, it was impossible to answer him with anything less than a modicum of honesty.

"It's just that I fear Orlov will be more trouble than he is worth."

The gloom did not hide the flutter of Lynsley's brow. "Yussapov has assured me of his courage and his cleverness."

"I don't doubt the man's professional skills, sir. However, we know he is a wolf when it comes to women. Such personal peccadilloes may prove to be a dangerous distraction."

"To whom?" said Lynsley softly.

Shannon fingered the Andalusian dagger that she had recaptured from the Russian. Sharp as two-edged steel, truth cut both ways. She was not quite as innocent of undisciplined desires as she wished to believe. "If you and Prince Yussapov are confident of Orlov's ability to control his impulses, then I most certainly defer to your judgment."

He took a moment to answer. "Neither the prince nor I would entrust any mission to an agent who did not have our full confidence, Shannon." The tiny lines etched at the corners of his eyes seemed to grow deeper, darker in the changing light. "Too much is at stake. So if, in your heart, you have any doubts about working with him, I want you to say so. Otherwise, I expect you to trust Orlov as you would a fellow Merlin."

Did she merely imagine the flutter of a pause?

"Unless he proves himself to be unworthy of it," finished Lynsley. "If that is the case, you will have to . . . improvise."

"Yes, sir." Steeling her resolve, she tossed the weapon in an arcing spin and caught it by the point. "I assure you that the Academy training has equipped me to handle any problems that may arise. I won't let anything—anything—threaten our chances of success."

"Very well. Then Godspeed." He touched her shoulder, a feathery graze that she might well have missed had she not seen the flick of his hand. "May Luck indeed prove to be a lady."

"Oh, she is, sir. And she looks after her own."

Chapter Nine

Despite her assertions to the contrary, Shannon had not quite conquered her misgivings about working with Orlov. Indeed, during several of the more uncomfortable moments of the journey up through the North Sea squalls, she had wondered if Lynsley's intention was to draw up the most diabolical punishment imaginable for her past transgressions.

If so, he had succeeded. In spades.

Grimacing at the thought of the coming days, she squinted through the mizzle and watched the craggy Scottish coastline materialize from out of the mists. So far, at least, she had not been obliged to endure a forced intimacy with the Russian. It had been a rough passage, and the steep seas and buffeting winds had kept them both confined to their cramped cabins.

Where, to her consternation, she had spent the greater part of her waking hours stewing over the dratted rascal and the indignities she had suffered at his hands, rather than mapping out a more precise strategy for confronting the dangers ahead.

Damn the man. He had played her for the fool. From the very beginning, he had known her official identity, yet had kept silent about his own. He had let her think he was naught but a thief, a rake, a scoundrel with no qualms about committing murder if the deed promised a profit. Though why that should bother her was cause for question—

"Enjoying the scenery?"

Shannon slanted a stony look from the gunmetal gray rocks to Orlov's profile. "I was until now." She took some consolation in seeing that his face was white as marble.

He made a clucking sound. "Come, come. Can't we bury the hatchet . . . though preferably not in the back of my skull."

"We will likely have need of all the weapons at our disposal in order to counter a man as cunning as D'Etienne," she replied. "If one of those happens to be the need to cooperate with you, then I shall try to wield it to the best of my abilities."

Orlov's expression hardened in response to her uncivil tone. "Still smarting over the pique to your pride? Perhaps females have too thin a skin for this line of work."

She made a face. "I need not ask what profession *you* think suitable for those of my sex."

"Resentment does not become you, Shannon. I was not at liberty to reveal my identity or the details of my mission. Under the same circumstances, would you have done any differently?"

She bit her lip, admitting to herself that he had a point.

Taking her silence as surrender, he propped his elbows

on the railing and cocked a sidelong smile. But to her surprise, he did not press his advantage.

Like her, he seemed content to tilt his face to the sharp salt breeze and allow his gaze to drift over the rainswept inlets and rocky strands that dotted the granite cliffs. The sounds of the sea, punctuated by the slap of the waves and the rattle of the rigging, made for a strangely companionable interlude as the ship tacked its way closer to land.

As did the tendrils of heat rising up from his cloak and the subtle scent of bay rum clinging to his freshly shaved cheeks. Suddenly aware that her shoulder had sloped perilously close to his, Shannon inched back.

"Oddly appealing, isn't it?"

"W—what is?" She hoped she didn't look quite as flustered as she sounded.

His brow rose ever so slightly. "Why, the landscape, of course."

She didn't answer.

"According to my map, we will be seeing quite a bit more of the Highlands once we head inland. It will take several hours by coach to reach the McAllister estate."

"Nigh on four by my reckoning. The roads are little more than cart tracks once we quit Dornoch, and they turn even rougher as they climb into the moors." She smoothed at her skirts, inwardly cursing the flapping folds of wet fabric. She much preferred the utilitarian comfort of her breeches and boots, but the role of governess allowed no deviation from straitlaced propriety. "We have orders to hire a conveyance at the sign of the White Gyrfalcon."

"Any reason?" he asked. "They cannot be expecting

us. We have traveled here faster than any message from Lord Lynsley—unless he sent it by carrier pigeon."

Heeding the marquess's parting reminder on trust, Shannon did not hesitate to share her information. "The proprietress of the inn is a past student at Mrs. Merlin's Academy for Select Young Ladies. Once I make mention of my time spent there, we shall be assured of encountering no delay in our travel plans. Prime horses, a trustworthy driver, and any other supplies we might need will be ours for the asking."

"Birds of a feather," murmured Orlov.

"Precisely."

"Very clever. And just how large a flock does His Lordship have nesting around the world?"

"That particular information has no bearing on the present assignment," she said primly. "If there is any other winged woman you should be aware of, I shall let you know."

"Ah."

The insouciant waggle of his brow was growing tiresome, but Shannon checked her annoyance. "Just as I shall make you privy to the other important arrangements made by the marquess, now that our arrival is imminent. In my reticule is a letter from McAllister to Lady Octavia, explaining his reasons for engaging a London tutor and governess for the children."

"Do you mean that the dowager is to be told the truth?"

It was her turn to exaggerate a sardonic arch. "Of course not. The letter is a convincing forgery. McAllister himself is completely unaware of our intentions, or the circumstances surrounding them."

"Convincing enough to fool his mother?"

"Lynsley's operatives are extremely good at what they do," replied Shannon with a touch of pride.

"That I can well believe." An oblique compliment? She ventured a peek at Orlov's profile, but this time his expression gave nothing away. "Perhaps I should become familiar with its details, and with any other documents that pertain to our mission."

It was a fair request, and one she should have thought of herself. "There are a few maps you ought to see, and some sketches of the house and property. I had counted on the carriage ride giving us ample time to go over the material," she added somewhat defensively. "But you might as well see it now." After a glance at the quarter-deck, she turned for the aft hatchway. "Meet me in my cabin in a quarter hour."

"An assignation?" Though seasickness rendered his grin a pale imitation of its usual self, the effect still stirred a strange little lurch of her own insides. "I am charmed."

"Don't be," she muttered in passing. "This is strictly business, not pleasure."

For an instant, his eyes darkened to a stormy blue and whitecaps seemed to swirl up from their depths. Just as quickly, the squall settled to a flat calm. "As if I need any reminder that this is not a match made in heaven."

Counting the minutes, Orlov drummed an impatient tattoo upon the chart table. Though in truth the ticking of his nails sounded ominously like a time bomb waiting to go off.

Bloody hell. He should not let the woman get under his hide. He didn't like the situation any more than she did, but her anger seemed sparked by something deeper than a disagreement in strategy.

It was personal. Passionate. He grimaced. With women it always was. Their minds seemed to work on the same principles as a naval chronometer—a bewildering mechanism of spinning gears and temperamental levers. Intricate and incomprehensible to mortal men.

He had not intentionally made sport with her misconceptions. The brutal game they both played had few hard-and-fast rules. Secrecy was one of them, and an agent who did not understand the basics would not be very long for this life. Her resentment was unfair.

Orlov rubbed at his shoulder. It wasn't that he expected a medal for his actions. However, a touch of gratitude would be nice, he told himself, unable to keep from remembering how surprisingly soft her lips had felt against his. They had tasted of spice and sunlight. Warm, enticing. And her whisper had been like a gentle zephyr caressing his cheeks.

Flushed with anger, for both her unjust accusations and his own traitorous longings, Orlov swore aloud.

And now, to add insult to injury, she was acting as though *she* was in charge of the mission. *Hah!* Beneath his clenched fingers, he felt his muscles knot. He did not intend to be relegated to a subservient role, simply because Scotland was her turf, so to speak.

Sod their superiors. In the field, an agent had to stand on his—or her—own two feet. Which, unfortunately, was impossible within the hunched confines of his so-called cabin. His skull ached from innumerable cracks on the overhead decking, and his spine was likely to have a permanent crink to it by the time they made landfall.

By the bones of St. Rurik, may Yuri Yussapov rot in the

bilge of a leaky galleon if the next assignment had any-
thing to do with the sea!

Adding an oath in Russian to his English invective,
Orlov stumbled through the narrow passageway. Like
the weather, his mood was growing more foul by the
moment.

"You might try to practice a bit of discretion. Mr.
Orlov. A tutor does not go around barging into a closed
room unannounced. Especially if it is the bedchamber of
an unmarried female."

Brushing her aside, he drew the door shut. "I don't
need a lecture on English etiquette."

The swinging lantern caught the flicker of uncertainty in her eyes. She was confused? Good. He should
not be the only one off-balance. His next step cornered
her against the bulkhead. Setting his hands on either side
of her shoulders, he leaned in closer. "And speaking of
practice, you ought to get used to the fact that my name
for this charade is Mr. Oliver, not Orlov."

She tried to slip out from his arms but Orlov captured
her chin. "Just a moment," he said softly. "Before we sit
down to study your papers, I wish to ensure that we are
on the same page."

"I am not at all sure I know which book you mean,"
she countered.

"Then let me recite chapter and verse."

Her eyes narrowed, but not enough to hide the fire of
molten jade.

"The first rule of this venture is that neither party as-
sumes the role of command. As we are equally dissatis-
fied with the arrangement, we shall each have an equal
say in how it is planned."

"I did not mean to assume any such thing. With you, it is a waste of time trying to predict how you will act."

"Which brings me to my next point," he replied. "Enough of your oblique insults. I saved your life, you saved mine. Once again, we are equal. As we begin this masquerade as tutor and governess, it would make things a great deal easier if we agree to wipe the slate clean. We must learn to work together."

"What you suggest makes sense," she said haltingly.

"Then we have a bargain?"

Shannon had stripped off her wet woolens and changed into breeches and a linen shirt. The collar was open, revealing the throb of a pulse at her throat. In the sliver of silence, he was acutely aware of her heartbeat, her scent, her heat. Every pore seemed alive. Gloriously alive. Her masculine attire only accentuated her feminine allure.

Hard and soft. Orlov braced his hands on the rough planking to keep them from seeking to twine in the silky strands of hair curling at her neck.

The rasp of his breath nearly drowned out her whisper.

"Yes, we have a bargain."

He knew he ought to leave it at that, but his palms stayed pressed against the blackened oak. "Among Cossack warriors, an oath is not considered binding until it is sealed in blood."

"Such rituals seem a trifle primitive. I shall take your word for it, if you take mine."

Orlov lowered his lips. "We Russians are not quite as civilized as you English."

She didn't flinch. "If you are looking to use your blade, you had better turn your eyes elsewhere."

His low laugh was edged with more than mere humor.

He could not help admiring her strength, her spark. They were so different, and yet so alike. *As if that made any sense.* But then, it was not reason ruling his actions, but a more elemental need.

"No need to do that, *golub.* I shall settle for something in between words and sharpened steel."

Her chin rose, as if in challenge. No longer in control of his desires, he was only dimly aware of shifting his stance and closing the gap between them. Lithe muscle, pliant curves—her body molded against his with exquisite ease. Her breasts were like points of fire, igniting a groan deep in his chest.

"*Vodyanoi,*" he whispered. A sea witch, drowning all coherent thought.

Shannon made no move to avoid the crush of his mouth.

Waves crashed against the hull, echoing the wild thudding of his heart as he coaxed her lips open. She tasted of seafoam salt, of fresh rain, and of a searing need that seemed to match his own. Hot, hungry, his tongue slid inside her, desperate for a deeper draught.

Her hands tangled in his coat, somehow finding a way through the wool and linen. As bare flesh met bare flesh, he felt the welling of a cry. A soft, vulnerable sound.

"Shannon," he murmured, slanting his kiss to the curve of her cheekbone. Her eyes widened, and for an instant she looked at him with the longing of a woman, not a warrior. "I'm not the enemy. You must trust me on that."

Her palm flattened on his chest, skimming lightly over the knife scar—a memento of a mission in Venice—to the twist of bandage at his shoulder. "Yet duelling and deception are a way of life for you."

"Aye, I bear the wounds of what we do," he said. "But like you, I do not fight for the mere thrill of the kill."

"What *do* you fight for?"

Already embarrassed by how much he had revealed, Orlov was not quite ready to bare his soul. Physical scars were obvious enough. His spiritual state was something he kept guarded even from his own gaze. "I have my reasons, *golub*. But they are private, personal."

"Honor?" she asked, her voice tentative.

"I am a man, not a saint." He had never regretted his actions before, yet at that moment he found himself wishing he were not quite so flawed. She made him wish to be better than he was.

Her half smile was luminous in the lamplight. "I—I believe you are more noble than you care to admit."

Orlov hid his longing with a sardonic shrug. "What you see is flesh and blood, not a suit of shining armor."

Was it disappointment he saw reflected in her eyes? He blinked and forced his gaze away.

The surging seas rocked him forward. Orlov tightened his grip to keep her from being tossed against the narrow berth. The squall seemed to be gathering momentum. Overhead, the timbers groaned and canvas snapped. The wind howled through the tarred hemp and taut rigging.

With his own gruff growl, he kissed her again, reveling in the feeling of peace that came over him in spite of the raging storm all around. Angling his body to shield her from the shifting trunks, Orlov coaxed her legs apart. She gasped as his thigh slid between hers, lifting her stockinged feet from the floorboards. There was something exquisitely intimate, erotic, about having her mounted on his person. A wild force of nature. A bold handmaiden of Neptune, resplendent in her bellicose beauty. All she needed was a trident . . .

"Damn." Her whispered oath pricked at his conscience. Loosening his hold, Orlov reluctantly freed her lips.

"The sea seems to have a tempestuous effect on your senses. And mine." With trembling fingers, Shannon stroked the damp hair back from his brow. She looked shaken.

But no more than he felt himself. She was right—a potent force was at play with his reason and resolve. But it was more complex than a simple chemical reaction of salt and water.

Awkward, unsure, she slid down from her perch, looking more like a lost waif than a hardened warrior. The shadows smudged the green of her eyes to a shade of bruised confusion, making her appear smaller, more vulnerable.

"W—we must be on guard that such moments of madness do not follow us to the moors."

"So you mean to play the role of proper governess to the hilt?"

"It is not a question of choice." Tugging her shirt back in place, Shannon turned and groped beneath the chart table for her reticule. "One little slip could easily betray us." Like her words, the crackle of papers as she unfolded the documents was a sharp reminder that it was duty and not desire that had paired them together.

Yet he sensed her resistance was not simply a question of strategy and tactics. Mirroring the surrounding seas, her eyes revealed a turbulent swirl of crosscurrents in their depths.

He looked away, unable to fathom her reaction. Or his own. "Then let us begin with your map." Perhaps she was right—it was best to use business to smooth the waters. "I imagine Lynsley has had his contact draw in all the possible routes of escape."

"Of course. He believes in being prepared for every exigency."

As he eyed the precise pen lines and shadings, Orlov wished that his own path through unknown territory was so clearly delineated.

Chapter Ten

*L*ike a merlin, a long-ago laird of the McAllister clan had chosen a remote spot in the Highland hills for his aerie. Angling her gaze, Shannon took measure of the surroundings as their hired coach lurched through the last, steep turn of the climb and came to a halt.

Perched high on the moors, the ancestral home—which looked more like an ancient Viking fortress than a lordly manor house—overlooked sloping stands of pine and rocky meadowland, thick with gorse and wild grasses. Far below, she spotted the glimmer of a river cutting through a narrow gorge. In another moment, however, the view was obscured by a heavy shroud of mist. Fast-moving clouds had been gathering force over the past hour and a storm now seemed imminent.

"Isolation can be a defensive strength," murmured Orlov as he stepped down from his seat and stretched his legs. "And a—"

"And a weakness," she finished.

He nodded. "In this case, yes."

Shannon took a last look around, though there was little to see, save for rock. Both the courtyard cobblestones and the castle walls were hewn from the same unrelenting shade of gray granite. But after a few yards, even those solid shapes quickly dissolved in a mizzle of swirling fog and spattering raindrops. A closer inspection of the grounds would have to wait until later.

Shielding her face from the gusting wind, she followed Orlov to the front door. It took him several tries with the ancient iron knocker to summon any sign of life.

The massive slab of blackened oak finally swung open a crack. "Ye have come a long way for naught," said a raspy voice from within. "The turn for Braeantra is some miles back."

"We are not lost," replied Orlov. He took a small oilskin packet from his coat and passed it over. "Kindly give this to the lady of the house."

There was a slight pause and a shuffle of feet. "Auch, ye best come in out of the wet while ye wait."

Shannon shook out her cloak. The entrance hall was rather gloomy, an impression accentuated by the slate tiles and dark wood paneling. A large hunt tapestry on the far wall did nothing to lighten the mood—it depicted a wounded stag being dragged down by a pack of hounds. The only other decorative touch was a large oil painting hung above a heavy pine sideboard.

"The old laird did not appear to look kindly on creature comforts," observed Orlov as he regarded the stern-faced gentleman staring down from the canvas. "Perhaps it was the haggis that spoiled his appetite for having any fun in life."

"Sssshhh," she warned. "Not everyone considers personal amusement the primary purpose of life. The Scots are a serious people, and many of them feel they have a moral responsibility to put duty before pleasure."

"Duty to what? Making everyone around them miserable?"

Shannon did not have time to frame a reply, for the butler reappeared from the shadows and beckoned for them to enter a small sitting room across from the main staircase.

"Hmmph. How strange." Light winked off the gold-rimmed lenses as an elderly lady looked up from the letter she was reading. According to Lynsley's dossiers, Lady Octavia McAllister, widow of Laird John McAllister of Skibo, was nearly seventy and something of a recluse. She was also said to have been quite a beauty in her day, and Shannon could see why. Despite the silvery hair and encroaching wrinkles, her fine-boned features and expressive mouth still possessed a captivating vitality.

"My son Angus appears to have been in a dreadful hurry to make these arrangements." Lady Octavia's lips suddenly pursed. "I wonder why?"

"The agency did not say, milady." With his scuffed boots and frayed coat, Orlov looked the very picture of an impecunious scholar. A tincture of walnut leaves had dulled the gleam of his fair hair, which was tied back in an old-fashioned queue, and his slouch softened the lines of his muscular frame, adding to the appearance of bookish reserve.

"They did mention that Mr. McAllister was engaged to lecture at an important scientific conference," he went on. "So perhaps a last-minute change of scheduling required him to act quickly."

"Hmmph." The dowager's eyes narrowed, and despite the thickness of her spectacles, Shannon had the impression that age had not dimmed her vision. "A very reasonable reply, Mr. . . ."

"Oliver," supplied Orlov.

"And yet, when it comes to the children, he is always very meticulous about making his choices."

"Our presence only confirms his due diligence." Orlov's smile could have charmed the stone basilisks standing guard atop the carved fireplace. "The Woolsey Agency is the best in the business, and with all due modesty, milady, allow me to say that Miss Sloane and I have impeccable credentials. If you would care to examine our references, I am sure you will find everything in order."

The pinch of the dowager's mouth softened. "No doubt, young man. Angus has likely gone over your qualifications with a fine-tooth comb, so if he caught no snarls, I daresay I shall be satisfied."

Shannon decided it was time for her to speak up for herself. "Thank you, milady. Mr. Oliver and I look forward to earning your approval."

"Don't thank me, gel. You have yet to meet the little hellions." Though it was said with a slight twinkle in her eye, Lady Octavia's expression clouded for an instant. "But first things first. Here I am doddering on like an old fool when you are likely tired and hungry from the rigors of the trip. I shall arrange for tea to be set out in the drawing room while you get settled in your quarters."

With a thump of her stout walking stick, the dowager recalled the butler, who looked as ancient as the Celtic symbols carved in the stone lintel. "Rawley, show Mr. Oliver to the first-floor guest room in the east wing. Miss Sloane, you come with me."

Orlov inclined a graceful bow and offered his arm.

"Don't imagine you can buy my good graces with

glittering manners, young man." She did, however, accept the attention. "I have seen enough rascals in my day to know Spanish coin from true gold."

"Wouldn't dream of it," murmured Orlov. "I cannot imagine anyone would dare try to pull the wool over your eyes, milady." Leaning a touch lower, he added, "Which are, if I may say so, a most striking shade of aquamarine."

She laughed and whacked her stick lightly to his shin. "Doing it too brown, Mr. Oliver. Now off with you." She paused in the hallway and pointed him to the stairs. "Before your outrageous flirtations land you in the briars."

He winked.

"Has he tried to lift your skirts, gel?" asked Lady Octavia as Orlov walked away.

Taken aback by the unexpected question, Shannon felt her face flame. "I—I, that is, Mr. Oliver understands that our relationship is to be a purely professional one, milady."

"You aren't a Methodist, are you?" The walking stick poked gingerly at the valise by Shannon's feet, as if expecting fire and brimstone to flare up from its depth.

"Er . . . no."

"Good. Presbyterians are dour enough."

Staring down at the toes of her half boots, Shannon maintained a tactful silence.

"So, you aren't warming Mr. Oliver's sheets?"

Her head jerked up. "No."

Lady Octavia removed her spectacles and carefully polished the lenses on her sleeve. "Perhaps you ought to get a pair of glasses, gel. If I were your age I should seriously consider tossing propriety to the wind. He is a *very* attractive man." Settling the frame back on the bridge of her nose, she gave an owlish squint. "Do I shock you, Miss Sloane?"

Shannon was careful to control the curl of her mouth. "Very little shocks me, Lady Octavia."

"Then there is some hope for you yet." The dowager turned for the center hallway. Despite her gnarled limbs, her movements were surprisingly spry. "Well, don't just stand there—come along."

An awkward silence, punctuated by the rap of the brass-tipped hawthorn wood, hung over their steps as they recrossed the entrance hall and passed into the east wing. The rooms there reflected the rustic grandeur of the Highlands. Stag antlers crowned carved stone fireplaces that were large enough to roast an ox. In the carved bookcases, stuffed birds sat cheek by jowl with leatherbound tomes on falconry and fishing, while underfoot a scattering of thick sheepskin rugs kept the damp chill at bay. And in keeping with the fierce traditions of the old clans, an impressive array of weaponry, from medieval to modern, decorated nearly every square inch of the walls.

Shannon slowed as they came to an armorial display bristling with old crossbows and quarrels. Fascinated by the razored edges and powerful gears, she felt her eyes widen.

Her reaction drew a small snort from Lady Octavia. "You aren't one of those milk and water misses who swoons at the mere thought of violence, are you?"

"No, milady. As I told you, my sensibilities are not quite so delicate," replied Shannon dryly. She thought she detected a glimmer of approval.

"But as a well-trained governess, you are no doubt a firm believer in rules?"

The Inquisition? There were certainly enough lethal-looking implements hanging around to create a combative mood. What was it the elderly lady wanted to know?

Aware that a misstep could set her on the wrong path with the dowager, Shannon determined to feel her way slowly. "Rules provide a necessary framework, but I am not so rigid as to refuse a bit of bending."

"Hmmph." The frail shoulders relaxed ever so slightly. "I am glad to hear it, Miss Sloane. My granddaughter is a lively child, exceptionally inquisitive, delightfully energetic. I would hate to see anyone try to stamp the spirit and spunk out of her." The dowager set a fist on her hip and tipped up her chin to meet Shannon's gaze. "The young ladies of London may be considered perfect patterncards of propriety, but if you ask me, they've had all the life and color leached out of them. Diamonds, they call them. Ha! To me they look like overpolished bits of brittle glass. Can't tell one from another."

Shannon bit back a smile. "I am all for encouraging a girl to have a bit of color and individuality."

The dowager sighed as she eyed the drab hue and severe cut of Shannon's dress. Her face did not express much hope on that score.

"Not all employers have quite such an enlightened view of how a female should appear," said Shannon softly. "Especially a governess. I hope to prove to you that I am not so much of a dry stick as you fear. I assure you, I have your granddaughter's best interests at heart."

"I have been rude, and overbearing, haven't I?" Lady Octavia leaned a bit heavily on her stick, then suddenly lifted it with a small flourish. "However, what good is getting old if you can't be just a little bit naughty."

To Shannon, the gleam in the dowager's eye was more one of relief than contrition.

"Come along, gel, just a few more twists and turns in this moldering maze." *Tap, tap.* "Perhaps you will fit in here after all."

"Sugar, Mr. Oliver?" Lady Octavia peered over the ornate silver tea set that the housekeeper had just set on the table.

"Yes, milady." Orlov dropped his voice to a conspiratorial whisper. "Quite a bit of it, I'm afraid. A bad vice, but there you have it."

"Your secret is safe with me, young man." The dowager passed him a cup, along with a platter of buttery shortbread still warm from the oven. "Though if that is your worst sin, you have led a far too virtuous—and boring—life."

He smiled.

"However . . ." She regarded him through the tendrils of steam rising up from the teapot. "Somehow I would guess you haven't a boring bone in your body."

Orlov heard Shannon choke back a gurgle. "I hope my person will stand up to such scrutiny. I should be gravely sorry to disappoint you."

Lady Octavia looked ready to continue the bantering exchange when her housekeeper approached and murmured something in her ear.

"Ah." Folding her napkin, the dowager rose with the help of her stick. "If you two will excuse me, Mrs. Mac-Argyle and I need to go over the new arrangements of the household."

The two of them withdrew to the far end of the drawing room, leaving Orlov free to compare initial impressions of the situation with Shannon. Without preamble, he angled his chair a bit closer to hers and muttered, "The house is like a damn sieve. With all the windows and quirky alcoves, there are far too many ways in and out."

She nodded. "And the staff is quite small. A cook, a housekeeper, a butler, a nursemaid, and a footman—and none of them looks to be much under the age of eighty. A girl comes up occasionally from the village to help with the charwork, along with two locals who tend to the gardens, but that is it."

"I managed a quick walk around the grounds. As we guessed from the carriage, the surrounding moors could not offer a more perfect cover for someone looking to creep up to the house unseen." He let out a sharp sigh. "Short of keeping the children and Lady Octavia confined to a small section of the house, it is going to be well nigh impossible for us to mount an adequate guard. The place is too big, too rambling."

"The dowager does not strike me as someone who would take kindly to having her freedom curtailed." Shannon made a wry face. "Besides, Lynsley was very clear about not wanting to alarm her with any hint of our true identities, or the danger lurking close to home."

"Alarm her? Hah!" It was no laughing matter, but Orlov couldn't help a harried chuckle. "Why, the old battle-ax would probably grab an ancient blunderbuss from the display of weapons and demand to man the ramparts in defense of her castle."

The image stirred a smile from her. "I fear you are right. She appears to possess more spirit than most ladies a quarter of her age. She already has hinted that she finds me a stick-in-the-mud." Shannon smoothed at her skirts, which were, he noted, a hideous shade of brown.

No wonder the dowager had experienced a sinking feeling on meeting the new governess. He muttered something in Russian, which thankfully Shannon did not ask him to translate. "We shall have to request that our quarters be moved to the nursery wing."

"That might present a problem." She bit at her lip, a rather endearing mannerism that she had when she was mulling over a particularly thorny problem. "Propriety, you know. Though Lady Octavia does seem to have a distinct aversion for the dictates of Society."

Out of habit, he started to rub at his jaw, then caught himself. "Perhaps that can be turned to our advantage." As a sharp rapping signaled the dowager's return, he turned away from Shannon. "Leave the lady to me."

"If anyone can disarm her, it is you."

Was that meant as a compliment, or did its meaning have a more cutting edge? Her expression as she stared into her tea was inscrutable.

He was left with little time to think on it, for as he rose, Lady Octavia waved away the proffered chair. "Now that you have fortified yourselves with a spot of sustenance, shall we go meet the children?"

"Prescott, make a bow to Mr. Oliver. And Emma, show Miss Sloane that you know a proper curtsey. You would not wish them to think their charges are wild savages, would you?"

"No, grandmama," they dutifully chorused. However, Shannon did not miss the sidelong looks that the two siblings exchanged. The rolled eyes and pinched grimaces did not express much enthusiasm for the new arrangement.

"My grandson is quite proficient in mathematics and science for a lad of eleven," continued the dowager.

"Though I fear he has neglected his study of history and literature."

"A deficiency that is easily remedied," replied Orlov.

Shannon saw that the remark earned the new tutor no favor with the lad.

"What do you know of navigation, sir?" demanded Prescott. "I am very interested in furthering my knowledge of the discipline."

"That is because Scottie means to be a pirate," announced his sister. "And he'll be a corking good one, seeing as Papa has taught him all about gunpowder and ballistics."

"Emma," chided Lady Octavia. "It is not polite to interrupt your brother."

"A pirate," repeated Orlov, after the little girl had mumbled an apology. "Not an admiral, like Lord Nelson?"

"Pirates have chests of gold and get to drink bottles of rum all day," said Prescott with a leer.

"Admiral Nelson was pickled in a barrel of brandy after the Battle of Trafalgar," replied Orlov. "Ensuring that he was pleasantly foxed for all eternity."

As the children giggled, Lady Octavia tried to cover her own twitch of amusement with a raised brow.

"History, milady," he said gravely. "You did say you wished Master Prescott to fill in the gaps of his knowledge."

"Not with fermented sugar cane or Blue Ruin," she said dryly.

Shannon was surprised that Orlov appeared to have a natural rapport with children. She hadn't known what to expect, but certainly it was not this easygoing banter. He was a man of many facets, as she was quickly discovering. *Killer, thief, spy.* Was he here as a protector? Or were his orders to play another role?

Damn. Lynsley's parting whisper had warned that for all the hearty handshakes and professions of friendship, the new alliance had to be taken with a grain of salt. She must never forget that his charm could turn deadly in the blink of an eye.

She looked up to find Emma studying her intently. The girl was about the same age as the youngest students at Mrs. Merlin's Academy, and had the same air of wariness at finding her life about to undergo a profound change. Did all orphans have such a guardedness to their gaze? It wasn't as if these children lacked a loving home, but could anything replace a mother and father?

"Do you wish to be a pirate like your brother?" asked Shannon.

Prescott made a rude sound. "Females aren't allowed to swing from the yardarms or brandish a cutlass. It isn't ladylike."

"Says who?" retorted the little girl.

"Parson Greeley's wife. And Mrs. Leith," answered her sibling. "They nearly swooned when you mentioned sailing the seven seas."

"I don't know why boys get to have all the fun," grumbled Emma. "Grandmama isn't such a stickler," she added after a pause, sneaking a tentative peek at Shannon as if to gauge her reaction.

"Nor am I. A lady should know how to defend herself," she said. "Though steel is not always the most effective weapon. There are methods of hand-to-hand combat that can throw the brawniest man on his . . . posterior."

Prescott's smirk squeezed to a more uncertain expression. "You are bamming us."

She winked at Emma. "We shall see."

"Have the ladies just issued a challenge?" Orlov dusted his sleeve. "We shall have to consider what measures we can come up with to match their prowess. After the textbook lessons, of course."

"May we start tomorrow, sir?" asked Prescott eagerly.

"I don't see why not. But of course, Miss Sloane is free to set her own schedule."

Emma looked up, her eyes widening in a mute appeal.

"Well, we certainly can't let the men steal a march on us, can we now?" answered Shannon, glad to see her words brought a glimmer of a smile to the little girl's face. "However, as Mr. Oliver rightly reminded us, the daily lessons must be attended to first."

"I can already do sums nearly as well as Scottie." Emma's chin took a stubborn jut. "Papa said I am very clever with numbers."

"I am sure you will prove an excellent student in all disciplines." Shannon paused. "For history, perhaps we shall begin our studies of the British Isles with a look at Grace O'Malley, the Irish firebrand from the sixteenth century, who was the first female pirate."

Lady Octavia coughed. "Let us leave any further tales of bloodshed and mayhem until the morrow. Children, it is time for your supper."

"But, grandmama—" they began in unison.

A crack of her cane cut off the pleas. "Any mutiny aboard this ship and the guilty party shall be made to walk the plank."

Grins and giggles greeted the threat.

"Now be off with you rascals." Once they had scampered away for the nursery stairs, the dowager turned her gimlet gaze on the two new teachers. "Hmmph . . ."

It was unclear whether the rasp of air was an unceremonious dismissal.

"London must have changed a great deal since my days in Town," she remarked. Her focus suddenly shifted to Shannon. "Where did you say you studied?"

"Mrs. Merlin's Academy for Select Young Ladies."

"Never heard of it."

"I am not surprised, milady," she responded quickly. "It does not count any daughters of the *ton* among its students, but I do assure you that the training is quite rigorous."

"The Woolsey Agency is very discriminating in its choice of teachers," murmured Orlov. "It prides itself on having a progressive educational philosophy."

"Don't get too far ahead of yourself, young man. Before you begin the first lessons, I should like to know just what sort of curriculum you have in my mind for my grandchildren?"

Unsure of how much Orlov really knew about academics, Shannon was about to speak up. However, her intervention proved unnecessary.

"We certainly intend to teach all the traditional subjects, along with encouraging a healthy dose of vigorous outdoor activity. *Mens sana in corpore sano*—the ancient Greeks were firm believers in a healthy mind in a healthy body."

An assassin who could quote from classical theory? Shannon was getting quite an education in the Russian's knowledge. She could not help wondering what other talents he was keeping under wraps.

Without missing a beat, Orlov leaned down and

replaced the dowager's hawthorn stick with the support
of his arm. "Speaking of traditional views, milady, I
would like to discuss another matter with you . . ."

Shannon was content to bring up the rear. A rakish
rogue, she admitted, could prove a useful ally. Just as
long as she did not allow herself to be seduced by his
golden tongue. Or the sleek stretch of corded muscle that
rippled beneath the frayed serge.

Hidden talents, indeed. Along with keeping a close
watch on the children and the surrounding Highland
moors, she didn't dare take an eye off Alexandr Orlov.

"A walk on the moors?" Lady Octavia looked strangely
troubled at Shannon's announcement. The first day in the
schoolroom had just ended and the children had gone off
to the kitchens. "I would have thought you would still be
tired from your journey here."

"Oh, I am made of sterner stuff than that," she replied.
"Seeing as our lessons are finished, and Emma is having
her supper, I thought I would take the opportunity to become more familiar with my surroundings while there is
still a bit of daylight left."

"Hmmph."

Shannon sensed the elderly dowager had still not decided whether she was up to snuff. Unlike Orlov, who
had clearly charmed his way into the lady's good graces.
"But if you feel that I ought not abandon my charge, I
will of course remain here."

"I am not questioning your diligence, Miss Sloane. I
am merely reminding you that Scotland is quite unlike
the gentle countryside around London. It is a wild and
rugged terrain, with many hidden pitfalls. For someone
used to a more pastoral setting, it could be daunting."

"I am quite at home in rugged country."

"You don't look it," said the dowager bluntly.

Deciding it would do no harm to show she was not such a timid little mouse, despite the drab brown dress, Shannon lifted her skirts to reveal the small dagger strapped to her calf. "Appearances can be deceiving, milady."

A glint flashed in Lady Octavia's eye. "Is it real?"

"You can shave the hairs on your forearm with its blade."

"And likely lop off a few limbs while you are it." The dowager waggled a brow. "God help Mr. Oliver if he gets too randy, eh?"

Shannon could not help but like the elderly lady's earthy bluntness. Matching the dowager's grin, she chopped at the air with her hand. "He has been warned not to come too close for comfort."

As her chortle died away, Lady Octavia turned a bit more pensive. "And yet, you readily agreed to the rascal's suggestion that the two of you be allowed to change your quarters and sleep in the same hallway. I was under the impression that you and he . . ."

"Oh, that." Shannon decided the best explanation was the one nearest the truth. "I think Mr. Oliver imagines that given time, I shall eventually succumb to his charms. Which are undeniably attractive. However, our primary concern is truly for the children. In a large and rambling house such as this one, it seemed prudent to request a closer proximity to their rooms at night, in case we are needed."

"Needed?" The dowager's voice suddenly seemed sharper.

"Nightmares, strange sounds in the dark. Such things can be frightening to young children, especially ones

who have recently experienced the loss of their parents."
She paused for a fraction. "I, too, was orphaned at an
early age, so I understand how traumatic it can be."

Lady Octavia appeared to be contemplating the silver top of her walking stick. "I am impressed by your
concern. The Woolsey Agency is to be commended for
finding such conscientious young people."

"They are, I am told, experts in the field and take their
reputation very seriously."

"Then no wonder Angus chose them. He wouldn't entrust his niece and nephew to just anyone."

"He hasn't."

"Hmmph."

Shannon was learning that the low snort could mean
anything from displeasure to delight. She hid her own
thoughts behind a polite smile.

"Well, go on, gel, and enjoy your tramp through the
heather. Mind you watch your step on the path above the
stable. A deep gorge cuts below the ridge and the footing
can be very treacherous. And if you choose to wander as
far as Loch Morie, avoid the southeast bank. There is a
peat bog close to the shoreline."

"I shall exercise great caution."

"Do." A hesitation seemed to hang in the air. "As
Angus has gone to all the trouble of dispatching you
here, I should hate to think of losing your services before
they have rightly begun."

Chapter Eleven

*T*wilight had faded to a purple mist over the moors, leaving the manor house half in shadow. But rather than retreat to her own rooms after supper, the dowager had invited Orlov and Shannon to take tea with her in the drawing room, ostensibly to go over the proposed program of lessons for the children. But privately, Orlov thought she simply wanted the company.

Indeed, the discussion on schooling did not take long, but as the last points were agreed upon, Lady Octavia seemed loath to let the conversation end. "Tell me something of your background, Miss Sloane."

"There is not much to tell, I'm afraid. I've led a rather sheltered life," answered Shannon. "I am from London, and after my parents passed away, I was fortunate enough to be offered admission to a small educational institution outside of Town."

"Yes, yes, so you said . . . Mrs. Merlin's Academy for Select Young Ladies." The dowager pushed her spectacles back up to the bridge of her nose. "I wonder that I have never heard it mentioned before."

"It is but a small school, established to train girls of modest background to be useful in Society," she said softly. "There is nothing grand or glamorous about its faculty or students, but its reputation is above question. The patrons include the Marquess of Lynsley."

"Hmmph. Well, I suppose it must be respectable." Lady Octavia appeared lost in thought for a moment. "His aunt and I were bosom bows in school. A lively gel. Ever so sharp. And outrageously funny. However, I hear her nephew is a bit of a stick in the mud."

Orlov saw Shannon bite back a smile. "I would not describe Lord Lynsley in such terms. He is a serious gentleman, to be sure, but that does not mean he is lacking in character."

The dowager gave a small snort. "A diplomatic reply, Miss Sloane."

"His Lordship would be pleased to hear you say so. He has cautioned me that I have a tendency to speak a bit too frankly."

"Nothing wrong with a bit of fire in a gel. Don't let them douse all spark of life in you."

Shannon looked down at her demurely folded hands. "I shall keep your counsel in mind."

Any further questions were forestalled by the entrance of the ancient footman, who shuffled in with a packet of mail. "Betty brought the weekly post up from the village, along with a basket of fresh eggs, milady."

"Hmmph. Likely nothing much of interest," said Lady Octavia as she began to untie the twine. "Don't know why I bother to have *La Belle Assemble* sent up from

London. It's not as if I have any need to keep up with the latest fashions."

She gave a gruff cough as Shannon started to rise. "No need to hare off. The two of you might as well stay and enjoy a game of chess while I have a look through this."

Orlov dutifully set up the pieces, while the dowager shifted the brace of candles.

Like the shaggy gray hound curled at the foot of her armchair, her bark was far worse than her bite, he reflected. Loneliness could make anyone snappish. Not for the first time, he found himself wondering why she chose to live for most of the year with no companions, save for her aging dog and three marmalade cats. McAllister and the children spent the winter months in Edinburgh—

"Hmmph!"

He looked up from the chessboard to see Lady Octavia ball the letter she had been reading and toss it into the fire.

"Sylvia has always exhibited an unfortunate lack of common sense," muttered the dowager. "But in this instance, her bird-witted notions have soared to new heights."

"I hope you have not received bad news, milady."

"Hmmph." The elderly lady's wrinkled cheeks flushed to an angry pink. "The nerve of the gel! Hasn't shown a whit of interest in the children before. Too busy gallivanting about London, enjoying her elegant soirees and French champagne. But now, out of the blue . . ." She frowned as the paper turned to ashes. "I wonder what would motivate her to make such a long and uncomfortable trip with her fancy friends."

As Orlov moved his rook out of danger from Shannon's knight, their eyes met.

Had the game just taken a new turn?

His fingers lingered on the carved ivory castle, which suddenly looked small and starkly vulnerable in its corner of the black and white squares.

"A safe play," murmured Shannon. "But I, too, am of the opinion that in the early stages of a game, it is wise to be conservative."

"As in any duel, it's best to feel out an opponent's strengths and weaknesses before moving in for the kill." Orlov sipped at his tea, deciding on how to tactfully maneuver the dowager into elaborating on her announcement.

However, the dowager needed no encouragement from him to go on. "Money," she muttered. "What else but a dire need of blunt would bring Sylvia haring to the Highlands." Although Lady Octavia was speaking to herself, the words cut through the crackle of the coals in the hearth. "Mr. Oliver, will you be so kind as to pour me a glass of sherry—no, on second thought, make that good Scottish whisky."

"The prospect of guests seems a source of some distress," observed Orlov politely as he splashed a bit of the amber spirits into a glass.

"I am not somewhat distressed, young man. I am seriously annoyed," she replied grimly. "If you had met Sylvia, you would understand why."

"Is the offending person a friend, or family?" asked Shannon.

"Family. Of a sort." Her lips puckered as she took a tiny swallow of whisky. "Lady Sylvia St. Clair is the sister of my late daughter-in-law. And like our Highland malts, she is best served in small doses." She sighed. "Do help yourself to a glass, Mr. Oliver. And pour one for

Miss Sloane while you are at it. An old lady ought not drink alone."

Orlov gave an appreciative chuckle as he did as he was asked. "I confess, you have piqued my interest, milady. She sounds like a potent force to contend with."

Lady Octavia jabbed her walking stick in his direction. "You will certainly pique hers. Sylvia has an insatiable appetite for handsome rogues."

He arched a brow. "Indeed?"

"But her tastes change even more quickly than her fashionable gowns and hairstyles."

"From what you say, it does seem odd that she would suddenly have a hankering for Highland air," observed Shannon. The whisky sat untasted in her hands. "Unless, of course, she simply misses her niece and nephew."

The statement was greeted with a muffled snort. "Ha! More likely, what she misses is money for her many indulgences. Angus has been most generous in the past, lending a brotherly hand. But she ought to know I am not such a soft touch."

"Likely she is unaware that he is absent."

The dowager's furrowed brow dug to deeper depths. "Strangely enough, she seems informed of that fact. Which only makes me more convinced that her situation is extremely pressing."

The spirits took on a sharper burn in Orlov's mouth. *Mere coincidence?* Cynicism had long ago sharpened his suspicions that such chance occurrences were rarer than hen's teeth.

Shannon seemed to be of the same mind. "You say she is bringing a party of friends. Are you acquainted with them as well?"

Lady Octavia shook her head. "Sylvia makes no mention

of their names. But I am sure they will be her usual entourage of silly fribbles and Tulips of the *ton*."

"Is she pretty?" he inquired.

"Before you get any ideas, young man, be warned that she hasn't a feather to fly with."

Fearing that perhaps their interest in the impending visit was appearing too sharp for mere strangers, Orlov decided to add a more frivolous note to the mood. "If I were looking to marry—for money or for beauty—I should not have to let my gaze stray too far."

"Have a care with your flirtations, Mr. Oliver." She waggled a bony finger. "I might say yes, and then where would you be?"

"In heaven," he replied with an air of angelic innocence.

"Hmmph!" Try as she might to be stern, her snort sounded suspiciously like a chuckle. "The devil you say."

Out of the corner of his eye, Orlov saw that Shannon appeared to be listening to the exchange with only half an ear. Her gaze had swung around to the alcove overlooking the stone terraces. The interior was unlit, but he knew from an earlier exploration that a narrow doorway, locked and barred from the inside, allowed access to a small walled herb garden.

She suddenly rose, and without explanation disappeared through the darkened doorway.

"Fie, sir!" Lady Octavia twisted at the fringe of her India shawl. "I fear you have wounded Miss Sloane's feelings with your silliness."

"Miss Sloane is all steel beneath those dowdy gowns. She has no tender sentiments toward me. And even if she did, she is quite capable of defending her heart from errant thrusts." He said it lightly, but his muscles tensed, and he shifted in his seat, ready to spring to action at the slightest hint of trouble.

"Really, Mr. Oliver. I have seen her little dagger, but I can't quite picture her wielding one of my forefathers' Viking broadswords."

"She might surprise you," he murmured, slipping a hand inside his coat to loosen the hidden knife.

"The young woman is trained as a governess, not a Death's Head Hussar." The dowager sighed. "A very competent one, so far as I can tell. But an embroidery needle is probably the only weapon she has wielded with regularity. More likely she is shedding a private tear or two."

More likely she was shedding her shawl and climbing around the manor walls to see if she could spot any trouble, he thought wryly. But in the next instant, the humor of the situation quickly faded. At the idea of her encountering D'Etienne alone, he could not longer sit still.

"I had best go see if she is in need of . . . comfort." Cold comfort it would be if she stumbled up against the Frenchman's ruthless blade.

But before he could move, Shannon slipped back into the room. "Forgive me." The smudge of dirt on her sleeve was almost imperceptible, as was the scrape on her knuckles. "I felt a sudden draft and thought I should check that the windows were all properly fastened before you took a chill, milady."

He quirked a brow in question.

"And indeed, a latch had come loose. I set it back in place, and checked that the others are snug." She smiled at Lady Octavia before slanting him a meaningful look. "No harm done. But we should ask the gardener to tighten the hinges and bolts. I will make a note of it."

"How very thoughtful of you, Miss Sloane. It appears that my son has hired not only a governess but a guardian angel."

"You might need divine intervention, milady, to keep you safe from my advances," murmured Orlov, seeking to divert the dowager's attention before she spotted the telltale leaves clinging to the hem of Shannon's skirts.

Catching his glance, Shannon reached for her notebook and pencil, shifting just enough to cover the bits of brown.

The teasing earned him another sharp reprimand from the dowager. "Though with my advancing age and infirmities," she added with a sigh, "I would not mind being swept off my feet. I am finding it deucedly difficult to move around like I used to."

"You don't appear to have slowed a whit."

The elderly lady met his wink with a thoughtful look. "Another splash of whisky, if you please. My ancient bones cannot bear too much excitement in one evening."

Shannon rose to refill Lady Octavia's glass. The man could charm the scales off a snake. And it seemed that no female between the ages of eight and eighty was safe from his flirtations. Save, of course, for herself. But then, she knew the truth about him.

"Now, it's time you tell me something about your history, Mr. Oliver." The dowager squinted through the cut crystal. "Miss Sloane has given an accounting of her background, but you have yet to give any hint of your credentials."

Shannon set down her glass, curious to hear how he would explain himself.

He didn't bat an eye. "My mother's family is from

Yorkshire. I attended Oxford where I studied philosophy and the classics, along with a spot of English literature. I had hopes of reading for law or perhaps the church, but as my family suffered a series of severe financial setbacks during my first year, I was forced to give up my scholarly endeavors and make my own way in the world."

"A pity. I imagine you would have been quite good at either profession," mused the dowager. "So you became a tutor?"

"No. As I was quite skilled at riding, I joined a traveling circus of acrobats. Our travels took us through the Low Countries and along the Baltic coast. Where, I confess, in Hamburg I became enamored with a merchant's daughter and signed on as driver for a trade caravan headed East. Alas, it turned out she was engaged to the head purser, so I found myself stranded in Warsaw."

"And then?" urged the dowager, clearly fascinated by the tale.

"I worked at a number of odd jobs which allowed me to travel to even more exotic places. I spent quite a bit of time in St. Petersburg and Moscow."

"Doing what?"

"Oh, serving as a secret agent for Tsar Alexander, among other things," he replied with a perfectly straight face. "Then I made my way down to the Black Sea and Constantinople. It was quite an education in itself."

Lud, the man ought to turn his hand to writing horrid novels, thought Shannon. Her own pencil paused on the page. With such a fanciful imagination and uncanny ability to lie through his teeth, his outrageously romantic tales would no doubt have the ladies of the *ton* swooning for more.

"After all that, I would think that teaching would be a trifle boring," remarked the dowager.

"I have had my share of excitement in life." As Orlov lowered his lashes and assumed a soulful smile, he looked innocent as a choirboy. A look he no doubt had perfected in the cheval glass. Shannon almost found herself believing his story. "I am quite content to put my experience to work on Master Prescott's behalf."

"How fortunate to have found you. Or rather, for you to have found us." Lady Octavia set aside her glass and slowly rose from the leather armchair. "Much as I have enjoyed the evening, I shall leave you and Miss Sloane to work out the fine points of the weekly lessons while I seek my bed. Haven't the stamina I once had."

"What a bouncer," hissed Shannon as the dowager tapped her way down the hallway. "How did you ever come up with those stories?"

He fixed her with an inscrutable look. "What makes you think they are lies?"

"Oxford?" She said it with pronounced skepticism.

"Merton College, to be more precise. Professor Henry Gilmartin is a renowned scholar on the Socratic tradition."

"I thought . . ."

"Think what you will."

He was right, of course. She really knew nothing about him, save for the bare-bones facts of his last few exploits. It had been her own imagination that had fleshed out the man. Assumption had shaped his character, sculpted his features to fit her own perceptions. *Art and reality.* She had painted a portrait of him in her head. Maybe she needed to look a bit more closely at the actual shape of her subject.

"Have I a bit of haggis on my chin?"

Caught staring, Shannon quickly looked back down at her notebook and resumed sketching a floor plan of the manor house. Yet somehow the pencil moved from the straight lines and right angles of the walls to scribing a fanciful curling of squiggles. A lock of hair took shape, then an ear, a nose, a sinuous curving of lips. *Damn.* Her impulsive doodlings were likely no more accurate than the other views. Her skills were too clumsy, his character too complex to capture on paper.

"Anyone I should know?" He had moved swiftly, silently across the carpet. "With fangs like that, it looks to be a wolf in sheep's clothing. Or, perhaps, the other way around."

She snapped the pages shut. "We have wasted enough time in frivolous banter. The moon is full tonight. I mean to make a more careful survey of the grounds and see if I can spot any signs of surveillance."

"I'll come along. Two pairs of eyes are better than one."

"No." Her objection was a touch shrill. Somehow his closeness caused her body to tighten, her breath to quicken. "We ought not leave the children's rooms unguarded. In fact, we had better be extra vigilant. There was no sign that the window had been tampered with, but it was a chilling reminder that D'Etienne can strike at any moment." She drew a deep breath. "In the morning, we ought to see about setting up a series of trip wires to signal an alarm in one of our bedchambers. It won't be easy with children and the animals, but some of the access points can be covered."

A change came over Orlov. Subtle but sure. He no longer looked the lounging drawing room rake. His body tautened, taking on a coiling of muscle, a predatory alertness that sharpened his gaze to a frightening intensity. *A wolf.* Though he had left off wearing the gold earring, its bared fangs seemed to glint from the loosened strands of hair.

"I'll go, while you keep a watch over the corridors," he said. "I am at home prowling over wild hills such as these."

"I'm quite capable of making my way over the moors," she said tartly. "As you should well know."

His eyes narrowed at the reference to Ireland. "I recall your exploits. Just as I recall that in hand-to-hand combat, *I* was the one who came out on top."

Their gazes locked, a silent clash of steel and will.

"Damnation," he said softly, seeing that neither of them was willing to flinch. "Let us not be at daggers drawn with each other, Shannon. Pride must give way to pragmatism. I am asking you to be reasonable—I am not questioning your strength or skills. But if you look at the situation with a dispassionate eye, you have to agree that it makes more sense for me to venture out while you stay here. Both tasks are equally important." He paused. "If we are to make this mission successful, we must work together."

She wished she could counter his logic, but no arguments came to mind. "Very well. But let us set a time for the surveillance. An hour should be sufficient. If you haven't returned by then, I will assume the worst and act on one of our alternative plans."

"If I fail to come back, don't try to be a bloody hero. Get the children and Lady Octavia into the carriage as quickly as possible and drive hell for leather to your comrade's inn at Dornach." Orlov took her arm, lightly, but

Shannon was aware of the force pulsing from his fingertips. Beneath the casual show of grace, they were hard, callused from constant contact with roughened steel. "Despite what you may think of me personally, *golub*, I am very good at what I do."

"I trust that is so." *Trust.* Lynsley's word echoed in her ears, a chill reminder that she must always be on guard.

"It is." Releasing her, Orlov turned for the hallway, moving quickly, quietly. In an instant he was naught but a blur in the shadows.

Shannon crossed her arms, goosebumps prickling her flesh. The draperies fluttered, mirroring the strange shiver running down her spine. She was suddenly glad he was not stalking her.

Whatever his faults—and they were legion—Orlov was a formidable adversary.

Mano a mano.

She hoped it would not once again come down to that.

Chapter Twelve

*O*rlov looked over Prescott's copybook exercises. "Excellent. Your penmanship is already quite good." A dappling of sunlight from the mullioned schoolroom window danced across the page. "We will move on to a longer passage . . . but not until the morrow." He capped the bottle of ink. "I think we have had enough scholarly lessons for the day. Care to try your hand at some more vigorous activity?"

The lad moved like a flash to put his books back on the shelves.

Chuckling, Orlov set the box of pens and rulers beside the varnished globe and followed his pupil down to the gardens.

"Are we going to learn to duel with pirate cutlasses?" asked Prescott eagerly.

"Not just yet, Blackbeard. As we are landlocked at present, let us begin with some other skills." Seeing the lad's face fall, he added, "Boxing and riding will come in very handy when you go ashore seeking plunder."

The thought seemed to cheer up Prescott considerably. "Aye, aye, sir. Where do we start?"

Orlov spelled out a program of drills. There was an ulterior motive to the games he had planned. It wouldn't hurt to have the children trained in the rudiments of self-defense. An unexpected move, a sudden twist or slip, might take even a trained killer like D'Etienne by surprise. It could even mean the difference between life and death.

Stripping off his coat, Orlov demonstrated a few balancing exercises before moving on to the basics of throwing a punch. "Hold your hand just so, Master Prescott." His fist angled upward. "And jab with the knuckles. Here and here. Hard as you can." He straightened. "Now you try."

"Like that, sir?" Prescott's blow landed flush on target.

"Exactly," he wheezed. "Try it again. It's a useful trick to know if, say, a stranger ever seeks to grab hold of you."

"And as you can see, Emma, it is quite effective, even against a far bigger opponent." Shannon and her student stepped out from the shadows of the boxwood hedge. "I do hope you are not suffering too many bruises, Mr. Oliver."

Orlov hadn't heard them approach. He looked up, rubbing at his ribs. "Only to my pride," he murmured as she held out a hand and helped him to his feet. "This bloodthirsty buccaneer would put Captain Morgan to flight."

Prescott grinned. "Will you show me another punch?"

"On the morrow, lad. For now, go practice the balance exercises I just demonstrated while I have a word with Miss Sloane."

"Mr. Oliver is going to teach me some riding tricks,

too," confided Prescott to his sister. "I want to learn how to flip backward off of a galloping horse."

"Let's not put the tail before the head, lad. That will take a good deal of practice," said Orlov wryly.

Emma slipped free of Shannon's hand and ran over to him. There was, he noted, an elfin, ethereal air about her. Finespun curls, pale as northern moonlight, danced in disarray from her loosened braid, framing porcelain features and light blue eyes whose hue was soft as a rain-washed dawn. She might have been a swirl of Celtic fairy mist, save for the look of fierce resolve peeking out from the fringe of quicksilver lashes.

"Will you show me, too, sir?" she demanded.

He smiled inwardly. The similarities between the newly paired teacher and student were uncanny—the same jutting chin, the same stubborn stance, the same utter fearlessness.

"If Miss Sloane agrees," he answered, lifting her into his arms. Her skinny little body felt so fragile against his chest. *Vulnerable.* Overpowered by a sudden surge of anger that anyone might threaten such an innocent life, Orlov hugged her tighter, breathing in the fresh scent of lavender soap as her fairy curls brushed his cheek. "However, like your brother, you will have to prove yourself ready for such a feat of acrobatics."

Emma's hands fisted in his collar. She looked up, shy, solemn, and nodded.

Orlov smoothed a smudge of dirt from the tip of her nose. Then, suddenly embarrassed at his odd reaction to her tentative smile, he tossed her high up in the air, catching her in tangle of muslin and wool. "It will take a good deal of hard work," he said gruffly, bringing her back down to earth, "before either of you are ready to attempt it."

Emma straightened, trying to look very tall. "I can keep up with Scottie, I know I can."

"Then go with your brother and have him show you the exercises I taught him."

Shannon, meanwhile, had perched a hip on the stone wall and was eyeing him with an odd expression. "Is your shoulder troubling you? I saw you grimace just now."

Damn. She didn't miss much.

"Not at all," he replied somewhat snappishly.

Her brow quirked slightly at his tone, but she merely asked, "How are you finding the duties of a tutor?"

"More exhausting than jumping through hoops at Astley's," he admitted. "Are children always so energetic?"

She cocked her head. "Have you not had much experience with them?"

"God, no." He exaggerated a grimace.

"Yet you seem to have an excellent rapport. I would have guessed that you had younger siblings."

He shook his head. "Nor any progeny of my own—that I know of." The offhand words quickly chased the smile from her lips. "The truth is, I've no idea how to treat the bantlings, other than as I would any adult."

"Which is what they prefer." Her voice was taut, all trace of camaraderie banished by his rakish remark.

Orlov had known the comment would be like steel striking flint. Why did he wish to throw up a shower of sudden sparks when the heat between them had shown signs of banking to a comfortable glow?

He backed up a step, under the pretense of watching Prescott and Emma trip through one of the exercises in footwork. Perhaps because of late he had experienced the oddest longing for a steady warmth that would penetrate to the bone. It was, he knew, a dangerous desire. In his profession, it was a grave mistake to get too cozy.

"On your toes," he called loudly, though he might well be speaking to himself. "And the key is to focus on some point in the distance, not the earth at your feet."

Avoiding Shannon's eyes, Orlov scanned the hills. No sign of the enemy. Unless he was looking in the wrong direction.

Perhaps he ought to be staring at his own traitorous soul. From the very beginning, he had been plagued with questions about this mission, doubts about his powers of detachment.

Was his nerve finally failing him?

Looking back to the children, he suddenly felt old. And unsure of whether he was the best man for this job. When he had set out for Ireland, his fears were that he had grown too jaded to care about anything anymore. Now, he worried that perhaps he had come to care too much.

Rubbing absently at his shoulder, he dismissed his leaden spirits as an aftereffect of his most recent brush with death. His resilience was not yet at full strength, and no doubt that was why he was feeling such a strange churning of emotion. Perhaps the bullet had been an uncomfortable reminder of his own mortality. A life with precious little of value to show for it. He had always been a devil-may-care rogue, reveling in his freedom. The notion of domesticity had always sent shudders through every fiber of his being.

To feel an unaccountable need to keep two orphans— no, three—safe was . . . absurd.

That Shannon's closeness—her long-legged lean body,

her sweetly seductive scent—stirred a more potent fire than mere protectiveness was also chafing at his resolve. Balefully aware of his physical reaction, a tightening, a yearning that he was unable to control, Orlov shifted his stance, until his back was nearly turned to her. All that accomplished was to stir a sharp prickling between his shoulder blades.

"If you will stand watch here a little longer, I will take a walk around the gardens and finish connecting the trip wires around the terrace." Shannon's brusque tone jarred him from his mordant reveries. "Any breach of the perimeter will now set off a small bell in my bedchamber. I take it you mean to continue with your nightly patrols?"

"Yes." After all, he was at more at home walking in the dark shadows than in the light of day.

"I have made a map of the ridge above the stables, showing where the crumbling rock has turned the path treacherous. I shall slide a copy under your door. The dangers would be easy to miss in the dark."

Orlov imagined her head bent over her notebook, the spill of tresses exposing the graceful arch of her neck. *Damn his rebellious body.* A wolf and lioness—no wonder that the fur should fly.

His breath, rough with a repressed curse, escaped in a low growl.

Shannon stiffened, interpreting the sound as a reprimand. "Any other precaution you wish to suggest?"

"Not for the moment. We are doing all we can. Let us wait and see what the next few days bring."

Rain. Shannon brushed the sodden locks from her cheeks and ducked away from the torrential downpour. The slate-gray clouds, blowing in from the North Sea, had brought with them a lashing wind, sharp as slivered stone. Her cloak was scant protection from its cutting edge. She quickened her steps, just as a gust nearly knocked her off her feet. Frigid water pooled along the graveled path. Already her half boots were soaked through, numbing her toes to the bone.

Only a madman would venture out in such a storm, she thought, knowing the trip to the stables had been an exercise in futility. She hadn't really expected to find D'Etienne lurking in the stalls. But she had been too restless to remain indoors for yet another day, staring at the impenetrable muddle of mists.

The moors were not the only surroundings shrouded in gloom. Orlov had unaccountably wrapped himself in an arctic silence, an enigmatic solitude. He had been avoiding all but the most cursory of conversations with her. Not that she had any desire to deepen their friendship—if the uneasy truce could be described as such.

Circumstances had made strange bedfellows of them. Just as quickly as the Scottish weather, the enforced intimacy could change to an adversarial confrontation. Shannon tightened her grip on her windswept hood. Along with his vocal support of forming a strategic alliance with Russia, Lord Lynsley had, in private, added a last whisper of warning. If the partnership with St. Petersburg did not live up to its promises, it was up to her—and her alone—to look out for England's interests.

Friend or foe. Perhaps Orlov was right in keeping her at arm's length. Emotion could not be allowed to cloud duty. And well she knew that her own ungovernable passions might well be her worst enemy.

Wrenching open the scullery door, Shannon shrugged out of her dripping cloak and wet stockings, determined to shed her black mood as well. With the school lessons done for the day and Orlov keeping watch over the children, she was free for another hour or two. She meant to put the time to good use, studying the local maps she had found in the library. Strategy was often dictated by surroundings. In a battle of wits with the deadly Frenchman, she meant to leave no stone unturned.

Laughter drifted out from the open drawing room doors. Though barefoot and shivering in her damp dress, Shannon paused in the hallway to peek in. Orlov was teaching the children to play chess while Lady Octavia napped by the blazing fire. A hard lump started to form in her throat, but she quickly swallowed any regrets at having no home, no family, apart from the Academy.

It wasn't often that she let herself think about her early life in the slums of St. Giles. Even now, the memories were painful, like daggerpoints prickling against her flesh. Scavenging for scraps of food in the alleys. Sleeping in cellars teeming with other urchins and lice. And sharpest of all, fending off the predators who saw small girls as fair game. Fear had been the one constant companion through those years. Other friends had fallen victim to illness, to—

Enough. Shannon closed her eyes for an instant.

Life was unfair, but at least she was trained to fight back.

Unlike Scottie and Emma, she had had her innocence stripped away at a young age. Which was all the more reason she would give her life to protect them. No matter the cost.

Another giggle, this one from Emma as Orlov whispered some secret in her ear.

Shannon was surprised that he was so kind with chil-

dren. She wondered whether his offhand remark on progeny was true. Or did he have babes . . . a towheaded son
with blue eyes, a little Nordic princess with a smile that
could slay dragons.

Her heart lurched. Oh, why was she torturing herself
over the cursed man? He was a rake, a rogue who by his
own admission cared for little in life but himself. This
was simply another job. For which he was undoubtedly
being well paid.

"Ha, sir, I have your knight surrounded!" She saw
Prescott push an ivory pawn to a black square.

"Ah, but you are forgetting that a skilled rider can spur
over the most daunting obstacles." Much to the children's
delight, Orlov picked up the carved horse and rider and
tossed it up in an arcing somersault before plucking it
out of the air. "Of all the players on the chessboard, the
knight is the one who can attack from different angles.
You must always keep a sharp eye on its moves."

As he set the ebony figure back in place, he slanted a
look at the shadowed doorway.

A challenge? A warning?

Their gazes met for an instant before Shannon turned
away.

She was halfway down the hallway when she heard
soft footfalls behind her. There was no mistaking the sure
step, the long stride.

"Anything to report?"

Shannon shoved back the snarl of hair from her forehead, suddenly aware that she must look like a drowned
marmot. Her nerves already on edge, she was about to
snap a sharp rebuke when she saw his face. In the low,
smoky flicker of oil sconces, the smudged shadows under

his eyes looked more like bruises, and the lines at the corners of his mouth dug deeper than just a few days ago.

"Come to my room," she said softly. "I have a balm that will help ease the pain of your wound."

"Which one?"

He suddenly sounded weary, his usual self-confidence worn thin. She had grown so accustomed to his air of arrogance that the note of uncertainty took her aback.

Forgetting her earlier assessment of his character, she reached out to touch his jaw. The golden stubble was like a thousand points of fire in the half light. Beneath her palm, she felt a tiny muscle twitch.

"You see, I've a thorn in my backside from the damn gorse," added Orlov quickly. He forced a sardonic laugh, but its echo did not ring quite true. "Dare I hope that you are offering to remove it, *golub*?" He tried to shake off her hand but she stood firm.

"Don't push me away. What is wrong?"

"Nothing," he said. "I am not used to sitting and waiting like a helpless lamb staked out for slaughter."

"You have been pushing yourself too hard. From now on, I insist that we share the nightly rounds."

"No," he said tersely.

"That is not your decision to make, remember? We are equal partners in this mission. You have no right to bark orders at me."

"It was more of a growl," he said, adding what sounded suspiciously like an oath in Russian. "Would it help if I prefaced it with a 'please'?"

Shannon shook her head. "Not a whit."

This time, the curse was considerably louder and in English. "Damnation, why the devil must you insist on taking such risk?"

"And if I asked the same of you?"

He drew in a harsh breath, only to let it out softly in a reluctant laugh. "Touché."

"Let us hope that no Frenchman can slide his blade in under your guard, Mr. Orlov."

"You are a far greater danger to me," he said cryptically. "And you had best use Alex for the present, rather than my surname."

Talk about dangers. They were already intimate enough without giving voice to it aloud. *Alexandr.* It had a sinfully seductive sound on the tongue. Exotic. Enticing. Even shortened, it was far too . . . personal.

"Don't worry. I won't make a slip in public, Mr. Orlov."

"My dear aunt! I thought we would *never* get here!"

Rawley stepped aside from the open door to admit the dowager's relative and her two companions into the entrance hall.

"What a pity," murmured Lady Octavia with a cool irony that bordered on sarcasm.

Lady Sylvia St. Clair's smile gave an uncertain twitch before she went on. "The roads turned dreadful once we reached the border, and from there, it is almost impossible to find decent lodging and food." She shuddered as she unfastened the clasp of her cloak and passed it to the elderly butler. "One would think the Scots survive on naught but whisky and mutton."

From where he stood in the small side parlor, Orlov had a clear view of the new arrival. She was a statuesque brunette, whose fitted carriage dress was designed to show off her voluptuous curves. A stylish shako crowned a heart-shaped face, and from beneath its fur trim, a profusion of glossy ringlets artfully accentuated the porcelain smoothness of her complexion. Sable lashes fringed eyes of a deep topaz brilliance.

At first blush, her looks were breathtaking. But there was, he decided, a certain brittleness to her beauty.

"It is an austere country, with few of the comforts you and your Town friends are used to." The dowager's expression remained stony as Highland granite. "Knowing that, I am surprised you would wish to make such an arduous trek."

"La, what are a few trifling hardships in the face of a family reunion? It has been far too long since we have seen each other." Pursing her rosebud lips, Lady Sylvia circled the dowager's bony shoulders in an awkward embrace. "I have missed you and the children greatly, so when Randall—Lord Jervis—announced that he could not put off a visit to family lands in Sunderland, we decided to make a grand adventure of it."

"Hmmph." Lady Octavia recoiled from the peck to her cheek. "Well, I do hope you have warned your friends not to expect much excitement. There is, as you know, little to do here save tramp through the moors."

"Which shall suit us perfectly!" Orlov noted that Lady Sylvia recovered from the rebuff with admirable aplomb. She could not be oblivious to the frosty reception, but seemed determined to ignore it. "Arnaud—Comte De Villiers—is a great admirer of Rousseau and has longed for some time to experience the natural splendor of the Highland hills. The men mean to hunt and fish while we ladies enjoy the simple pleasures of hearth and home."

"Hmmph." The dowager shook her stick at the two gentlemen who stood behind Sylvia. "Well, don't just stand there, sirrahs! Start bringing in the baggage so that we may get everyone settled."

Lady Sylvia's eyes narrowed in irritation for an instant before she trilled a soft laugh. "You have left off your spectacles, my dear Octavia. Those are not our servants." In a louder voice she added, "Allow me to present my dear friends, Lord Jervis and Comte De Villiers. Lord Robert Talcott is accompanying his two sisters in the other coach, which should be arriving soon."

"I can see quite clearly," retorted the dowager. "As the gentlemen each appear to possess two arms and two legs to go along with their titles, they ought to have no trouble hoisting the trunks up the stairs. Rawley's rheumatism no longer allows him to lift heavy objects."

Stifling a grin, Orlov moved out from behind the half-opened door. "Might I be of some assistance, Lady Octavia?"

Lady Sylvia's pique took a more speculative curl as her eyes slid over his person.

"You have enough duties to shoulder, Mr. Oliver, without being asked to play valet to my visitors," replied the dowager.

"And pray, what duties are those?" asked Lady Sylvia, flashing her first real smile.

"Mr. Oliver has been engaged as a tutor for Scottie," snapped the dowager. Turning to him, she softened her tone somewhat. "You need not worry that a party of guests will disrupt the daily routine of studies. Angus takes the notion of education very seriously and would not wish for any distractions."

Orlov inclined a small bow.

"Angus made no mention in his letter of having hired a teacher." Lady Sylvia was casually peeling off her gloves, but the tautness of her mouth showed she wasn't quite as relaxed as she wished to appear.

"Not one, but two," added Lady Octavia. "A governess for Emma accompanied Mr. Oliver from London. And like him, Miss Sloane comes with the highest recommendations. Angus would, of course, insist on no less."

Was it merely a quirk of light, or did a shadow of distress flit over the younger lady's brow? "La, he is taking the children's education very seriously, indeed." She pressed a hand to her breast, her ringed fingers winking with jewel-tone hues of ruby and emerald.

For a lady without a feather to fly with, she did not appear to be lacking in fancy plumage, observed Orlov.

"I do hope they will be given some respite from their books to spend time with their aunt." A sigh punctuated the request. "You know how I simply *dote* on Westcott and Emily."

Thump. Despite her advanced years, the dowager was capable of wielding her cane with remarkable force. "I am sure that *Pres*-cott and Em-*ma* will be delighted to discover such devotion in a relative they haven't seen for over three years."

A stain of red ridged Lady Sylvia's elegant cheekbones.

The dowager had drawn first blood, but Orlov did not underestimate her opponent. For all her pampered prettiness, Lady Sylvia St. Clair had the look of someone who was not going to be easily vanquished. It was not that he saw strength in her eyes, but rather fear.

"Hmmph! Well, let us not just stand here in the doorway. My aging bones do not tolerate the damp and chill like they used to."

Orlov took the snort as his cue to withdraw, before the agitated arc of the dowager's stick included him as well. He wished to remain in the lady's good graces. "If I might offer an arm, milady," he murmured.

"La, Octavia, surely you would rather that Mr. Oliver's muscle were put to more practical use." She turned, favoring him with a brilliant smile. "Might we impose on you for a moment?"

"Oh, go on," snapped Lady Octavia. "You might as well help get things settled while I inform Cook of the new arrivals. Rawley will show you up to the guest rooms. Tea will be served in the drawing room." She stomped off with a speed that drew a faint smile to Orlov's lips.

"The spiteful old bat." Lady Sylvia's mutter chased away his amusement. "She's more outrageously awful than ever. Lud, I wonder that Angus is addled enough to trust her to care for the children."

"She does not appear to welcome the prospect of guests." Lord Jervis, who along with the other gentleman had remained tactfully silent until then, shrugged out of his overcoat and tossed it carelessly over one of the carved sidechairs. He was tall and trim, but there was a softness about his well-manicured hands and handsome features that bespoke a taste for Town pleasures.

"Lady Octavia has always had an unreasonable dislike of me," said Lady Sylvia darkly. "No doubt from jealousy, seeing as . . ." Biting back further comment, she smoothed the scowl from her face as she turned to Orlov. "You have my sympathies, Mr. Oliver. You and your unfortunate colleague will likely be making the arduous journey back to London in the near future."

"Oh, I am not easily intimidated," he replied pleasantly. "In my profession, one learns to deal with all manner of difficult situations."

"Indeed." Her gaze remained on him for a touch longer than necessary. "Still, I cannot imagine anyone—not even a saint—putting up with her whims for long." She toyed with an end of her shawl, slowly twisting the fringe around her fingers. "Are you, perchance, a saint?"

"Just a humble tutor, milady."

"Then you won't mind carrying the bags up to our quarters?" With a gesture as silky as his accented English, the Comte De Villiers withdrew a purse from his waist-coat and shook out a coin. "As a token of gratitude—"

"Lord McAllister's generosity is quite enough to cover extending hospitality to his guests," replied Orlov.

"Ah, but in my experience, a man in your position always finds an extra bit of money welcome."

Orlov had already taken up two of the traveling valises, leaving no hand free. "Thank you, but consider it a gesture of goodwill, sir."

"A saint, indeed."

Jervis said nothing but flicked open his snuffbox and inhaled a pinch. "Do try this blend, Sylvia. It was made up especially for me by Lord Brimfield, who is, as you well know, the leading arbiter of taste in such things."

Orlov maintained a suitably subservient expression as he moved to follow the dowager's butler up the stairs. Through lowered lashes, he noted that the other two men were, despite their assumed nonchalance, watching him. Had they noticed Lady Sylvia's undisguised interest?

Whatever their pedigree, men were wont to revert to animal instinct when a female was involved.

Like dogs sniffing around a bone, he thought sardonically. De Villiers had been almost comically condescending, the deliberate wave of white-laced cuff and well-tailored sleeve no doubt meant as a marked contrast to his own frayed coat. The other gentleman's reaction was a touch more subtle perhaps—he had merely ignored the existence of a servant.

But of course, the air of tension could be due to an even more primal force of nature than sex—the urge to be King of the Jungle, the dominant male.

As the new arrivals followed, Orlov heard Lady Sylvia reply to her friend. "That Lord Brimfield has singled you out with a special mixture is a mark of particular favor. He is quite influential with the Carlton House set." Orlov heard the soft rustle of silk. "Do give me your arm, Randall. I find myself utterly fatigued from the journey."

"A rocky road," murmured Jervis. "But now that we are here, things should become smoother."

"Hmmph," she replied in unconscious imitation of the dowager.

"*Mais oui,* Sylvia . . ." assured De Villiers.

The rest of the words trailed off as Orlov walked across the carpeted landing and into the hallway leading to the guest quarters. Yet the echo of the Frenchman's accent was amplified to an unpleasant pitch with every step.

Damn. His penchant for irony was quick to collide with the need to view anything out of the ordinary as highly suspicious. All the cursed comte needed was a black velvet cape—lined in blood-red satin—to appear the perfect villain stepped straight from the pages of a gothic novel. Truth could be stranger than fiction, he reminded himself grimly. The scene he had just witnessed raised a number of unsettling questions.

He would have to keep his eyes and ears open in order to read between the lines.

"The lady is in here, Mr. Oliver," said Rawley, his reedy voice a trifle breathless after the climb. "While the rooms set aside for the gentlemen are just ahead."

Orlov placed her valise in front of the painted pine armoire, then stepped aside as Jervis escorted Lady Sylvia into her quarters. After a barely perceptible hesitation, De Villiers continued with the butler, passing through a set of doors to the far end of the hallway.

"I had forgotten how horribly rustic the place was," said Sylvia under her breath. "But then, Lady Octavia has always been lacking in any sense of refinement."

"Thank you, Mr. Oliver." Jervis dismissed him without a look. "The other bag belongs in my chamber. And do have a care, please. There are several porcelain snuff jars which are exceedingly fragile."

The cheval glass reflected a picture of languid grace— an impression heightened by the gentleman's pose. Bracing a shoulder against one of the carved bedposts, he crossed his legs and ran his fingers through his hair, carefully combing the fair curls back into the *à la Brutus* style currently in vogue with the bucks of the *ton*.

"Oh, after that, perhaps you would be so good as to give the coachman a hand with the rest of our luggage," he added. "The coach carrying our servants was delayed this morning by a cracked wheel, and won't be arriving for another hour or two."

Nodding agreeably, Orlov withdrew, but paused outside the door to refasten a buckle on the gentleman's valise. Just as he expected, Lady Sylvia was quick to resume her complaints.

"Perhaps this was not such a good idea after all," she muttered. "I had hoped that age and encroaching infirmities would have softened Lady Octavia's attitude somewhat. But it appears she is still as spiteful as ever."

"I have yet to meet someone who is immune to your

charms," said Jervis. "Do not abandon your efforts just yet."

Orlov could not make out the reply.

"Is there a reason for the bad blood between the two of you?" continued the gentleman.

"The dowager dislikes most everyone! But I think she has taken a particular dislike of me because I am welcomed into the highest circles of Society. While she is not."

"Indeed? You had not mentioned that before." Jervis prodded her to go on. "Have you any idea why?"

"On account of a youthful indiscretion." There was a degree of malicious satisfaction in Lady Sylvia's voice. "And she dares to look down her nose at *my* activities in Town." Orlov heard her reticule thump down upon the dressing table. "*I* was not forced to leave Town in disgrace. The gossip has it that her family had no choice but to marry her off to a hairy, half-heathen Scot, no matter that his title was a minor one and his only lands this godforsaken estate."

Godforsaken lands that the younger lady had just taken great pains to come visit. Orlov grimaced. The new information added yet another unexpected twist to the mission. Whether it was meaningful or not was impossible to tell, but at this point, nothing could be ignored . . .

"Trouble, Monsieur Oliver?"

"Nothing I can't deal with easily." He rose from his knees, slowly and deliberately enough to provoke a spark of annoyance in the comte's eyes. "There—the buckle is now as good as new."

"You are very clever with your hands?" It was phrased more as a question than a statement.

"Necessity inspires ingenuity." Of all the roles he

had played in his profession, that of *agent provocateur* fit him like a glove. A good many people—Shannon included—would agree that he had a real knack for getting under a person's skin. "And I like to fix things."

"You must be very useful to your employers." Up close, De Villiers was not quite as foppish as he first appeared. Beneath the exaggerated lapels of his sky-blue coat and the intricate folds of his starched cravat, his shoulders were solid slabs of muscle. And though his height was only average, the chiseled taper to a narrow waist made him look smaller than he really was.

He slapped a kidskin glove lightly against his thigh. The snug buckskins revealed the contours of more than male pride. "I wonder that you would wish to endure the hardships of this part of the world when your services would be welcome far closer to London."

"One man's paradise is another man's purgatory."

"Chacun à son goût," said the Frenchman softly before moving on to rendezvous with his friends.

Each man to his own taste, translated Orlov silently.

If the comte had come here expecting to savor an easy victory, he was in for a rude surprise.

Chapter Thirteen

$\mathcal{T}$he arrival of the two other traveling coaches heralded a flurry of unusual activity in the castle. While Rawley oversaw the serving of a cold collation of refreshments for the London lords and ladies, the personal maids and valets set to sorting out the luggage and seeing it conveyed to the upper floors.

Not without a fair amount of grumbling over work that fell beneath their dignity, noted Shannon. Drawn by the sound of strange voices, she had left the children doing sums in the schoolroom to take a quick peek into the entrance hall. By the load of baggage still remaining on the slate tiles, it looked as though a regiment had taken up residence, rather than a half dozen members of the beau monde.

They were, she imagined, already in the drawing room. As for Orlov, he was nowhere to be seen.

It was not until the supper hour that she caught her first glimpse of the guests. The harried butler had paused in his puffing just long enough to convey Lady Octavia's request that she and Orlov continue to take their meals with her. The positions of governess and tutor were often awkward ones when it came to protocol. They were not quite servants, not quite social equals. In the end, it was left to the discretion of the family on how to treat the relationship.

That the dowager was not one to stand on ceremony was fortunate, thought Shannon. It afforded the opportunity to subject the guests to a closer scrutiny than circumstances would otherwise have permitted. She scraped her hair back and fastened it in a prim bun at the nape of her neck, then stepped back from the looking glass to assess the effect. A governess was supposed to appear colorless. Her dress, a shapeless design cut in a drab shade of iron gray, was suitable for her station. And after adding another few hairpins to tame an errant curl, she decided she looked the part.

The bulge of the small pistol was hidden by the heavy folds of wool. As was the blade strapped to her leg.

"Ah, there you are, Miss Sloane." A rap of the dowager's cane summoned her closer. "Come meet the guests."

Shannon crossed the drawing-room carpet, aware of a momentary lull in the conversation.

"This is Lady Sylvia St. Clair, Angus's sister-in-law."

If the lady in question was annoyed by the breach in proper etiquette concerning the introductions, she hid it well.

"Her companions are Miss Helena Talcott and her sister, Miss Anna." To the three ladies, the dowager added, "Allow me to present Miss Sloane."

They acknowledged her with tiny nods.

The gentlemen, who had been examining the old

fowling piece hung above a painting of a hunting scene, proved rather more forthcoming as the exchange of names was made.

"My sisters are Helen and Annabelle," murmured their brother with a quick wink. He had a broad, friendly countenance, though the redness of his nose and a puffiness around the eyes seemed to hint at a tendency to overindulge in spirits. He had a glass of whisky in hand rather than sherry.

"Sloane?" he continued after a sip of his drink. "Are you perchance related to the Shropshire Sloanes?"

"No," murmured Shannon. "I doubt you are acquainted with my branch of the family."

"The ladies are all enjoying champagne. May I pour you a glass, Miss Sloane?" Shannon thought she detected a flicker of annoyance in Lady's Sylvia's gaze as Lord Jervis moved to the sideboard.

"Just water, thank you."

"Ah, but we are celebrating."

What? she wondered.

He went ahead and filled a crystal flute with the wine, prompting yet another question. Was he the sort who refused to take no for an answer?

"Miss Sloane has very strict notions of propriety." Orlov moved in quickly and lifted the glass to his own lips. "While I, on the other hand, confess to having slightly less lofty standards."

Biting back a titter, the younger Miss Talcott fixed the tutor with a bold stare that was a bit forward for a young miss just out of the schoolroom. The gentlemen did not look quite so amused.

As for the dowager's relative, her topaz eyes seemed

to reflect the same mysterious effervescence as the champagne.

"A man after my own heart," announced Lady Octavia. "Come here, Mr. Oliver. And bring the bottle with you."

"Allow me to propose a toast." Lady Sylvia raised her glass. "To family, and to friends, both old and new." Her gaze never left Orlov.

"*Santé,*" said the Frenchman, his mouth turning up at the corners, as if savoring some private jest.

"*Móran làithean dhuit is sìthm,*" countered the dowager in Gaelic.

De Villiers offered a silent salute.

"Lead me in to the supper, Mr. Oliver, before the soup gets cold."

The dowager's demand once again upset protocol, forcing Talcott to offer his arm to Shannon. He did so with good grace, and indeed, he seemed loath to relinquish his hold on her when they came to her chair.

"Lady Octavia says you attended school near London." He seated himself beside her.

"Where?" asked Helen quickly. "Perhaps we have mutual friends."

Shannon did not wish to keep the attention focused on herself. "I cannot think so. It is a very small academy, and one that does not attract students from the higher circles of Society."

"Your family does not come to Town for the Season?" asked the comte.

Shannon kept her eyes on her plate. "I am a governess, sir, not a belle of the beau monde."

Good manners demanded that the subject be dropped. De Villiers tried to draw the dowager into conversation, but his attempts were rebuffed with brusque replies. To relieve the stirring of silver and china, the Londoners fell to discussing the highlights of their journey—a topic that only seemed to drive Lady Octavia deeper into her uncharacteristic silence.

Intimidated? It was not like the dowager to retreat from any challenge. And yet, the elderly lady was definitely subdued. Once or twice Shannon even noticed the soup spoon shake in her hand. She wondered if Orlov had any inkling why. They had not yet had the opportunity to confer about the new arrivals.

Was he as surprised as she was to find a Frenchman making up one of the party?

"What of you, Mr. Oliver?" Jervis suddenly directed his attention to the tutor, his tone taking on an edge of mockery. "Did you, too, attend an obscure institution of higher learning?"

"I suppose, milord, it would depend on how familiar you are with the educational offerings in England."

The subtle barb did not miss its mark. Jervis colored ever so slightly as Lady Octavia answered, "Mr. Oliver attended Oxford."

Shannon wondered if he was deliberately tweaking the London lords. Most likely the answer was yes, she decided. His arrogance was like a second skin, and the ladies seemed to be finding his attitude intriguing. Especially Lady Sylvia.

"Ah, a serious scholar," remarked De Villiers. "Are you, perchance, fluent in French, monsieur? I should find it pleasant to converse in my native tongue."

"I know Greek and Latin, of course, but modern languages are not my field of expertise."

"Which is?" inquired Lady Sylvia.

"English literature and ancient history," he replied smoothly.

Jervis patted a napkin to his mouth. "Rather dry subjects, to say the least. I prefer more active pursuits than holing up in a library to study moldering manuscripts."

"Those who do not recall history are doomed to repeat it."

"Bonaparte would agree with you," remarked the comte. "By all accounts, he is a keen student of the subject."

Before Orlov could form a reply, Lady Sylvia interjected her own comment. "Mr. Oliver does not have the look of a man who spends all of his time in a dark, stuffy room."

"Do you hunt?" asked the elder of the Talcott sisters. Like her brother, Helen had thick auburn hair and wide hazel eyes. Her features were pretty enough, but her face was a bit full and her nose a trifle sharp—she would never be thought beautiful, especially in comparison to Lady Sylvia. Perhaps that was why her mouth appeared pursed in a perpetual pout.

"On occasion," answered Orlov. "Do you—"

"Then you must join us on a shoot," interrupted Jervis as he sliced off a morsel of pheasant. "Tell me, have you noticed much game in the area?"

"I have seen plenty of grouse on my morning walks."

"I was thinking about something more challenging than birds."

Orlov allowed a small smile. "I would imagine that these moors offer plenty of sport."

"Excellent. I look forward to seeing how well scholarly skills translate to stalking roe deer."

Shannon sipped her mushroom bisque. *No, you do not.*

The meal proceeded without further incident. As Lady Octavia remained unresponsive to polite conversation, the London contingent turned to discussing the merits of a recent exhibit of landscape painting among themselves. Though Orlov listened politely, he was aware of how pinched the dowager's expression had become, and how deeply her eyes had sunk in their sockets. As if she had withdrawn to some inner place of refuge.

Why? It was yet another unanswered question. He felt his grip tighten on his knife. And there were too damn many of them for his taste.

When she rose abruptly and suggested that the ladies leave the gentlemen to their port, he pushed back his chair as well. "Allow me to assist with the tea service, milady. I am sure that these gentlemen would prefer to relax in some privacy."

Jervis seemed to realize that such an arrangement would leave the tutor alone with the ladies. "Let us not stand on ceremony," he announced. "We will take our postprandial drinks with you in the drawing room, if that is agreeable, Lady Octavia."

She shrugged her bony shoulders. "Suit yourself. But be advised that if you wish to blow a cloud, you will have to do it on the terrace."

After escorting the dowager to her favorite chair by the fire, Orlov contrived to brush by Shannon. "Keep the gentlemen occupied here for the next quarter hour."

"Why?" she whispered.

"I want to make a quick search of the comte's quarters, while his servant is still at supper."

She looked uncertain. "I am not sure how—"

"Think of something." He moved away quickly as Helen approached, and took the tea tray from Rawley. "Would you prefer to pour, milady? Or might you like one of the ladies to serve as hostess."

"I am sure Lady Sylvia would take pleasure in presiding," answered the dowager. "I find myself rather exhausted from the day's commotion and prefer to retire for the night."

Bowing, Orlov offered his arm.

"You needn't abandon the company on my account, young man. I have my stick to lean on."

"I was about to take my leave as well. I have several sections of Homer's *Odyssey* to review for Master Prescott's history lesson."

The Talcott sisters looked disappointed. "La, we were hoping you might join us in a hand of whist," said Annabelle. "We have all grown far too familiar with our usual partners."

Steam from the teapot obscured Lady Sylvia's reaction. "Do you play, Miss Sloane?"

"Cards? No, not well at all." Shannon had already moved past the table to where the ancient firearm hung on its bracket. She ran a hand along its varnished stock. "Monsieur De Villiers, you seemed so *very* knowledgeable about the working of this weapon earlier in the evening. Might I ask you to explain again just how the firing mechanism works?" The request was accompanied by a flutter of lashes. "I confess to being absurdly ignorant on these things. I hardly know which end is which."

So the warrior hawk could metamorphose into a flirtatious dove? Seeing this side of her nature for the first time, Orlov was torn between amusement and a more primal irritation.

"But of course, mademoiselle." All smiles, the comte came to her side, standing a bit closer than was necessary. "You see here . . ."

"Hmmph." Once in the hallway, Lady Octavia recovered enough of her usual aplomb to voice her opinion. "Miss Sloane certainly exhibited no such ignorance the other day, when I observed her take that weapon off the wall and subject it to a thorough test of its working." She paused for a fraction. "And do *not* imply that I had left off my spectacles, lest you wish to be digging the point of my stick out of some vital portion of your anatomy."

"You are too sharp by half," he murmured. "I would not dare question your sight or your sleight of hand."

"I wonder why she would take pains to hide her skills with firearms," mused the dowager. Candlelight flashed off her lenses, casting a kaleidoscope of patterns across her wrinkled face. Her hand suddenly felt cold upon his sleeve.

"I imagine she has her reasons."

"Which, I take it, you are not about to reveal?"

Orlov sought to slice a fine line between truth and lie. "I cannot claim to be in the young lady's complete confidence. We are not . . . intimate friends."

"Hmmph. I wonder why a man as clever and charming as you are has not found a way to penetrate her defenses." Her steps seemed a bit labored as she climbed the stairs. "Well, I am afraid you are on your own. Do not expect *me* to invite you into my boudoir." Her stick tapped his toes. "Run along, Mr. Oliver. I can find my way from here."

*   *   *

". . . and so, when you pull the trigger, the flint strikes the pan, and *voilà*! The powder goes up in smoke." The comte's fingers curled around hers, drawing them down to the smooth curve of steel. "Here, you try it."

Shannon did not have to feign a maidenly hesitation. Though the Academy trained all of its students in the art of allure, she had always felt awkward, unsure of her skills in flirtation. Her roommate Sofia had an innate knack for wrapping men around her little finger, while she, on the other hand, was far more comfortable with a length of leather or steel pressed in her grip.

A warrior or a woman. In her, the combination seemed to clash.

Surely Orlov was aware of her lack of charm. And yet, she thought wryly, his curt command had likely not meant that she should challenge De Villiers to a bout of fisticuffs in the middle of the drawing room. Given her limited options, she had no alternative but to exercise her feminine wiles. No matter how tentative.

"Don't be afraid, mademoiselle." The comte's touch sent another small shiver down her arms. "It is not loaded. And I have firm hold of the barrel. It will not slip from my grasp."

"Arnaud fancies himself quite an expert on hunting birds, Miss Sloane. But his technique can be a trifle too heavy-handed." Jervis, who had joined them, gave a cocky smile. "Allow me to demonstrate." Plucking the old fowling piece from his friend, he took mock aim at one of the winged cherubs adorning the carved ceiling.

"Do put that down, Randall, before there is an unfortunate accident," snapped Lady Sylvia.

Her friend laughed. "I doubt it has been fired since Cromwell's time."

"Sylvia is right," announced Annabelle loudly. Shaking off her sulky silence, the younger Talcott sister sought to draw some of the attention to herself. Flaxen curls set off a heart-shaped face and lush, rosebud mouth. She was far prettier than her sister, and with another year or two of polish to round off the adolescent edges, she would be a Diamond of the First Water.

But patience did not seem to be one of Annabelle's virtues, noted Shannon. Throughout supper, the girl had seemed greatly annoyed that the gentlemen were not making more of a fuss over her.

Exaggerating a shudder, Annabelle added, "How you can bear the touch of it is beyond me. Weapons are far too dangerous. The mere sight of such horrid things sends chills down my spine." A flutter of lashes seemed to invite the comte to offer his soothing support to her, rather than a lowly governess.

De Villiers did not appear to notice.

"Only in the wrong hands, Bella." It was her brother who answered. "Sylvia is made of sterner stuff. I can vouch for her skills in archery."

"She is a crack shot with a bow and arrow," agreed Jervis as he set the old musket back in its place. "As I can well attest. She beat all of us gentlemen soundly at Lord Henniger's house party."

How interesting. Shannon shot the lady a sidelong glance. So those graceful hands were not quite as dainty as they seemed.

"Perhaps we should organize a rematch." The comte perched a hip on the edge of the console table and began buffing his nails on his sleeve. "Seeing as the choice of entertainments here promise to be rather sparse, it would provide a source of amusement."

The others applauded the suggestion.

"Are you adept with a bow and arrow, Miss Sloane?" he asked.

"A governess is not ordinarily trained in such skills," she replied obliquely.

"Not ordinarily." The rich scarlet hue of his coat—strikingly similar to the color of British regimentals—set off his dark coloring to perfection. A choice, no doubt, as deliberate as the flash of pearly teeth. "But being a country miss, I thought you might have some experience with such sport," he continued. "You *did* say you were from the country, did you not?"

Lady Sylvia proved an unwitting ally in deflecting the question. To Shannon's eye, she looked none too happy with the fact that her gentlemen friends were paying attention to a mere servant. "Lady Octavia was adamant about us not distracting Miss Sloane from her duties in the schoolroom. I should not like to cause my dear aunt any distress."

"Oh." Looking disappointed, Annabelle nibbled a sugary bit of cake. "I was hoping to see Mr. Oliver display his prowess at hitting the bull's eye. He looks to have an admirable form for sport."

"Your eyes ought not be straying to the tutor," began her brother. "Your infantile infatuation with Lord Norbert—a country nobody was bad enough, but—"

"He is *not* a nobody," responded Annabelle hotly. "He is a perfectly respectable gentleman. You have no right to look down your nose at a barony, just because it is located in Yorkshire."

Her brother's voice rose, too. "I'll not permit you to squander your chances of making a good marriage in London by allowing some feckless fribble to come sniffing around your skirts. If you thought to ask him to follow you here, be advised I will boot his—"

A stirring of Lady Sylvia's silks nudged Talcott to silence. "Let us not begin squabbling in front of strangers," she said with a pointed look at Shannon. "Miss Sloane will think us ill-mannered savages."

Glancing at the clock, Shannon decided her delaying tactics had served their purpose and it was safe to withdraw. It would not do to make an enemy of the dowager's relative so early in the game.

"Not at all," she replied softly. "Indeed, you have all been more than kind to tolerate my presence with such good grace. I am well aware that Lady Octavia's notions on the social status of the household help are not shared by a majority of the *ton*." That yet another stranger might soon be arriving at the castle was unwelcome news, but she dared not ask any questions about the Talcott family argument. "If you will excuse me, I, too, have lessons to go over for the morrow."

Looking somewhat mollified by the humble tone, Lady Sylvia unbent enough to offer a slight nod. "Good evening, Miss Sloane. Pray, do not feel intimidated by our arrival. You have a formidable enough adversary to cope with in my aunt. We should hate to add to your travails."

"How kind." She could not quite read in the gentlemen's faces whether they seconded the sentiments. Talcott's features were too slurred with drink to reveal much of anything, but the other two looked as if partridge and grouse were not the only birds they intended to stalk.

To many men of wealth and rank, servants were fair game.

The comte left off polishing his person to escort her

to the door. "*Bon soir*, mademoiselle." He lifted her hand to his lips. "And *beaux rêves*."

Sweet dreams, indeed. For the moment, let him think she was naught but a pigeon ripe for the plucking. When the time came, he would learn how quickly she could unsheath her talons.

Much to her dismay, Shannon did not move quite fast enough the next morning to catch Orlov in the breakfast room. Distracted by all the questions she had concerning his nocturnal forays, she rushed through the morning lessons with Emma, hoping to have a word with him before nuncheon, only to have the housekeeper call her to the kitchen for an opinion on whether the London ladies would prefer roast beef or leg of lamb for the supper meal.

When she returned to the schoolrooms, the tutor and both children were gone.

Damn. Damn. Damn.

Taking the back stairs two at a time, she hurried through the scullery and took the shortcut out to the gardens. The sun, playing hide-and-seek among the thick clouds, had not yet warmed the chill from the air. It caught in her throat, like a sliver of ice.

Where had Orlov taken Prescott and Emma?

The path forked and she plunged on to the right, passing under a low pergola covered with climbing roses. Thorns caught at her cloak. Had she been wrong to let her guard slip? Looking to the distant moors, she was about to turn for the stables when a raucous cackling sounded from behind the nearby boxwood bushes. Sliding cautiously along the line of the hedge, she peered over the curling leaves.

"In Russia, they are called wolf birds." Orlov was coaxing one of several big black ravens closer with a crust of bread. "But despite their predatory looks, they are quite gregarious."

"Th—they won't bite? Or peck out my eyes?" Emma flinched as the bird flapped its glossy wings, her clenched little fists turning white at the knuckles. But seeing that her brother didn't budge, she kept her seat on the low stone wall.

"No, my little elf." Circling her shoulder, he drew her closer to his side. "Here." He turned her palm upward and crumbled a bit of the bread into a fine powder. In a deep voice, he uttered a few Russian words. "There, I've said the magic spell. If they come any closer you can throw Druid dust in their eyes, and turn them into tiny sparrows."

She giggled. "There are no such things as spells and Druids. Papa says it's just the stuff of old legends."

"Perhaps. But it never hurts to keep an open mind. As a scientist, your father would no doubt agree." Orlov tossed the raven a crumb. With a hop and jab, the bird caught it in midair and gobbled it down, setting off a flurry of protest from the others.

Forgetting her fears, Emma clapped her hands together. "They look so funny, with their bobbing heads and great big feet."

"Aye, they do." He mimicked their motion, drawing more laughs from the children.

Shannon smiled, in spite of her still-pounding heart. The Russian was a contradiction, a conundrum. A cold-blooded killer, a kind-hearted guardian—the two seemed hard to reconcile. Which was a truer measure of the man? She had a sense that there was no easy answer. And yet . . .

The errant thud of her pulse, fast and furious as a stallion's gallop, warned her to rein in her wild speculations. She had promised Lynsley to keep her impetuous emotions from riding away with her. Alexandr Orlov was a man of hardened will, tempered arrogance, carnal appetites. Whatever inexplicable attraction sparked this powerful heat in her veins, she must fight it at all costs. Losing control could be dangerous to all concerned.

"Is something wrong?" To a chorus of aggrieved squawks, Orlov suddenly looked around to meet her gaze. He swung Emma up into his arms and rose. A blur of black wings cast a momentary shadow over their faces.

Aware of her wind-snarled hair and thin muslin dress, Shannon felt rather foolish. "Cook is looking for the children. She has baked a special treat of hot mutton pasties and they are fast growing cold."

Would that the same thing could be said for her burning cheeks. The man had an uncanny knack of making her feel . . . naked beneath his raking eyes.

His mouth curled up at the corners. "I do hope she has made an extra batch. I am famished."

"I missed you at breakfast."

"I rose early and decided to take a walk while the weather held. I did pocket a few slices of bread, but I fear they have now gone to feed our winged friends."

"St. Francis of Assisi would be impressed."

Orlov flashed a choirboy grin. "Lord knows, I have little claim to sainthood. However—"

"Scottie was teasing me about being afraid of ravens," piped up Emma. "And Mr. Oliver offered to teach me that they aren't so bad, once you see past the black feathers and sharp beaks."

"Yes, appearances can be deceiving." Shannon resisted the urge to sneak a peek at the Russian. "It is an excellent lesson to keep in mind. Now run along, the two of you, before Cook's feelings are hurt."

"I take it the invitation does not include me?" said Orlov as the children scampered away.

"Stay a moment," she replied a touch sharply. "I wish to know what transpired last night."

"Precious little of any import. I found nothing incriminating in De Villiers's rooms. Most gentlemen would pack a brace of pistols for such a journey." He made a face. "However, his taste in cologne is grounds for being shot on the spot."

"The carriage—" she began.

"I checked it this morning, while the coachman was still sleeping. Again, I saw no sign that anything is secreted within the paneling or the upholstery."

"No maps." She frowned in thought. "No hidden messages, no stash of money."

"That is not to say that a more thorough search would not turn up something of the sort. I will keep my eyes open for any opportunity to dig deeper. But so far, there is nothing to arouse suspicion."

"Save for their very arrival."

"Save for their arrival," repeated Orlov.

The furrow between Shannon's brows deepened. "Then you are not fully convinced that is it merely coincidence?"

"Oh, as I told you before, *golub,* I take a rather jaded view of the world and those who people it." He looked to the moors as the sun gave way to shadow. Mist was beginning to blow in from the coast, hazing the hills with austere shades of windswept gray. A breeze, redolent of approaching rain, ruffled the twisting ivy and from far away, the growl of distant thunder rumbled against the stones. "That way I am rarely disappointed."

Fallen leaves rustled against the gravel.

"In this case, I am inclined to agree—" she began.

Orlov suddenly shoved her up against the stone archway and kissed her hard. "Look outraged . . . but not too outraged," he murmured, angling his mouth to nip at her earlobe.

She gasped, her anger hot against his flesh.

"Yes, that's it."

Struggling, Shannon freed her arms. She clawed at his shoulders, then her hands softened as they slid into his hair. He felt the burr of callused fingertips, the stretch of sleek muscle as her body molded to his. She had not been neglecting her training. Her lethal grace—all long limbs and lithe curves—once again brought to mind a lioness. A regal huntress. Matching him strength for strength.

With a low groan, he kissed her again on the lips, the pretense of passion deepening to a more primal need. *So fierce, so feminine.* His tongue thrust inside her, touching, teasing, tantalizing.

Shannon shivered as she arched back and entwined herself in a more intimate embrace. Emboldened, Orlov slid his hands over her breasts, feeling the tips harden against his palms. Shifting his stance he nudged a knee between her skirts.

She appeared to be taking his orders to heart. Rather than fight him, she opened her legs to his scandalous advance. In another moment . . .

He pulled back.

"Hit me," he whispered, bemused to find his voice strangely fuzzed. "Hard."

Her palm came across his cheek in a stinging slap.

They froze, facing each other in stiff-armed silence. Surprise held them still for some moments.

"Well played," he finally murmured, slowly brushing a tangle of curls from the nape of her neck. "If ever you tire of your current employment, you might consider a career on the stage."

"What the devil was that all about?" Her face was flushed and her breath was a bit ragged.

"The ladies were watching." With his eyes, Orlov indicated the screen of yews bordering the upper terrace. "They are gone now."

"Why—" she began.

"By playing the role of a rake, I mean to see what hidden tensions I can stir up among the London party. This little scene will help to convince Lady Sylvia and the Talcott sisters that I am not quite a gentleman."

"Isn't that exactly the sort of male a gently bred young lady is taught to avoid?"

"Ah, but a taste of the forbidden has been an irresistible attraction since the Garden of Eden was put on this earth . . ."

Shannon's kiss-swollen lips pressed together.

Was it his imagination, or did they quiver ever so slightly? "You won't be jealous, will you, if I flirt with them?" he asked.

She swore, drawing a small laugh from him. "No, I didn't think so, *golub*." He turned, then hesitated as an unwelcome thought came to mind. "But no doubt they will gossip to the gentlemen about your own availability.

Be aware that they may seek to take the same liberties as I just did."

"I can handle myself, Mr.—"

"Alex," he interrupted. "Remember that we had agreed to dispense with formalities. And it suits our intimacy. If we were carrying on an illicit affair, we would hardly be calling each by our surnames."

"I—it is only an act."

Orlov found himself savoring the sight of her blush. Color spread slowly over her cheekbones, the dark crimson hue pooling in the hollows, then lightening to a more nuanced shade of pink as it crept toward her eyes. "Ah, but they don't know that, do they, Shannon?"

"Let us hope it is not the only falsehood they fail to discover," she muttered. The temperature was dropping, and Orlov felt the pebbling of goosebumps beneath the thin fabric of her sleeve. "De Villiers was awfully attentive during our little *tête-à-tête* last evening. He even inquired where in the country I was raised."

"How did you keep him occupied?"

She exaggerated the flutter of her lashes. "By asking him to explain the mysterious workings of a seventeenth-century fowling piece." The thick fringe of gold seemed to spark flecks of fire in her emerald eyes. "By the by, his discourse on ballistics was woefully inaccurate. It was the Bavarian necromancer Moretius who wrote a treatise on the principles of rifling, not some Benedictine monk from Savoy. In 1522, not a century later."

Orlov couldn't help but smile at the thought of the Frenchman's expression had she gone ahead and tossed the facts back in his face. "You didn't correct his error, I trust?"

Her gaze turned slitted. "You are not the only one who

can play the game of flattery. The Academy's training includes expert instruction on the arts of seduction as well as weaponry. I am well aware that men cannot bear to be wrong in anything."

His humor suddenly darkened to match the clouds overhead.

"You won't be jealous, will you, if I flirt with him and his friends?"

He swore, surprising himself with the vehemence of his oath.

"No, I didn't think so." Hugging her arms to her chest, Shannon turned into the teeth of the wind.

"Be careful," he warned. "Don't get too close to De Villiers. He may be naught but a pompous prig, but if he is in league with D'Etienne, he is a trained killer."

"Then it will be a match made in heaven," she shot back. "I shall take pleasure in sending him straight to hell."

"Take care you don't get burned."

"As you saw in Ireland, I am very good at handling lucifers."

"Playing with fire is always unpredictable—in case your damn training failed to make that clear." Her announcement had taken him by surprise. Though why he should be disturbed to learn of her schooling in feminine wiles was odd. It was merely another weapon in their arsenal, and if she could wield it well, all the better for their chances of success.

"I know full well the dangers of what we do."

Orlov wished he could feel so sanguine. "Well then, you need no further counsel from me."

"Indeed not. As I said, I can take care of myself." She patted at her skirts—no doubt checking that her knife had not shifted during their amorous interlude. "I would rather you worry about how we can make any further progress in securing the house from intruders. The terrace is now protected by trip wires, but there are a good many other ways into the place."

"I, too, am not in need of a lecture to alert me to the dangers lurking at our gates," he snapped. "After a wee dram of spirits with Rawley and Euan last night, I was able to learn which side doors and cellar entrances are never used. I've shut them with my own set of padlocks, so that cuts down on the number of ways into the house."

She nodded. "And all jesting aside, your earlier comment about nailing the windows shut is not a bad idea either."

In defensive strategy, at least, they saw eye to eye. Orlov held her gaze for a moment longer before turning for the terrace. "I'll see to it before supper if you will take my place at the chess board."

"One other thing—I also overheard a squabble between Annabelle and her brother. Apparently she began a flirtation with a Yorkshire baron they met on their way north. From what I could gather, there may be a moonstruck young man on the way north, hoping for an invitation to join the house party here."

"Damn, there are too many strangers as it is," he muttered.

As for any offensive gambits by their enemy . . . he would have to stay on guard.

Chapter Fourteen

*S*o many questions, so few answers.

Shannon drew a piece of chalk in random circles across the schoolroom slate, wondering how she had let herself be so distracted that she had neglected to ask Orlov about several pressing concerns. His kisses, however fake, had left her momentarily robbed of reason. The why of it was proving as elusive as all the other answers they sought, she thought glumly. But personal concerns, however nettling, could wait.

Lady Octavia was a far more important mystery. The dowager's reaction to the visitors from London had so far been marked by an odd combination of feistiness and fear. The acquaintance was admittedly a very short one, but Shannon was willing to wager that the elderly lady did not shrink from confronting a difficulty head-on. And with her trusty stick held firmly in hand.

For the dowager to looked defeated by anything less than a fire-breathing dragon . . .

The sharp scratch caused Emma to look up from her

lettering exercise. "B is devilishly difficult to get right," she sighed. "It comes out all lumpy, no matter how carefully I try."

"You must not say 'devilish,'" corrected Shannon.

"Scottie does." The little chin, now liberally smudged with ink, rose a fraction higher. "And so does Uncle Angus."

"If Prescott does so within hearing of Mr. Oliver, he may feel a birch on his backside. As for your uncle . . ." She drummed her fingers on the desk. "Perhaps we will wash his mouth out with soap."

As she had hoped, Emma giggled. But the sound was fleeting. All too soon, the little girl was looking wistful. And wary. "I miss him very much. Grandmama says he has been delayed in England, and that we must be patient." The little girl brushed a knuckle to her cheek. "It is devilishly hard to be patient."

"Yes, it is." After squeezing the hunched little shoulders, Shannon leaned in for a look at the letters. "You are doing very well. Try holding the pen a bit closer to the nib. That way, I think you will find the stroke easier to control." Turning to a fresh page in the copybook, she added, "Now write the passage one more time. Practice makes perfect."

As Emma sighed and set to work again, she could not resist sneaking into the corridor for a quick peek at the adjoining schoolroom. Orlov and Prescott were engaged in the study of the globe. Its slow spinning beneath the tutor's touch seemed an apt metaphor for her own unsettled emotions. The Russian had a knack for keeping her off balance.

War is the Tao of deception.

Recalling one of Sun-Tzu's basic precepts, Shannon

was once again reminded of how the smallest slip could spell disaster.

Between Orlov's explosive kisses and the Frenchman's smooth flirtations, she had better find a way to keep a firm footing.

"What a lovely little folly you have down the by the loch, Lady Octavia," said Helen brightly as she wandered around the drawing room, waiting for the evening tea to be served. "We took a short stroll there this morning and spent a very pleasant hour enjoying the view."

"The fourth Laird McAllister was a great admirer of Greek architecture," replied the dowager without looking up from her book.

"There is a charming little boat tied to the steps," continued Helen, her words now directed to the gentlemen of her party. "Might we convince you to take us out on the waters some afternoon?"

"I would be happy to handle the oars if your friends prefer to devote their leisure hours to hunting," offered Orlov quickly.

Jervis, who along with Talcott and the comte was perusing a folio of bird engravings, set aside the print of a gyrfalcon. "What an amiable fellow you are, Mr. Oliver," he said with an ill-concealed sneer. "But I thought that your duties in the schoolroom did not allow such liberties."

"Oh, I am sure I can arrange my schedule to attend to the needs of the ladies as well as my pupil." As he had hoped, his offering of his services had struck the London lord as presumptuous.

"Amiable, indeed." Lady Sylvia appeared to have no such objections. Her murmur was more of a purr. "We shall be delighted take advantage of your kind offer. Perhaps tomorrow?"

"But my dear Sylvia, I thought we had agreed on holding our archery challenge in the morning," reminded the comte. "We gentlemen ought to sharpen our skills before setting out for the moors."

"Ah, yes. Quite right, Arnaud. I don't know how it slipped my mind." Lady Sylvia seemed aware of the tension she had stirred. And in no hurry to smooth any ruffled feathers. "Another day then, Mr. Oliver."

"I am at your service, milady. You have only to say when."

"Well, then." She toyed with the ends of her sash. "Perhaps you would agree to serve as a second for the ladies in tomorrow's competition. As the gentlemen are determined to see us defeated, we cannot count on them to play fair."

"I would be delighted to be of assistance."

"Would that my brother had such solicitous manners. But he cares more for his clubs and his card games than his sisters." Annabelle's mouth pursed to a petulant pout. "I vow, he thinks only of himself and never of *our* pleasures. He so rarely offers to take us driving in the park, or to escort us to a ball, even though he knows how much we enjoy such activities."

Talcott stalked to the sideboard. "Perhaps if you behaved more like a proper lady than a spoiled schoolgirl I would be inclined to accede to your whims. However, your behavior on the trip here did not augur well for that ever happening. Your outrageous flirtations were extremely embarrassing." He scowled. "It was bad enough that a broken wheel forced a delay of a day at that dreadful inn, but to have you encourage the attentions of a mere baron was outside of enough. Lord Nobody—"

"Stop calling Lord Norbert a nobody!" exclaimed Annabelle.

Orlov saw for himself that Shannon had not exaggerated the ill-will between siblings. The chit's choice of suitors apparently did not please her brother.

"A Yorkshire title glitters just as brightly as one from London," she continued. "And his charm is certainly a good deal more polished than yours. *He* was gentlemanly enough to ensure that the landlord saw to the comforts of us ladies while *you* became foxed on the local ale."

Ignoring her retort, he added another splash of whisky to his glass. "Really, Helen, can't you exercise a bit of restraint on the chit? I am beginning to think Aunt Georgianna was right in saying she needs a more steadying influence than you and Mama if she is to avoid dragging the family into scandal."

Helen drew in a sharp breath at the rebuke. "It is not *I* who have the tabbies wagging their tongues. Your recent luck—or rather the lack of it—at the gaming halls around Town is the only family foible giving rise to gossip."

"Bite your tongue," growled her brother. "My personal affairs—"

"That's quite enough," said Lady Sylvia. "From all of you."

"But Helen is right." The youngest Talcott seemed to think the command did not include her. "The only reason Robert agreed to this trip was not out of concern for *our* wishes, but to escape from his creditors."

"Right or wrong, one does not discuss such private family matters in public." Lady Sylvia's smile did not quite reach her eyes. "You ought to have learned that much by now."

Orlov hid a smile on seeing the look of sulky defiance Annabelle directed at both her brother and the other lady. A headstrong little hellion. With the right sort of encouragement, she might well be coaxed into making more indiscreet revelations about the London party.

"You see what I have to put up with?" said Talcott with a long-suffering sigh. "While you are up, do pour me another measure of that excellent malt, Jervis. Unpleasant arguments always give me a thirst."

Annabelle looked about to retort, but a frown from her sister warned her to silence.

"Indeed, it is a trifle warm in here," murmured De Villiers. "I think I shall step outside for a breath of fresh air. Would you care to join me for a turn around the terrace, Miss Sloane? Given your educational expertise, I was wondering whether you might be able to tell me the English names for several of the specimen plantings."

Shannon hesitated, then set aside her book. "I would be happy to try, sir, though plants are not my field of expertise."

The tension in the room eased slightly, yet Orlov was aware of a constriction in his own chest. So, she had been deadly earnest about her intention of using her sex as a lure. It shouldn't surprise him. They were both trained to use an enemy's weakness as a weapon. Still, though his mask of good humor remained unflinching, he could not quite shake off the unsettling sensation—an odd mixture of irritation and apprehension.

"The reading material here is all so boring," groused Annabelle. "The only copy of Ackermann's fashion plates is at least a decade old."

"While the gentlemen enjoy their drinks, perhaps the ladies would like to learn the basics of a board game from India." Turning away from his inner misgivings, Orlov flipped a pair of ivory dice into the air and caught them with a show of bravado. "I came upon a backgammon set in the card cabinet, and think you will find it a most interesting combination of luck and strategy."

"You intrigue me, Mr. Oliver." Lady Sylvia gave the sisters no time to respond. "I should be delighted to match wits with you."

"A regrettable lapse in manners," murmured the comte. "Please accept my apologies for my friends."

"You have nothing to apologize for." Shannon allowed him to lead her to the railing. The night was cool, but clear, the stars sharply luminous against the sable skies. A crescent moon cast a soft light over the decorative urns and twists of ivy. "It was not you who misbehaved."

"So I am not guilty by association?"

"I believe in judging people on their own individual merits."

"You are kind, Miss Sloane." He touched her hand, his meaning unmistakable. "More than kind."

Shannon leaned back against the stone balusters, slipping her fingers free from his.

"Ah." A smile played on his lips. He seemed more amused than angry at having his advances snubbed. Everything about him—his gestures, his dress, his way of tilting his face to show off its best angles—suggested a man supremely confident that no one could long resist his charms. "Speaking of individual merit, what is your relationship to Monsieur Oliver?"

"Why do you ask?"

"Far be it from me to repeat idle gossip, but the ladies observed a rather intimate scene this morning. I am simply curious as to how deep the attachment is."

She lifted her shoulders, imitating his Gallic shrug. "We have no formal understanding, if that is what you mean. What happened today was merely a whim of the moment. He has a very high opinion of himself, as I am sure you have noticed. And with some reason. There is no denying that he is a very handsome man."

"Handsome, indeed." The comte toyed with his watch fobs. "But a humble tutor nonetheless. One who likely has little to offer an intelligent young woman like yourself, save for his kisses."

"And you do?"

"Most certainly. A snug little nest in London, stylish gowns, enough money to keep you in comfort."

"Why me?" she asked after a moment. "We have only just met."

"Why?" he repeated. "You are extremely lovely, and have a certain *je ne sais quoi* about you."

She arched a brow.

"An aura of mystery. An intriguing hint of steel in your spine. I confess, the idea of convincing you to unbend to pleasure is rather provocative."

"You seem quite sure of yourself."

"When I put my mind to something, I am not in the habit of failing," replied the comte.

"Some might call that arrogance, Monsieur De Villiers."

"And some might call it honesty. What, pray tell, might you say, Miss Sloane?"

Shannon smiled and answered in the same soft whisper. "In all truth, I have not yet decided just what to think, sir."

"A woman who takes time to deliberate on all her options." He nodded. "How very wise."

"There are a great many pitfalls for one in my profession. I would not survive on my own if I were not careful."

"And yet, I do not detect any note of bitterness," said the comte slowly. "Even though the cruel vagaries of Fate have left you alone in the world, and forced to labor for a living."

"Whining is a waste of breath."

"There are those who could profit from your example."

Shannon acknowledged the compliment with a light laugh. Strangely enough, against all reason, she was finding it hard to dislike the man. He had a certain . . .

Je ne sais quoi, she repeated silently, savoring the mellifluous echo of his native tongue. Part of it was a quick wit and disarming frankness about what he wanted.

But then again, she reminded herself, an experienced agent would know all the little tricks of appearing charming. Given a sword, she could cut through any clever spins and distractions. With words as her only weapon, she was not nearly so confident.

Feeling his eyes intent on her face, Shannon quickly composed her thoughts. "I imagine that you, too, could rail against the unfairness of life. It can't be easy—a gentleman of title, and no doubt of wealth. And yet here you are, forced to abandon your homeland, your heritage, and take refuge in a foreign country."

"Not easy, no. But like you, I am a pragmatist, and make the best of the situation. There are worse places to land than in London. And several of the more influential émigré families saw to it I was introduced into Society."

"Have you known Lady Sylvia and the others for long?"

"We are casual acquaintances." His answer evaded the question. "When Lady Sylvia invited me to join in the journey to Scotland, I accepted. It appealed to my sense of adventure."

"So, you are not intimidated by the unknown."

"Nor are you. It is another thing we have in common, Miss Sloane." His dark lashes were long and thick, and he used them with the same subtle skill as a lady. "There had to be a great many other teaching positions available closer to London."

"None that offered the same rewards."

"Back to money."

"They say it is the root of all evil. But I daresay that those who have it would not be quite so smug if they were to awake one morning and find themselves penniless."

De Villiers let out a low bark of laughter. "I am sure that one of Aesop's fables says much the same thing. However, as I am not nearly as erudite as Mr. Oliver, I cannot recollect it. No doubt he could recite it to us verbatim."

"Actually, I believe he said that his expertise does not include French."

"Quite right." As he shifted his hand on the stone, the winking of moonlight caught the flash of gold. The crest cut into the burnished metal looked to be a gryphon. On his pinkie was a smaller ring, the single ruby appearing nearly black in the shadows.

"As Miss Annabelle remarked, the man does have an admirable set of muscles for a scholar."

"Mr. Oliver believes in the ancient Greek ideal—*mens sana in corpore sano.*"

"A healthy mind in a healthy body." De Villiers paused. "Yes, he did mention his expertise in the classical languages. Speaking of which, I cannot quite place his accent? Has he studied abroad?"

She, too, could dodge direct query. "Even to an English ear, a Yorkshire accent sounds quite exotic."

"Ah. That must explain it."

After exchanging a few more trifling pleasantries, the comte offered to escort her back to the warmth of the blazing log fire. Shannon was quick to accept, and once inside, she took her leave from the rest of the party, pleading fatigue and the need to rise early for lessons.

She *was* tired, and the day had left her with much to mull over. Draping her shawl over her dressing table, she began to pull out her hairpins. For a moment, she found herself staring at her own face in the looking glass. In the flicker of candlelight and half shadows it was hard to reflect on exactly what she saw. Was it a subtle shift in perspective, or were her eyes not as sharp as she thought?

Perhaps in the morning things would appear clearer.

Moving to the window, Shannon took a last look out over the gardens as she tied her hair back in a simple plait. The sky was still clear, allowing a wash of pale moonlight to cast a silvery shimmer over the ornamental plantings. There was a stillness to the leaves, an air of quiet—

Out of the corner of her eye, she caught a sudden slip of movement. A flutter of lace beneath a dark cloak.

Lady Sylvia. And she was not alone.

Shannon dropped her brush and shot for the back stairs. Hurrying down to the kitchen, she passed through the pantries and eased the scullery door open. Her slippers were soft and she managed to creep noiselessly around to the privet hedge in time to hear Sylvia's tone turn more agitated.

". . . of course I did not know they would be here!"

The man's reply was low, and too muffled for Shannon to make out the voice.

"Well, I suggest you think of something, and fast. Miss Sloane is too bloody sharp for my liking. She has eyes like daggers."

Flattening herself to the ground, Shannon slithered closer to the edge of the shrubbery, trying to identify the lady's companion.

"I am *not* imagining things." Lady Sylvia's shrillness carried clear enough through the chill, but the man had his back to Shannon. Blurred by the fluttering leaves, his size and height were too indistinct to make out. He could have been any of the three male guests. Or a stranger.

"Oh, easy for you to say," said Lady Sylvia in response to his muddled words. She listened for a moment longer, then gave a grudging nod. "Very well, I'll trust you to handle things. But try to do it without delay. The sooner we can quit this moldering pile of rocks, the better."

Her companion shifted, throwing himself deeper in shadow.

"We had better not linger out here any longer. Someone might spot us." Clutching at her cloak, Lady Sylvia nearly stumbled over a twist of ivy vines in her haste to retreat.

Shannon made a sure-footed return to her own room without being seen. As the door closed silently on its freshly oiled hinges, she decided that Orlov ought to be informed immediately of this latest development. If he had not yet left on his nightly patrol, perhaps he could—

She stopped short at the sight of Lady Octavia sitting on the bed with an ancient pistol in her hands.

"Who are you?" demanded the dowager.

Shannon didn't answer right away.

"And don't bother repeating that farrididdle about being a governess arranged by my son. I have stayed silent, trying to decide what it is you are up to, but now that Sylvia and her party are here, I dare not sit back any longer."

"Lady Octavia, it is very late, and perhaps you have become a trifle confused, what with all the recent upheaval of your quiet routine. If you would care to have another look at the letter—"

"I have *not* been tippling at the sherry," said the dowager grimly. "I may appear a doddering old fool to someone as young as you, but I'm still sharp enough to know my own son's handwriting."

Shannon drew a deep breath, then let it out in a wry sigh. "I shall inform Whitehall that its forgers are not quite as good as they think."

The weapon wavered just a touch. "You have been sent by Whitehall? Prove it!"

"I cannot," she replied. "I work strictly undercover. Nothing must connect me in any way to the government."

Lady Octavia's eyes remained narrowed. "And Mr. Oliver? He works for Whitehall as well?"

"No. This is a joint venture, so to speak. I am not at liberty to say who he works for, but I assure you he is—"

"A friend, not foe."

Shannon looked around to see Orlov silhouetted in the doorway.

He stepped into the room and drew the door shut. "And like my lovely colleague, I cannot produce any official orders from my superiors in St. Petersburg. I can only offer my word as a gentleman." He raised his candle, just enough to illuminate a gold-lashed wink. "In a manner of speaking."

The dowager's frail shoulders relaxed, and her weapon dropped. "Demme, why didn't you say so in the first place?"

"We were under strict orders not to alarm you," replied Orlov.

She made a rude noise. "As if your skulking around in the night was not cause for concern, young man. Though I did wonder whether the two of you were simply covering up your amorous exploits."

"Alas, my colleague is of the opinion that this assignment must be all business, no pleasure."

Shannon was glad that the dim light hid the flush of color rising to her cheeks. "As you see, Mr. Orlov—that is, Oliver—has enough serendipitous wit for the two of us. In any case, there is nothing remotely pleasurable about the situation."

Orlov's expression turned deadly serious. "No, indeed. The children and you may be in grave danger, milady."

"I suspected as much." If anything, the glint in Lady Octavia's eyes grew a touch brighter. "From that sly puss Sylvia?"

Shannon and Orlov exchanged looks. "We cannot say for sure."

"What *do* you know?"

She hesitated, but he merely shrugged. "No sense in

keeping it a secret." Moving a step closer to the dowager, he dropped his voice to a low murmur. "The French are desperate to stop your son from working with the British military. They have dispatched one of their top agents to come here."

"To kidnap the children?" asked Lady Octavia.

"Or worse," answered Shannon. "To be blunt, we believe he will do whatever he thinks is necessary to achieve his goals."

Out of the corner of her eye, she saw Orlov's profile take on a harsher line in the limning of moonlight.

"We are not exaggerating the danger, milady," he said. "Monsieur D'Etienne is a remorseless killer."

"Hmmph." Lady Octavia blinked and then checked the priming of her pistol. "Then we shall have to make sure that he never gets the chance to do his dirty work."

"Precisely. *We* have been working diligently to ensure just such a thing." Orlov softened his words with a slight smile. "Miss Sloane and I are heartened to know we may count on your firepower should it come to that. But for now, we would like to ask you to leave the offensive forays to us."

The dowager set aside the pistol—quite reluctantly. "So you wish for me to act as if nothing was amiss around our guests."

"An ancient Chinese general wrote a little book that is still considered the bible of warfare, milady," said Shannon. One of his precepts states 'Be tranquil and obscure.'"

"And if I remember correctly, another one says, 'Although capable display incapability.'" Lady Octavia mused for a moment. "Angus is also an admirer of Sun-Tzu, Miss Sloane. And I suppose the man's thinking makes a great deal of sense. Even if he was a heathen foreigner."

"So, in the spirit of international harmony, I propose we follow the fellow's teachings," suggested Orlov.

"I will do my best," replied the dowager solemnly.

"As will we, milady." Shannon repressed a shiver as she carefully removed the flint from the ancient firearm. "As will we."

Chapter Fifteen

Weapons were much in evidence the following morning, as the London party insisted on arranging their archery games immediately after breakfast. With Euan, the elderly footman, as a guide, Jervis and the comte headed to the attics and soon reappeared with an armful of sturdy yew bows and leather quivers filled with arrows.

"Lud, these were probably used against our forefathers at the Battle of Culloden Moor," quipped Talcott as he fingered the feathered shafts. "They look as if they could penetrate a suit of armor."

"And most likely did. The Scots have a rather bloodthirsty history," said the comte.

"Neither the English nor the French have a spotless reputation when it comes to violence." Stepping into the entrance hall, Orlov bowed to the ladies before adding, "One has only to look at the current conflict."

"Are you, perchance, a Quaker, Mr. Oliver?" asked Jervis in a needling tone. "For you certainly sound like a man who shies away from a fight."

"Alas, no. Though I admire their patience and pacifist principles, I am of the opinion that violence is sometimes a necessary evil."

Lady Sylvia smiled in approval. "A very gentlemanly sentiment, Mr. Oliver. It is hard to find fault with your thinking."

Jervis flushed, while the comte seemed to be taking amusement in some private joke. Talcott, who did not look at all happy at having been roused before noon, gave a peevish grunt. "Are we ready?"

"Yes. Why don't you help Randall and Arnaud with the bows, while we ladies fetch the picnic hampers prepared by Cook." She turned, pausing just long enough to flash a coy appeal. "Seeing as you are on our side, perhaps you would be kind enough to lend us a hand, Mr. Oliver."

Lady Sylvia seemed to be taking a conspicuous delight in goading her London friends into an ill-humor this morning. The reason was not clear to Orlov, but as it suited his own purposes for the moment, he had no objection to playing along.

"I would be delighted to do so," he replied, offering his arm with a flourish. He did not miss the dirty look darted his way by Jervis.

And by Annabelle. Robert Talcott's fondness for the bottle was no doubt exacerbated by his youngest sister. She was a little hellcat, spitting adolescent anger and frustration. Clearly she thought her beauty ought to have men groveling at her feet. That the ones around her were paying more attention to an aging widow and a prim governess was obviously infuriating.

As he escorted Lady Sylvia to the kitchen, Orlov reminded himself to seek a private moment or two with the girl. In her present mood, she might easily be coaxed into talking about others in intimate detail.

The chance came during the walk to the orchards. Still in a childish snit, Annabelle had refused to keep pace with the other two ladies. On the pretense of checking that he had remembered to add a wood file and carving knife to the last basket, Orlov dropped back and waited for her in the shade of the walled herb garden.

"I could not help but see that you seem to have little enthusiasm for the upcoming game, Miss Annabelle. Are you feeling out of sorts?"

"I am surprised you noticed aught but Lady Sylvia's walking dress," she replied rather waspishly. "Really, a lady of advanced years ought not wear such a low-cut bodice."

"When a lady is past the lush bloom of youth, she must resort to desperate measures," murmured Orlov.

"*You* do not appear to think she has withered on the vine." Her voice was still sulky.

"I must go out of my way to be polite. As a hired servant, I can hardly afford to offend my employer's relative."

Annabelle's face brightened as she thought on his words. "Yes, I see what you mean. How very boring for you, sir."

"Sometimes." He flashed a rakish smile.

She sidled a step closer. "Except when you are stealing kisses from that stiff-rumped governess?"

"I overstepped the bounds of propriety. As you saw, she quickly put me back in my place."

"Silly cow. Be assured *I* wouldn't kick up such a dust over a little harmless flirtation." Clutching at his shirt, she suddenly lifted herself on tiptoes and planted an awkward, open-mouthed kiss on his lips. The picnic basket swung wildly, striking a glancing blow to his leg before tangling in her skirts.

Easing back from her embrace, he gently pried it from her grip. "Allow me."

Annabelle's eyes had a dangerous glitter. He quickly took her arm and started to walk. "Much as I would like to deepen out acquaintance, this is neither the time nor place," he whispered.

"My friend Catherine is tupping her Papa's head groom," she said boldly.

"Risky."

"Cat says it is ever so . . . exciting to do something risky." He saw the erratic flutter of pulse at her throat. "I allowed Johnny Wollton to put his hand up my skirts last month, but he's only a boy and is not half so handsome as you." She pressed her hips against his. "Would you like to touch me, Mr. Oliver?"

"What do you think?" His own mind was racing as he added a throaty laugh. He would have to handle the little hellion with kid gloves, else the situation could turn embarrassing. Or worse. *Damn.* If one of the London party caught him ravishing a highborn young miss, there would be hell to pay. A duel, an arrest on charges of assault—there were any number of ways the mission could be compromised.

Annabelle gave a toss of her head and smirked.

She was like a headstrong filly, he thought. Someone ought to take the reins and offer some guidance before it was too late. Wildness was not the same as spirit. And with her unbridled recklessness, the chit could well end up hurting others, as well as herself.

"However, I have to be very, very cautious," he warned.

"Your brother could have me transported if he catches me with you. Not to speak of Miss Sloane." He couldn't resist adding, "She watches me like a hawk. I fear any transgression will be reported to the dowager."

"Oh, pooh!" she chided. "Have you never taken a chance in life, Mr. Oliver?"

"One or two," he said with a straight face.

"That's more like it." As they crossed the grass to where the rest of the party was waiting, Annabelle gave a sly flounce of her skirts as she passed Lady Sylvia.

The lady did not look amused.

Talcott swore, and Jervis snapped his bowstring before turning away.

Orlov was tempted to laugh aloud. He had meant to stir up a few waves, not a full-blown typhoon. The waters were looking dangerous at the moment. He would have to steer a careful course to avoid being caught in the crosscurrents.

"It rained arrows?" Prescott's eyes widened and Emma shuddered.

Shannon paused in reading from the history book. "It is a figure of speech," she explained. "But according to eye-witnesses, the sky was darkened by their numbers. And to the French soldiers on the field of Agincourt, it must have felt as if the heavens had turned against them."

Prescott rolled his pen between his fingers. "Mr. Oliver says the English archers were the most feared warriors in the world until someone figured out how to use gunpowder in firearms."

"Indeed."

"Papa is a wizard with gunpowder," said Emma. "Is he a feared warrior?"

"He is a famous scientist," replied Shannon evasively.

The little girl seemed satisfied with the answer. Her brother, however, looked up from his quill with a pensive expression.

She quickly turned the talk back to arrows. "Even today, the Red Indians of America are extremely skilled with a bow. With one shot they can bring down a buffalo, which is said to be even bigger than one of your great, hairy Highland steers."

"Might we watch Mr. Oliver in action?" Like countless other females, Emma had been won over by Orlov's charm, thought Shannon. He needed no weapon to slay hearts, save for a sinful smile.

Shaking off very ungovernesslike thoughts of his curved lips, she closed her book. "He is only advising the ladies on technique. But if you wish to watch the others display their prowess, I see no reason why we can't take a break from our classroom lessons."

Orlov tested the flex of the bow, then chose a thinner cord. "See how this suits you, Lady Sylvia. If it is too stiff, I could shave a bit off the ends."

She drew back on the string. "It is perfect."

"As is your technique," he replied. "I am glad I am not on the opposing side in this battle."

"Lady Sylvia is a veritable Diana," said De Villiers with a smile. "A graceful goddess of the hunt."

"I should say she is more like an Amazon," said Jervis loudly. "Bold and beautiful. But like the ancient figures of mythology, doomed to go down in defeat to the men."

"Actually, the Amazons were said to cut away one breast in order to better shoot their bows," murmured

Orlov. "I, for one, am immensely pleased that Lady Sylvia is a more modern female."

Jervis flushed with anger. "A gentleman does not make mention of bodily parts in the presence of ladies," he snapped.

"Forgive me." He grinned, taking care not to look the least bit contrite, and bowed low to the ladies. "I seem to have forgotten all the rules that Polite Society plays by."

Annabelle smothered a laugh in her glove.

Jervis clenched a fist, only to have Talcott place a restraining hand on his arm. "It was just a jest that flew awry, Randall. The fellow didn't mean any insult."

Muttering darkly about manners, Jervis stalked away.

"First we must decide the placement of the target," said Lady Sylvia. "Shall we start at thirty paces and move them back after each round?"

The suggestion was met with approval from both sides. The stableboy helped Orlov carry the wooden easel and sack of straw the appointed distance. As he squared the painted canvas on its bracket, he saw Shannon and the children cutting across the field. Her sweeping stride set the tall grasses to swaying, giving the illusion that she was floating on a shimmering sea of greens and golds. No amount of gray serge could disguise the bellicose beauty of her bearing. Lady Sylvia might bear passing resemblance to Diana, the Goddess of the Hunt, but Shannon was Athena personified. A flesh-and-blood Goddess of War as well as Wisdom.

The archery match momentarily forgotten, Orlov stood at attention, savoring the sight of the sunlight setting off sparks of gold in her windblown hair.

"A magnificent creature, *non*?"

He turned.

"Toiling as a governess seems a poor use of her talents." The comte's smile had a wolfish quality that set his own teeth on edge.

"I doubt that the position of *cher amie* would be any more appealing to a female of Miss Sloane's temperament." Orlov knew he ought to be encouraging an intimacy, but the thought of the Frenchman's hands or lips anywhere near Shannon's body was repulsive. "She is fiercely independent."

De Villiers leaned an elbow on the cross bar. "*Oui.*"

"Her services are not for sale." He kept his voice even, but some flare of emotion must have shown in his eyes, for the Frenchman drew a thumb across the painted circles, letting it come to rest in the center of the bull's eye.

"Ah, but perhaps you did not offer the right price, Monsieur Oliver."

A sudden fury welled up inside him. Orlov went very still, willing it to subside. *Jealousy?* Surely not. Cupid's arrows would never find their mark in him.

Still, for an instant, his hands clenched so tightly that he feared the bones might crack. But then he mastered his feelings and was back in command. Loathing—for his own momentary weakness and the comte's hauteur— gave him the strength to appear amused by the Frenchman's retort.

"In for a penny, in for a pound." Baring his teeth, he barked a cold laugh. "You are welcome to try your luck," he said. "But it may cost you more than you think to penetrate Miss Sloane's defenses."

De Villiers was no longer looking so smug. Where a moment before the comte had smelled blood, now he was not so sure. Still, his reply had an arrogant edge. "My purse is deep."

Flashing a mocking grin, Orlov resumed his adjustments to the target. "I was not speaking of money."

The children's approach put an end to the *tête-à-tête*.

Emma reached him first, her face flushed with the effort of racing through the meadowgrass. "Are you going to play Robin Hood and vanquish the evil sheriff?"

"Nay, my fair maiden." He swung her up in his arms, feeling the softness of her sun-warmed curls touch his cheek. "I am sorry to disappoint you, but no heroics for me. I am simply assisting the ladies in a friendly competition with the gentlemen."

"Miss Sloane had us studying about famous archers in history." Prescott skipped away from Shannon's side, eager to share his morning's lesson. "Did you know that William Tell shot an apple off of his son's head? And that five thousand English bowmen defeated a force of twenty thousand Frenchman at the Battle of Agincourt?"

"Lud, you are a bloodthirsty little buccaneer." He chuckled, ruffling the lad's hair. "The only target at risk today is this sack of straw."

"They begged to be allowed to watch the match." Shannon shot him a look of apology. "I saw no harm in it."

He nodded. "A practical display of skills is always educational. But keep them well off to the side." To the children he added, "Mind Miss Sloane. No larking about, or you will find yourselves back in the classroom."

"Yes, sir," they chorused.

"I will take her, and let you get back to your duties." Her hand brushed against him as she gathered Emma in her arms. She must have felt the coiled tautness of his muscles, for her brow furrowed in silent question.

Orlov shook his head ever so slightly. Whatever her inner misgivings, she heeded the warning and turned away without comment.

"Mr. Oliver!" Lady Sylvia gave a wave. "Are you about ready?"

All of the London party looked to be growing impatient to begin. The Talcott sisters were fussing with their skirts while Jervis stood with their brother in the shade of a live oak tree, flexing his shoulders.

He walked slowly back to the line that had been drawn with powdered chalk.

"Fraternizing with the enemy?" Even in teasing, Sylvia's tone had a brittle note to it.

A strange choice of words. He looked up sharply. Or had all the waiting and watching pulled his nerves to the snapping point?

"De Villiers," she added. "Arnaud has been insufferable in asserting that the ladies do not stand a chance against the gentlemen. I am counting on you to give us an extra advantage."

"An unfair advantage," called Talcott as he peeled off his coat. "There was nothing said about expert advisors. It seems unsporting of you, Sylvia . . . unless, of course, Miss Sloane would like to offer us her services."

"You don't need a governess, Mr. Talcott," replied Shannon.

"Indeed, let us not be childish in quibbling over the fine points of the competition," said De Villiers. "We are willing to take our chances against Mr. Oliver, *mes amies*. Aren't we?"

The thrum of a bowstring punctuated the rustling of the leaves. "Yes, let us see just how well the tutor translates theory into practice." Jervis snapped off another imaginary shot, then waved a mocking salute at Orlov. "Would your protégés care to go first?"

"Why not?" Lady Sylvia stepped to the line and held out her hand.

Drawing several arrows from the quiver, Orlov sighted down each shaft in turn before choosing one. "The breeze is blowing in from the right. I would factor in at least a hand's span to your aim," he murmured.

Sylvia fingered the feathers, then nocked it in place. In one smooth movement, she drew back the bowstring, drew a bead on the bull's eye, and let fly.

"Oh, bravo!" Helen clapped. Sylvia's shot looked to have lanced through the target just outside dead center.

"Your turn, Lord Jervis," said Orlov. "You will be hard-pressed to equal the lady's shot."

Jervis pretended not to hear the barb as he fussed over his choice of arrows. When he finally made his selection and took aim, his hands were surprisingly steady.

Interesting, noted Orlov. So the London lord was able to keep anger from interfering with his performance.

A sharp *whoosh* signaled his shot. A moment later, the arrow hit home, matching Lady Sylvia's accuracy.

"A point for the gentlemen," announced the comte as Jervis strutted away from the line.

Neither Helen nor De Villiers could come closer than the outer ring. Annabelle and her brother missed the target completely.

Another round ended with nearly the same results.

"Archery is hot work." Talcott patted his flushed face with his handkerchief. "Shall we take a break for lemonade?"

"And perhaps a quick review on the basics of grip and aim," said comte dryly.

"Will you show me how to hold a bow, Mr. Oliver?" It was Emma who asked, earning a look of undisguised annoyance from Annabelle, who had just opened her mouth to make the same request.

"Very well, my dear." Orlov dusted a bit of powdered sugar from his hands. "Finish your biscuit and then let us move over there, behind the apple trees, where we won't disturb the adults."

"I should be happy to offer my advice, Miss Annabelle," said De Villiers. "Seeing as your advisor has deserted you."

Jervis spread a blanket, removed his coat, and loosened his Belcher neckerchief. "Come have some lemonade, Sylvia. We have no need to sharpen our prowess."

"A temporary truce? Oh, very well." She accepted the proffered glass and sat down beside him. "Miss Sloane, would you be so kind as to bring the baskets over here."

It was not phrased as a request, but Shannon made no objection. After giving Prescott permission to climb into the branches of the shade tree, she dutifully set to work laying out the collation of cold meats and bread.

"Mr. Oliver." A tug on his hand brought his gaze back to Emma. "I am ready. May I try a shot at the target?"

"First you must show me that you have mastered the basics of handling a bow." Orlov flexed the length of yew, which was half again as tall as she was. "Then you must be able to draw the string."

Her chin rose. "I'm very strong."

"And very determined." He laughed. "For now, I shall show you the proper grip. Later, we shall see if we can find a more suitably sized weapon in the attics. Then you and Scottie can have your own competition."

She flashed a gap-toothed grin, seemingly satisfied

with the compromise, and carefully wiped her palms on her skirts.

"Put your hand here," he instructed. "And here."

Emma's stubby little fingers struggled to keep the bow upright.

"Try again," he murmured. But much as he tried to pay attention to her efforts, Orlov found himself distracted by the rising discord between Annabelle and De Villiers.

They seemed to be arguing over some fine point of technique. The girl's voice turned from a tone of whining to outright defiance, and the comte was clearly losing his patience. He snapped a sharp rebuke and out of the corner of his eye, Orlov saw her try to jerk away. Both were gripping the feathered end of the arrow, while its tip cut a dizzying pattern through the air.

"Fie, sir. I really don't need any more pointers from you," cried the young lady.

Annabelle Talcott would do well to listen to someone, he thought. Before she got herself into real trouble. But neither her sister nor her brother appeared to be paying her ill-mannered outburst any heed.

A giggle drew his wandering attention back to Emma. He smiled and shifted her fingers on the bow, but for some reason, the hairs on the back of his neck were standing on end. Puzzled, Orlov angled a quick look over to the nearby woods. An inner alarm warned that a threat was lurking nearby. Yet nothing seemed amiss.

"Watch out!" It was Shannon's voice, sharp as steel.

Orlov ducked, knocking away the bow and instinctively shielding the child with his body. For a moment, he heard only the soft swish of the long grass, the gentle rustlings of the leaves, and Emma's squeak of protest.

Then the sound of racing feet.

He tensed and twisted, trying to spot the danger. He saw a blur of brown skirts, Shannon's spinning limbs . . .

His own arms and legs suddenly went numb as Annabelle screamed, "It slipped!"

At the same instant, Shannon dove, flattening him to the ground. The buzz of the arrow, like an angry bee, cut through the roaring of blood in his ears. He was dimly aware of fabric ripping.

"For a man with no claim to sainthood, you came perilously close to playing the role of Sebastian." Shannon rolled off his back and sat up.

He saw a small gash on her arm through the torn sleeve. "So you rushed in where angels should fear to tread? Damnation, that was dangerous—"

She tugged down her cuff. "A critique of my tactics can wait until later." Her voice dropped a notch. "Let us make light of the incident. There is no sense in frightening the children."

A reminder to keep an emotional distance from the danger? Orlov knew she was right, but the soft stirring of Emma's fragile little body against his chest made detachment impossible. His heart was still pounding with a fury that threatened to fracture his ribs.

Never had he faced such a diabolical adversary. He felt helpless fighting shadows and suspicions. It seemed that any one of the London party—including a spoiled young miss—must be viewed as a threat.

But perhaps the most dangerous enemy of all was himself. This mission had become personal. Was his nerve finally betraying him?

A sidelong glance at Shannon sharpened his resolve. Time enough after this mission to decide whether the moment had come to hang up his dagger. Right now, he had a job to finish.

Red-faced and gasping for breath, Jervis and De Villiers were the first to reach them.

"Good Lord, is the child hurt?" demanded Jervis as he dropped to his knees in the tall grass.

"No. Thanks to Miss Sloane," said Orlov, his body still clenched in a protective cocoon around Emma.

"Mr. Oliver, Mr. Oliver, let me out! I don't like this game!" came a muffled little voice.

He unbent enough to allow her face to peek out over his arms. "You are right, elf. It's a silly game. We won't play it again."

"Mr. Oliver is more used to rough-and-tumble wrestling with boys," said Shannon, gently lifting Emma from his grip. "Here, let me wipe a smudge from your cheek."

Suddenly reminded of Prescott, Orlov jerked his gaze along the edge of the orchard, finally spotting the lad still in his perch overlooking the picnic.

"Scottie, come down from the crow's nest," he called. "Our ship is about to set sail for home."

Talcott huffed to a halt, trailed by the ladies.

"I—it was an accident," cried Annabelle, her voice wavering between fear and defiance. "Monsieur De Villiers wouldn't let go of my hand. I—I didn't mean—"

Shannon silenced her with a stare. "No hysterics, please. None of us imagines you did it on purpose." Turning to Helen, she said, "Kindly take your sister away and wave a bottle of vinaigrette under her nose if she is in danger of fainting."

The two Talcott ladies retreated in a swish of silks and sobs.

"I had better go and see if I can keep the floodgates

from bursting," growled their brother. He blotted the sheen of sweat from his brow. "Bloody hell. There are times that I think the chit is more trouble than she is worth."

"Miss Annabelle has an unfortunate tendency to exaggerate," said the comte tersely. His face was so bloodless it looked as if it was carved from marble. "And to allow her violent emotions to go unchecked. I feared her temper was getting out of hand and was trying to remove the weapon from her grasp." A flicker of his gaze was the only sign of his own emotion. "Are you sure the child is unharmed?"

"Quite." As he spoke, Orlov signaled a silent warning to the comte to say no more about the danger in front of the little girl.

Lady Sylvia looked shaken, but her eyes were on Shannon rather than Emma. "Where did you learn such astounding moves, Miss Sloane? I swear, I've never seen such a display of acrobatics—not even at Astley's Circus. You flew over that wall as if on wings."

"It was nothing nearly so dramatic. In the heat of an emergency, everything seems to be moving fast. Things often become blurred."

Orlov knew it was no such thing. He, too, had seen her hit the wall at a dead run, vault into a spinning handspring flip, and land on her feet without missing a stride. An instant later, she had flung herself forward, flattening him and Emma in the nick of time. The arrow had whizzed by harmlessly. Or nearly so. The cut on her arm looked to be only a scratch.

"And yet you sound so calm, mademoiselle," observed the comte. "As if you have a great deal of experience in handling a crisis."

Shannon answered without hesitation. "I am a governess, Monsieur De Villiers, so of course I am trained to deal with all sorts of contingencies." She smoothed a tangle of hair from Emma's cheek. "Dealing with children is a dangerous assignment. They are always straying into trouble, so I have been taught to always stay on guard."

"Ah. Of course. When you put it that way, it makes a great deal of sense." De Villiers inclined a slight bow. "You are a credit to your training. mademoiselle."

Lady Sylvia looked less sure. Eyes darting from Shannon to Jervis, she bit at her lip. "No amount of training can explain how you managed to outrace an arrow."

"Indeed not," replied Shannon. "I had a quite a head start. Seeing how erratic Annabelle's actions were, I had a feeling that an accident was about to happen. So I decided to take action, no matter how foolish I might look. Better safe than sorry."

Jervis placed a hand on Lady Sylvia's shoulder. But whether it was meant as a comfort or a warning was unclear. The London lord had turned just enough to hide his expression.

"It was quick thinking on your part," replied Orlov. He rose to meet Prescott and swung the boy into his arms.

"What happened, Mr. Oliver? Miss Annabelle is crying and her brother is saying a number of bad words."

"A small accident. But unlike a stalwart Scottish lassie, the London lady is easily overset."

"*I* didn't turn into a watering pot," piped up Emma to her brother. "Not even when Mr. Oliver tumbled on top of me."

"Aye. I daresay you have proved that you are tough enough to fall off a horse. If you show equal resolve in finishing your daily lessons, we shall have a first riding lesson this afternoon."

"Hooray!"

As the children began a delighted discussion of what tricks they wished to learn, Orlov added a low aside to the London party. "I trust you gentlemen will see to everything here. Whether you choose to finish your game—"

"La, how can you even suggest such a thing!" Lady Sylvia leaned a bit more heavily on Jervis. "I can't bear the idea of touching those horrid weapons again."

For once, Jervis did not take umbrage at Orlov's addressing him as an equal. "Calm yourself, Sylvia. We shall call the contest a draw, and take our picnic down to the loch."

"An excellent suggestion," said the comte. "The sound of the waters and a sip of the excellent Moselle wine we have packed in the hampers will do wonders in soothing everyone's nerves."

Chapter Sixteen

*P*our yourself another whisky, Mr. Oliver. And one for Miss Sloane."

It was late, but the dowager had insisted that they join her for a glass of spirits in the private study adjoining her bedchamber.

"I think I have had enough," said Shannon, though the mellow warmth did feel good inside her.

"Bollocks," said Lady Octavia. "Trust me, gel, after a nasty shock, strong Scottish malt is the best medicine. One more shot won't hurt."

She flinched slightly at the word.

"An unfortunate turn of phrase, milady, considering what transpired earlier today. But I heartily second the sentiment," murmured Orlov. *"Za Zdorovie."*

The dowager replied in Gallic before tossing back a sip of the spirits. "What the devil *really* happened this morning?"

Shannon stared into the dregs of her glass. The whisky's heat began to burn in her throat. "I wish I could say." A glance at Orlov elicited no immediate comment. It wasn't like him to be at a loss for words, but then, he had been strangely quiet since the incident. "From where I was, I could not tell just how much control De Villiers had of the arrow. It's possible he aimed at Emma and Mr. Oliver on purpose, but I can't say for sure." She sighed. "As for the alternative, I confess that Miss Annabelle seems the most unlikely of the group to be a threat."

Orlov finally roused himself from his reveries and spoke up. "Don't be so sure the chit is harmless." He made a face. "I took her aside for a bit of flirtation, and was lucky to escape with my virtue intact. After thrusting her tongue inside my mouth, she all but forced my hand up her skirts." He was making a joke of it, but the deep lines cutting out from his eyes belied the bantering tone. "I had better put a lock on my door, lest the grasping little minx make another attempt to strip away my innocence."

Something was bothering him, but she decided to match his sardonic nonchalance for the moment. Orlov did not seem to react well to sympathy. He turned snappish, as if unused to any kindness. Shannon bit back a sigh. She supposed the same could be said for her.

"I imagine it's been ages since you had any such tender feeling to lose, Mr. Oliver," she said dryly.

"Alexandr," he reminded her over the dowager's throaty chuckle. "I thought we had agreed to dispense with formalities."

"It appears you have quite enough intimacies on your hands, sir. Let us stay at arm's length, so to speak."

His dark mood seemed to lighten somewhat as they traded quips. "Ah, and here I though we were bosom beaus."

Lady Octavia's snort of laughter ended in a wink of amber and cut glass as her gaze moved from Shannon to Orlov. "Your real name is Alexandr?" she asked as she sipped her Highland malt.

"It is."

"A fine, sturdy name. It suits you." The dowager's eyes swung back to Shannon. "And yours?"

She hesitated before answering. "Shannon."

"Irish, eh? I thought there was a spark of Celt in you."

Her shoulders lifted in a brusque shrug. "Haven't the foggiest idea what—or who—I really am. Shannon is merely a . . ."

"A *nom de guerre*," said Orlov softly.

"That is as good an explanation as any," she said curtly.

Behind her spectacles, Lady Octavia's eyes blinked. "You don't know your real name?"

She shook her head.

"Or your background?"

"My background was a muddy alleyway in the stews of St. Giles. Let us leave it at that." It was her turn to withdraw into herself.

Rising, she stalked to the window and surveyed the gardens. The room suddenly seemed too close, too confining. "Time to make the nightly patrol. I'll take the first turn."

Orlov excused himself as well. But once back in his rooms he was far too tense to sleep. His wounded shoulder ached, and the fresh bruises on his back were uncomfortable reminders of how close they had come to disaster. If not for Shannon's quick thinking . . .

He shook off the thought. She was doing her duty. As he must do his. Regardless of the dangers. But it was growing harder and harder to remain detached. His admiration of her professional skills was deepening to something he could not quite define. Orlov moved to the window and stared out at the mist-shrouded trees. Perhaps it was just as well that words remained elusive. He dared not dwell on what they might spell.

An end to the illusion of seeing the world through a prism of cynicism? In the past he had prided himself on his cold-blooded view of human nature. *Every man for himself.* Barbed humor, casual lust—those were all the feelings he needed to survive. Until Shannon stormed into his life, sparking a different need.

A fire-gold flame. One that was fast threatening to melt the ice of his indifference.

Orlov pressed his palms to the chilled glass, hoping to temper the strange heat coursing through him. He had thought himself impervious to foolish sentiment. The notion of romance was only a dribble of ink on a piece of paper—it existed only in the pages of a book.

And yet it was growing harder and harder to deny that the attraction was more than skin deep. A sound slipped from his lips, something between a laugh and a groan. Not that her glorious body, her explosive grace, weren't enough to set any man's flesh afire. But even more than the sinuous stretch of her limbs, he loved seeing her angry, aroused. *Passion, principle.* Somehow Shannon had rekindled his own desire to care. He found himself wanting to . . .

To be friends. He made a wry face. He wasn't sure she would welcome such an overture, even if he knew how to try it.

He stood a moment longer, staring at his own hazy reflection in the fogged panes, before setting out to take his turn at patrolling the grounds.

The next day dawned gray and windy, but by the afternoon break from classes, the clouds had cleared and the sun had warmed the chill from the air. Leaving her folded dress and shawl in the shelter of a rock outcropping, Shannon quickly worked through a series of yoga stretches. The small glade in the pines provided a private retreat, well hidden from the castle, and the daily exercises helped clear her mind, sharpen her focus.

After yesterday's near-miss, her nerves were on edge.

Breathing deeply, she pushed up from the cobra position and shook out her muscles. Barefoot and clad only in her breeches and shirt, she reveled in the unrestricted movement of her limbs. Skirts were such a cursed encumbrance, she thought as she cut a sapling as a practice sword for her fencing maneuvers. If only females were permitted the same freedom as a man—

"Aren't you cutting it a bit close for comfort?" Orlov stepped out from the screen of needled boughs. "It would raise a number of embarrassing questions if any of the London party should see you stripped to the bare essentials."

"They never venture off the beaten path." She raised her cudgel and snapped a quick swoosh through the air. There was a tautness about him that sent a frisson through her fingertips. Any doubts about his dedication to the children had been dispelled by seeing Emma in his arms yesterday. But even so, he was still . . . dangerous. "Which begs the question—what are you doing here? Shouldn't you be watching the children?"

"Lady Octavia is entertaining them in her tower rooms with stories of Viking plunder and pillage," replied Orlov. "The stairway is locked from the inside, so it's safe enough for the moment." He, too, broke off a slender length of yew and peeled away its foliage. She watched it cut a sinuous swath through the air. "Like you, I felt the need to work up a sweat. So far, we have had naught but an exercise in futility."

"You are in a strange mood today."

"Am I?" Orlov tested the snap of his stick. Then suddenly it whipped up, crossing hers with a soft *snick*. "Perhaps dueling with shadows is dulling my edge. Care to flex some real muscle?"

As the breeze rustled through the pines, Shannon could hear the echo of her fencing master's grizzled grunt. *Discretion is often the better part of valor, lionni.* But she wasn't very good at resisting a challenge.

"En garde." Her make-believe blade broke away and cut a hard slice at his ribs. Orlov spun back in the nick of time. "That was quick." Countering with a *quartatta,* he crossed to a *traverse.* "But not quick enough, *golub.*"

"I wouldn't crow just yet." Shannon feinted a *riverso,* then switched to a *terza* stance.

Orlov evaded the attack with maddening ease, then grinned as his *botta dritta* sailed past her cheek. "You appear to have been trained by a master."

"Il Lupino is one of the best blades in all of Europe." A hop lunge closed half the distance between them. "So you see, I am experienced in fighting a wolf."

"Allegretto Da Rimini?" His brows waggled. "I grant you he is good, but the wily old rascal is growing a bit long in the tooth. I daresay I am a step faster—"

She whirled aside at the last second. His point grazed

only the buckskin of her breeches. "Tit for tat." Her slash glanced off his forearm.

He parried the next cut as well, then suddenly grabbed her wrist. A flick sent her stick flying through the air.

"Unfair! I—" Her protest was cut off by the press of his mouth. His tongue slid over her lower lip, a soft, sensuous caress that sent a shudder through her steeled spine. He pulled her closer and deepened the embrace. In contrast to the lightning tempo of their swordthrusts, this clash of wills seemed to go on for an eternity.

Twisting, she finally freed herself from his kiss. "That's fighting dirty."

"What do you expect, given our profession?"

"Next time, I shall be on guard against any trick."

"Or any thrust?" He smiled, a sinful, sensual curling of his mouth.

Her cheeks, already flushed from the physical exertion, took on a deeper burn. *Damn the man.* And her own wicked body for yielding a sign of weakness.

She knew she ought to slap him . . .

As if anticipating her thoughts, he tightened his fingers around her wrist. "In chess, I would call this a checkmate, *golub*."

"But we are playing a different game." Shannon twisted out of his grasp and in a whirl of spins and steps threw him over her shoulder.

Orlov fell heavily among the pine needles. "Why, you little spitfire." He rolled quickly to a crouch and balanced on his toes. "So the Academy training also includes some of the esoteric Eastern disciplines?" His eyes gleamed, sharp as knifepoints. "How very clever of Lord Lynsley to ensure that his women know how to use their bodies as weapons."

"Against an opponent of superior size and strength, it is key to know how to turn those advantages into weaknesses." She stood firm, though her limbs were tingling from the way his gaze raked over her from head to toe. "Such skills give us a mental edge as well. Most men are overconfident when facing a female in hand-to-hand combat."

"An elemental mistake," he agreed, springing lightly to his feet.

Shannon shifted along with him, keeping her shoulders square to his moves. There was something strangely erotic about the sinuous dance. Though they were not even close to touching, she was acutely aware of his body.

"Did I mention that my travels took me to Bombay for a short time?" He slid in and out of the shadows. "Where I met a fascinating fellow who knew how to make cobras dance to the tune of his flute."

"Ah, so that is where you learned to charm the scales off a snake?" she countered.

Orlov laughed. "Among other things." His attack was quicker than a serpent's strike. Uncoiling in a blur of motion, he shot forward, lunging in low and hard with a flick of his foot that caught her hard on the knee.

Though she managed to dodge the full impact, the blow knocked her back.

He was on her in a flash.

She countered with a jab to the jaw, which snapped his head back. He grunted in pain, but kept hold of her wrist, turning sharply with a deft jerk that pinned it against her back. "You have only to cry surrender," he murmured, his breath hot and tickling against her neck. "I wouldn't want to hurt you like before."

"The hell I will." Twisting, she angled a glancing knee to his groin. Which drew a gratifying *woof*. His grip loosened for an instant and she pulled away.

"A low blow," he grimaced.

"It was you who said all is fair."

His eyes took on a wicked gleam. "So I did."

Shannon watched warily as he backed up a step and suddenly dropped to a crouch. An instant later he straightened again and flexed his shoulders.

Damn. Was he trying to distract her with the rippling of muscle beneath the light linen? She forced her eyes away and edged back, toward the outcropping of rock where she had left her garments.

Time to end the game before things got out of hand.

Orlov seemed of a different mind. His hand flashed out, and suddenly her eyes were filled with dust. Momentarily blinded, she froze, then felt his arms encircle her waist and lift her from the ground.

"Bloody hell." She struggled, but had no leverage. Still swearing, she tried a chop to his throat but drew only a muffled grunt.

"You should have remembered your Sun-Tzu—If they are strong, avoid them."

Her flailing fists caught his wounded shoulder, throwing him off balance. Still wrestling, they fell to the ground. Orlov angled to take the full impact, and Shannon landed atop him. She felt the hard heave of his chest, and caught a grimace of pain.

"I am sorry—I didn't mean to hurt you," she whispered. Her breathing was as ragged as his. "Are you injured?"

He rolled, and she suddenly found herself pinned between the soft earth and his hard, unyielding body. "A basic mistake," he murmured. "Show no mercy."

"In a real fight . . ." Her words died in her throat as he straddled her thighs and pinned her arms so that she lay spread-eagled on the bed of pine straw.

"In a real fight," he repeated, "the merlin would find her wings clipped and her talons useless against the ravening wolf."

"W—what would you suggest?"

"You will have to suffer the consequences of your slip." His lips were now just inches from hers. "I'm sure your instructors did not let you off lightly."

"No. I was usually made to run around the perimeter of the school grounds."

"Ah, corporal punishment." A wicked light glittered in his gaze. "The same is true in Russia." His fingers were toying with the fastenings of her shirt. "In St. Petersburg, cadets are sometimes made to stand naked in the snow to teach them a lesson."

"It is mild and sunny," said Shannon as the linen slowly slipped from her shoulder. *So why was a shiver skating down her spine?*

"Then I will have to think of some other physical test of—" He stopped short on seeing the tattoo above her left breast. Black as midnight, the hawk in flight was the badge of the Academy's full-fledged Merlins. "What have we here?"

"Our troops cannot wear their rank as gold braid and scarlet regimentals."

"How unique. As is everything about you, *golub*." Orlov paused a fraction, his stubbled cheek leaving a trail of prickling heat as he took a closer peek. "It gives you the look of . . . a pirate. Scottie would be duly impressed."

His breath tickled against her flesh.

"It's not something I'll be showing to him anytime soon." In reply, she could only manage a faint whisper.

"Far too provocative for a young boy," agreed Orlov. "It might encourage improper thoughts." Slowly but surely, his mouth feathered across the tracing of ink. "Immoral thoughts."

Shannon found herself helpless to resist. Should she beg for mercy? Orlov claimed to have no heart, but perhaps she might appeal to some lingering shred of decency.

However, when she opened her mouth, it was only to surrender to the moment. *Fire and ice.* It was chilling how easily Orlov could melt her resolve.

She moaned. His tongue was like a lick of flame, burning an indelible imprint on her flesh. Her shirt was now a tangle of limp linen around her waist, and as his nipping kisses slid down to the rosy peak of her breast, she tried to muster a last fight. *Duty versus desire.*

"Th—this is likely not a good idea."

"Likely not," he answered, his voice somewhere between a laugh and a groan. "But rational thought rarely triumphs over our more primitive passions."

Passion. Shannon tugged his shirt open and threaded her fingers through the finespun curls. In the slanting afternoon light, he looked like an icon. A work of art. Golden highlights gleamed in his hair, and the blue of his eyes and the bronze of his skin were luminous, lustrous as precious pigments. Angled cheekbones, a lean face, all shaped by a master's hand . . .

She felt the breath squeezed from her lungs as his touch slid over her ribs to the fastenings of her breeches.

"Alexandr." All of a sudden, her whisper was lost in the sound of other voices swirling in the breeze.

"Bloody hell." Orlov was quick to react. He shot to his feet and pulled her up. "Get dressed," he ordered, brusquely, indicating her folded gown and cloak. "And hurry."

He was right, of course. Her attire—what little was left on her person—would provoke a number of uncomfortable questions.

"Help me with the fastenings," she said, tugging the shapeless dress in place over her breeches.

His hands lingered for an instant on the nape of her neck before deftly tying the tabs.

No doubt he had a great deal of practice in such matters, Shannon thought as she snatched up her shirt and stuffed it beneath the tangle of herbs in her basket. Somehow the idea hurt, a sharp twinge that was far more painful than any physical cut or bruise. Turning, she stumbled.

Orlov steadied her slip. "Are you all right?"

She nodded mutely.

He hesitated, his eyes searching, then looked away. "Take the path that leads down to the gardens. I'll duck into the trees and see what I might overhear."

"Right." It was a good strategy.

"And Shannon . . ."

She looked around, expecting a tactical detail.

His mouth caught hers in one last lightning kiss. "Be careful."

A reminder of the dangers lurking close at hand? Shannon allowed a wry smile. "Don't worry. I'll not let my guard down a second time today."

He flashed a half smile and was gone.

Hurrying her own steps, Shannon ducked around a

thicket of gorse, unmindful of the thorns scraping her skirts, and cut through the copse of oaks. A few moments later, she was back on the footpath, her collection of cuttings ample explanation for her presence on the moors, should anyone think to ask.

She slowed to a leisurely pace, yet her breathing remained ragged. She had no right to feel possessive, no right to feel as though the damnable attraction that drew them together was anything more than skin deep.

Pleasures of the flesh. Orlov made no secret of his womanizing. A man of his virile appetites must be unused to going so long without a female sharing his bed. No doubt, the primal urges were coursing through his veins.

Strange, it seemed she too had urges, no matter that she wished to deny it. He set off the strangest longings in her. Though trained to be tough as tempered steel, she softened like putty in his arms. It puzzled her. And frightened her just a little.

But she was a Merlin. And Merlins were up to any challenge.

Chapter Seventeen

*S*haking off the sexual heat of Shannon's touch, Orlov was now fully alert. The steps had turned for one of the more secluded paths leading down to the loch. He took a shortcut through the trees, his feet moving lightly over the pine straw, and slipped into a rock crevasse overlooking the trail. Hidden from view, he went still. A few minutes later, the voices sounded again.

"I was sure you had forgotten me. And your ardent promises."

Annabelle. What mischief was the minx up to now?

"How could you think such a thing!" exclaimed her companion. From his angle of view, Orlov could catch only a partial glimpse of the fellow—sandy hair, slender build—but the burred Yorkshire accent made it clear he was not one of the London party.

"As if any man could forget you, my love," went on the stranger, his tone turning a touch reproachful. "I told you I would find a way to be together. But it was not easy finding a way to pass you a message."

The young lady gave a furtive look around. "My brother would die if he knew I was meeting you on the sly."

So, the loyal Lord Norbert had followed the young lady to Scotland? Orlov gritted his teeth to keep from swearing aloud. Yet another entanglement to trip up this mission. It was as if some great, malevolent spider was spinning a web around the McAllister castle.

"Forgive me if I have put you in an awkward position. I simply *had* to see you."

"My brother has threatened to turn you away if you show up at the castle doors."

"It doesn't matter, darling. I found lodging in the village of Boath. And I have a plan that will soon solve all of our problems."

"So you *do* love me?" Annabelle's tone was at once arch and unsure.

"With all my heart!" assured her admirer. "If all goes well, in another week I shall sweep you away from here, my dearest angel, and then we shall be married. I have it all arranged with a local justice in Inverness." A pause. "Please tell me you have not changed your mind."

"Never!" Annabelle let out a trilling laugh. "La, it is all so romantic. All my friends will be green with envy! Just think of it. A dashing adventure, a hint of danger . . ."

Orlov grimaced. Someone ought to have curtailed the silly chit's reading of horrid novels.

"And then I shall be Lady Norbert—a *grand dame* who no longer has to listen to the carping complaints and silly restrictions of my boring family."

So, Lord Nobody had proved to be a very persistent fellow. Orlov hoped the fellow possessed a great deal of patience as well. Though that seemed highly unlikely, given the mad rush on both of their parts to elope.

"We shall be very happy, Bella, just you and I," promised Norbert. "But for now, you must be very careful not to give away our plans. It must be our little secret." He hesitated a fraction. "You are sure you are not in danger of incurring the wrath of your brother? I worry that he may begin to suspect something and keep a closer eye on you."

"Pooh! I'm not afraid of Robert. Besides, he's usually so foxed by breakfast that he wouldn't notice if I showed up for my coffee in the nude."

"Oh, but I would, sweetmeat."

A giggle, followed by long, mewling moans. The kiss seemed to go on forever.

Orlov winced. The girl seemed desperate to offer herself up on a platter to any man who cared for a taste. Shifting his shoulders against the stone, he prayed they would quickly move on, so that he could get back to his own business.

Twigs snapped, pebbles crunched underfoot. Annabelle's laugh cut off in a high squeak.

Bloody hell. Surely they were not . . .

Orlov ventured a quick peek over the ridge of stone.

The fellow's bare arse was buried in a frothy swirl of petticoats as he braced the girl against a tree.

Swearing another silent oath, Orlov ducked back into his hiding place Perhaps with the right guidance Annabelle's wildness could be tamed into some semblance of common sense. But he did not have high hopes for her future happiness.

He could not help comparing the girl's utter lack of self-restraint with Shannon's disciplined devotion to duty. One born to privilege and pleasure, one born to pain and poverty. One was a spoiled brat, one was . . .

How to describe Shannon? His mouth crooked, her kisses still sweet on his lips. She defied capture in words. Adjectives like courage, strength, principle did not spell out the full depth of her character. A man might spend a lifetime in her presence and still find new surprises every day.

A shrill shriek cut off his musings. At least the tupping had been blessedly brief.

"Oh, *Stephen!*" Annabelle's voice melted to a tremulous titter. "Will we do this often when we are married?"

"As often as you like, my darling."

"Mmmmm." Her skirts rustled in the breeze. "The plan . . . you will come for me soon?"

"Yes, my love. Very soon, I hope. I need another few days to arrange everything. I'll send word as we planned. You will be ready?"

"Oh, yes." A girlish giggle. "I know just what you expect of me, and you need not fear that I will have a last-minute change of heart. This will be fun."

"That's the spirit." Her lover laughed softly as he brushed a kiss to her upturned face. "What a lucky man I am to have chosen such a daring darling."

"What does he look like?" Shannon checked the priming of her pistol, then tugged on a black knit cap in readiness for her round of the nightly patrols.

Orlov's mouth twitched in amusement. "Sandy locks, well-muscled thighs, and a hairy arse."

She bit back a laugh. "Well, if he points his weapon

at me in the dark, he is going to be singing his marriage vows as a soprano."

He chuckled, then abruptly changed his own tune. "In all seriousnes, be extra vigilant out there."

"You think the randy Lord Norbert is here to steal more than the chit's virginity?"

"The thought occurred to me." Orlov ran a hand through his hair. "We can't afford to overlook any possibility."

"True." Shannon thought for a moment. "However, I doubt a professional like D'Etienne would risk exposing himself to the opposition for a quick tupping."

"You have a point," he admitted. "Still, don't let down your guard."

"That goes without saying." After making a minor adjustment to hammer and flint she added, "You would think that the girl would have enough sense to wait for a ring on her finger before lifting her skirts."

"I would not have thought you such a stickler for propriety."

"I am not being prudish," she replied. "Merely practical. In negotiating a deal, you should never give away your most valuable bargaining chip without getting something of equal value in return."

"Ah." His expression was hidden by the flutter of the draperies. "So you have no moral objection to sleeping with a man out of wedlock?"

Shannon knew he was being deliberately provoking. Still, she could not keep a faint flush from coloring her face. "Seduction is part of our schooling," A blade slid into the hidden sheath of her boot. "It's all part of the job."

"And you are, of course, the consummate professional."

There was an odd sort of note to his teasing that made her look twice before turning for the open window. "As are you, Mr. Orlov."

"Indeed?" The Marquess of Lynsley looked up in some surprise from his study of the weekly military reports. "Show her right her in, Graves—" He rose as Mrs. Merlin marched by the startled secretary, her silk skirts a fluttering contrast to the starkly masculine furnishing of his ministry office. "Never mind."

"I would not normally intrude on your schedule, Thomas," she said, once the door had closed. "But I have just received news that D'Etienne has been spotted near the Scottish border."

"You are sure?"

The headmistress nodded. "He was positively identified by one of our former students. And seeing as Seville witnessed the assassination of our envoy in Holland, I am sure she would not mistake his face."

"The Amsterdam mission." Lynsley heaved a heavy sigh and fell silent for several moments. "This is a devilish dilemma. The question is whether to send word . . ."

"Or?" asked Mrs. Merlin.

"Or reinforcements. We can't afford any mistakes." His jaw hardened. "I don't want to let him get away this time."

"You are concerned about Shannon." It was more a statement than a question.

"We both know that she can be volatile. And while her handling of the Irish mission was commendable, I am unsure of how her passions will affect this particular assignment."

The headmistress withdrew a sheet of foolscap from

her reticule. "In reviewing what we know of this man Orlov, perhaps there is reason to worry." She hesitated. "Do you trust Yussapov?"

The marquess made a face. Despite his patrician air and elegant tailoring, he was no stranger to the cutthroat underworld of clandestine missions. "I trust no one in this dirty game we play, save for you, Charlotte. However, in this case, it seems that the prince's interests are the same as ours. So I don't expect a double-cross."

"But you cannot overlook the possibility," she said softly.

"You have had some time to contemplate the options," he said. "Any suggestions you care to offer?"

"If you wish to send one of our own as a backup, we could dispatch Sofia."

"In what guise?" Perching a hip on the edge of his desk, Lynsley began to drum his well-tended fingers upon the polished wood. "The area is quite isolated. Any new arrival at the McAllister Castle will not go unnoticed. We already have a governess in place, and the servants are all local folk."

Mrs. Merlin nodded. "The same concerns occurred to me. But given Sofia's dark looks and her talent with the tarot cards, I thought she could masquerade as a traveling Gypsy. With Marco, our assistant fencing instructor, playing the role of her husband, the two would make a formidable force to reckon with." She paused. "Assuming that Shannon is having any difficulty in completing the mission on her own."

His expression was unreadable as he turned and walked to the windows. A mizzled mist hung heavy over the spires of the nearby buildings, fuzzing the outlines of stone and slates to hazy shades of gray. "There is no clear answer."

"There never is."

He allowed a small smile. "Then I suppose we had best err on the side of caution. Can they leave by nightfall?"

"They are packing their bags as we speak."

Chapter Eighteen

*L*eaves stirred, their verdant hue gleaming bright against the muted heather hues of the moors. The breeze was mild, and the sun had dappled the stones of her vantage point with a mellow warmth. Shannon cast one more longing look at the craggy cliffs, then forced her attention back to the book on Scottish history. She felt compelled to do her best to further Emma's education, no matter that scholarly skills were not her strength.

But there was no denying that she would much rather be in the saddle, pushing herself and her mount to the edge of exhaustion through the twisting trails and steep climbs. The Highlanders had a fearsome reputation for savage strength and flinty resolve. Surveying the wild terrain, its isolated splendor both grim and grand, she could understand why.

Perhaps, she mused, there *was* a touch of Celtic blood in her veins—fire and ice—for she found a strange beauty in the harshness of the hills.

A sigh slipped from her lips as she watched a lone

hawk circling high overhead. The small knoll overlooking the stables was as far as her wings would take her this afternoon. A glance at the manor house, looking small and alone surrounded by untamed nature, brought her thoughts back to ground.

The presence of Annabelle's clandestine lover added yet another thorny problem to contend with. A randy English lord lurking in the bushes, coupled with Lady Sylvia's nocturnal trysts and the movements of the other guests, made the job of detecting any signs of the enemy's presence even more daunting . . .

"Have you not had enough studying in the schoolroom?" Orlov sounded bemused. His hair was tangled around his ears, and his collar was open, revealing a tanned V of flesh.

Shannon made a face. "Too much, in fact. I am not trained as a teacher. I am trying to find an appropriate lesson for Emma. Speaking of which, where are the children?"

"Safely ensconced in the kitchen, helping Cook prepare a batch of gingerbread. I took the opportunity to make a circuit of the grounds. No sign of surveillance."

"Damn. Waiting for D'Etienne to make his move is stretching my patience thin. Isn't there some way for us to take the offensive?"

"Remember that Sun-Tzu says warfare is the Tao of deception. And one of the cardinal rules is that although you are capable, display incapability." He softened his sardonic expression with the semblance of a smile. "Not that we have much choice. With our limited resources, we must wait for him to come to us." The slanting light picked out the lines etched around his mouth. They seemed to have deepened over the last few days.

Ashamed that it had taken her so long to notice the toll that the waiting was taking on him, she dropped her gaze.

"He might have been delayed," added Orlov. "Or he might be taking his time to decide how to deal with the unexpected additions to the household."

"Or he may be waiting for a certain signal." She sighed. "What of the London party?"

"They have packed a picnic and taken a carriage ride to view an ancient site of Druid standing stones. According to local legend, it is called 'The Sorceress and Her Apprentices.'"

She turned a few more pages of her book, giving a desultory look at the text. "Why is there not more mention of females in history, save as wives or witches?"

"Possibly because the books are mostly written by men," he said dryly. Burrs clung to his breeches and mud spattered his boots. His linen shirt, damp with exertion, clung to the contours of his chest. As he sat down beside her, Shannon caught the earthy wafting of sweat mingled with grass and leather. A masculine scent, and one she was coming to recognize as distinctly his own. "Then again," he went on. "There are few of your sex who possess the same martial spirit as Merlin's Maidens."

"We are merely proof of what women can do, if given half a chance. I imagine there are a great many unsung heroines from the past, whose brave deeds have long since been forgotten."

"An interesting point." Orlov seemed in a more reflective mood than usual. Rather than make any attempt to rekindle the sexual heat of yesterday's outdoor encounter, he leaned back on his elbows and tilted his face to the warming rays.

Despite the dulling effects of the walnut rinse, his hair was still threaded with intriguing highlights of gold and honey. Shannon was suddenly not thinking of heroines, but of how the silky strands softened the planes of his face, somehow making him appear more boyish, carefree.

His grin, an impish curl of quicksilver humor, only added to the effect. "Why not make your next lesson about the great warrior women in history?"

"We have already covered Boadicea and her fight to defend England from the Romans."

"Ah, but that bold Queen had a great many sisters-in-arms throughout the ages."

"Sh—she did?" Shannon tried to recall her own classroom experience. "I'm afraid I did not pay as close attention as I should have to the history lectures. Our instructor was a dry stick, making the past sound dead rather than alive." She twisted a blade of grass between her fingers. "I was always more comfortable with steel than scholarly abstractions. Weapons were something I could get a grip on. While ideas . . ."

Surprised at the note of longing in her voice, she let the words trail off. Her roommates Sofia and Siena had always seemed so much smarter when it came to books and abstract concepts—like cause and effect. They seemed able to exercise logic, while all too often she allowed her explosive temper to get the better of her.

Orlov was regarding her oddly. "While ideas . . . ?"

"While ideas always seemed harder to hold," she admitted. No doubt she *was* an idiot for admitting to such a shortcoming. One of the basic rules of engagement—both physical and mental—was never show the enemy any weakness.

But strangely enough, Orlov did not seek to take advantage of her slip. "Most likely you had a good teacher for fencing and marksmanship. And a dull one for academics." He settled himself a bit more comfortably against the outcropping of rock. His shoulder pressed up against hers, and along with the frisson of sexual awareness that his touch always sparked, Shannon was aware of a mellower warmth, a bond of camaraderie.

"You might begin with such mythic figures as Rhiannon, horse goddess of the Welsh," he mused. "Or Queen Maeve, the Celtic sylph whose cunning and courage were matched only by her lust for . . ." His mouth curved upward for an instant. "On second thought, you will not want to mention that particular detail to Emma."

"Lady Octavia *does* believes in plain speaking," she murmured with an answering twitch of her lips.

He gave a mock grimace. "Emma's father is an expert in ballistics—I would rather not have my body parts blown from here to China."

"True—such comments might ignite his wrath." This good-natured teasing was a new tone between them. It might even pass for . . . flirtation? Their gazes held for an instant and she saw the same ripple of awareness. "Do go on," she added quickly, unsure of whether to feel embarrassed or amused.

"History holds a great many real women whose exploits are worthy of study."

Fascinated, she leaned in a bit closer. "Yes?"

"Take Catherine the Great of Russia. Voltaire was a great admirer, and in his letters, he called her the Semiramis of the North. Like her ancient namesake, she was hailed as a great sovereign and a great lover."

Shannon shifted slightly. Though the sun had dipped

below its zenith, her limbs were suddenly suffused with heat. "The amorous exploits of these Queens always seem rather exaggerated."

"Exaggerated? Ha!" Orlov chuckled. "You have not heard the stories surrounding her death?"

She shook her head.

"I shall not go into all the gory details, but they involved a stallion and a complicated creation of pulleys and scaffolding that suddenly collapsed."

"You are joking," she sputtered, once her laughter had died away.

"Even I could not make that up."

"Thank you for the suggestion. It was quite entertaining. And interesting." Her palm slid along the leather-bound spine of the book. "You are an excellent teacher. You make me want to know more. About . . . about a lot of things."

"Learning is for a lifetime."

Curious, she ventured a question. "So you were not lying when you told Lady Octavia that you attended Oxford?"

"That was all true. My family did indeed suffer some severe financial setbacks. My father, you see, was an inveterate gambler, whose lucidity and luck were slowly stretched to the breaking point."

"I see. And the part about the acrobats?"

"Again, all true. It was only when I came to the part about my infatuation for the young lady that I bent the facts a bit. I did not leave the circus on account of a broken heart, but a broken neck. I did not mean to kill the fellow, merely to stop him from asserting his conjugal rights over his new bride with the help of a bullwhip."

"She should have murdered him herself."

"Not every female possesses your indomitable strength and courage."

A compliment from Orlov—one that sounded sincere? She nearly slipped from her seat.

"In any case, the young widow was suitably grateful, but I found that my eagerness to don a leg shackle had waned considerably. So I took my leave, crossing the border of Prussia into Russia." He shrugged. "From there, my exploits went along pretty much as I told the dowager. I spent the last few years in Austria and Poland, but recently . . . well, you are aware of my recent assignments."

"Yes."

"What of your past?"

Her shoulders stiffened. "There isn't much to tell."

"You grew up in London?"

She didn't answer.

No doubt he would take her silence as one of their usual competitive challenges. Gritting her teeth, she prepared to defend herself from his scathing wit.

But rather than come at her with a verbal attack, Orlov reached out and touched the tensed muscles at the back of her neck. "A sensitive subject, I take it." His fingertips began a gentle massage. "Sorry."

There was nothing sexual in the intimacy. It was more a gesture . . . of friendship? She found herself relaxing under the light, swirling pressure.

"I grew up in the slums of St. Giles." The words slipped out in a soft sigh. "While you were roaming through Europe and Asia, my world was a few acres of filthy alleyways. The stories of those days are not half so entertaining as yours." She shrugged. "I was lucky—Lord Lynsley plucked me from the legion of other orphans and gave me a home at the Academy. My fellow students are my friends, my family. There is not much more to tell."

"I should like to hear about your roommates," he said.

"You have met Siena. She is perhaps the most . . . introspective of the three of us." Shannon made a wry face. "Or so it says in the report I found in the headmistress's private files. Sofia is by far the most ladylike. She has a natural grace about her. Indeed, I would not be surprised to discover she was the daughter of a duke and some poor servant girl, turned off without references."

Orlov looked thoughtful. "There seem to be few of the world's sordid realities that you have not been exposed to."

"In comparison to yours, my life has been very sheltered."

He choked back a laugh. "I doubt that many people would agree with your assessment. Trust me, it is highly unusual for a young woman to be trained in the expert use of weapons and explosives. Not to mention the equally lethal arts of intrigue and seduction."

Anxious to turn the talk from her past, Shannon saw her chance. "Look at the party from London. It seems to me that the ladies and gentlemen of the *ton* know a thing or two about the latter subjects."

"Polite Society is a perilous world unto itself," he agreed. "Lives can be ruined by a small slip in propriety, reputations slain by malicious gossip."

"It sounds daunting."

"The same could be said of what you do."

"There is a difference." She thought on it for a moment. "We fight as we do for principles."

"Lynsley must be very proud of you."

"Hah." The snort slipped out before she could help it. His brow quirked in question.

"The marquess thinks me rather hot-headed," she admitted. "I have had a number of disciplinary problems at the Academy. His patience has frayed. I am hanging on to my rank by a thread."

"If we fail here?"

Her laugh held little mirth. "Perhaps the Tsar could use a freelance agent."

"Yet the marquess chose you for this assignment."

"He had little choice. As you pointed out, I am very good with weapons. It's just when it comes to authority that I sometimes run into trouble."

"I can't imagine why."

"Stubble the sarcasm, if you please." However, a reluctant grin pulled at her mouth. "I suppose I tend to be a bit headstrong. But only when I am convinced that I am right."

"Which is more often than not." He grinned.

She rubbed her wrist. He was teasing, of course. But his banter was a painful reminder of how she had fallen short of the Academy's lofty standards. She had let herself down as well. "I can't say I blame Lord Lynsley for putting me on probation. He's extremely fair, and he is right to demand discipline and a steadfast devotion to duty."

Wind rustled through the oak trees, and a scattering of leaves floated to the ground. Shannon closed the book in her lap. What was it Orlov had said the other evening— that one must know history in order to avoid repeating it. It was, she supposed, another way of saying that one must learn from past mistakes.

A wise lesson.

"We had better be getting back to the castle."

"And face the battlefield of spilled flour and sticky batter?" said Orlov.

"You have vanquished far more formidable foes."

"Yes. However, sometimes it is wiser to avoid the direct line of fire."

"Cook is already a conquest. She may let you lick the spoon," replied Shannon.

"Tempting." He gave a lazy smile. "I am inclined to rest here for another little while." Seeing she was already on her feet, he rose, too. "Very well, if you are determined to charge into the fray, I can't very well let you do so alone."

"You need not stir. I know how much this enforced alliance goes against your principle of every man for himself."

"Whether we like it or not, we are comrades for the moment."

A fleeting friendship. A reminder not to get too comfortable with him. Whether the mission ended in victory or defeat, life or death, one thing was certain—they would go their separate ways.

Not so very long ago, she would have heaved a sigh of relief. Now, as she watched his wind-ruffled hair dance against his open collar, her breath seemed to catch in her throat.

"Comrades in arms," he amended, offering her a hand over the rough stones.

"Don't worry about me." Shannon didn't mean to sound quite so hard. "I am used to going it on my own."

As the afternoon remained gloriously clear and warm, Shannon suggested that they cut short the afternoon lessons and take a hike in the surrounding hills. Orlov readily agreed, and as they packed a picnic for teatime, she saw him slip a brass spyglass into the basket. His weapons, she knew, were hidden on his person. As were hers. If the enemy attacked they were armed and ready.

"Let us head for the top of Beinn Moran," he said. "I have not yet had a look at the far side of the valley."

"The choice is yours, sir." She added her sketch pad and pencils. Another detailed map of the surroundings might prove useful. Already she had memorized several possible escape routes through the rugged moors.

Once they had passed by the loch and started up the steep slope of wild meadow, the children raced ahead to chase the sheep. Emma scrambled to keep up with her brother, her skinny little legs tangling with her skirts as she climbed over the stone fence and tumbled into the grass. Orlov could not keep a straight face, though there was some hint of deeper emotion in the baritone chuckle.

"Fearless, isn't she?"

Shannon felt a ghost of a smile form on her lips, the sight bringing to mind a long-ago little orphan, undaunted by a challenge.

As if reading her thoughts, he said, "The imp reminds me of you, save that she is so tiny. She has the spirit of a lioness, though I fear her limbs will never quite catch up."

Shannon experienced a painful squeeze of her chest. "She may grow like weed in another few years. I was very small at that age."

He looked askance at her, allowing his gaze to linger for some moments. "I find that hard to believe."

"It is true." She closed her eyes. Darkness brought no

relief, only a rush of long-fought memories. Without her quite realizing what she was saying, the words slipped out in a ragged whisper. "Delicate might be a more apt description. Like a china doll. At least, that is what the drunks and dippers used to call after me in the alleyways. Said I'd earn a pretty penny if I put myself under their protection."

Strange how despite her hardened muscles and deadly fighting skills, the echoes of anther age still sent a frisson of fear down her spine. "I learned early on that the only hope for survival was to fight like hell. Even in the face of overwhelming odds."

She opened her eyes to find him studying her intently. "Were you . . ."

"Raped?" She shook her head. "No. But when you grow up alone in the stews, you don't remain an innocent for long. There are other lewd acts that a very large man may force upon a child."

"I am sorry," he said simply. She saw sympathy in the set of his jaw, the press of his lips. An understanding, born of a firsthand experience, that life was often not just or fair.

Yet another bond they shared.

"Don't be. He won't be subjecting any other young girls to such horrors." Realizing that she had stopped, Shannon turned quickly and forged ahead, determined to make up for her momentary weakness. The conversation was revealing too much, too fast. Anger, antagonism was an armor of sorts. Stripping away such defenses could leave her far too vulnerable.

"Is that what drew Lord Lynsley's eye to you?" asked Orlov softly as he caught up to her.

"He did not witness that particular example of my

prowess with a blade. Our paths crossed later, when I was fighting off a pair of pimps who were trying to drag away two of my friends. I expect he thought my savage instincts could be channeled to a more useful purpose."

"The marquess would likely describe those qualities as courage and loyalty."

Her lips quivered. "On the contrary, Lynsley is likely regretting the choice. While he values strength and skill with a lethal weapon, he puts a higher premium on discipline and devotion to duty."

Orlov had not yet answered when a high-pitched cry rang out from above. Drawing his pistol, he sprinted for the crest of the hill, motioning for Shannon to circle around the rock outcropping to their left.

Attack what they love first. How had she let Sun-Tzu's principles slip her mind, even for an instant? She had tried to make herself invincible. And had failed miserably.

The scrape of stone against her hand pushed aside all thoughts of self-pity. Nothing mattered, save Emma and Prescott. A silent, spinning leap brought her to the top ledge. D'Etienne would not find it easy to outwit or outfight Orlov. There would be an instant, an opening—and when it came, she would swoop in for the kill. Pistol cocked, she clamped her throwing knife between her teeth and dropped lightly into a narrow crevasse. From there she inched forward, muscles coiled, ready to spring into action.

"Damn!"

Shannon spotted the jagged gap in the footpath at the same moment as Orlov. Loosened by wind and rain, the shale and soil must have given way under the children's footsteps.

He reached the spot first and flung aside his weapon.

"Hold on, sweeting," he called as he flattened on his stomach and peered over the edge. "Don't try to move. I'm coming for you."

"I'm lighter—let me go," said Shannon, her teeth clenched to keep them from chattering. The drop was quite steep, broken by only a few narrow juts of rock as it tumbled nearly one hundred feet down into a slivered ravine filled with rushing water, shattered stones, and splintered pine. Emma had somehow managed to come to rest on a narrow ledge some thirty feet below them.

Her demand seemed to have been swallowed by the swirling gusts, for Orlov was already peeling off his coat. "That goes for you too, Scottie." The boy had bravely started down after his sister, but another shard had broken off, leaving him trapped just out of reach. "Stay still, lad. I'm going to knot my sleeve and lower it to you."

Shannon inched out for a better view of the situation. It was not looking good—

"For God's sake, stay back," snapped Orlov. Sweat was beading his forehead despite the wind. "If another piece breaks away . . ."

Rather than finish the sentence, he gave a last twist to his jacket sleeve, then slowly slid the garment down the rock face. "I want you to grab this, Scottie, and hold on tight. Miss Sloane will anchor it on this end while I come down and get you. Understand?"

The lad looked up, and though his face was ashen, he nodded.

Shannon saw what Orlov had in mind and quickly took hold of the tail end. "I've got it." Fisting the fabric, she added a silent prayer. "Go."

She held her breath as Orlov found a handhold and swung his weight over the edge. He was so solid, so strong, yet the rock was so fragile . . . Her own self-control started to crumble. If only she had kept her mind on the mission. If only she hadn't distracted him with talk of her past.

If only, if only. Perhaps Lynsley was right to question whether she was capable of learning from her past mistakes.

The wind stung her cheeks, bringing tears to her lashes. But she would not let them fall, she vowed. A tug tightened the cloth in her hands. Not when there was still a shred of hope to cling to.

"Hold fast!" Orlov's voice swirled.

Shannon dug deeper for a foothold in the wet earth.

After what seemed like an eternity, a hand appeared at the rim of rock, then a face . . . two faces. Reaching out, she grabbed Prescott's collar and pulled him to firmer ground.

Orlov loosened Shannon's hold on the boy. "No time for sentiment." He set Prescott in the shelter of a large boulder. "Stay here." He had meant the order to include Shannon, but she stayed right on his heels as he scrambled around to a different vantage point. He didn't waste his breath in ordering her back.

"See there . . ." He pointed to where a large fissure cut down the craggy rock wall. From where they were crouched, they could see that there was a narrow trail, barely wider than the span of his hand, leading down to where Emma sat hunched against the whipping wind.

"I'll—"

"Don't move," he ordered.

"But I am trained in gymnastics—"

"For God's sake, do as I say! One gust, and your bloody skirts will turn into a kite."

She had the sense to step back. "B—be careful, Alex."

His boots began to inch along the windblown rock. "Don't worry," he muttered. "Having made it made it this far in life, I have no intention of cocking up my toes now."

A sliver of shale broke away from beneath his boots and was quickly swallowed up by foaming waters. Through the linen of his shirt, Orlov was aware of the knife-edged rock against his back. As if he needed any reminder of his precarious position.

On finally reaching the ledge where Emma sat, he slowly inched to within arm's length. "You've been a brave lass, sweeting. We have just one more balancing trick to do."

"I—I remembered what you told me, Mr. Oliver. D—don't look down and you won't get dizzy."

"Exactly right."

"L—like balancing at the very topmast of a ship."

"Aye, no pirate captain could have done it better."

Fortunately, she was too scared to flinch as his fingers slowly curled around her sleeve and lifted her up. All it would take was one errant twitch to send them both tumbling onto the jagged teeth of rocks far below.

"Steady, lass . . . now put your arms around my neck."

Emma nestled against him. He could feel the beat of her heart.

So far, so good. Hugging the child to his chest, he started the agonizing climb back, taking care to keep his gaze from drifting downward.

Shannon's eager hands steadied his last few steps.

"Oh, Alex! You were absolutely magnificent!"

Orlov realized that he had never felt quite so proud of himself.

"I'm sorry," whimpered Emma as soon as her feet touched the ground. "I didn't mean to . . . but it looked so pretty sitting there."

Shannon reached out and took the small object the child had clutched to her chest. It was a lump of quartz, so clear and smooth that it appeared translucent in the pale sunlight.

"Very pretty," she replied.

"I spotted it first on the edge of the trail." Prescott's lip quivered. "And I challenged Emma to race me for it—first one there could keep it." He hung his head. "It's my fault."

"It's nobody's fault," said Orlov. "But it is a reminder to both of you that the hills can be dangerous. You must both try to exercise more caution in the future."

He saw Shannon examining the stone more closely. Her expression was grim. And with good reason. He, too, had noticed that there was not another piece like it within sight.

"But I'll hold my lecture until later," he went on. "Right now, let us bundle the two of you back to the castle and get you settled in front of a roaring fire."

Shannon slipped the quartz into her pocket. "You go on ahead. I'll retrieve our things and catch up." A meaningful glance at the verge of grass reminded him of the pistols lying in full view.

Orlov nodded, giving silent thanks that the children had been too shaken to notice them.

A few sweeping strides, and she had the weapons concealed in the waistband of her walking skirt. From there, he saw her circle around the rock outcropping to pick up the picnic basket. Checking, no doubt, that no other threat was lurking close by.

Scottie insisted on walking, but Emma allowed Orlov to take her in his arms. She was so quiet that he thought perhaps she had fallen asleep, sheltered deep within the folds of his upturned collar. Holding her tighter, he began to hum an old Russian lullaby.

It wasn't until Shannon rejoined them that Emma ventured to speak. "Mr. Oliver was a hero, wasn't he, Miss Sloane?" Her breath was sweet and warm on his cheek.

He smiled, but his blood went cold at the thought of how close he had come to losing her.

"Just like one of the knights in shining armor we have been reading about in the adventures of Sir Galahad," continued Emma.

"Indeed, a storybook hero," murmured Shannon. Her voice was cool, but a sidelong glance revealed that her gaze had a strange sort of blurred glitter.

Damn. The warrior was not weeping, was she?

"There was a scene in 'Bluebeard the Pirate' where one of his crew climbed a cliff to capture a Spanish cannon," offered Prescott. "I daresay Mr. Oliver was braver than that . . ."

Recovered from their initial shock, the children began to chatter like little magpies on the merits of knights and pirates. Orlov was glad to see that they were acting as if the outing had been a grand adventure rather than a traumatic ordeal. The young were resilient. As for their guardians . . .

He slanted another look at Shannon. Her face was still leached of color, and her spirits seemed as heavy as the clouds hanging low over the distant mountains. She refused to meet his eye and barely managed to respond to the children's questions.

He had little time to mull on her melancholy mood. As they entered the castle through the back doors of the kitchen, Cook guessed immediately from their dirt-streaked faces and disheveled clothing that something had gone amiss. The events of the afternoon were recounted in great detail, punctuated by enough gasps and dropped pots to draw Lady Octavia from her sitting room.

"Little devils," she snorted, once the tale was finally done. A "Hmmph" hid a small sniff as she squeezed their shoulders, then waggled a bony finger. "You were lucky to have two guardian angels hovering close by. Promise us that you will be more careful in the future."

"Yes, grandmama." Emma and Prescott looked dutifully chastised.

Under the dowager's basilisk eye, the children were plied with plenty of hot chocolate and freshly baked shortbread before being sent up to a bath and bed with the housekeeper.

"You two—follow me," she added, leading the way back to her sitting room.

Orlov nudged Shannon, who appeared lost in her own thoughts.

"Whiskey all around, young man. And make it more than a wee dram, if you please."

Obeying orders, Orlov poured three generous glasses. He made Shannon down a warming gulp before he took a seat by the fire.

"Accidents do happen, Miss Sloane," said the dowager softly.

"Yes," said Orlov, anxious to ease the anguish he saw etched on Shannon's face. It was unnerving to see her look so down, so defeated. "Even when one takes the utmost precautions, things can go wrong."

"That's just it—I didn't take the proper precautions. I let my guard down." Her voice was barely audible above the crackle of the coals.

"How the devil could you have anticipated what happened?" he growled. "You cannot be expected to read the future in your morning tea leaves."

"I can be expected to do my duty," she said bleakly.

He raised the glass to his lips, surprised to find his fingers clenched so tightly that the crystal was in danger of cracking. He wished he might wind them around Lord Lynsley's neck. Damn the man for sending a lone young female to fight England's deadliest battles. It was dangerous, dirty, depressing work, even for a cynic such as himself.

But thoughts of Lord Lynsley could wait until later. Right now, he must find a way to pull her up from the depths of despair.

After a moment's thought, he assumed his most offensive sneer. "For God's sake, Shannon, it's not like you to wallow in self-pity."

Shannon's head jerked up, indignation sparking in her gaze.

Finally, a flare of her usual fire. He hid a smile.

She looked about to speak, when Lady Sylvia burst into room. "What's this about my niece and nephew nearly coming to grief on the moors." She flung an accusing look at Lady Octavia. "I would be remiss in my duties as aunt if I did not inform Angus of this incident. I'm sure he will be absolutely appalled at such lax watch over the children."

Orlov had never in his life contemplated striking a female, but on seeing the look of self-reproach return to Shannon's gaze, he was sorely tempted to slap the smirk off Lady Sylvia's face.

"Seeing as you have accepted the gentlemen's invitation to join their hunting party on the morrow, Mr. Oliver, I thought I would take the children on a visit to St. Alban's Abbey. The trip will be an educational experience, and it would do them a world of good to get away from here for a bit."

"Not necessary," snapped Lady Octavia. "When it comes to the education of my grandchildren, I am convinced they are in capable hands."

"Who are *you* to judge," muttered Lady Sylvia under her breath.

"I think what Sylvia meant was that perhaps Miss Sloane might be grateful for a day off from her duties." His step matching the smoothness of his words, De Villiers came to stand by the lady's side. Turning his eyes on Shannon, he added, "After the recent events, mademoiselle, you must be feeling a trifle exhausted, non?"

"No." Her reply was curt to the point of rudeness.

The comte lifted his shoulders in oblique apology. "I intended no insult. But alas, I see I have—how do you English say it—stepped on your toes."

"We are all walking on pins and needles at the moment," said Orlov with measured politeness, though he was seething inside. Allowing his temper to run away with him would only exacerbate the tensions. "Lady Sylvia's offer is a kind one, I am sure. But Miss Sloane and I are of the opinion that the children have had enough excitement for the time being. A quiet day of indoor study and reading would be best for the morrow."

Sylvia did not look at all pleased at his defection from

her ranks of admirers. "I had thought *you*, Mr. Oliver, might be counted on to show some sense. I am surprised that you do not agree that a day away from this dark and drafty pile of granite would be a healthy change. I am only thinking of what is best for the children."

"As am I."

Left with no possible rejoinder, Sylvia was forced to concede. "Don't say I didn't warn you," she said with an ungracious huff. Her skirts flared as she turned for the doorway. "Come, Arnaud. Will you join us for a hand of whist in the drawing room? Lady Octavia and her hired help seem to prefer their own company."

"Hmmph." The dowager punctuated her snort with a rap of her walking stick. "I wonder what sort of game she had in mind with me?" she mused.

"Whatever it was, I think she now knows she cannot play you for a fool." Orlov raised his glass in salute, but Shannon saw that his smile looked strained.

She could not bring herself to second the gesture. "Let us not celebrate just yet. We have won a diversionary skirmish, if that. As for the real threat . . ." She pulled the shard of quartz from her pocket. "The truth is, we are desperately vulnerable. Despite all efforts, he can strike us at will."

"Let me have a closer look at that," said Orlov. Shannon passed it over. "There are no man-made markings on it." The translucent stone seemed to glow like fire in the light of the flames.

"We have both walked enough over the nearby moors to know that type of quartz is not from around here," she pointed out.

Orlov didn't argue.

Shannon drew a deep breath and continued. "And from what we know of D'Etienne's cunning, it would be just the sort of trick he would try." She suddenly shivered. "He's close. I know it."

He held the shard a bit higher. Shadows flickered against his face, sharp and snapping as a predator's teeth.

"Call it woman's intuition," she added.

"Aye." The dowager flexed her frail fingers. "I feel it in my bones as well—and do not say it's merely the aches of old age."

"Far be it for me to contradict either of you." Orlov finally spoke. "In these last few weeks, I have come to have the utmost respect for the feminine mind." He forced a wry grimace. "Though it is incomprehensible to mortal man."

"Your understanding of a wide range of subjects leaves most men in the dust," said Lady Octavia, her grim expression lightening somewhat. "For which I am profoundly grateful."

Giving silent thanks for how deftly he had rallied the dowager's flagging spirits, Shannon managed a ghost of a smile as well. She had come to appreciate how his humor was not always intended to be an offensive weapon.

Encouraged by Orlov's example, the dowager thumped her stick to the floor. "So, what do the two of you suggest we do to counter the dastard's latest move?"

The smile died as Shannon stared blankly at the fire. She did not trust herself to speak.

Orlov eyed her for a moment before assuming command. "According to Sun-Tzu, if the enemy is substantial, prepare for him. So it seems to me we must take up a more defensive position. Shannon is right—we are far too vulnerable, even here inside the castle walls. The place is too big, too rambling. I suggest we move the children in with Lady Octavia for the next few nights."

He turned to the dowager. "Your rooms in the central tower are accessible by just one stairway. There is a small parlor at its foot. We will set up our sleeping quarters there—in shifts, of course."

"That makes a good deal of sense," said the dowager. "There are still iron bars guarding the windows, left over from some ancient clan conflict." *Tap, tap, tap.* The rap of her walking stick took on a martial beat. "We shall rouse the children and tell them that the move is a special treat in light of the trying day. A grand adventure. And with a roll of blankets on the floor, they may pretend they are pirates, sleeping on the deck of a ship."

"Whitehall ought to consider offering for your services, milady," remarked Orlov. "Your talent for spinning a good yarn at a moment's notice would prove extremely valuable. Diplomats are often called upon to explain delicate situations."

"My talent for lying through my teeth is probably not nearly as good as yours. Still, I have told enough bouncers in my life to be reasonably adept at improvising."

The scuff of the stick sounded as Lady Octavia started to rise. Ashamed at her own lack of spirit, Shannon forced her shoulders to square. What was wrong with her? She had never been afraid of a fight. If anything, her desire for action had been too driven, too devil-may-care. *Reckless.*

Again she wondered whether Lord Lynsley was right in doubting whether she deserved to wear the badge of a Merlin. Her hand crept to her breast, touching the hidden tattoo. Beneath it she could feel the drumming of her heart, unsure, erratic. The marquess had warned her that duty demanded dispassionate resolve.

Her fingers curled in a clench around the small silver hawk and fine-link chain, a sharp reminder of the Academy and all it stood for. Sofia had thought her worthy to wear it. She must not let them down. Or herself.

"Ready to go?" Orlov had moved to her side, his gaze catching hers in a deeper unspoken question.

She set aside her unfinished whiskey. "I'll rouse the children and gather the blankets while you check that the doors and latches of the Tower stairwell are in good working order."

"I will recheck the window bars," offered Lady Octavia. "And perhaps order up a few buckets of boiling oil." A waggle of the polished hawthorn emphasized her snort. "Hmmph. Just let the fellow try to breach these walls."

"I doubt the devil himself would dare do battle against us." Orlov smiled. "I certainly wouldn't."

"I'll bring extra blankets for the guard room," said Shannon. "Let me take the first watch."

"You are sure?"

She didn't blame him for questioning her fitness for duty. He was far too sharp to have missed the signs of self-doubt. Both comrade and enemy must see only unflinching courage.

"I am ready." *I am a Merlin.* She would prove to everyone—including herself—that she was worthy of her wings.

Chapter Nineteen

The locks are secure, and as an extra precaution, I've added a second deadbolt on the Tower door." Orlov angled his light over the window, checking that the latches were fastened. "The children?"

"Safely stowed away in Lady Octavia's bedchamber," answered Shannon. "Though I'll not vouch for their getting a wink of sleep during the night."

"Leave it to the dowager to run a tight ship." A mattress had been made up in a corner of the small parlor room at the foot of the stairs. He came and sat down beside her, shoulder to shoulder, with their backs against whitewashed plaster. "She found a book on the pirates of the Caribbean that is guaranteed to frighten even the most bloodthirsty buccaneer into slumber."

"The last thing the children need is a fright." Even to her own ears, her voice sounded perilously close to cracking.

"They are resilient, Shannon."

"And you think I am not?"

"I did not say that."

"You didn't have to." Hunching away from his touch, she drew her knees tighter to her chest, though there was no hope of hiding within herself. "I know it's my fault. I should not have been distracted."

"Don't be so damnably hard on yourself, Shannon."

Surprised, she looked up.

"Do you think you are the only one wracked by doubt, by fears of not being up to the job?" Orlov crooked a weary smile. "Trust me, it gets even worse as you get older."

"As if *you* have ever suffered a moment of self-doubt."

He twisted a lock of her hair between his fingers. "Only a fool or an ass does not question himself. I know you think me both. But if it's any consolation, there have been times when I wondered whether an enemy blade or a bullet would have been a less painful alternative to my own thoughts."

Orlov had never allowed such an unguarded glimpse of his feelings. Shannon blinked before answering, "I—I would never have guessed you to have such doubts. You hide them well."

"Mental discipline is no different from swordplay. In both, we must master the art of feints and deception."

"You are far more skilled than I am."

His laugh was little more than a whisper. "You underestimate your skills, Shannon. They are far more formidable than you imagine." His broad, warm palm cupped her chin. "Your courage and compassion make me ashamed of my own selfish weaknesses."

Her breath caught in her throat. His voice, stripped of its usual caustic edge, sounded nearly as vulnerable as her own.

"You have nothing to be ashamed of, Alexandr." As his hand drew away from her face, Shannon reached out and twined her fingertips with his. Through the calluses and cuts she felt the warm, steady beat of his pulse. "You are a kind, caring man, though you take great pains to hide it."

"You give me too much credit, *golub*."

"I have seen the look on your face when you have Emma cradled in your arms."

His mouth crooked. "Perhaps it's merely the scars of past battles twisting my expression of their own accord." He touched the tiny nick at the corner of his mouth. "This was from a tavern brawl in Cracow—hardly a heroic exploit."

Shannon leaned closer and pressed her lips to the spot.

Orlov stiffened for an instant, then let out a whispery laugh. "This was from a Venetian spy, who was trying to sabotage one of our trade agreements with Constantinople."

She kissed the razor-thin line above his brow. "What happened to him?" she murmured.

"He's feeding the fishes in the Grand Canal."

"And this?" Shannon touched his knuckles.

"Ah. You wish to know my deepest, darkest secrets?" He sighed. "My puppy bit me when I tried to take away his bone. You see, even at a very early age, I had a penchant for thievery."

And how very good he was at it. He had taken her heart without her realizing just when it had gone missing.

Orlov slowly put his arms around her. "And yet it is you who have stolen my will to resist."

Shannon made no protest when he tilted her chin

and took her mouth in a gentle kiss. It was strange how passion could spark in different ways. She felt a burning need for him, but tonight it was a slow flame, rather than the crackling intensity of their earlier encounters. Those had been fueled by a volatile mix of aggression and attraction.

And this? How to describe their relationship?

A clash of competitive wills had slowly but surely softened to mutual respect. Perhaps they had recognized in each other that despite the outward differences they were very much alike. Lost souls with a certain darkness in their hearts, looking for some missing piece to make them whole. What they had found was each other. And matched together, their strengths seemed to conquer the weaknesses.

"Alexandr." She had been drawn to him from the very first time her steel had crossed with his.

His mouth, softer than velvet, was now nuzzling the hollow of her throat. The fastenings of her shirt had come free, baring her shoulders.

She undid the buttons of his placket and slid her hand against his chest. The dusting of curls was like finespun silk beneath her palm, the flat planes of his breast smooth as polished marble. Seized by a sudden urge to see the flicker of firelight on his flesh, she tugged the linen over his head.

It might only have been a quirk of the candles, but Orlov's expression appeared oddly tentative. "Are you sure this is what you want, Shannon?" he murmured. "I don't wish to take advantage of the moment and have you do anything that you will later regret."

She mustered a laugh. "Thank you for the warning, but I know how to defend myself—if I so desire."

"And what is it you desire, *golub*?"

You.

She wasn't quite brave enough to say it aloud, but her eyes must have spoken for her. His grip was surprisingly gentle as he laid her down across the counterpane and covered her body with his. The scent of him, an overtly masculine mix of smoke, leather, and pine, was intoxicating. She could not resist tracing her tongue along the ridge of his shoulder.

"You taste of salt and Scottish malt," she whispered.

"You taste of wild honey," he said, after drinking in a more intimate embrace. "And a sweetness beyond words."

There was no way to describe the sudden flare of heat that his kiss ignited inside her. Rough with need, the rasp of his stubbled jaw was like a thousand points of fire against her cheek, and the press of his mouth, hard yet soft, a tongue of flame.

"Then no more words, Alexandr," she begged. "No more warnings. God knows what the morning will bring. The only certainty is that we have this moment. I want you, beyond reason, beyond regret." *Beyond yearning.* "Please."

"I fear I am beyond the point of turning back, no matter that I should." His hands framed her face. "You deserve better, Shannon. So much better."

"But I want *you*." In the firelight, his hair had a whiskygold gleam. She threaded her fingers through the curling strands. "Only you."

Guiding his grip to the remaining fastenings of her shirt, she wriggled her breasts free of the fabric. With a ragged groan, Orlov ripped it open all the way, sending a flutter of linen threads across the counterpane. Her breeches yielded to his hands, then her stockings.

A last tug left her naked beneath his gaze. Unashamed, Shannon met his gaze. The gleam in his eye sparked a fierce joy deep within her.

"Have you any idea how lovely you are?" Orlov's callused palms slid over her hips.

She edged closer, so close that the peppering of golden hair on his chest tickled against her skin. "Not nearly as magnificent as you are." The breadth of his shoulders, the sculpted muscles, tapering to a narrow waist, were smooth and hard as marble. Chiseled perfection. "Like a Greek god."

"Lud, I am all too human, Shannon. All too flawed." His hands came up to cup her breasts. She tingled all over as he teased their tips.

"Not to me." She fell back against the pillows, drawing him with her. "You are . . ." All coherent thought dissolved in a gasp of delight as his mouth closed over a nipple, laving, suckling the flesh to a hard little point of fire.

"Perfect." The last word crescendoed into a cry. Arching instinctively, she wrapped her arms around his neck, reveling in the silky tangle of his hair, the slope of his back. The bedcover fell away as he hitched her higher, their legs entwining in the sheets. His erect shaft brushed her thigh, and the thought of him wanting her was wildly arousing.

Somehow she *did* feel beautiful. Feminine, sultry, seductive. All the things she did not think were a part of herself. Her hands tightened. She meant to hold on to the moment, savor the splendor of his shape, his strength, his scent.

Everything about him.

"Please!" she whispered, as his lips slanted to the hollow of her throat. The pounding of her pulse echoed her need. In another instant she feared she might shatter like crystal.

His eyes, swirling like liquid steel, met hers.

Shannon felt another jolt of heat course through her. "Don't wait any longer. Come inside me, Alex."

Orlov lifted her hips, driven on by her plea and his own ruthless need. He could no longer leash the Russian wolf deep within him—his baser instincts now overpowered what few scraps of gentlemanly English scruples he still possessed.

Damn him for a beast, but he meant to have her. To mark her irrevocably as his own.

"Open yourself to me, Shannon." He coaxed her thighs apart. "Yes, like that." All pliant curves and creamy flesh, her long legs responded sweetly to his touch. He nearly came undone.

A sigh, soft as spun silk. Had she ever had a man inside her?

Slowly, slowly, he thought, holding himself in check. More than anything else, he wanted to make this joining of their bodies a memory that they could hold forever.

Her honeyed curls, gleaming gold in the dancing light, were damp to his touch. Sucking in his breath, he found the nub within her feminine folds of flesh and circled a slow caress.

"Oh, Alexandr!" Her voice—wild, wondrous—urged him to quicken his stroke.

Shannon pressed hard into his hand, and he took a wicked satisfaction at having awakened her to her own innermost passions. Another cry, as his finger found her passage and slipped inside. *So tight. So trusting.*

And so innocent.

Damn. For all her virago strength, it seemed she was still a virgin. With a low groan, he eased back, though it took a considerable effort.

"Please," she begged, grabbing at his wrist. "Don't stop. Not now."

"Not so fast, *golub*," he said through gritted teeth. His self-control was perilously close to going up in smoke. "I mean to make this right for you. I don't want to hurt you."

Her eyes were luminous in the flickering light, as if the sun were shining on a clear blue sky. "You could never hurt me."

It was still not too late. A true gentleman would have come to his senses. But he had never claimed to be a saint. Primal passion had taken possession of him, body and soul. Angling higher, Orlov braced his weight and entered her, slowly, gently as he could.

But after a momentary flinch, Shannon surged to meet him, sheathing his shaft deep in her warmth. He gasped, fighting to keep from going over the edge.

"A-am I doing this right?" Her smile turned tentative.

"Oh so right," he rasped. *And oh so wrong.* He ruthlessly thrust the thought aside. Cynicism, his usual shield, had unraveled, leaving him tangled in a hopeless snarl of emotions. *Hope, guilt, fear, longing.* But need overpowered all. Somehow he would sort the others out later.

Orlov withdrew slightly, giving her body a moment to adjust to his, then eased forward again.

"So right," he whispered again, tipping her face to take her in a long, lush kiss.

Clinging to his shoulders, she eagerly matched his rhythm. Limbs entwined, he felt her heart pounding, in perfect harmony with his own. So close. Her touch awakening hope, even though he had sworn never to make himself so vulnerable.

"Hold me tight, Alexandr." The words feathered against his cheek. "I shall be lost without you." He could feel the tension mounting within her, straining to break free.

"I have you, Shannon." His hands guided her hips higher, joining them more deeply. Like liquid honey, her warmth enveloped him. Two as one, cresting in yet another exquisite wave of pleasure, before she shuddered beneath him and gave voice to a cry of ethereal sweetness.

His own limbs trembling, Orlov was not sure whether to laugh or cry. Reveling in her wonder, he was only dimly aware of the darker note of warning thrumming through his head. Had he made the cardinal mistake of allowing lust to deepen into love? Emotional attachment was the kiss of death in their line of work.

And yet rather than heed the danger, he surged forward, his own hoarse exultation echoing the thunder rumbling through the distant moors.

"Are you awake, *dorogaya*?"

Shannon was roused from her reveries by a feathered kiss to her brow. "Mmmm . . . yes." She gave a languid stretch, reveling in the sleek warmth of Orlov's body pressed against hers. "But only barely." His skin was still redolent with musky scent of their lovemaking, and as she snuggled closer, she was intimately aware of every nuanced texture. The smoothness of his muscles, the hardened contours of his chest, the stubbling of whiskers along the lean line of his jaw.

The first rays of dawn lit a flare of gold beneath her outstretched caress. "It's still early."

"Aye. But loath though I am to mix business and pleasure, duty calls." Orlov's smile was sweet but fleeting. "I had better not linger here in bed any longer."

Duty. Shannon shot up with a guilty start. "The children. Lady Octavia. I should have—"

He pulled her back down to the pillows. "All is well. I checked on them a half hour ago. You need not rush to dress. However, I have a few things I wish to do before I join the London gentlemen for the hunt."

"Alexandr, can I not convince you to reconsider?"

The ice-blue resolve melted, but only for a moment. "No."

"Then please be careful. Three against one, stalking through steep moors thick with gorse and pine? The odds are stacked against you."

"Assuming there is a conspiracy." He cocked a brow. "You think them in league?"

"The idea had crossed my mind," she confessed. "We cannot dismiss it, no matter how far-fetched it might seem."

"I, too, have given it some consideration. It's unlikely, but I will be on guard." His fingertips brushed at the corners of her mouth. "Don't frown, *golub*. A hunting rifle will not be my only weapon."

"A pistol or knife is little protection at long range. And an attack may come from two angles."

"Sun-Tzu says if your enemies are substantial, prepare for them. My true advantage lies in knowing what I am up against. On the other hand, the London gentlemen cannot know for sure what sort of threat I represent."

Shannon caught hold of his hand. "Don't be too sure of that. D'Etienne will have heard about Ireland. He is far too clever not to put two and two together."

He was no longer smiling. "Would that our own surmises would add up to more than guesses."

Palms pressed as one, she could feel the warm pulse beneath his toughened flesh. *Hard and soft.* She no longer felt them as two contrasting elements, but as part of a whole.

He broke away, but only to lift her fingers to his lips. "I promise I will be careful, *golub.* Tell me you will do the same."

"You may rest assured that I won't take any unnecessary risks. I mean to keep the children indoors for the day. Lady Octavia says there is a trunkful of old games stored in the attics. Between lessons and skittles I should have no trouble keeping them occupied."

"Stay here in the Tower. It's is the safest part of the castle."

"Yes, safe as a merlin's eyrie," Shannon stared out at the distant moors. "It is you who are alone and vulnerable."

"That is exactly what we are trained to do, Shannon—work on our own. Danger is the one constant companion of our lives." Untangling his legs from the rumpled sheets, he rose. A dappling of light skimmed over the contours of his naked body. "Remember, I am a professional. I am used to taking care of myself."

The reassurance did nothing to still her fears. The play of sun and shadow showed not only chiseled strength, but past scars, stark white against the tanned flesh.

"You are flesh and blood, Alexandr. And what I remember all too well is how easily a bit of lead cuts through the toughest muscle and sinew."

"The trick is never to think of the past, Shannon. Only the future."

He was right, of course. A warrior must always stay a step ahead of regrets and recriminations. Shielding her face from the flare of the flint, Shannon lit the single candle by the bedside.

Don't look back.

No doubt Sun-Tzu had an aphorism for such a situation, but Shannon couldn't think of a one. No heroic lines from Homer, no poetic quotations from Shakespeare. She said the only words that came from the heart. "Keep your eyes open."

"And you, *golub*." Orlov finished dressing and slipped out the door.

Chapter Twenty

We may as well pack some birdshot, but I for one would prefer to see if we can pick up the trail of a Highland stag," announced Jervis as he handed out the hunting rifles from the gun room. "I've heard much about their size and stealth. It would be a prize to bring one down."

The comte lifted his shoulders. "I am perfectly amiable to stalking whatever prey you choose."

Were the gentlemen simply making the usual small talk before a hunt? Or was there a more menacing meaning to the exchange? Orlov stood to one side, assuming an attitude of casual indifference as he readied the cartridge bags. The comment did not include him, which was just as well. He was in no mood for any more games—verbal or otherwise.

"Sweet Jesus, I'm not sure I could hit the broadside of a barn," groaned Talcott. His eyes were red and his sallow skin resembled the underbelly of a cod. "I would cry off, except I'm sure that if I stay here, I will be pestered to accompany the ladies to whatever cursed pile of rocks they are so keen to see." He pressed a hand to his brow and winced. "I would rather risk a fit of apoplexy in traipsing the moors than endure several hours of Annabelle's whining. Bloody hell, you would think that the world had ended simply because the chit had to put off her coming out for a season."

If he were a gentleman, he might feel obliged to give warning of the youngest Talcott's plans, thought Orlov. However, his scruples were not so finely honed. In truth, he had little sympathy for any of the family, save perhaps Helen. Caught in the middle between a dissolute wastrel and a spoiled hellion, she was more to be pitied than disliked.

"All young ladies dream of fancy balls and handsome suitors. It is only natural that she is disappointed," observed De Villiers.

"You are far more tolerant than I would be," replied Talcott. "She behaved like a simpering schoolgirl, making calf's eyes at you throughout the journey."

"There are worse things than having a pretty girl bat her lashes at you." The comte turned. "Would you not agree, Monsieur Oliver?"

"I can think of a great many," he replied politely.

"And then, of course, there are even better things, *non*? For example, bedding a beautiful woman like Mademoiselle Sloane." De Villiers winked at his London friends. "Now there is a bird I wouldn't mind pursuing. Have you perchance had the pleasure of plucking her feathers?"

Orlov willed himself to stay calm. "I was under the impression that a gentleman does not discuss his private dealings with a lady, *non*?"

"But you are no gentleman, Mr. Oliver. And Miss

Sloane is no lady," sneered Jervis. "The rules don't apply."

"Thank you for the reminder." Orlov ran a hand down the barrel of his rifle and tested the action of the trigger.

For a moment, the only sound in the room was the echo of the sharp *snick*.

"Ready, gentlemen?" Jervis shouldered his weapon and marched for the mud room. "My valet will follow along with food and drink for the day."

Orlov waited for the others to file out, then fell in step behind Talcott.

"Might I have a word with you, Aunt Octavia?"

"Hmmph." Turning away from the leaded windows, the dowager relaxed her grip on her walking stick—this one a stout length of yew topped with a heavy brass ball—and gestured for Lady Sylvia to enter the sitting room. "Well, don't just stand there, gel. Come in."

To her surprise, Lady Sylvia was carrying a silver tray with two tea cups and a bowl of sugar. The dowager's eyes narrowed even more on seeing her relative's cat-in-the-creampot smile. "What's this?"

"A peace offering," replied Lady Sylvia. "I wish to apologize for my outburst of last night."

"Hmmph."

"And for the air of tension surrounding the entire visit. I had hoped that perhaps we might . . ." She shrugged as she placed the tray on the sidetable. "But there is no use in crying over spilled milk. My party will be taking its leave soon, and while I know it is too much to ask that we part as friends, I should at least like to do so without animosity."

Lady Octavia eyed the steaming brew with some skepticism. She would sooner expect hemlock than Oolong from her relative, but as Lady Sylvia seemed sincere, accepting the goodwill gesture seemed a small concession to make.

"It is a special mix I brought from London—a blend of Indian spices and black tea." A splash of cream lightened the deep chocolate color. "It's best enjoyed with a liberal helping of sugar. May I?"

The dowager gave a brusque nod as Lady Sylvia held a heaping teaspoon over the cups. "Just don't expect to turn me up sweet," she murmured. "At my age, I am too old to change, gel."

A laugh. "Oh, I have no illusions of altering your opinion of me. I know you think me shallow and far too extravagant in my taste of fashions and friends." Lady Sylvia stirred her tea. "But truly, do you never miss the gaiety of London Society? The glamour of the *ton*, the glitter of the ballrooms?"

The dowager took a long sip before answering. "Fool's gold. Beneath the lustrous veneer is nothing of real value. Perhaps one day you will understand what I mean."

"Perhaps." Lady Sylvia was saved from having to say more by the pelter of small feet on the stairway landing.

"Miss Sloane says we may end lessons early." Prescott shot into the room a half step ahead of his sister.

"She says you have found a grand set of skittles in the attics and that we may play with it in here with you, grandmama," added Emma, a bit breathlessly.

"If you keep your voices down to a dull roar." Shannon followed on their heels. "And if we are not interrupting a private family conversation." Her brow rose in question. "I can keep the children occupied in the schoolroom if you prefer."

"No need, Miss Sloane. I was just leaving." Shannon was surprised to see Lady Sylvia take up the tea tray as she swept by. "As the weather looks to be holding, we will be leaving shortly to view the ruins of St. Alban's Abbey."

"She's finally come to the conclusion that her presence is best served in small doses," said the dowager dryly, once the door had fallen shut.

"What did she want?" Shannon's gaze remained on the panels of polished oak.

"To offer an apology, if her words are to be believed." Lady Octavia fingered the knob of her walking stick. "She is not quite as featherbrained as I thought. Indeed, had she ever spoken to me with as much candor as today, things might have been different between us."

"I wonder what prompted a change of heart."

"As do I. She didn't ask for money. But likely she is just trying to butter me up for later."

"Sugar and spice," murmured Shannon. "I believe there is an old nursery rhyme—"

A snort interrupted her words. "Hmmph. She tried that already." A glare glinted off the dowager's spectacles. "But I didn't bite."

Whatever schemes Lady Sylvia had brewing, they seemed trivial compared to the threat of a cold-blooded French assassin.

Shannon shivered in spite of her shawl. "While the London ladies feast on a picnic of cold pigeon pie and old Town gossip amidst the Abbey Ruins, our concerns are closer to home."

"Indeed." Though she spoke with some force, Lady Octavia was forced to stifle a yawn.

"Did the children keep you up all night?" she asked in

some concern. "If you wish to take a nap, I am perfectly capable of keeping watch."

The dowager waved off the suggestion. "Slept like a babe. And you?"

She hoped her cheeks did not betray the telltale flush of heat. "No disturbances to speak of."

"Miss Sloane, will you come show me the proper way to play skittles?" called Emma from the far corner of the parlor. "Scottie is making up his own rules."

"I am not," retorted her brother. "Mr. Oliver taught me how the Russian Imperial Guards play."

"I had better mediate an international truce," murmured Shannon. She was not sorry to have something to take her mind off Orlov. The gentlemen had been gone for several hours, and she couldn't help imagining all the terrible things that could befall an individual out on the moors.

Even one as wily as a Russian wolf.

"If you tire of games, I brought down the book on pirates." Lady Octavia rubbed at the bridge of her nose. "I think I shall ring for some more tea."

But it was one of the local gardeners who appeared in the doorway, rather than Rawley. "Excuse me, milady, but I've been sent with a message. Right urgent, I was told." Hat in hand, he tugged at a shock of ginger hair. "From the tall gent—the tutor."

Shannon forced a show of calm as she waited for the man to go on.

"Well, don't just stand there, man, spit it out!" said the dowager.

The man swallowed in some confusion. "Auch, he asked that Miss meet him as soon as possible by the loch. At the old laird's boathouse."

"You spoke with him?" Shannon rose. "When?"

"Not me, miss." He ran a hand over his grizzled chin, leaving bits of dirt clinging to the rough stubble. "It was Jock who passed the word."

She looked to the dowager, who nodded in answer to her unspoken question. "He's a steady enough fellow," added Lady Octavia, after dismissing the gardener with a brusque thanks.

Still, she hesitated. Her foremost duty was to the McAllister children. As for Orlov . . .

"He wouldn't ask you to leave the children unless there was a demmed good reason." The dowager's low whisper echoed her own sentiments. "He left me a loaded pistol, and made sure I knew how to use it."

Her mind raced through a few hurried calculations— the distance to the loch, the time it would take to make the round trip. "You are sure?"

"Go."

"You will stay here in the Tower? And bar the stair-well door until I return?" she murmured.

"Never fear. These old fortress walls have held off hordes of wild Highlanders. They won't give way to a Frog assassin, no matter how slippery a reptile."

Shannon dared not vacillate any longer. Lynsley might question her judgment, but it would not be the first time they had disagreed on strategy.

"Mind your grandmother while I am gone," she called to the children. "I must run an errand for her, but I shall be back shortly." *And if she was not?* No, she would not even think of it. Lady Octavia had been told about the inn in Dornoch, run by one of Lord Lynsley's operatives, and knew it was where she must go in case of disaster.

Giving thanks that she had taken to wearing her

breeches and shirt beneath her dress, Shannon turned for the door.

"Damn. Another miss," growled Jervis.

"Perhaps the gunsights need to be readjusted," said De Villiers. "None of us has had any luck today—and my last shot was at nearly point-blank range."

"Shoot *me* and put me out of my misery," wheezed Talcott. Dropping his rifle, he slumped to a seat on a pile of stones. His face was a mottled red, and his shirtpoints and Belcher neckerchief were soaked with sweat. "Jervis, where the devil is your man with the refreshments? I need a swig of brandy to fortify my strength."

Still fiddling with the powder pan, Jervis looked up in annoyance. "He will be along in a moment."

"We might as well take a break for some sustenance. The last beat through the heather was a trifle steep." The comte did not look at all winded from the climb, noted Orlov. His step had been sure over the uneven ground, and he had handled his weapon well on flushing a brace of partridge. That he had missed bagging the birds was simply a bit of bad luck.

Their eyes met and De Villiers smiled. "You have yet to take a shot, Monsieur Oliver."

"I did not wish to interfere with your sport. Perhaps later."

"Afraid of matching your skills against those of a gentleman?" said Jervis with a lordly sneer.

"I'll take my chances."

The comte laughed. "He is right. We have nothing to crow about."

Jervis did not appear to find the observation amusing. "Enough of damn birds. Let us cross that ridge and head into the stand of pine trees. It seems a likely place to pick up the trail of a stag."

"The Highland variety prefer a more open terrain," murmured Orlov, more to goad the other man into a temper than to offer accurate advice.

"If I wanted a schoolroom lecture on the flora and fauna of Scotland, I would have hired a lackey for myself."

"I am sure Monsieur Oliver was only trying to be helpful." De Villiers moved quickly to smooth his friend's ruffled feathers. "Ah, here is your man now with the food and drink."

The valet unslung the large canvas sack from his shoulder and began unwrapping the oilskin packages of cheese and cold ham. Orlov watched, seeing for the first time the man's misshapen knuckles and scarred fingers. They looked more adept at throwing a punch than knotting a gentleman's cravat.

"Some claret, Hartley, and be quick about it." Jervis accepted the bottle from his servant and took a long drink. "Come, gentlemen, don't tarry too long. If we are to have any hope of downing a prize, we cannot waste any time."

Talcott groaned. "I will wait for you here, if you don't mind."

"There is no guarantee we will pass back this way again," snapped Jervis, a rather nasty smile curling the corners of his mouth. His mood seemed to be growing edgier by the moment. "So unless you can find your own way back to the castle, I suggest you follow along."

Swallowing a hasty bite of cheese and bread, Talcott swore again. "Christ, don't leave me here in this godforsaken place."

"Then don't lag behind." Jervis seemed to be taking a

malicious pleasure in venting his ill-humor on his friend. He allowed a few more minutes to pass, then signaled to his valet to begin packing up.

Talcott swore and struggled to his feet.

"Hartley, give his lordship a hand." Brushing the last crumbs of cheddar from his fingertips, Jervis took up his cartridge bag. "Let him carry your rifle," he said to Talcott.

His friend gratefully passed over the weapon.

Orlov slowly gathered his own gear, straining to over-hear the exchange as Jervis drew his servant aside for a few words. They spoke too softly, however, and he was forced to back off.

"Ready, gentlemen?" Jervis did not wait for an answer as he started up the steep trail.

Faster, faster. Her heart was outracing her feet as Shannon beat a path back to the castle. Vaulting the garden wall, she sprinted across the cobbled courtyard. There had been no sign of Orlov—or anyone else—around the loch.

Even a child should have seen through the ruse. But she had been looking with the starry-eyed gaze of a lover rather than the hawkish stare of a Merlin.

She barreled through the front door and rushed blindly down the hallway, praying there was still time.

Up ahead, the Tower door hung wide open on its heavy iron hinges.

Taking the stairs two at a time, Shannon yanked the pistol from her waistband. Shadows cut across the landing, dark as the iron bars guarding the narrow window. From inside the parlor came an ominous silence.

Drawing a steadying breath, she slowed to a measured

step and cocked her weapon. A nudge of her boot inched the door open a crack.

"Lady Octavia."

There was no answer . . . save for a whispery snore.

Thank god. She gently shook the dowager's shoulder. "Lady Octavia, you must wake up."

A flutter of lashes, and finally a peek of blue showed behind the glass lenses. "Hmmph." The snort was soft and slurred and the eyes looked rather glazed.

"You've been drugged," muttered Shannon.

The dowager struggled to raise her chin. "It must have been the tea. The taste was strange but I thought it due to the spices," she said thickly. "Demme me for a fool."

"And me." Shannon spun around at the sound of approaching steps.

"Is something amiss?" Rawley shuffled into the room. "Cook and I saw Miss Sloane flying across the courtyard like a bat out of hell."

"The children—have you seen them?" she demanded.

"Why, Lady Sylvia and her friends took them along on their picnic." His face fell. "She said milady was napping, and that you were running an errand. I thought nothing of it."

"You had no reason to." The carriage had less than an hour's head start, but it could be headed anywhere. Shannon closed her eyes and recalled the maps she had memorized. Fortunately, a vehicle of that size had few choices. There was still a chance.

"Rawley, stay with Lady Octavia."

The only horse left in the stable was an old Highland gelding used for the occasional cart ride into the village. Shannon grabbed a bridle and a moment later was astride the animal's bare back, urging him into a rawboned gal-

lop. Cutting across the orchards, she crested the hill overlooking the loch. From there she had two choices—the
road leading down toward Dornoch, or the way winding
south through the moors to Inverness. Shading her eyes,
she saw no sign of movement. She would have to act on
intuition.

The abbey ruins were situated deep in the hills, on a
small lake at the foot of Beinn Tharsuinn. Five miles by
road, but no more than two as the crow flies.

Or the Merlin.

Praying that she was right, she turned her mount
south.

It was slow going through the thick pines, and what
little sun trickled through the heavy boughs did nothing
to lighten the mood of the hunting party. Talcott had fallen
into a sullen silence, punctuated by wheezing gasps and
an occasional oath. Even De Villiers had dropped any attempt at small talk. The only sound was the crunch of
dried needles underfoot.

Under Jervis's direction, they spread out, and within
minutes Orlov lost sight of the others through the tangle
of dark tree trunks and twisted branches. He paused. The
woods seemed wary, watchful. Even the songbirds had
ceased their twitter.

After waiting a little longer, he angled through the underbrush, intent on keeping the others in front of him.
The stalk was on. But what game was being hunted?

A twig snapped. Orlov looked around and saw a
shape backtracking down the hill. He moved quickly to
catch up.

"Lost your way, Mr. Hartley?"

Startled, the valet spun around. Talcott's rifle was still

in his hands, but before he could bring it to bear, Orlov caught its barrel. "Careful." A sharp twist pulled it free of the man's grasp. "It's imperative to exercise great caution when handling a loaded weapon."

Hartley glowered. "Lord Jervis asked me to return to the castle for more wine and brandy."

"I think that would be a grave mistake. Shooting requires a clear head and a steady hand, don't you agree?"

"Orders are orders," grunted the valet.

Orlov shouldered the second rifle. Not that it added any real firepower to his arsenal. He had taken the precaution of removing the bullets from all the cartridges earlier that morning. "Come, let us find His Lordship and ask him to reconsider."

Hartley shot him a disgruntled look, but after eyeing the weapons a moment longer, he seemed to think better of further argument and reluctantly started back up the hill.

A puff of dust swirled up ahead. Shannon reined to a halt. The top of the carriage, a black speck against the heathered greens and golds, was visible for an instant before dipping down into a wooded swale.

Coaxing a last burst of speed from her lathered mount, she caught up with the vehicle as it slowed for a bend in the road. Coming abreast of Lady Sylvia's coachman, she called at him to halt.

He turned to answer, but a sharp crack cut off his words. His mouth hung open for an instant, then he slumped forward, revealing a gaping hole at the back of his head.

From the underbrush across the road, Shannon saw the glint of gun barrel swivel her way. Jerking back on the reins, she flung herself sideways. The shot whistled by her ear.

Another few inches . . .

She dropped lower—only a handful of horsehair kept her from falling beneath the pounding hooves. As her frightened mount reared, she pushed off from its flank and grabbed for the carriage door latch. The brass gave a wild lurch as the wheels hit a rut, but her grip held.

Pain shot through her shoulder as her body slammed into the varnished wood. From behind the paned window came a piercing scream. Swinging her legs up, Shannon kicked in the glass and crawled inside.

Lady Sylvia, her face bloodless as marble, was trying to crawl out from under Helen Talcott, who had fallen into a dead faint. Ignoring her sister's plight, Annabelle started to scream again. "Stephen! Stephen!"

Shannon elbowed her aside and crouched by the far window. "Stop that caterwauling," she ordered. Knocking out one of the panes with her pistol, she scanned the roadside. *Nothing.*

"Are two you all right?" She slanted a quick look at the children. Prescott had his arm around his sister, but other than that, they looked remarkably calm.

"Yes, Miss Sloane," they answered in unison.

"But you have a cut on your wrist," said Emma in a worried voice. "And on your cheek."

"Mere scratches, elf." Shannon wiped at the blood. "Nothing to worry about."

"Why do you have a pistol?"

She hesitated for a fraction. "Pirates. Of a sort, that is. They are trying to board and hold us for ransom. I mean to fight them off."

The driverless team had slowed to a shambling walk.

"Stay very quiet, children, and don't move." She cracked the door open. Still no sign of the enemy. Which one of them would make the first move?

The answer came in a flash. Breaking out from behind a thicket of gorse, a figure darted between the harnessed horses.

Damn. She had no angle for a shot. Stepping to the ground would make her an easy target. But if he reached the coachman's box, he would have the upper hand.

Do not move unless it is advantageous. It was one of Sun-Tzu's basic precepts. Her hand tightened, and the door hinges creaked. Caught up in a deadly game of chess, she must make a split-second decision on how to counterattack—pawn, rook, queen, knight.

Knight. Holding the door like a shield of old, she swung out, gaining just enough arc to see her attacker reaching for the perch.

They both fired at the same time.

He dodged away with lightning quickness but her bullet caught the butt of his weapon, knocking it from his hand. His shot shattered the door panel. Its force spent, the lead ball bounced harmlessly into the grassy verge.

Drawing her second pistol, Shannon leaped to the ground and edged around the front wheel. The man's pistol lay in the dirt, its splintered butt stained crimson. So, she had drawn first blood.

At the sound of retreating footsteps, she ventured another step, just in time to see a loping figure disappear into the woods.

She drew in a deep breath. And let it out in a sharp oath. The harness had been sliced through, leaving it useless. *Clever bastard.* But two could put a blade to imaginative use. Her own horse had bolted, but she wasn't about to wait around to see what other tricks he had up his sleeve.

Choosing the strongest-looking of the matched bays, she cut the animal free of its traces. On horseback they would make better time and have far more freedom to improvise. A lumbering coach, confined to a twisting road, was too easy a target. She knotted off a set of reins and led her makeshift mount around to the side of the carriage.

"Toss me that blanket, Scottie." Shannon folded it across the horse's withers. "Now help your sister over to me."

Annabelle's sobs started up again, a high keening whine. Helen still lay in a swoon.

"Well done." Holding Emma steady, she reached for Prescott. "Give me your hand."

"W-what are you d-doing?" Lady Sylvia finally roused from her dazed silence.

"Taking the children back to their rightful guardian."

"You can't be meaning to leave us stranded here! We shall be at the mercy of any predator."

"You will just have to take your chances." Shannon took a moment to reload her spent weapon. "Be grateful I don't shoot you on the spot. Perhaps your cohort will be as forgiving."

Lady Sylvia blanched. "I didn't . . . it wasn't . . ."

Ignoring the halting explanation, she swung up behind the two children. "Hold tight to the harness. We are going to take a hard gallop, but I won't let you fall."

"I bet none of the acrobats at Astley's could match your riding," said Prescott. "That was a corking good trick. Will you teach me how to do it?"

Shannon's lips twitched. "Thank you, Scottie. However, it's not one I care to repeat." The wind had risen and the skies were beginning to darken with clouds from the North Sea. Turning the horse in a tight circle, she made one last survey of the surroundings. "We will choose an even better one once we are home."

The lengthening shadows cast the trees in an ominous light. Leaves rustled, roughening the whistling through the moorland heather. Still, there was no sign of the enemy, nor of any reinforcements. By all accounts, the Frenchman worked alone. But in Ireland, he had found temporary allies with the O'Malleys. Scotland, too, was a hotbed of intrigue. There were many diehard clansmen who considered Napoleon the lesser of two evils. Indeed, they would side with the Devil himself if it offered the chance to throw off the English yoke.

"May we go home now?" asked Emma in a small voice. "I'm hungry. And Mr. Oliver promised to read me a Russian fairy tale about a little girl and a magic hawk after tea."

Leaning low, Shannon set her heels to the big bay's flanks. "We shall fly, elf, as if we were on wings."

Chapter Twenty-one

*J*ervis was in a truly foul mood by the time they broke out of the trees and started around the loch. "That damn rabbit was close enough to kick," he snarled, sending several pebbles skittering across the footpath.

"Perhaps the cartridge misfired," suggested the comte.

Orlov allowed a small smile. Though in truth, there was little enough to laugh about. He felt a bit like the shards of stone, bouncing aimlessly about the moors. Yet another day spent in a wild goose chase. He stretched the tension from his shoulders, suddenly feeling weary to the bone. This hide-and-seek mission was taking its toll. He would be heartily glad when it was over.

Would he?

His step slowed at the thought of parting from Shannon. She would return to her Academy and await Lord Lynsley's next assignment, while he would go . . . God knows where. St. Petersburg, Baden-Baden, Vienna— wherever the glitter and gaiety offered a respite between Prince Yussapov's calls to duty. The tickle of fine champagne, the thrill of a torrid affair, the challenge of purloining some rich peer's baubles. A wild life, perhaps, but one that had always been perfectly suited to his temperament. Never linger long enough to care.

But he knew Shannon was no passing dalliance, no wanton whim.

His cynical words to Yussapov on settling down came back to him in mocking clarity. By nature, he had been a solitary beast all his life, and there was an old adage that said an old dog could not learn new tricks.

Yet Shannon had taught him more about loyalty and courage in the last few weeks than he had learned in a lifetime. And about love.

He cringed at the word, hearing Yussapov's roar of laughter ring in his ears. *Love.* He was tempted to laugh himself. But there was no denying the twinge in his heart, sharp as a knife, at the thought of never seeing Shannon again. Did she ever have leave from her duties? Would she consent to taking a week in the countryside with him, an interlude where they might talk about what the future could hold?

His mouth crept up at the corners. Maybe an old dog could manage to grovel. Or sit up and beg.

"You find something amusing, Mr. Oliver?" Jervis looked over at him, a dangerous glint in his eye. He had polished off one bottle of claret on the trek through the pines and was now well into a second—this one of brandy.

Alcohol added to anger and frustration was a volatile mix. Stirred from his own broodings, Orlov realized that the combination was now threatening to blow up in his face.

"Merely my own thoughts," he replied. There seemed no point in sparking a fight at this late hour in the day.

"Wipe that sly smirk off your face." Jervis suddenly swung his rifle around.

"*Attendez-vous,*" said the comte in a low voice. "You are tired, *mon ami*. We all are."

Jervis brushed him off. "What am I am tired of is this man's infuriating insolence." The hammer drew back with an audible click.

"Come now, surely you English, with your finely honed sense of honor, don't believe in shooting a man for smiling." De Villiers exaggerated a grin, looking to crack the tension with a joke.

"The cursed fellow ought to be taught a lesson in civilized manners," huffed Talcott. "He has been acting far too bold with his betters."

Orlov was suddenly keen to see just how far Jervis was willing to go. The comte was right—a man didn't murder someone over the curl of a mouth. Not unless his nerves were stretched to the point of snapping.

"Civilized manners?" He lifted a brow, adding an extra measure of sarcasm to his voice. "And which of you honorable gentlemen am I to look at as a paragon of manly perfection?"

A rush of fury flooded Jervis's face. "You dare to mock me, you cur?"

"Randall—"

Before the comte could stop him, Jervis shoved the rifle barrel hard against Orlov's chest and pulled the trigger.

The explosion drowned out De Villiers's cry. Sparks flashed, illuminating Talcott's look of mute shock.

Orlov looked down at his coat, and for a heartbeat no

one moved. The smell of gunpowder swirled as the shot echoed through the surrounding trees. He waited for another instant, then wrapped his hands around the smoking muzzle and smiled.

"Hartley!" gasped Jervis. "For the love of God, help!"

Wrenching the weapon from the gentleman's grip, Orlov pivoted and in the same motion swung the butt up, catching the valet with a blow to the head. Stunned, the man slumped to the ground.

Jervis turned in a panic, lunging for De Villiers's weapon. Orlov spun the rifle in his hands, a lethal blur of limbs and steel, and whipped around, slashing the barrel across Jervis's ribs.

No longer looking so lordly, Jervis sank to his knees, groaning.

Tossing aside the weapon, Orlov drew his hidden pistols. "Help your comrades to their feet," he ordered.

"S-spawn of Satan," stuttered Talcott. "No one but the Devil himself could survive a point-blank shot."

"Or someone who took the precaution of removing the bullets from your cartridges," answered Orlov. "But I assure you, my own barking irons have plenty of bite, so don't attempt anything rash."

"*Sacre coeur,* you sabotaged our shot and powder?" exclaimed the comte. "Why? What is going on?"

He seemed genuinely puzzled, but then, thought Orlov, D'Etienne would be capable of great cunning. A master of duplicity, deception. "That is exactly what I intend to find out." He took up position behind them, keeping a careful distance. "Hands on your heads, gentlemen. March."

The crunch of stones set a grim cadence for the walk through the walled gardens.

As the party rounded the corner of the courtyard, Orlov saw the lone bay standing by the front entrance, the remnants of a leather harness hanging from its flanks.

"Why, isn't that one of Sylvia's—" began Talcott.

"Quiet." Orlov felt every muscle clench. Had he made a fatal mistake by allowing Shannon to face the London ladies by herself? By now he ought to know that females could be formidable opponents. Far from being the weaker sex, they were capable of physical strength. *And diabolical cunning.* His mind began to race through the possibilities . . .

"Slowly now, and stay together." They crossed the courtyard, Orlov's mood turning more murderous with each step.

"Open the door." He gave a savage shove to Jervis as he slid a step to the side. If they were walking into a trap, let His Lordship take the full brunt of it. Indeed, he would almost welcome bullets or blades. It would save him from having to kill the man with his bare hands.

Jervis hesitated, but seemed to sense that the lesser of two evils lay behind the blackened oak. He took hold of the latch and swung it open.

Silence greeted them. The branch of candles stood in its usual spot on the sideboard, casting a whispery light over the deserted entrance hall. Orlov swept the room with a quick glance. Nothing seemed out of place.

"Monsieur," murmured De Villiers.

Orlov pressed one of his pistols to the back of the comte's head. "Not a word." With the other, he signaled for Jervis's servant to step into the small cloakroom beside the main corridor. The valet was but a pawn in whatever game was being played, but it was best to remove him from the board.

Still slightly dazed, the man made no protest as Orlov closed the door and turned the key.

"Now to the Tower," he ordered.

The open portal and darkened stairway sent a cold shiver up his spine. "Shannon," he shouted, deciding stealth served no further purpose. If the enemy was here, he was no doubt well aware of their presence.

His own hoarse voice, amplified by the mortared stone, was the only reply.

Talcott drew a ragged breath.

Footsteps suddenly sounded from above. "Mr. Oliver . . ."

Orlov felt the air leach from his lungs as Shannon took shape from the shadows. She was wearing her dowdy dress, but the collar was badly askew and muddied riding boots peeked out from beneath the hem.

"It appears that you, too, have had a spot of trouble."

"Is everyone all right?" he demanded, seeing the cuts on her cheeks.

She nodded. "Aside from a little wooziness from the drug in her tea, Lady Octavia is quite unharmed. As are the children." Her own weapon kept dead aim on the others. "But it was a near miss."

"Lady Sylvia," whispered Jervis, his face pale as death.

Shannon's lip curled in contempt. "I can't vouch for her safety. Or that of her friends. The moors can be even more dangerous at night."

"What happened?" asked Orlov.

She gave a terse account of Lady Sylvia's trickery and her ensuing chase. "I caught up with the coach just in the nick of time."

His heart skipped a beat as she calmly described the

attack. "I managed to hit him—no more than a flesh wound. He will be back."

"M-my sisters," moaned Talcott. "You cannot leave them out there to die."

"Damn," growled Orlov, a mixture of rage and relief giving his voice an odd edge. As she shot him a quick look, he had to restrain the urge to gather her in his arms and kiss the smudges of gunpowder and grit from her face. "I am tempted to let them suffer the consequences of their own chicanery."

Shannon gave a slight shake of her head.

"But I suppose we cannot in good conscience leave them to the mercy of the wilds," he finished. "No matter that it is what Lady Sylvia deserves."

"Better to collect them," agreed Shannon. "And then question everyone at the same time. It seems we are finally coming close to fitting this puzzle together."

Orlov nodded, though he could not shake a nagging feeling that some key piece was missing. "You can hold out a little longer by yourself?"

"Lady Octavia has the children settled in her quarters with hot chocolate and cakes. With the door barred they will be safe enough." Her eyes flashed with a hellfire light. "Don't worry about me. If our adversary thinks he can get under my guard, he has another lesson coming."

Orlov smiled in spite of himself. "If I were him, I would be quaking in my boots."

Talcott gave a nervous titter. "Lud, one would think you two were trained for the battlefield rather than the classroom."

Shannon silenced him with a quelling look.

"Come, I'll leave you to stand guard over these gentlemen in the drawing room. A fire is already laid in the hearth, and the double doors give you clear view of this corridor," said Orlov. Though loath to leave her alone, he had little choice. "I'll have Rawley bring some rope, if you wish to ensure that they don't cause any trouble."

"I sent Rawley and the others away to the village with the gardeners," she replied. She gave a thin smile. "I am sure our London visitors will comport themselves like perfect gentlemen."

"Else they will answer to me." He signaled for the men to turn around. "Be advised that any transgression will be punished with more than a birch to the backside."

"Take care, Alex," she said softly. "A wounded predator is even more cautious. And cunning."

He touched her cheek, a gesture so swift that it was lost in the half light of the fading day. "Two against one—I like our odds, *golub.*"

"Help yourselves to some brandy." Shannon chose a vantage point by the sofa. "Then perhaps one of you would be so good as to light the fire."

De Villiers went to the sideboard and poured a glass. Jervis joined him. Talcott made a half-hearted attempt with the flint and steel, but his hands were shaking too badly to strike a spark.

"Sorry," he mumbled, seeking to still the tremors with a splash of Scottish whisky.

Sighing, she set aside her pistol and took up a taper. She was halfway to the hearth when Jervis suddenly broke away from the two other gentlemen and snatched a sword from the wall. With a menacing slash, he advanced toward her.

"Out of my way. I had nothing to do with what happened this afternoon—if Sylvia made a change in plans, let her answer for it. I don't intend to wait around for any magistrates."

Shannon quickly reached for one of the rapiers on display and blocked his path to the door. "You aren't going anywhere, Lord Jervis."

"Don't try to be a bloody hero, Miss Sloane." Seeing he was cornered added a note of shrillness to his voice. "I don't want to hurt you, but I swear, I won't hesitate to use this if I must." He wet his lips. "I've trained with Ludwig von Mulenberg, the renowned Prussian swordmaster. So trust me, you will only end up as mincemeat if you dare to stand in my way."

"Von Mulenberg?" The stones suddenly echoed with the clash of steel against steel. "He couldn't cut his way out of butter with a hot blade."

Jervis fell back a step under the force of her attack. Sliding sideways, he feinted, then sought to slash her sword arm.

Shannon parried the blow with ease. "You will have to muster a more imaginative combination than that, sir."

His eyes betrayed a flicker of confusion. "Who the devil *are* you?"

"No one you should wish to toy with." Her blade cut a deadly *arrebata* through the air. "Sit down, Lord Jervis, while your legs are still attached to your torso."

A tentative *punta sopramano* probed for an opening. She countered with a spinning combination that nearly knocked the sword from his hand. "*You* ought to be the one wearing skirts."

Swearing furiously, he lunged forward, the point of his weapon aimed straight at her heart.

A deft twist of her wrist deflected the blade. Before Jervis could recover his balance, she angled a hard kick

that knocked him to his knees. A flurry of lightning cuts
flashed out, and a last sharp slash sent the sword flying
from his grasp.

He stumbled back against the wall. Sweat had plas-
tered his fashionable curls to his forehead, and his air of
arrogance had dissolved into a look of stunned disbelief.

"Go back with the others, Lord Jervis." Lowering her
weapon, Shannon had already begun to think on what
other precautions she might take in order to secure the
castle from attack. As she had told Orlov, she had no illusion that a flesh wound had driven D'Etienne off. If
anything, it would be a pique to his pride.

Mano a mano. The Frenchman was not used to losing
a one-on-one fight to anyone, much less a female.

As she turned, she saw Jervis's eyes still darting about
in desperation. Spotting her pistol atop the curio cabinet,
he made a run for it.

Damn. There was no chance to catch him.

A whirlwind spin set her skirts aswirl. Whipping the
knife from her boot, she threw it in the same deadly motion. A silvery blur, a lethal whisper—like a hawk, it flew
through the air with unerring accuracy.

Thwack. Its point cut through flesh and bone, pinning
Jervis's hand to the wood.

He screamed in pain and crumpled, arms splayed,
upon the inlaid mahogany.

Shannon was on him in a flash. "Stop whimpering like
a stuck pig," she muttered, yanking out the still-quivering
steel and hauling him to his feet. A shake of his collar
strangled his moans. "You'll live."

"I am glad I did not decide to attempt any liberties
with your person, Mademoiselle Sloane." De Villiers
shifted his stance against the stone, his expression un-

readable. "I was not aware that hand-to-hand combat was part of the basic curriculum for English governesses. Perhaps the Prince Regent should consider forming a special regiment—"

"Save your *bon mots* for some other time," snapped Shannon. She shoved Jervis toward the comte. "Bind up his hand, before he bleeds all over the expensive carpet."

Talcott made a small retching sound and pressed his handkerchief to his quivering lips. "God Almighty. She is quite mad."

"On the contrary, she is quite *magnifique,*" murmured the comte.

"I doubt you will think so in a moment." She motioned to a set of heavy oak straightback chairs set along the wall. "Have a seat, all of you."

They did as she ordered, though Talcott had to help a half-dazed Jervis to his place. Once there, Jervis slumped against his friend with a low groan—a sound promptly echoed by the other man. Shannon turned in disgust. She would get nothing coherent out of them for the moment, she decided.

The comte was a different story. He had remained remarkably cool throughout the fight. Perhaps too cool. It was time to test his Gallic *joie de vivre*—if he wished to live for another day, he was going to give some honest answers.

"Alors." Flicking with a lethal grace, her swordpoint sliced off the two tails of his neckcloth. As the linen floated to the floor, the steel kissed De Villiers's neck. "How do you fit into this sordid plot?" she demanded.

The comte didn't flinch. "As naught but an observer, mademoiselle."

"You like to watch innocent children be murdered?" Her voice was deceptively soft.

He stiffened. "I have seen far too many people marched to the guillotine to take any pleasure in bloodshed, mademoiselle. The street of Paris were often awash in crimson—a sickening sight that any civilized man should be ashamed of."

"So you deny that you are working with one of your countrymen—a man by the name of D'Etienne?"

"I am not familiar with the person in question. Who is he?"

"You are in no position to ask the questions." Shannon drew the blade across his throat. "If you are not in league with him, or Lady Sylvia, then why did you come to Scotland?"

"To be honest, I was a bit bored in London. English Society is rather dull—the fashions are gauche, the food is terrible, and the ladies have little *savoir faire*." He made a wry face. "When Lady Sylvia suggested I accompany her party to Scotland, it seemed like a chance for a little adventure."

"So you claim you are innocent of any intrigue." Though Shannon was inclined to believe him, she pressed the point. "Prove it."

"I cannot." De Villiers shrugged. "So I suppose you will simply have to go ahead and kill me."

It was hard not to admire such *sangfroid*. "You seem awfully nonchalant about the prospect."

"Merely a bit cynical," he replied. "Having escaped from the Terror by the skin of my teeth, I consider that I am living on borrowed time. I should not like to shuffle off my mortal coil, but if I must, I shall try to do it with a show of grace."

"I am not as ruthless as Robespierre." She drew back her blade. "I shall give you the benefit of the doubt."

He released his breath in an audible sigh. *"Merci."*

"De rien."

He laughed. "My previous offer still stands. In fact, I am tempted to make it a proposal of matrimony."

"I'm married to my job," she replied with a twitch of her lips. "But thank you all the same."

"Teaching children their lessons seems such a sad waste of your talents, mademoiselle."

She winked. "But as you see, sometimes I get to spank the naughty adults."

Chapter Twenty-two

*O*rlov herded the distraught ladies into the drawing room, feeling rather like a harried border collie trying to keep a bunch of frightened lambs under control. The torrent of tears had made him appreciate Shannon's stoic courage even more. For all their fancy airs and graces, highborn ladies could use a lesson in true nobility.

"Randall!" Lady Sylvia clutched at her sodden skirts. Her black hair, wet with rain, had come loose from its pins, and hung heavy around her pale face. She looked like a drowned crow. And sounded even worse. "Do something!" she screeched.

Jervis sank a bit lower in his chair.

"He's not feeling up to polite conversation," said Shannon.

"I need some laudanum," he croaked. He held up the wrapping of blood-stained linen. "She nearly cut off my hand."

"Only a finger or two," she murmured.

Orlov's mouth twitched as Lady Sylvia's lips formed

an O of horror. She sat down rather heavily on the chair next to her friend.

"Now that we are all together, milady, I suggest you tell me what is going on, and without delay," said Orlov. "Otherwise, I shall have to turn the interrogation over to Miss Sloane."

Lady Sylvia shrank back. "No, no, I'll tell you everything!" She took a gulp of air. "I admit that we came here planning to kidnap the children. Randall helped me think of it . . ."

Jervis made a feeble protest.

"But I swear, we never meant them any harm. You two added an unwelcome complication. At first, we were not sure what to do. Then Randall came up with the idea of asking you to join the hunting party. He was to keep you out on the moors for the day while I found a way to spirit the children away from their grandmother and Miss Sloane."

"Drugging an elderly lady was a dangerous move," said Shannon. "You could have stopped her heart."

"It was only a few drops," said Lady Sylvia.

"Why go to all the trouble?" he asked, though he could guess the answer.

"I need money. Desperately." She looked at Orlov with pleading eyes. "My debts in Town were mounting and my creditors were growing more impatient. You have no idea how clutch-fisted my aunt is. Just because *she* was shunned by Society, she has no sympathy for the great expense required to be part of the *beau monde*. I was left with no other choice."

Sensing the coldness of his stare, Lady Sylvia left off the litany of complaints. After a moment of silence, she went on.

"It was all meant to be harmless. Disguised so that Helen and Annabelle wouldn't recognize him, Randall's valet was to stop the coach and take the children to an abandoned gamekeeper's cottage that we discovered during our morning rides. A ransom note would follow, instructing Lady Octavia where to leave the money. The amount was not so very great—and by handling all the details of the exchange we thought to gain her good graces as well." She bit her lip. "It all seemed so simple on paper. You must believe me that we never planned to use any weapons. I swear, I have never seen the fellow who attacked the carriage."

"And yet, your coachman lies murdered in cold blood." Orlov frowned. "It seems too much of a coincidence that some stranger chose your carriage out of the blue. Did anyone else know of your plans?"

A sudden hiccup from Annabelle drew his attention. An unpleasant sensation skated up his spine.

"Miss Annabelle?" he said softly. "Have you something to say?"

The girl looked scared to death by the mention of a killer. "No, no, no, it couldn't be," she stammered. "He's *a gentleman.*"

Shannon swore under her breath, echoing his own sentiments.

"The gentleman you were secretly meeting in the woods? Lord . . . Nobody?"

Talcott roused himself enough to snarl at Helen. "*You* were supposed to be keeping an eye on the chit, not letting some Yorkshire looby lift her skirts."

"I'm bloody tired of trying to keep scandal from our door. *You* try taking some responsibility for this mess, rather than reaching for a bottle of brandy or a deck of cards."

They eyed each other with mutual loathing, too exhausted to continue the fight. No doubt it would resume again, now that the first overt salvo had been fired, thought Orlov. It was about time that Helen mustered the backbone to stand up for herself.

But that Talcott skirmish was not the main battle. He looked back to Annabelle and nodded for her to continue.

She dabbed at her red-rimmed eyes. "Y-yes. He said he wanted to m-marry me. But first he needed to wrest his rightful inheritance from that spiteful old bat, Lady Octavia. He never said anything about m-murder!"

"Lady Octavia?" repeated Shannon, her expression turning incredulous.

"Yes. You see, she is his grandfather's sister, and a clutch-fisted miser who has kept a generous bequest from dear Stephen . . ." It took much stuttering and gulping, but the story finally came out—a woeful tale of an impoverished gentleman, denied his due by a rich, spiteful dowager. All her swain needed was his true love to help right a wrong in order to have a fairy tale ending.

"He was working out a plan to take the children, and then return them in exchange for the money that was rightfully his. So when I heard last night that Sylvia meant to bring the children along on our ride to the abbey, I left a note for him in our secret spot, telling him of the outing . . ."

Shannon's disbelief grew more evident with each tearful word. "For god's sake, you have been reading far too many horrid novels," she finally snapped, cutting short the last, woeful wail.

"Stephen," muttered Orlov, trying to sharpen the vague stirring of disquiet hovering at the edge of his conscious thought. "He called himself Stephen."

"Etienne in French," offered the comte. "Is that not the name you mentioned earlier, Mademoiselle Sloane?"

"D'Etienne," said Shannon.

Everything suddenly snapped into focus.

"Damn! How could I have missed—"

Before he could finish, Orlov found himself thrown against a glass-front cabinet as a deafening explosion rocked the room. Shards crackling under his boots, he skidded across the floor to where Shannon lay wrestling with a large marble plinth that had fallen on her leg.

"Are you all right?"

She nodded, though her face was a mask of pain. "The Tower—we must get to the Tower."

He helped her up. Through the first swirls of acrid smoke, he saw that Jervis had been knocked unconscious by a section of ceiling molding. The ladies—for once mercifully silent—were huddled in a circle, while Talcott had taken cover under a chair. Only the comte, his face dusted with crumbled plaster, was making any attempt to clear away the debris.

"De Villiers!" cried Orlov over the rumble of a second blast. "The carriage is still outside. Gather your friends and servants and try to make your way to Boath. Alert the authorities there!"

The comte signaled his understanding.

"Alex!"

He jumped aside at Shannon's warning, just as a ceiling timber came crashing down.

"Come on!" She paused just long enough to take down a small crossbow from the wall of weaponry. "This way!"

The corridor was filled with a black, billowing smoke. Mixed with the moonlight, it had a strange, otherworldly luminance. Beautiful but deadly. Tearing his gaze from the spectral sight, he saw Shannon was limping.

"It's not so bad," she said, catching his glance. "Bruised, I think, not broken." She quickened her pace. "Hurry."

"A moment." Orlov caught her sleeve and spun her around into his arms. He held her for a heartbeat, brushing his lips to her cut cheek. She tasted of smoke and salt, of blood and valor. *"Ya lublu tebya."*

Her singed lashes fluttered, hiding her eyes.

Had she heard him? The words "I love you" were so foreign on his tongue that he wasn't even sure he had spoken aloud.

"We must hurry," she repeated.

He took her hand and broke into a run.

The oaken door to the tower stairs was still intact and locked from within. A good sign, hoped Orlov, as he pounded on the paneling. "Lady Octavia! Open up!"

The deadbolt slid back. "About time, young man. I was beginning to think I would have to take matters into my own hands." The dowager, her walking stick held at the ready, had possessed enough presence of mind to bring the children down to the first-floor parlor.

"It sounds like one of Uncle Angus's experiments," said Emma.

"Or the broadside of a pirate ship. Are we under attack, Mr. Oliver?" asked Prescott.

"Aye, lad," he answered grimly. "But the boarders will soon see they are no match for our crew." He felt his pockets. One pistol, and a blade in his boot. Added to the dowager's stick and the medieval mechanism in

Shannon's hands, it was not much of a match for the enemy's firepower.

As if reading his thoughts, Shannon said, "The first order of business is to get the children and Lady Octavia to a safe place."

"Right." Ignoring the dowager's snort of protest, Orlov thought for a moment. "We'll head back through the kitchen and out to the gardens. They can take shelter in the root cellar while we circle back to finish the fight." He was already making a mental calculation of the distance. He should be able to carry both children and still help Lady Octavia, if need be.

But as he reopened the door, a wall of flames drove him back. "Bloody hell," he swore over the heated roar of sparks. "He's used naphtha."

"Greek fire," muttered Shannon. "Damn, we've no hope of extinguishing it. Not with the resources at hand." She eyed the way leading back up to the dowager's quarters. "We can't stay here—the smoke and heat will soon be overpowering. Much as I hate to say it, I don't see any alternative but to retreat to the upper floors."

"Wait! There is a hidden set of stairs leading to the cellar behind the far bookcase," piped up Lady Octavia. "The first laird was a Papist and built this castle with a number of secret priest holes and escape routes."

"God bless him," murmured Orlov, wiping the smear of soot and sweat from his brow. "Show me where."

"All the doors in this section of the cellar are locked shut," reminded Shannon. "We made sure no one could break in—or out. Even the connecting passages have been closed off. The forged steel is made to military specifications. It won't yield to picks or hammers. Without the keys we will be trapped."

"Perhaps not," replied the dowager. "We will come out in the area Angus used as a workroom and wine cellar. If you shift the casks of ale, you will find an iron grating that can be removed with a knife blade. Behind it, there is an underground passageway that leads to a trapdoor by the edge of the lower terrace."

"How on earth did you discover that?" asked Shannon.

"With two mischievous lads to keep track of, I daresay I know every nook and cranny of this place." She tapped her walking stick on two of the intertwined acanthus leaves carved into the molding. "Press here, Mr. Oliver, and here. It takes a bit more muscle than I possess these days."

He did as he was bade, and a section of shelving slowly pivoted on groaning hinges, revealing a sliver of space between the tiers of waxed wood.

"Quickly now," urged Orlov. A noxious smoke was already seeping into the room. He helped the others to squeeze through, then hit the molding again and ducked inside.

Setting down the weapon she had grabbed from the medieval display, Shannon loosened her bodice and fumbled for the candle she had stuck inside her shirt. The layers of wool and linen were a cursed encumbrance. Her leg was aching, and the tangle of singed skirts was only slowing her down. As the wick flared to life from the spark of her flint, she stripped off her gown and tossed it aside.

Orlov paused in passing to eye her snug-fitting buckskins. "Has anyone told you how lovely you look in leather?"

"Stop ogling my legs and pry that lock off the gate to the wine cellar."

"I would rather drink my fill of your luscious form." His light laugh tickled at her ear. *Soft, sensuous.* Too sensuous. She needed to keep her mind on military tactics, not the way his lips had felt on her scraped cheek, whispering a few words. Strange, but for a fleeting moment back in the corridor, she thought he had said . . .

Amidst all the crackle and thunder, she must have misheard his murmur. Alexandr Orlov had made no bones about his aversion to emotional entanglements. They were friends, yes, and lovers. But when the smoke cleared, he would drift off to some new adventure, some new mistress.

She drew back. "Linger too long in flirtation, and we all may end up with our throats cut."

"A sobering thought." Orlov looked around the aureole of light cast by the candle. Spotting a length of iron lying among a jumble of old wood balusters, he grabbed it up and thrust it through the iron loop. A quick twist and the hasp snapped open.

"Scottie, come hold this flame aloft," he called.

Shannon handed over the candle to the lad and moved awkwardly to Orlov's side. Together they shifted the barrels of ale away from the wall. The grate was thick with rust and the tunnel entrance was covered in cobwebs and mouse droppings. Peering closer, she saw the passageway was barely more than a crawl space.

"When was the last time this was used?"

"A number of years ago," admitted the dowager.

"I don't like the looks of it," she said slowly. "In a wet climate such as this, the earth is likely to be unstable. The smallest bump could cause it to collapse."

Orlov loosened the last screw and set the metal covering aside. "It looks to be carved out of rock," he called as he dropped to his belly and slithered inside. His voice sounded strangely muffled, as if swathed in silk rather than stone. "An easy traverse. The distance can't be very great."

"Alex, come out of there," she snapped. It was, she knew, unreasonable to feel so uneasy. "At once."

He reappeared a moment later, his hair matted with mud and several substances she did not care to identify. "What's amiss?"

"I—I am not sure." She shifted her stance, feeling a fool. Lud, her nerves were so jumpy that it seemed the earth was moving under her feet. She eased the weight off her injured leg, hoping to steady her thoughts. But the tremors grew more pronounced. An ominous rumbling, like the thunder of fast-approaching stormclouds, reverberated off the walls.

Her knee buckled as the force of a deafening explosion pitched her forward. Orlov caught her and took the brunt of the blow as they fell against the iron gate. Smoke and ash billowed from the tunnel, the acrid smell of burnt chemicals mixing with the earthier scent of decayed leaves. The sound deadened to a dull roaring in her ears.

"Lady Octavia!" It took a moment for the gun-gray swirls to dissipate.

"Here!" Her silvery head bobbed up from under the workbench. "And all in one piece."

"We all are, thanks to Shannon," said Orlov. "How did you know?"

She couldn't explain it, not even to herself. "I sensed you were in danger."

"A magical Merlin," he murmured. His fingers twined

in the delicate chain around her throat, caressing the silver hawk. "It seems you are my lucky charm."

Her pulse thudded against his palm. The thought of how close she had come to losing him made her shudder.

"D'Etienne obviously had a chance to make a careful survey of the terraces while we were otherwise engaged," said Orlov in a louder voice. "His eye doesn't miss much."

The reminder sent a shiver down her spine.

"Sit down," murmured Orlov. "Your leg needs a rest." He dusted a corner of the workbench.

"I don't need to—"

"Sit!" he commanded. "Or must I sweep you off your feet?"

Shannon perched a hip on the scarred wood.

Orlov leaned in, his hand resting lightly on her thigh. His touch had come to feel like a part of her. When this mission was over . . .

She would worry about that when the time came. *If* the time came. Despite the bantering humor, she had seen in Orlov's eyes that he, too, recognized the seriousness of the situation. It seemed that D'Etienne had switched tactics. He was no longer concerned with taking the children alive.

Her hands fisted in frustration. Their own expertise had come back to haunt them. With the tunnel sealed off, they had no way out.

D'Etienne could break his way in. But why would he bother to risk a hand-to-hand confrontation? It would be hours before any help could be mustered from the village. Given his deadly skill with explosives, he could take his time in setting a number of charges that would bring this part of the castle crashing down on their heads.

Dismay must have shown on her face, for Orlov began to whistle a spirited tune. *Handel. Music for Royal Fireworks.*

She felt her eyes light with silent laughter.

"Don't be alarmed, Lady Octavia," he said in between stanzas. "We shall find a way out of here, if I have to dig our way to China with a teaspoon." He took a turn around the perimeter of the workroom, pausing at the door leading out to the firewood shed.

"Alarmed? Hmmph." The dowager had lost her stick but not her doughty resolve. "If he imagines he can frighten the mother of Angus McAllister with a paltry display of fireworks, he can think again."

Emma shook the soot from her braid. "Uncle's pyrotechnics make a much louder bang," she said with some pride.

"That's because he takes special care preparing the ingredients," added Prescott. "He says it is an art as well as a science."

An all-too-lethal art. Shannon watched as Orlov probed at the latch and the thick doorframe with his knife.

"No use," he said without looking up. "It would take a strong explosion to knock the door off its hinges." He shook his head before she could ask. "I have only a small bit of powder for the pistol. Not even enough to make a dent in the oak."

Prescott cleared his throat. "Mr. Oliver?"

"Yes, lad?"

"Would it help if we could make up a batch of our own gunpowder?"

"It would help a great deal."

"I've seen where Uncle Angus keeps a supply of saltpeter, sulfur, and charcoal."

"And where he hides the key to the lockbox," chimed in Emma. "Though we're not supposed to know he has such things in the castle." She bit her lip. "I know we were wrong to peek. Will Uncle birch us?"

"Don't make a habit of spying," said Shannon. McAllister had obviously taken a great deal of trouble to hide the hazardous material from his nephew and niece. However, he ought to have remembered from his own hairraising exploits that children had an uncanny knack for uncovering secrets. "But in this case, I think we may show a little leniency."

The siblings looked greatly relieved.

"The case is stored in the crate marked 'Wool.'" Prescott pointed to a workbench piled high with assorted boxes and baskets. "The key is tucked inside the glove on the wall."

Orlov dug a large iron box out from its sheepskin wrappings while Shannon took the old hawking gauntlet from its hook. It was stiff with age, but sure enough, when she turned it upside down and shook it, a small brass key fell out.

The oiled lock on the box opened with a soft snick. A marble mortar and pestle, much blackened from use, lay beside three brass canisters.

Saltpeter. Sulfur. Charcoal. The Chinese called their invention "firedrug," a potent elixir of *ying* and *yang*— the cool essence of the female mixed with the hot spark of the male. *Fire and ice.* Shannon felt a bit giddy with hope that such alchemy would be their salvation.

"I've never actually made my own powder," murmured Orlov. "Have you?"

"It was a basic requirement in my school," she replied. "We were put through a rigorous course of study."

"I should like to attend *that* school," said Emma from her seat in the shadows. "Rather than the horrid places that Mrs. Kelso describes, where young ladies must learn things like how to curtsey to a duke."

Shannon smiled as she broke up a piece of charred willowbark and began to grind it to a fine powder. "Mr. Oliver and I will talk to your father about what school would be best for you, elf, if ever he feels you should be sent to a boarding school."

"Is there a school for pirates?" asked Prescott hopefully. "The curate says all lords must go to Eton for their education, but it sounds very boring."

"I have some other recommendations I shall discuss with your Papa, lad," replied Orlov. He watched her open the sulfur canister and add several pinches of the pungent yellow substance to the pestle. His tone turned a bit more tentative. "I trust you received a passing grade."

"I wouldn't be here if I had failed." Shannon looked up to find the children had crept closer to the table and were watching the procedure with great interest. Giving silent thanks for their eccentric upbringing, she decided that a lesson might be the best way to keep their attention occupied. They were, after all, a captive audience, so to speak.

"What I'm doing here is combining these three ingredients—charcoal, saltpeter, and sulfur—in just the right proportions to make an explosion strong enough to blow the shed door from its hinges."

The children nodded solemnly.

"It was the Chinese who invented gunpowder, you

know," she continued. "For centuries it was used for magic tricks and celebrations."

"While Western civilization decided to put it to a more practical use," said Orlov dryly.

"The Chinese experimented with its use in warfare, too," replied Shannon. "They created fire arrows, rockets, and incendiary bombs for their catapults." She took a moment to make an inventory of the other items in the lockbox. Fuses, a wad of sticky pine resin, an oval corning screen—all the basics were there.

"And cannons," said Prescott. "Uncle Angus said one of the very first ones was called the 'Nine-Arrow-Heart-Piercing-Magic-Poison Thunderous Fire Erupter.' "

"But it was quite crude," commented Emma.

"Quite," repeated Shannon. Molding the pine resin into a squat cylinder, she lit it with the guttering stub of the candle. The substance would burn brighter and longer than wax. "Will you pass me the saltpeter, elf?" She reached for a measuring spoon. "One of the first great European battles won with the help of gunpowder was Crecy, where King Edward III used his new firepower to rout the French knights."

Prescott mustered a martial scowl. "We will beat them this time, too. Though Uncle Angus says Napoleon is a very clever general, because he was first an artillery officer."

"He's not nearly as clever as your uncle," said Orlov. "Or Miss Sloane. As you see, Scottie, females are every bit as capable of military prowess as men." Leaning back on his elbows, he waggled a brow. "Perhaps we ought to retreat to the wine cellar and uncork a fine claret, seeing as the ladies are doing all the hard work."

The lad's eyes lit up. "Or a bottle of rum?"

Shannon rolled her eyes at Orlov. "Be grateful I did not order you to drain McAllister's brandy collection and then piss in a pot."

His arms nearly slipped out from under him. *"What!"*

"I'm deadly serious." She kept up her grinding. "The best gunpowder is said to be made from the chamberpots of bishops who imbibe brandy. The contents were boiled down for the nitrates and then . . . never mind the rest of the details."

"Thank god," he muttered. "If celibacy is part of the mix, we would have been doomed."

"What's celerbercy?" asked Emma. "Does Uncle put it in his powder?"

"I would rather you didn't ask him," said Shannon quickly, slanting a reproving look at Orlov. His look of unholy amusement had returned.

"Forgive me for raising another uncomfortable question, but ought we try to stop the smoke that is coming in under the door?" Lady Octavia, who had been unnaturally quiet for the last little while, pointed to the thick white fingers of vapor that were creeping in from under the doorway to the woodshed terrace. "It has a most unpleasant smell."

"Damn." Wiping the smile from his face, Orlov pulled off his coat and stuffed it in around the crack. *"Sal ammoniac,"* he muttered after a tentative sniff set him to coughing.

A powerful poison, used in early smoke bombs. Shannon's lips set in a grim line as she hurried her final preparations. So D'Etienne was also well-schooled in the alchemy of death.

"Find a metal container and cover," she said to Orlov. "Something heavy."

"Are you going to blast the bastard to Kingdom Come?" demanded Prescott in a muffled voice. The dowager had gathered the children and covered their faces with the silk skirting of her gown.

"First we are going to try to blow this door open, Scottie." Deciding to overlook the lad's bad language, Shannon scooped out a small indentation in the earthen floor by the outer door. "Then we will deal with the, er, bad—"

"The bastard won't stand a chance against Miss Sloane. She will gut him like a lake trout if she gets her hands on him," said Lady Octavia through the lace of her handkerchief. "I hope you will allow me to hand you the fillet knife."

"For now, would you mind tossing me the coil of matchfuse by your elbow? And Scottie, will you please fetch the crossbow I left by the foot of the secret steps?"

"Would that you had grabbed a blunderbuss from the wall," quipped Lady Octavia. "I fear that old-fashioned arrows aren't going to be much good against the Frenchman's firepower."

Shannon kept up her grinding. "One never knows."

"Speaking of firepower, have we a plan, once we blow the door open?" asked the dowager.

"Our original idea still seems the safest bet. Mr. Oliver will help you and the children to the shelter of the root cellar, while I create a diversion to draw D'Etienne's attention."

"I was beginning to think I was considered quite superfluous here," drawled Orlov. His tone was nonchalant but his movements were swift, sure.

"Men have some useful purposes." She grinned, in spite of the fact that her lips were so encrusted in cordite they felt about to crack.

Orlov grinned back, a half-moon sliver of pearly white against the blackness of the cellar walls.

"I am glad to see you have finally discovered that, Miss Sloane." Lady Octavia chortled. "I was beginning to worry about you."

She hoped the coating of black powder on her face was thick enough to hide her blush. Did the dowager know of their new intimacy? Or was it merely a shot in the dark?

Shifting the light closer to her work, Shannon ducked down to examine the texture. Not perfect, but it would do. "Any luck with a container?"

A cast-off cooking pot thunked down upon the work-table. The handle was broken but the walls were over a quarter-inch in thickness. "I found a roll of baling wire as well," added Orlov. "Once everything is ready, I'll make sure the lid is tied on tight as a drum."

"Excellent."

He cut off a length of the fuse. "Thirty seconds?"

"More than enough time." She emptied the contents of the mortar into the pot. "Lady Octavia, kindly take the children into the wine cellar and take cover behind the ale casks. We shall join you momentarily."

Moving to the doorway, Orlov made a few quick measurements. "I've moved your hole slightly to the left and added an inch of depth," he said as he returned to wire the lid in place.

After a few mental calculations, she nodded.

He carried it over and positioned it in place, carefully patting the dirt around the base. The fuse lay like a languid snake upon the earthen floor, waiting for a spark to ignite its strike.

"Ready when you are."

Shannon drew in a deep breath, and set the flame to the tail.

Chapter Twenty-three

*T*he silence seemed to go on forever.

Orlov held his breath, trying to hear the hiss of burning cordite above the pounding of his heart. Was the air too damp? The fuse too old? A myriad of things could go wrong.

His palms flattened against the rough wood as he ventured a peek around the barrels. *Fifteen . . . sixteen . . . seventeen . . .* Shannon shifted, too, her shoulder tensed against his.

"Damn, perhaps the spark did not catch."

He held her back, still mouthing the silent count.

She tried to wiggle free. Limned in the light of the burning resin, her profile had a Mars-like glow. A Warrior Queen, unflinching, unafraid of anything but her own imagined weaknesses. "The fuse may have fallen—"

The *BOOM* threw them back against the wall. Above their heads, bottles shattered, filling the air with flying glass and spattered wine.

"A pity to waste such a lovely Moselle," muttered

Orlov as he shielded his pistol from the drops. Shoving Shannon aside, he sprang up and raced for the gap in the wall. He had a plan of his own for dealing with the Frenchman.

He forced his pace to slow as he edged through the smoking remains of the doorway and up the stone stairs. Red-hot embers crunched underfoot, in stark contrast to the ice-cold fury he felt for the man who would murder innocent women and children.

No misstep now, he warned himself. Sliding out from the archway, he crept along the weathered retaining wall cut into the sloping ground. Ahead was a small, steep-roofed storage shed for firewood, set in the shadows of the narrow scullery terrace. Granite stairs led up to the yet another expanse of stone.

Cat-and-mouse. Time to see who was the predator and who was the prey.

Picking his way around the smoldering debris, Orlov paused to look back. No sign of the others. As he had hoped, Shannon was slowed by the need to sort out the confusion and assist the elderly dowager and the children. It would likely take her several more minutes to emerge from the cloudy chaos. By which time he was determined to engage the enemy alone.

No more need for stealth. Orlov gauged the numbers of steps to the far set of stairs, then decided on a direct challenge to draw D'Etienne into the open.

"As you see, your cowardly way of murder did not succeed, *mon vieux*," he called. "Do you dare meet me man to man, or are you only capable of fighting women and children from afar?"

His words echoed dully off the sooty stones.

"Ah, well, I suppose I, too, would be afraid to show

my face if I had been bested in hand-to-hand combat by a female." He paused. "Perhaps you are losing your edge."

A laugh floated down from mist-shrouded terraces above. "I am sharp enough to send you to *le diable,* monsieur. And mademoiselle as well. A pity I must do it quickly, rather than make you suffer for all the trouble you have caused me."

Orlov strained to see any sign of movement in the swirl of smoke and shadows. It was nearly nightfall and the fading twilight had blanketed the moors with a purpled haze. The fires burning in the castle tower added a scudding of charcoal clouds that deadened any sound of footfalls.

"Rather, it is *you* who have been most annoying. You have made me chase you across Ireland and now Scotland. It's grown most tiresome."

The scrape of a boot, almost lost in the crackle of burning wood, sounded from overhead. Orlov allowed an inward smile as he crept a step closer to the shed. From behind its shelter, he could gain an angle—

A pattering behind him caused him to whirl around.

"Mr. Oliver!" He watched in dismay as Emma bolted past Shannon, her little fists outstretched. "You forgot your knife!"

"Go back, elf!" But he saw his shout was too late—a wink of steel flashed at the terrace railing.

Flinging himself at the racing child, he caught her in a rolling hug. One turn, two. A bullet whizzed by his ear, cutting a furrow through the slate tile. All was a blur of flailing limbs and flapping skirts. Somehow he managed to push Emma clear, into the sheltering safety of the shed wall.

In making the desperate lunge, he had lost hold of his pistol. It lay not far away, scant inches from his reach, but as he stretched out to grab it, everything went black.

"Emma!"

Between lighting the way for Lady Octavia and loosening the cord of the crossbow, Shannon had momentarily let her grip on the little girl's hand slip.

Orlov reacted in a flash, shielding Emma's skinny form with his own body. They hit the ground at the same instant that a shot rang out. The flare from the muzzle illuminated a lean face—a high forehead, aquiline nose, and full lips pulled taut—before darkness swallowed the feral smile.

"Stay back, Scottie." Shannon caught the boy's collar and thrust him back into the dowager's grasp. "Guard your grandmother."

Cursing her limp, she hurried up the last step. The reddish glow from the tower windows showed D'Etienne as a slim black shape, moving with hellish precision as he took aim with one of the marble urns and launched it at Orlov.

It hit with a sickening thud and shattered just inches from his head. He appeared stunned by the shards of flying rock, for after a spasm of his fist, he lay unmoving on the terrace.

Emma cried out, her high-pitched voice punctuated by the Frenchman's deep laugh.

"It's *you* who have grown too dull for this sort of work, *mon ami*." D'Etienne was taking his time in reloading his pistol for the *coup de grace*. He had his back angled to her, and in the swirl of mist and moonlight she could just make out the heavy rucksack slung over his shoulders.

Damn. Setting down the makeshift resin candle, Shannon sighted along the stock of the ancient crossbow, desperately searching for a clear shot. But the thick canvas—bulging with enough explosives to blow half the Highlands into the North Sea—served as a shield.

"Having a heart is a fatal weakness," called D'Etienne. Still gloating, the Frenchman rammed a fresh bullet down the barrel. "*Moi*, I don't dwell on the fine points of morality. A skilled banker or artist is paid for his expertise—why should I not profit from my god-given talents as well, eh? The Emperor is extremely generous in rewarding merit over rank or privilege." In another moment, he would curl his finger around the trigger.

Though her own hands were shaking, Shannon fought off despair. Surely there was some strategy from all her training. Sun-Tzu, the Chinese military master—

Chinese. Something from her earlier history lecture suddenly sparked an idea. She grabbed the flaming pine resin, jabbed it onto the point of her arrow, and let fly.

The small dart barely made a sound as it bit into the canvas. The Frenchman must have felt a quiver, for he whirled around.

Shannon dropped the crossbow and backed up a step.

D'Etienne laughed again. He took up a deliberate stance atop the terrace railing. "English archers may have won the Battle of Agincourt. But this is a new age, a new dawn . . ." A flicker of light, white then pink, rose from behind his head.

Shannon held her breath.

Suddenly aware of the danger, D'Etienne spun round and round, arms flailing, dancing a macabre ballet as he tried to peel off the rucksack and its deadly contents.

A last pirouette exploded in an ear-splitting boom,

followed by a burst of brilliant light. Flames shot up, red and orange streaks against the black velvet sky. A shower of white-hot gold sparks, glittering like a myriad lethal little stars, hung for a moment in silent splendor before slowly drifting back down to earth.

"Bravo!" From the ruins of the stairwell came Lady Octavia's applause. "Bravo, gel! I've witnessed countless pyrotechnics over the years, but none so deserving of accolades as that one."

Orlov stirred and sat up. "High praise indeed, coming from the mother of Angus McAllister." His face was streaked with blood from the cut on his brow, but through the grime and the gunpowder he flashed a lopsided grin. "Perhaps the military ought to enlist your unique expertise as well as his. That was certainly a highly unusual strategy. But highly effective."

"Wellesley and his generals don't need my help. They have only to read their history books—the Chinese have been using fire arrows for centuries." Shannon sat heavily on the stone wall, overcome by a sudden weariness. "It was a lucky shot. And not one I would want to try again."

From down in the valley, the tolling of the village church bells rose up in counterpoint to the dying thunder of the blast. The flames from the castle must have been visible for miles. Help would soon be on the way.

Hardly daring to believe it was over, she closed her eyes.

Things had not gone exactly as planned, but she had accomplished all that Lord Lynsley had asked of her. Would he see the mission as a success? Or would he find fault with the decisions she had made in the field?

Too exhausted in body and spirit to contemplate the future, Shannon lifted her face to the cooling night breeze. Consequences be damned. For now, she would savor the light lilt of the children's voices, the soft "Hmmph" of the dowager's cough, and feathery warmth of . . .

As her lashes fluttered opened, she was surprised to find them pearled with tears. "Warriors aren't supposed to be watering pots," she whispered against Orlov's lips. He tasted of salt, of sweat, of fire. She drank in his warmth.

"Do you recall the illustrious list of Warrior Queens we discussed?"

His touch was making it impossible for her to think clearly.

"Your name ought to be added to their ranks."

"I am merely an anonymous foot soldier," she managed to reply. "My exploits can never be written down."

Orlov framed her face with his strong, capable hands. "My brave and bold Valkyrie, you and your exploits will always be etched on my heart." His kiss tickled at the corner of her mouth. "Though I confess it's becoming rather a sore point that you keep on having to save my skin. A blow to my manhood, you see."

She hugged him closer, reveling in the contours of their closeness. "There doesn't appear to be grievous injury to your manhood, Alex."

"I am sure with a bit of nursing, it can be coaxed into making a full recovery." His chuckle was echoed by Emma's giggle.

"Mr. Oliver, are you *kissing* Miss Sloane?"

Loath though she was to leave his arms, Shannon stepped out of his embrace.

"I was, elf," answered Orlov. "But I have one for all my brave ladies. Here is yours." He lifted the little girl against his chest and planted a noisy smack on her fore-head, earning a peal of delight. "And yours, milady."

"Hmmph." The dowager touched her wrinkled cheek and tried to disguise a sniff with a snort. "If I were half a century younger, Miss Sloane might have to watch *her* back. But let us save any further display of sentiment for later. We had better take shelter in the stable before we catch our death of cold. I daresay Squire Urquhart and the villagers will be along shortly."

"Just as long as *I* do not have to kiss anyone," muttered Prescott.

"I shall remind you of that statement in several years," said Orlov dryly. Arm in arm with Lady Octavia, he started across the terrace.

Sighing, Shannon flexed her aching leg and made to bring up the rear. The sight of his broad shoulders and tapered waist was a rueful reminder that in a few days they would turn their backs on this job and head off to new missions, new challenges, new dangers.

Surely nothing was as dangerous as ice-blue eyes and a devilish smile. The man was indeed a master thief, for he had stolen her heart . . .

She looked up abruptly to find he had sent the others along and was waiting for her.

"You didn't really think I was going to leave you on your own, did you?"

Her mouth quivered. "Every man for himself."

"Those rules went up in smoke the first time around." His stone-roughened fingers caught hers, pressing their palms tight. "Come Hell or Lucifer himself, we face the fire together, Shannon."

Chapter Twenty-four

$\mathcal{T}$he hired coach kicked up a cloud of dust as it jolted through the winding turn. Orlov flexed his raw hands and shifted his grip on the reins. Though bone weary and bleary-eyed, he and Shannon had decided it was best to move the dowager and the children away from the area as quickly as possible. It did not appear that D'Etienne had any accomplices, but they were not about to take chances. Not after all they had been through.

The previous night had gone by in a blur after the arrival of the local magistrate and a troop of the local farmers. The fires had been put out, the family shepherded to the shelter of the village rectory, and an explanation made of the events. Not the exact truth, of course, but a story that seemed to satisfy the authorities. Angus McAllister's experiments with gunpowder were well known in the area.

In deciding what to do about the London party, the dowager had agreed with the suggestion to avoid any public scandal. No doubt some of them deserved further punishment, mused Orlov. But perhaps seeing their own selfish faults so clearly would have some effect. De Villiers—the only one of the group who had nothing to be ashamed of—had offered to see to the arrangements for the long journey home.

As for their own travels, the mood had been strangely subdued since setting out from the village. Despite their triumph, he hadn't felt much like talking and Shannon seemed lost in her own thoughts.

Was she finding the fruits of victory as bittersweet as he was? Soon he would be back to his old haunts, his old life—wine, women, waltzing until dawn. The prospect left a stale taste in his mouth.

"Another hour should bring us to Dornoch." Rousing from her reveries, Shannon shaded her eyes to the scudding sun. "We can shelter at the White Gyrfalcon while we decide on how to proceed."

"The damage to McAllister's eyrie will take months to repair, so return to the family estate is not an option." Orlov glanced back at the creaking cab, where Lady Octavia and the children sat swaddled in layers of sheepskins and tartans. "And in any case, I am of the opinion that they shouldn't remain in Scotland. Lynsley ought to consider reuniting them with McAllister, wherever the military has him sequestered. Napoleon does not suffer defeat gladly."

But that was not his problem, he reminded himself as he guided the team of horses around a tumble of rocks. He had done his job. It was time to move on. No matter that the road ahead looked suddenly bleak, the granite and gorse leached of all color by the harsh wash of sunlight.

Shannon's squint suddenly deepened. "There are two riders coming our way at a fast gallop."

Orlov felt her stiffen and reach for her pistol. He drew the horses to a halt. "You go guard the dowager while I handle things from here."

She started down, then stopped for another look. "Gypsies, judging by their brightly colored wraps and flowered headscarves. They won't usually attempt an attack on a coach of this size."

"Anyone may tie a garish rag around his head." He checked the priming of his own weapon, then covered it with his coat. "Besides, I traveled for a time with a tribe in Westphalia. Those two do not ride like Romany."

"True." She swung out from the footrail for a better vantage point.

"Let us not fight over the honor of standing in the line of fire." But before Orlov could say more, Shannon broke into a smile and shot her hand up to wave a quick signal.

"No bullets will be flying. It's one of my fellow Merlins."

"What the devil—"

"Greetings, Fifi," said Shannon as the lead rider brought her lathered stallion alongside the coach. "What brings you so far from the nest?"

"Things were far too quiet without you setting off sparks." From beneath the wild tangle of raven curls flashed a pair of thick-lashed emerald eyes. Orlov saw them quickly slant his way.

"So you decided to gallop off into the fire?" Shannon assumed an air of nonchalance, but he didn't miss the note of underlying tension in her voice.

Damn Lynsley. He knew what she was thinking. And

while the marquess could not be faulted for taking precautions, at that moment Orlov itched to punch him senseless for doubting her.

"We thought you might need a hand," said Sofia.

Her friend's gaze shifted slightly, allowing Orlov a quick study of her face. This was the third member of Merlin's Maidens he had met, and if anything, the rumors of their striking beauty had been underexaggerated.

Catching Sofia's questioning look, Shannon replied, "As you see, I'm not alone. Allow me to introduce Alexandr—"

"Orlov." The flowing folds and riotous colors of the exotic garb half obscured the fine-boned features, but he saw her sultry mouth thin to a hard line. "The rascal who nearly bungled Siena's mission. And then nearly broke your arm. Mrs. Merlin has also filled us in on a few more of his recent exploits."

"This is my roommate, Sofia," murmured Shannon. In a louder voice she added, "Let bygones be bygones, Fifi. Mr. Orlov is now an ally."

Sofia raised a brow. "The Emperor's Eastern campaign has certainly made for strange bedfellows."

Shannon colored slightly, but was saved from having to answer by the approach of the second rider, who had come on at a more leisurely pace.

"*Ciao, bella!*" He blew a kiss to Shannon, then cocked a jaunty salute to Orlov. "*Ciao,* Allessandro."

Shannon blinked in surprise. "You two know each other?"

"Oh, *sí, sí,*" answered Sofia's companion. Like her, he was layered in bold colors and his leather bandoleers were bristling with brass ornaments. "Sandro and I are old friends. We met several years ago in a house of . . . lovely ladies. The loveliest in all of Milano, eh, *amico*."

It took a moment for Orlov to recognize the fellow as Giovanni Marco Musto—a rogue whose exploits with women made *him* look like a choirboy. His eyes narrowed. Little wonder he had needed a second look. He had rarely seen *Il Serpente* with all his clothes on.

"I seem to recall there were twin sisters who had taken a fancy to you that night," continued the Italian. "Sicilians, dark as sin, with sweet, ripe *melones*." As Marco was speaking with his hands, translation was unnecessary. "Who were only too happy to share their fruits—"

Orlov cut him off with a sharp cough. "Any chance you might have brought along some bread and water? It's been a dry and dusty journey down from the moors."

Sofia gave Marco a shove, setting off a tinkling of bells. "The provisions are packed in your saddlebags. Have a look, and quickly, while I explain our presence." She flashed a wry smile. "We *are* here under official orders, in case you were wondering."

"Of course—I'm the only one hot-tempered enough to break the rules." Shannon managed a short laugh, but there was uncertainty in her eyes. "So, Lord Lynsley did not think I was capable of getting the job done?"

Her friend's expression turned serious. "Mrs. Merlin assured me this is no reflection on you, Nonnie. Rather it is a mark of how much the marquess wants to be sure that D'Etienne will no longer threaten England or her allies."

"He won't."

"Shannon saw to that," said Orlov. "See to it that she gets the credit she deserves."

She shook her head. "No—it was a joint effort."

Orlov started to speak, but Shannon quickly changed the subject. "I take it Lord Lynsley planned a contingency for getting the family out of Scotland. He never leaves anything to chance."

"Of course." Sofia straightened in the saddle. "In the event of an emergency, Marco and I were to escort the McAllister family to the fishing village of Tain. The naval frigate that brought us here is anchored there, waiting to whisk them to the North Sea Squadron base at Middlesbrough." Sofia's brow quirked in question. "But seeing as you are in command of the situation . . ."

"The enemy is no longer a threat, but the castle has been reduced to smoldering cinders," said Shannon. "It seems the logical choice to follow Lord Lynsley's plan."

Orlov could not argue. Her reasoning made perfect sense. *So why was he feeling so perfectly miserable?* It was not merely the thought of rough seas that had his stomach churning.

But a thump from inside the carriage reminded him that he had more important considerations than the stormy state of his emotions. "All is well, Lady Octavia. These are friends, not foes," he called. "We will soon be on our way."

"Yes, we had better not linger. The tide will soon be turning," said Sofia. "Take the unmarked turn ahead. It's a shortcut down to the south shore of Dornoch Firth. Then follow the right fork to Tain. We will ride on ahead and inform the captain that he should make ready to weigh anchor."

Marco finished rummaging in his saddlebags and tossed over a small sack. "Sorry, no sweet *melones*, Alessandro. Only cider and cheese." His grin was nearly as brassy as the thick chains looped around his neck. *"Arrividerci* for now, *bellas."*

Had he been a bit closer, Orlov would have been sorely tempted to throttle him on the spot.

Seeming to sense he was treading on dangerous ground, the Italian gave a flick of the reins and danced his stallion back a few steps. "I've a bottle of *prosecca* in my sea bag. I shall look forward to sharing a laugh or two during the voyage, while we reminisce over our misspent youth."

"How did your friend come to be working with a snake like *Il Serpente*?" he muttered as the man gave a last little flourish of his bejeweled hand and galloped off.

"Marco?" Shannon watched the riders for a moment longer before turning his way. "He is one of the instructors at the Academy."

Orlov grimaced." I shudder to ask what he teaches."

"He's very skilled with a sword," she answered with straight face. "And spurs."

Orlov knew he was meant to laugh, but somehow sound stuck in his throat. Given the Italian's lust for lovely women, it seemed likely that he had given Shannon a private tutorial in anatomy, She had, after all, mentioned that her classes included the art of seduction.

"If he keeps on acting like an insufferable prick, he will be fishing his cods out of the North Sea."

"That would be a pity—his *gioielle di famiglia* are quite a treasure."

The carriage gave a sudden lurch. Swearing, he loosened his grip on the reins. "You mean to say you have seen him naked?"

"Of course." A pause. "In *art* class. Marco sometimes served as a model for our drawing lessons." Shannon shot him a quizzical glance. "Is something wrong? Your usual sense of humor seems to have deserted you."

He didn't answer, fearing his attempt at a sardonic drawl would come out as a sulky snarl.

She waited a moment before going on. "You must know that his braggadocio is greatly exaggerated. At heart, Marco is a good friend, unwavering in his courage and loyalty."

"Then no doubt the two of you will enjoy the chance to spend so much time in each other's company."

Shannon looked about to speak again, then fixed her gaze straight ahead and maintained a stony silence.

Damn. In contrast to the Italian's bright color, he felt cloaked in unrelenting black. It seemed his Russian penchant for melancholy brooding had returned. With a vengeance. Strange, but over the last few weeks Shannon had made him forget his many faults, his many failures. And where in the past, he had often felt aimless, she had helped him rediscover a sense of purpose.

Now, he was about to be back on his own.

His mood was even darker after another hour of contemplating the coming days. "I am damn sick of sea voyages," muttered Orlov to himself as the horses rounded the last turn into Tain. Adding an oath in Russian, he stared out at the small harbor tucked in the lee of a spit of stone.

A lone ship was riding at anchor, and he watched with sinking spirits as a longboat was lowered and began the short row to shore. With its rakish masts and narrow hull, the naval vessel was clearly designed for speed. Flying on wings of canvas, it would carry him that much faster to port—and to his parting with Shannon.

"Next time I see Yussapov, I may carve his grin into

gills." It was a cruel cut of fate that he must share her with the others during the voyage. What chance was there for any privacy in the crowded confines of a ship? That he would likely be too seasick to take advantage of their last bit of time together only rubbed salt into the wound.

His ill-humor was not shared by the others. The children raced to the longboat, eager to be aboard a real fighting ship. Even the dowager did not look displeased to be leaving Scottish soil.

"Look, look, Mr. Oliver!" Prescott was beside himself with delight on spotting the line of bright yellow gunports below the main deck. "A real broadside. Isn't that smashing!"

"Smashing." His voice had a rather hollow echo.

"Try not to look as though you have just swallowed a mouthful of seaweed," murmured Shannon as they climbed aboard the frigate.

"A whole platterful of the slimy stuff would be more palatable than the prospect of another ocean voyage."

"Come, it will only be for a day or two."

What little resolve he still possessed ebbed out with the tide. She sounded excited to be heading homeward.

A strange constriction took hold of his heart. And his tongue. Without a word, he turned and went below deck.

Shannon leaned on the ship's railing and watched the coastline dip beneath the wind-tossed waves. The deck began to pitch beneath her feet, the up-and-down motion matching the crosscurrents of her own thoughts.

She felt a certain elation at having triumphed over a difficult, dangerous enemy. Yet, there was a deeper, darker side to victory. A lowness of spirit she could not quite put into words. She had come to care for the McAllisters. And for Orlov. Likely she would never see them again.

"You look blue-deviled." Sofia took up position by her shoulder. "Any reason?"

"I . . ." As she tugged her cloak a little tighter, her fingers brushed over the silver chain beneath her blouse. "I ought to return this to you," she said, unclasping the charm. "I've no more need of lucky talismans. My mission is done."

Sofia made no move to take the tiny merlin. "You keep it."

"But—"

"It seems to suit you. Besides, I've chosen something else to take its place." Her friend parted the collar of her dress to reveal an oval of burnished gold.

"You've decided to wear your childhood locket?" asked Shannon. Sofia was the only one of the three who had any memento linked to her past.

"It's as good a talisman as any, I suppose." Sofia shrugged. "I've had it so long, the tiny portrait inside feels like a friend, though I've no idea who it is. Perhaps the lady, whoever she is, will serve as a guardian angel." Her friend refastened her cloak. "So you hold on to the set of wings."

"Thanks, Fifi." The silver charm felt cool and comforting as Shannon slipped it back in place around her neck. She hadn't realized how much a part of her it had become. She would have felt a little lost without it. Turning away from the sting of the salt spray, Shannon wiped her cheek.

"You did well." Sofia smiled. "But I knew you would."

"Did you?" Shannon sighed. "Despite all my troubles with rules and regulations?"

"You have caused your share of fireworks, that is for sure. But you have always known in your heart what is the right thing to do." A curl came to the corners of her friend's mouth. "So always follow your heart. It won't lead you astray."

"You have always been the wisest of us three. And the steadiest."

"Oh, I have my ups and downs. But someone had to take charge of keeping you and Siena out of trouble."

"You are the best of friends."

They shared a moment of companionable silence, watching the setting sun paint the horizon with soft shades of pink and purple, before Shannon stepped away from the rail. "Will you excuse me. I—I had better go check that the dowager and children are comfortably settled below."

But once down in the narrow passageway, she found her steps veering to the starboard side of the ship. A knock on the cabin door drew no answer.

Setting her shoulder to the planking, she nudged it open. The lamplight was barely more than a flicker, and in the yawing shadows all that was visible was two boots protruding from the tiny berth.

"Alexandr?"

"Go away."

She entered anyway and balanced herself on the edge of the bunk board. "Just like old times, with you snapping and snarling at me."

"If you want more convivial company, go seek that damn Italian snake. I'm sure he would be delighted to keep you amused."

"Surely you are not *jealous* over Marco?" The rhythmic thud of the waves against the hull seemed to echo the sound of her own heartbeat. Her hand found his beneath the thin wool blanket. "Don't be."

He slowly sat up, and in the smoky half light his face looked oddly vulnerable. Shadows smudged the hollows of his cheeks and his eyes were flat, colorless circles of gray.

"I'm sorry the sea makes you feel so wretched." Shannon slid her hand up over his wrist. His muscles were tense under her touch and she began a gentle caressing, up and down the length of his arm.

He gave a wordless groan.

"At least there is no bullet to remove, no torn flesh to stitch up." Her kneading moved to the knot in his shoulder. The fastenings of his shirt were open, the linen loosened to expose the curve of his neck, the ridge of his collarbones. Tracing the shape of the scar, she felt the heat of the puckered flesh tingle through her fingertips.

"The damage this time around is to my heart." He gave a sarcastic laugh, sounding almost like his old self. "Maybe it's been struck by an arrow." He pressed her palm to his chest. "Do you think it might prove fatal if left to fester?"

"Ah, a glimmer of the Orlov I am used to." Shannon smiled, a little uncertainly. "Whatever was ailing you, it seems you are well on the road to recovery."

The shipboard sounds of creaking timbers and pounding seas hung heavy in the air, uninterrupted by any words from Orlov.

"I shall miss your sense of humor," she continued.

He pulled back from her touch and withdrew as far as his berth would allow. The distance was only a matter of inches but it felt like an ocean between them. "And not much else," he growled.

His expression was shrouded in shadow but the self-mockery in his voice cut through the damp chill with piercing clarity. Her heart ached for his pain, and yet the hurt held a twinge of hope. Was he sorry to see her go?

He swore softly in Russian, then didn't speak again.

One of them must dare to reach out across the chasm, before its depth grew unfathomable. Shannon felt a flutter of fear in her chest. Where was the daredevil hellion of old? She drew in a breath, then let it out in a rush.

"I shall miss the light in your eye, and the tiny scar at the corner of your mouth that gives your smile a rakish bend. I shall miss you singing Russian lullabies to Emma and the gentleness in your hands when you help Lady Octavia to stand."

His boot scraped against the planking but she wasn't about to stop. "I shall miss your laugh and your snarl and . . ." Her words were muffled for a moment. "And yes, you incorrigible rogue, I shall miss your kisses." She framed his face with her hands and pressed her lips to his cheek. "I shall miss *you*."

"Shannon . . ." He hesitated. "I—I am said to have a glib tongue, but at the moment I feel bereft of clever comments or scathing wit. I have so very little experience in speaking from the heart."

She wasn't sure whether the echoing in her ears was the pounding of the waves against the hull or the thud of her pulse.

"I can only say that when I left ship that morning in Southampton, I thought I would never see you again. And it hurt like hell—far more than blades or bullets." His mouth crooked as he leaned into the light. "Is that love? The poets seem to think that suffering is involved. So I must be deeply, madly in love."

"Alex—" she began.

"Let me finish, *golub,* before my nerve fails me." Scraped and scarred, his hands tenderly traced the line of her jaw, the curve of her neck. "Fate brought us back together. But Fate can be fickle—I don't want to trust in chance."

"If you are suggesting that Lynsley and Yussapov can be convinced to coordinate an occasional time off from duty, I think we may be able to negotiate a deal."

"Lynsley and Yussapov can go to the devil. I am speaking of a permanent alliance, Shannon."

"You mean—"

A rap on the door cut off her question.

"Hmmph." Without standing on ceremony, Lady Octavia entered the cabin, her walking stick steadying her against the roll of the ship. "You looked a bit green around the gills earlier, Alexandr. I thought I had better check and see how you were getting on." A bottle of spirits materialized from the folds of her shawl. "The captain was kind enough to offer this from his stores. It may not calm a queasy stomach, but it may help dull the pain." She squinted through her spectacles. "Though perhaps you would have preferred a bit of privacy to port. Am I interrupting something serious?"

Orlov's mouth crooked in a faint smile. "Just my feeble attempt to convince Shannon to marry me."

"Well, it's certainly taken you long enough to get around to it." She tapped at her chin. "But come to think of it, the timing is not bad. No need to go through all the folderol of posting the banns or procuring a special license. The ship's captain can perform the wedding ceremony on the morrow. Emma will adore being the flower girl, and Scottie will bear the ring . . ."

"I—I don't have a ring," blurted out Shannon.

"I don't have a 'yes,'" murmured Orlov.

Lady Octavia ignored the second statement. Her frail fingers slipped inside her bodice and extracted a thin filigree chain. A simple gold band, burnished with age, hung from its links. "This served me well, gel. I would be happy for you to use it until you have a chance to choose one of your own liking."

"But I couldn't possibly . . ." Shannon stammered in confusion, overwhelmed by the dowager's kindness. "I'm not even family."

"Hmmph. Perhaps not by blood, but by heart, you will always be family to me, Shannon." Lady Octavia's wrinkled countenance glowed in the lamplight. "Though perhaps you would rather not consider yourself related to an old dragon and two little Highland heathens."

Family. A few moments ago she had been on her own, and now she was surrounded by love. She blinked a tear from her lashes as Orlov chuckled.

"We certainly make for an unconventional clan," he said. "I doubt that Debrett's would approve."

"Debrett and all his distinguished dolts can go to the devil," replied the dowager. "Once the castle is rebuilt, I trust you two will visit Scotland often, as often as your work allows."

"You may count on it."

Lady Octavia thumped the deck. "Excellent. Let me go confer with the captain and see if he is willing to arrange things."

Orlov chuckled. "He will not dare disobey."

"Naughty man." Stifling a snort, the dowager waggled

her stick. "One last bit of wisdom, gel. A reformed rake makes the most interesting husband. He will never be boring—in bed or out."

As their laughter died away, Orlov found himself once again turning tentative. "Shannon, all joking aside, I would have a rather large void in my heart were you to leave me. You make me feel whole. I can't promise to be a perfect husband. You know my faults all too well. But I shall try."

"Are you sure?" Her lips quivered. "I love you, Alex, More than I can say. But I also love the wind in my hair and the feel of steel in my palm. I don't wish to retire to the domestic duties of a conventional wife." She made a face. "I don't think I'd be very good at darning or dusting or . . . whatever it is that proper females do all day."

"You wish the partnership to be professional as well as personal?" Orlov felt his eyes spark with unholy amusement. "God help any enemy who dares stand in our way."

"Be serious." Shannon turned very solemn. "I am hardly the ideal sort of bride for a man of noble birth. I have a hellfire temper, and am more comfortable in buckskins than a ball gown."

"You do look lovely in leather," he murmured. "And even lovelier in nothing at all."

He watched her cheeks turn a glowing shade of pink despite the coolness of the cabin. How he loved her face, her fire.

"However, my memory may need a bit of refreshing."

"Alexandr! That *tickles*." Shannon's squeal dissolved in a throaty laugh. "Do stop. The children might enter at any moment."

"Don't worry—I intend to nail the door shut." He

resumed removing her garters. "And if the little devils dare filch any gunpowder from the gunnery mate, I shall make them walk the plank." Her stockings slithered to the floorboards. "Now please say yes."

"Yes."

He drew her closer, only to pull back as another sharp smack rattled the door.

"Bloody Hell," he swore as Shannon hurriedly straightened her skirts and rushed to open it. A red-faced midshipman held out a letter. "The captain's compliments, ma'am. A courier ketch just pulled alongside to deliver this. The order was that you were to have it without delay."

Shannon stared down at wafer of black wax, crested with a merlin in flight. "Thank you." She held her breath and waited until the latch clicked shut before cracking open the sea-damp parchment.

He watched as her gaze skimmed over the contents. "Trouble?"

She passed it over without comment.

Lord Lynsley wrote in a neat copperplate script:

A matter of the utmost urgency has arisen. You are hereby requested to change ships at Middlesbrough and continue on to Hamburg. Events in Prussia require immediate attention. As time is of the essence Yussapov and I have agreed to pool our resources once again. I hope you will not mind, but Mr. Orlov seems the natural choice as a partner, given the talents that are needed. I trust the new orders are not too objectionable. If so, you may ask Sofia to take your place, though I would rather use her talents in a different mission. The choice is yours.

It was signed with a looping "L."

There was a postscript, written in a different hand.

Tvaritch, I hope you found that working with a partner is not so onerous. You are, after all, not getting any younger. A little fire may warm the ice from your Russian bones. By the by, this next mission should not take the pair of you long to complete. After all you have been through, Lynsley and I agree you both deserve a short leave of your duties. I hear that the spa at Baden-Baden makes a fine place for an interlude of uninterrupted relaxation. No wonder it is such a popular spot for a wedding trip. Put the champagne on my bill.

Orlov could not contain a bark of laughter. "I'll drink to that." The crumpled paper fell to the floor.

"Now, where did I put those nails?"

About the Author

ANDREA PICKENS started creating books at the age of five, or so her mother tells her. And she has the proof—a neatly penciled story, the pages lavishly illustrated with full-color crayon drawings of horses and bound with staples—to back up her claim. Andrea has since moved on from Westerns to writing about Regency England, a time and place that have captured her imagination ever since she opened the covers of *Pride and Prejudice*.

A graduate of Yale University, she lives in New York City. Her work lets her travel to a number of interesting destinations around the world—but her favorite spot is, of course, London, where the funky antique markets and used-book stores offer a wealth of inspiration for her stories.

Please visit Andrea's Web site at www.andreapickens online.com. She loves to hear from her readers!

THE DISH

Where authors give you the inside scoop!

From the desk of Amanda Scott

Dear Reader,

The idea for BORDER WEDDING (on sale now)—which is about a Scottish Border reiver, who is captured and forced to choose between marriage and hanging—stemmed from an ancient Scott family anecdote that has also inspired authors such as James Hogg, Sir Walter Scott, and Lady Louisa Stuart, among others. Most authors include the capture, the threat of the hanging, and the captor's demand that the wedding take place at once. Then, optimistically, the authors simply declare that the pair lived happily ever after.

I decided to tell the rest of the story.

Since the reiver of that ancient tale was a nobleman and the bride a lady, one might like to understand something about the nature and identity of Border reivers. They existed on both sides of the ever-shifting line between Scotland and England and were, by definition, "raiders" or "marauders." But reiving was also, for nearly 350 years, the basis of the Borderers' economy. And, since the landowners were nobles, it was not rare for the leader of such a raid to be a nobleman.

The minor seventeenth-century poet/historian Walter Scot [sic] of Satchells, who published the first known history of the Scott family in 1688, said of the reivers,

> "*I would have none think that I call them thieves. . .*
> *The freebooter ventures both life and limb,*
> *Goodwife, and bairn, and every other thing;*
> *He must do so, or else must starve and die,*
> *For all his livelihood comes of the enemie* [sic]."

Mind you, that enemy might be anyone other than his own family, Scot or Englishman, a neighbor, or someone fifty miles away.

In the case of Sir Walter "Wat" Scott of Rankilburn and Lady Margaret "Meg" Murray in BORDER WEDDING, the reiving began with Meg's father taking Wat's cattle. Wat is just taking them back (along with a few of Murray's for good measure). Nevertheless, on both sides of the line, the penalty for capture was hanging. That was simply the way of the fascinating Scottish and English Borderers, who feuded and married amongst each other, and who accepted such a life and its risks as normal.

I do hope you enjoy BORDER WEDDING.

Suas Alba!

Amanda Scott

http://home.att.net/~amandascott

♥ ♥ ♥ ♥ ♥ ♥ ♥ ♥ ♥ ♥ ♥ ♥ ♥ ♥ ♥ ♥

From the desk of Andrea Pickens

Dear Reader,

I learn many interesting things whenever I visit Mrs. Merlin's Academy for Select Young Ladies. As you may know, the school does not teach an ordinary curriculum of study. Oh, to be sure, there are lessons in dancing and deportment. But swordplay and seduction are by far the most important classes, along with basic training in yoga and Eastern martial arts.

Needless to say, the students are not your usual Regency debutantes. They are, well, the truth is, they are swashbuckling secret agents, trained to defend England from its most dangerous enemies. And as proof, I offer the following snippet of conversation between two "Merlins" overheard outside the headmistress's office as I was researching their exploits for my latest book, SEDUCED BY A SPY (on sale now).

Sofia: Bloody hell, you are really in trouble now.

Shannon: To the devil with rules. If Lord Lynsley and Mrs. Merlin wish to expel me for riding to Siena's rescue, so be it. I believed her to be in dire trouble, and though it turns out I was wrong, I would do it again in a heartbeat.

Sofia: I know, I know, but do try to keep a rein on your temper during the meeting. Remember our lessons in discipline and duty.

Shannon: [*Expletive deleted.*]

Sofia: If you are going to ask for a second chance, I would suggest a different choice of words.

Shannon: Never fear—I will be a paragon of reason and restraint.

Sofia: Ha! And pigs may fly.

Shannon: Thanks for the vote of confidence, Fifi. [*A long pause.*] I'm awfully good with blades and bullets. Shouldn't that be a mark in my favor?

Sofia: Hmmm.

Shannon: Perhaps I could offer to go after the Russian rogue, who eluded Lord Lynsley's forces at Marquand Castle. The dratted man is a menace to our country—not to speak of every woman within its borders.

Sofia: Nonnie, I am getting a bad feeling about this.

Shannon (blithely ignoring her friend): Oh, what I wouldn't give to get my hands on Mr. Orlov.

Sofia (rolling her eyes): Be careful what you wish for . . .

Unfortunately, the door fell shut at that moment and I heard no more. However, be sure to visit www.andreapickensonline.com, just in case I discover further news about Shannon and the mysterious Mr. Orlov.

Enjoy!

Andrea Pickens

Want to know more about romances at Grand Central Publishing and Forever? Get the scoop online!

GRAND CENTRAL PUBLISHING'S ROMANCE HOMEPAGE

Visit us at www.hachettebookgroupusa.com/romance for all the latest news, reviews, and chapter excerpts!

NEW AND UPCOMING TITLES

Each month we feature our new titles and reader favorites.

CONTESTS AND GIVEAWAYS

We give away galleys, autographed copies, and all kinds of fun stuff.

AUTHOR INFO

You'll find bios, articles, and links to personal websites for all your favorite authors—and so much more!

THE BUZZ

Sign up for our monthly romance newsletter, and be the first to read all about it!